BEHIND THE VEIL

BAEN BOOKS by JOHN RINGO

TRANSDIMENSIONAL HUNTER (with Lydia Sherrer)
Into the Real • Through the Storm
Behind the Veil • Beyond the Rift, forthcoming

SHADOW'S PATH
Not That Kind of Good Guy • Welcome to the Jungle, forthcoming

BLACK TIDE RISING
Under a Graveyard Sky • To Sail a Darkling Sea
Islands of Rage and Hope • Strands of Sorrow
The Valley of Shadows (with Mike Massa)
Black Tide Rising (edited with Gary Poole)
Voices of the Fall (edited with Gary Poole)
River of Night (with Mike Massa)
We Shall Rise (edited with Gary Poole)
United We Stand (edited with Gary Poole)

TROY RISING
Live Free or Die • Citadel • The Hot Gate

LEGACY OF THE ALDENATA
A Hymn Before Battle • Gust Front • When the Devil Dances
Hell's Faire • The Hero (with Michael Z. Williamson)
Cally's War (with Julie Cochrane)
Watch on the Rhine (with Tom Kratman)
Sister Time (with Julie Cochrane) • Yellow Eyes (with Tom Kratman)
Honor of the Clan (with Julie Cochrane) • Eye of the Storm

COUNCIL WARS
There Will Be Dragons • Emerald Sea
Against the Tide • East of the Sun, West of the Moon

INTO THE LOOKING GLASS
Into the Looking Glass • Vorpal Blade (with Travis S. Taylor)
Manxome Foe (with Travis S. Taylor)
Claws that Catch (with Travis S. Taylor)

EMPIRE OF MAN (with David Weber)
March Upcountry • March to the Sea • March to the Stars • We Few

SPECIAL CIRCUMSTANCES
Princess of Wands • Queen of Wands

PALADIN OF SHADOWS
Ghost • Kildar • Choosers of the Slain • Unto the Breach
A Deeper Blue • Tiger by the Tail (with Ryan Sear)

STANDALONE TITLES
The Last Centurion • Citizens (ed. with Brian M. Thomsen)
Beyond the Ranges

To purchase any of these titles in e-book form, please go to www.baen.com.

BEHIND THE VEIL

JOHN RINGO & LYDIA SHERRER

Behind the Veil

This is a work of fiction. All the characters and events portrayed in this book are fictional, and any resemblance to real people or incidents is purely coincidental.

Copyright © 2025 by John Ringo & Lydia Sherrer

All rights reserved, including the right to reproduce this book or portions thereof in any form.

A Baen Books Original

Baen Publishing Enterprises
P.O. Box 1403
Riverdale, NY 10471
www.baen.com

ISBN: 978-1-6680-7278-3

Cover art by Kurt Miller

First printing, August 2025

Distributed by Simon & Schuster
1230 Avenue of the Americas
New York, NY 10020

Library of Congress Control Number: 2025017953

Printed in the United States of America
10 9 8 7 6 5 4 3 2 1

To my husband, and all the
2 a.m. grilled cheese sandwiches
he made me while I was writing this.
—L.S.

~

As always
For Captain Tamara Long, USAF
Born: May 12, 1979
Died: March 23, 2003, Afghanistan
You fly with the angels now.
—J.R.

Chapter 1

"EDGAR, MACK, LAY DOWN COVER FIRE. RONNIE, MOVE ACROSS the open area when he's got it suppressed and take over. Dan, need you to dash up the stairs as soon as you can and give top cover. On three. One, two, three..."

Lynn took prone with Edgar standing and started pouring 6.8 fire down the main lobby of the Chattanooga Convention Center.

The Possessed returned fire but it was slacking. They seemed to be running out of ammo. Which was good because so were Skadi's Wolves.

Ronnie darted across the lobby to the doors at the front. If the group flanked them, he could get hit from the outside and he'd be in a bad spot. But the Possessed didn't seem to want to leave the building.

He made it to position and started firing down the lobby.

"Reloading!" Edgar shouted, dropping the box from his Squad Automatic Weapon. Mack leaned in and started the reload.

"Wait for reload, Dan," Lynn commed.

"Got it," he replied. "I'm in position. Gonna be a hell of a run."

"You can do it," Lynn said. "Make the angle as fast as you can."

"Firing!"

"I've got TDMs coming in!" Ronnie shouted. "I need fire!"

"Mack!" Lynn replied.

Mack, the only one currently armed for TDMs, took a knee and launched a barrage of Dark Energy bolts from his energy bow. The Ghosts were coming right through the sunlit glass windows fronting the Center. Not that it was necessary since most of the doors were broken from the fighting.

"Go, Dan!" Lynn said as she finished her own reload.

Dan darted out of cover and made a record on the fifty-meter dash to the escalator. Because it was around the corner he was mostly out of sight from the Possessed as he pounded up the long immobile stairs.

Once up there he took a covered position and started servicing the Possessed.

As their opponents started to drop, Lynn assessed the situation.

"Edgar, get ready to fall back," she said.

"Not until you go," Edgar said.

"Come on, Edgar! I'm faster than you are. Move when I tell you!"

"Listen to the Boss," Mack said. "The Boss is wise..."

"Edgar, go!" Lynn shouted.

With a "hmmph" the big Samoan hoisted his SAW and began humping to the escalator.

"Give us cover fire when you get up top!" Lynn shouted as she reloaded. She was down to two mags. They really needed to find some ammo. And it didn't sound like most of their opponents had much.

As soon as the SAW started barking she waved to Ronnie. "Move!"

"Oscar Mike," he replied, pulling out of position and loping across the lobby, headed for cover.

"Mack! Get ready! We're pulling out together."

"Got it," Mack said. "I've got the Ghosts suppressed but there's more coming."

"Worry about Ghosts later," Lynn said. As soon as she heard Ronnie's fire coming from upstairs, she gestured. "Our turn!"

Lynn reached the top of the escalators with her stamina bar dropping like a rock.

"We need ammo!" Ronnie said.

No shit, she thought.

"Copy," Lynn replied. "Check these side rooms as we cross."

At the top of the escalators was a large gathering area, then a flyover that led to the Marriott. On the left side of the flyover were windows, mostly broken. On the right side were doors, presumably leading to rooms.

The way things were going, rooms filled with either TDMs or Possessed.

"Pull back," Lynn said. "Check the rooms."

The first door was locked and they didn't have access keys. The second was broken in.

And lo and behold not only had an ammo store but med kits and food.

"Jackpot!" Mack yelled. "Oh, blue food, lovely blue food!"

"Leave some for the rest of us," Dan yelled. "And we still have company!"

Lynn picked up a case of SAW ammo and ran it to Edgar's position.

"That should help with the company," Lynn said.

"Oh, yeah," Edgar said as Lynn dropped to the prone next to him and reloaded his SAW.

With the additional ammo, meaning he didn't have to be careful with his fire, he terminated the rest of the Possessed with extreme prejudice.

"Ronnie, keep watch, Dan, Mack, Edgar, take everything not nailed down," Lynn said.

"Just me to watch?" Ronnie said, angrily.

"No," Lynn said. "I'm still here. Right?"

"Sure," Ronnie snapped.

"What's eating you now?" Lynn asked over their private channel.

"That you keep putting me in the spot of maximum danger?" Ronnie said. "Having me run across the open area when we barely had them suppressed? Leaving me to be almost the last one out?"

"Because you're the best guy in the squad, Ronnie," Lynn said. "You're the one most likely to survive."

Next to me, she carefully didn't add.

"Sure," Ronnie said. "More like you're trying to get me killed."

Lynn rolled her eyes but didn't reply, just kept watch as the other three hooted and hollered over all the cool loot they were finding.

"Guys, hurry it up," Lynn said. "We need to find a safe point by dusk. Not tomorrow."

"Working on it," Edgar said. "But there's a bunch of stuff to pick up."

"Well, if there's 6.8 it's mine and Ronnie's," Lynn said.

"Here you go," Edgar said, transferring rounds to her inventory. "Might want to reload."

"Done," Lynn said.

"You're full of it too, Ronnie," Dan said, transferring 6.8mm penetrator and explosive ammo to his inventory.

"Screw you, Dan," Ronnie said. "There'd better be more food. My health meter is low."

"Food, lovely blue food," Mack said, transferring same to Ronnie's inventory. "All the blue food gel you could need, want or desire. There's more than we can carry."

"Nice to finally see a decent cache," Ronnie said, grumpily.

"Dan, Mack, Edgar, hold this point while we go fill our inventories," Lynn said.

They both entered the room and picked over the remaining loot. Ronnie picked up some grenade launcher ammo as well. They hadn't found one of those, yet, but it might come in handy in the future.

When they were done they exited and joined the team.

"Suggestions," Lynn said. They weren't currently under fire, so it was worth taking the time for input.

"Use the cache for our safe point," Dan said.

"You just want to eat more blue gel," Ronnie said.

"Blue gel is the best gel," Dan pointed out.

"Mack?" Lynn said.

"Cache," he said.

"Edgar?"

"We've got sun for a while. Staying here doesn't get us closer to the objective. Keep moving."

"Ronnie?"

"Keep moving," Ronnie said.

"We're moving," Lynn said. "What Edgar said. Ronnie, point. Edgar, me, Dan, Mack. Watch the glass area. There might be issues. Move fast. Ready? Go."

Ronnie started trotting across the flyway followed by Edgar and the rest of the squad. When they were about halfway across, Edgar suddenly jerked sideways and his armor flared damaged.

"I'm hit!" Edgar yelled.

"Sniper!"

"Dan!" Lynn said, continuing across the fire zone.

Dan took position at one of the support beams, giving him full cover, and started scanning the rooftops across the street.

"I don't got him!" he shouted.

As soon as Edgar was across the flyover and had cover he pointed the SAW around the corner and started laying down fire in the general direction of the roof.

"He's not on the roof," Ronnie said looking out one of the side windows. "He's in the building. Third window from the left." He shot twice. "And so much for needing a sniper."

"Leave some for the rest of us," Dan said. "Is it clear?"

"We'll know when you stand up," Mack said, a grin in his voice.

"Oscar Mike," Dan said.

"And now I'm down on SAW ammo," Edgar said. "We could go back and get more...?"

"Keep moving," Lynn said. "Down escalator this time. Sweep the area first."

Restaurant, bar, few more health and food packs. No ammo repair material for Edgar and no more ammo.

"Down the escalator," Lynn said. "Ronnie."

"Why do I always have to be point?" he grumbled.

"Let's move," Lynn replied.

There was no more fire on the way down the escalator and no enemies apparent on the ground floor. It was almost without incident until...

"What the hell?" Mack said, facedown on the floor. "I did not go prone! Why am I prone?"

"I think you just tripped," Lynn said, laughing.

"I hate this game!" Mack said, as his avatar stood up. "How the hell do you trip in a game?!"

"'Cause you're clumsy?" Dan said.

"My freaking leg is showing injured!" Mack said. "I am not taking a med pack for tripping!"

"You are if you're slowing down our movement," Dan said.

A notification pinged in Lynn's ear. It was from her mom.

Lynn, you asked me to remind you when it got late. Early day tomorrow.

Okay, Mom, she messaged back. "Guys, it's been fun, but we've got a lot of work to do tomorrow. Time to bug out."

"Ugh, fine," Mack said. "We need a safe point, though."

"There's a niche around the corner here," Dan said.

"Assemble there," Lynn said. "We'll continue to the objective next time."

"This is why we should have stopped at the cache," Dan said.

"You just want more blue food," Mack replied.

"Good game, guys," Lynn said, getting her avatar situated. "See you tomorrow." She exited the new TransDimensional Hunter–themed crossover mode WarMonger had just dropped and took off her AR glasses to rub her eyes. As usual, going from the immersive in virtual world of WarMonger back to her quiet, dark bedroom was a bit of an adjustment.

The world ended in a tidal wave of TransDimensional Monsters destroying the power grid, wiping out electronics and killing by what people called the 'Ghost Touch,' then possessing the dead who rose as TD Zombies.

"In the hellish aftermath, survivors battled not only the invisible TDMs but each other as well, desperate to find some safe haven, some food, some shelter against the thousand-year night."

That was the ad copy for the new WarMonger TD Hunter mode, anyway. What it came down to was fighting people and TDMs with WarMonger sets and engine.

Lynn cracked her neck and stretched out her back.

"Man, it's so much easier to fight when it's just electrons," she muttered, standing up and grimacing at the thought of her butt-crack-of-dawn workout she had to look forward to in the morning.

Whoever invented running was evil.

Like, really evil.

"Freaking—hate this—kill me—now."

"That's the spirit, Miss Lynn. It is always good to start your day with a positive mindset."

Lynn Raven would have liked to call Hugo, the TD Hunter service AI running her exercise scenario, a great many vulgar names. But she was too busy using her air to stay upright and conscious, and had none to spare putting her sarcastic AI in its place.

"Only thirty more seconds until your cooldown."

Lynn gritted her teeth and strictly commanded her legs to keep pumping. It wasn't as bad as usual, since she was on a treadmill in the apartment complex weight room. She preferred running outside, but the cold weather and aggressive flocks of paparazzi drones had conspired against her. Normally there were only one or two drones, if that, especially during the winter months. But mere days ago, she had led a group of twenty-two TransDimensional Hunter teams to destroy a massive TD boss in their area, and they had streamed most of the fight on the mesh web.

It had apparently been quite the viewing experience.

Streams and gaming forums all over the mesh web were in an uproar about "General RavenStriker" and her horde of hunters. Clips of it had gone viral on multiple platforms. Lynn had even gathered enough courage to watch some of it herself and had to admit it looked pretty impressive. The TD Hunter augmented reality overlay was otherworldly. Truly groundbreaking and next generation.

It all looked so... real.

But that was probably just because the camera view was coming from an actual person physically swinging, jumping, and rolling to fight the augmented overlay TD Monsters.

Which was why she was up at the crack of dawn doing the thing she hated most in the entire world.

Well... maybe second most hated thing. The first would be doing interviews, which was sucky because GIC, her PR company, was receiving more and more requests. So many that she really couldn't keep refusing them all. She'd embarked on this quest to win the TD Hunter International Championship to earn money for her and her mom and ensure a future for herself. And interviews absolutely made her money.

"Well done, Miss Lynn!" Hugo chirped in her earbud. "You have successfully completed your Stamina Booster workout!"

The treadmill slowed from its sprint pace, and Lynn grabbed the handles on either side to hold herself up as the muscles in her legs finally gave her the middle finger and ceased functioning. She'd been doing a HIIT routine—High Intensity Interval Training—that the TD Hunter app had in its extensive database of fitness resources. According to her ER nurse mother, Matilda, they were very well-designed exercise regimens, and since Lynn didn't want to do any of them anyway, having a program lead her through them was easier than trying to keep track of it all herself.

Of course, the bigger question was why, in the name of all

that was holy, was she doing HIIT training at seven in the morning during her senior year spring break.

She had considered the possibility that she was a masochist, otherwise known as a workout junkie. But she really didn't enjoy working out. There was no high afterwards or a glowing sense of accomplishment. Just lots of groaning and foul curses under her breath.

What she did crave, though, was being able to breathe while fighting TDMs, and stamina was built by one thing and one thing only: exercise. And exercises only worked as well as the effort you put into them. Lynn wasn't a workout junkie, she just hated wasting effort, so there wasn't much point in taking a vacation from her normal workouts only to make it harder on herself when she got back to them.

The treadmill finally got down to walking speed and Lynn drank water while she did her cooldown circuit. Hugo rattled off her workout numbers, from heart rate to calories burned, to peak records in time and distance. The AI was annoyingly supportive and chipper about it all, probably because the collected wisdom of the mesh web informed it of the benefits of a positive attitude. It was wasted effort on Hugo's part, though, because the day she felt anything positive toward running was the day she bleached her hair and tried out for her school's cheerleading team. Instead of informing Hugo of that fact, Lynn simply mopped her face with a sleeve and tried to enjoy the fact that she no longer wanted to stab herself in the face.

That was what she got for aspiring to be the world-class champion of an *augmented*-reality game. Playing virtual reality games felt oddly lame by comparison.

Well, maybe not WarMonger.

Lynn smiled at the thought, remembering her latest conquests as the Tier One mercenary Larry Coughlin. WarMonger didn't give her the same full-body satisfaction that a day of hunting TDMs did, but there was something uniquely delectable in proving her superior skill, tactics, and sheer ferocity in a first-person shooter game like WarMonger.

It was also a frustrating but unavoidable fact that Larry Coughlin was respected in ways that Lynn Raven never would be, no matter how many competitions she won. Part of that was her age, of course. It was natural that a grizzled war vet would garner more respect than a fresh-faced teenager. But the main factor that she'd experienced over and over in her years gaming was the resistance to seeing girls as serious and capable gamers.

Most guys, and even a lot of girls, simply didn't respect a female gamer the way they respected a male one, no matter how skilled the female was. It made her fantasize sometimes about revealing that Lynn was Larry and Larry was Lynn, just to see the proverbial jaws drop across the mesh web. It would truly blow people's minds—at least for those who believed her. A significant subset of the gaming population would write it off as a hoax, even with evidence to the contrary. Some people simply had no desire to challenge their assumptions. It was human nature, and she couldn't change it, so she tried not to dwell on it. She refused to let bitterness or resentment take a single iota of energy away from her achieving her goals.

So, instead of getting worked up about the stupidity of human nature, she simply enjoyed playing Larry when she could, and focused on pushing herself to the very top of her game in TD Hunter.

To that end, she had some tactical data to review from her recent "Operation Boss Bash," so she needed to take a shower and get to it. Just because it was spring break and most high school seniors were on a beach in Panama City didn't mean she and her Skadi's Wolves TD Hunter team got to take a break. They had to use every spare moment to train and hunt in order to reach Level 40 by mid-June.

Despite the workout from hell she'd just finished, her heart rate picked up again at the thought of the championship, drawing ever closer. She tamped down on the thread of anxiety that came with it and focused on the here and now.

She couldn't let future distractions ruin her present performance. That was a rookie mistake in gaming.

"Thanks for the pep talk, Hugo," Lynn said, now that she'd regained most of her lung capacity. "I'd be happier if you'd just stop torturing me, but I guess it's good you say nice things about me while committing crimes against humanity. You win the prize for world's most polite sadist."

"Drama and exaggeration do not become you, Miss Lynn."

"Oh, darn, and here I was hoping for your undying approval. I'm crushed, Hugo. Truly crushed."

"Sarcasm is hardly better," Hugo said primly.

"Just following your example."

"I beg your pardon? When have I ever—"

"Don't even finish that thought, smarty-pants. I like my eyeballs where they are, thanks, and they won't stay put with how hard I'll be rolling them if you try to deny what a snarky little bastard you are."

The AI did not reply, and Lynn grinned at the thought of it grumbling and muttering to itself.

She dismounted the treadmill and grabbed her water bottle, compact TD Counterforce backpack, and heavy jacket on her way to the door. With the backpack on and the hood of the jacket up, she dashed across her apartment complex's main courtyard, hoping to reach her apartment building without being subjected to flybys from nosey drones trying to dip down and get a shot of her face.

Honestly, Lynn thought paparazzi drones should be outlawed. But the culture's obsession with gossip combined with free market capitalism ensured *that* would never happen.

She made it back through her building's automatic doors without any mishaps and flipped back her hood as she headed for the elevator. Yes, the stairs were a healthier option, but her legs felt like wet noodles boiled so long they'd started to disintegrate. So, the elevator it was.

"Good morning, Lynn, how are you today?"

Lynn turned, a smile lighting up her face at the sight of her downstairs neighbor, Jerald Thomas, coming toward her leaning on his cane for support.

"Hi, Jerald! My workout tried to kill me, but I'm still alive. So, good, I guess?"

"Ah, the joys of youth. Just wait until you get to be my age, young lady. You will long for the days when something as simple as getting out of bed did not result in multiple minor injuries."

A snort escaped her and Lynn shook her head.

"Come on, it can't be *that* bad."

"I am not cruel, so I will not shatter your illusions, my dear. Let us just say that growing old is not for the faint of heart."

They shared another smile and Lynn stepped away from the elevator, offering her arm to Mr. Thomas for him to lean on while she walked him back to his apartment door. She knew how much his daily walks meant to him, and how much the cold made his bones ache. Since she was up early most mornings for a pre-school workout, she was used to running into Mr. Thomas on his daily circuit of their apartment building. He always asked her about school and how her TD Hunter training was going. He'd even started watching a few gaming streams to keep up with news about Skadi's Wolves—much to her embarrassment. But he just chuckled and waved off her awkwardness, saying that "all the drama" made him feel young.

They chatted about her recent successful Boss Bash, and he made her laugh with his incredulous descriptions of her athletic feats, as if he'd forgotten that the human body was even capable of such spryness. Jerald was always polite, interested, and supportive of her endeavors, even though she'd had no time for months to drop by and bring him some of her mom's homemade taco pizza or sit and play a hand of cards with him. He didn't seem to mind. Lynn couldn't help but think that if anyone needed a lesson in what it looked like to be a decent human being, they need look no further than Mr. Thomas.

Once she'd seen him to his door, she wobbled back to the elevator and headed up to her apartment, her mind singularly focused on the blessedly hot shower waiting for her.

Her focus was shattered by a ping notification on her earbuds, and she pulled up her LINC message list on her AR glasses. She didn't always wear them during her workouts, but she tried to at least half the time, since she had to be able to fight TDMs in them with ease and fluidity.

When Lynn saw who had pinged her she almost choked.

Voice call request from: Robert Krator.

Had she done something wrong? Had her recent boss victory broken some TD Hunter rule she didn't know about? Why else would Robert freaking Krator, CEO of Tsunami, be casually pinging her at eight o'clock in the morning? If it was something mundane, he had employees for that kind of thing, didn't he?

She was too sweaty and exhausted to focus on an important conversation, so she responded to the request with simple text:

Sorry, Mr. Krator, just finished a workout. Can I ping you after I take a shower?

Sure. And it's Robert.

Lynn smiled, anxiety fading a little.

Got it. Get back to you in a bit.

She took an only-slightly-shorter-than-normal scalding hot shower, because Mr. Krator might be a billionaire, but she wasn't capable of more than surface politeness without a certain amount of time to decompress under a pounding shower spray. Her apartment complex was only middling quality, but the water pressure was top-notch.

When she got out, her mom was busy fixing bacon and eggs for breakfast. Matilda Raven worked night shifts at St. Sebastian's Memorial Hospital in downtown Cedar Rapids, so this was dinner for her and she insisted on eating together as often as schedules allowed.

"Be ready in five minutes, honey," Matilda called.

"Okay, Mom. I need to call someone real quick, but it shouldn't take long."

Lynn went and hid in her room, making sure the door was firmly closed, before taking a deep breath and selecting the callback option on the voice request from Mr. Krator. She sat on the bed and began braiding her wet hair as she waited for it to pick up.

"Good morning, Lynn. I hope you're enjoying spring break so far?"

"Um, yeah, I guess?" Lynn said, grimacing.

"Too busy to enjoy your just deserts, is it?"

"More or less."

"I remember my senior year spring break. I made an ill-fated trip to Miami Beach on the advice of a friend. He was convinced it would change my life."

"Er, did it?" Lynn couldn't help asking.

"Yes...but not in the way he'd imagined," Mr. Krator said ruefully, and Lynn wasn't brave enough to pry further. "I would say I'm surprised you're working out during a school break, but then I've seen what you do, both in TD Hunter and WarMonger. You're a dedicated person, Lynn, a commendable quality that few have these days."

"Th-thank you, M— I mean Robert." Lynn could have slapped herself for tripping over her words. It wasn't as if Mr. Krator hadn't asked to speak to her before. He'd been the one to personally invite her to beta test TD Hunter in the first place, after all.

"That's why I was hoping you'd be willing to go a step further and do something unique to help promote TD Hunter—with compensation, of course."

"Uh... sure?"

Mr. Krator chuckled. "Wait till you hear what it is, Lynn."

"Yes, that's what I meant. So... what is it?"

"Well, we have a variety of marketing strategies promoting TD Hunter to the public as well as our current player base for all Tsunami games. As I'm sure you've seen, we frequently invite star players and stream influencers to do promos and sponsorships. There has been a particularly stubborn subset of WarMonger players that seem to enjoy mocking TD Hunter as 'lame' because of the augmented aspect, while discounting the mental and physical health benefits of gaming in the real. WarMonger players as a general customer base are a close target audience for TD Hunter, so I'd like to hire Larry Coughlin to promote TD Hunter to help win over that player segment."

Lynn nearly swallowed her tongue.

"W-what? You want me to do *what*?"

"Well, it doesn't *have* to be you personally, I suppose. After all, Steve Riker and some of my other employees have been doing an admirable job of keeping Larry involved and current despite your busy schedule."

Lynn gulped. Mr. Krator must have heard it, because he chuckled again.

"Don't worry, Lynn. Steve cleared the plan with me before he implemented it. It was a good idea, frankly. Larry Coughlin is a genuine asset to Tsunami. It's in the best interests of the company to maintain his presence as an active and valued member of the WarMonger community."

That made Lynn snort, and she covered her mouth with one hand.

"Sorry, I just—valued?—do you know how many players hate my guts? I *do* pound people into the dust for money, you know."

Mr. Krator chuckled softly.

"You've made your enemies, to be sure. But you are a legend in the player *and* fan community. Have you ever done a 'Larry Coughlin' search on the streams?"

"Yeah, made that mistake once," Lynn said with a grimace. "Won't do it again. Did you know some guy curates an open hit list that people can add fellow players to that they want to get fragged?"

"Hm, I did not. Sounds... pleasant."

Lynn shrugged, then remembered Mr. Krator couldn't see her.

"I'm sure for most people it's all in good fun, siccing Larry the Snake on their buddies. But it's kinda insulting, too. As if I'd waste my time killing people for free." She mentally added *unless they're Ronnie Payne*. Mr. Krator could easily look up the match data and see that she'd spent a significant amount of time over the years ruining Ronnie's day, but there was no point drawing attention to it. She had better things to do, now, and besides, Ronnie was... different these days. She no longer had the urge to slap him whenever he opened his mouth—a surprising and welcome change.

"Of course not, which is why you'd be compensated for your time promoting TD Hunter—or for the use of your profile, if one of Steve's team did it."

Lynn squirmed; not sure she liked the idea of someone else speaking on her behalf. Because Larry *was* her in enough ways that doing something like that felt deceptive, as if she was selling *herself*, not just her skills and services.

"I mean, I could probably handle it. What, er, would it involve?" She regretted her words almost as soon as she'd said them but stubbornly ignored the feeling.

"Don't worry, nothing difficult. The first stage would simply be to record some matches of you fighting TDMs in the WarMonger-TD Hunter crossover mode we introduced. Then we would take Larry's likeness from WarMonger and create an augmented reality version of him for the native TD Hunter part of the ad. For that portion, it would be ideal to have you fly down to Texas and do some takes in our marketing studio so we can use that to overlay Larry's skin onto your fighting moves. AI vid generation has come a long, *long* way from the early years, but it's not perfect, so a live recording we can overlay would work best."

"But how would that work? I'm a curvy, average-height teenage girl. Nobody would believe I'm a grizzled old guy even with an AI overlay."

"O ye of little faith," Mr. Krator chuckled. "The wonders of AI-generated graphics are quite jaw-dropping, but they're still lacking in two specific areas: the fluidity and the randomness of human movement. Pure computer generation, even guided by human creative design, is too perfect, and therefore inhuman. But your stature and body shape won't be the anchor points for the graphics. Rather, the recordings of your specific attacks, special moves, and body language are what our designers will use as input to enable custom footage to be created. In essence, we could make a promo ad using any old body double, but they would have no knowledge of how to move to look like Larry Coughlin. Using you brings accuracy and authenticity to the footage. As an added bonus, creating custom footage will put to bed all those rumors that Larry is confined to a wheelchair. Imagine how everyone will be quaking in their boots to see how dangerously competent Larry Coughlin still is."

The amusement in Mr. Krator's voice made Lynn relax as she thought the offer through. It wouldn't be that bad, really. It's not like she'd be out in public revealing her Larry Coughlin identity. All she had to do was a bit of fighting, and Tsunami's graphics team would do the rest.

"Um, what about my, you know, secret identity? Wouldn't people in Texas see who I was and put two and two together?"

"True, true. I trust my employees' discretion, but if you're worried about it, we could pull Steve and a few others from his team to handle the go-between and once you're in your green suit and AR glasses most of your identifying features would be covered anyway. We could come up with a neutral name for the project and ensure the footage and documentation is not connected to your or Larry's name. That way, by the time it got to the graphics department, they would have no knowledge of what stunt artist we used for the green-screen recording. But, if you're truly concerned about it, we could use a different stunt actor."

Lynn chewed her lip.

"Um...can we plan on me doing it in person but hang on to that as a backup? I'm also worried about, well, time."

"Yes, of course. Senior year, national competition, I understand. There is something else you can do for the promotion that does not involve travel, however."

"Oh?"

"Yes, I'd like Larry to do an interview."

Lynn's eyes widened.

"An *interview*? But—" She stopped and took a breath. He'd said no travel, so he didn't mean in person. She had her voice modulator, and it could be audio only, so no need to freak out. "I mean, that's, er, pretty bold, wouldn't you say? Larry is more of a shooting kind of guy than a talking one."

"Are you kidding me? The Snake's quips are legendary."

"That's just the thing," Lynn protested. "They're prepared, not spontaneous. You should see my wall at home, I've got sticky notes all over it with perfect zingers written out and waiting to be used."

Mr. Krator fell silent, which made Lynn nervous. Was he disappointed to see behind the mask? Just like the Wizard of Oz, she could never live up to the legend she had created.

"I mean, they're not fake or anything," she hurried to add. "I had to do a *ton* of research to figure out the perfect phrasing, military lingo, local pronunciations, and all that. It's just... I'm *not* Larry. I've never traveled the world. I've never fought in any wars. I've never, well, killed anyone, obviously. So... I don't think an interview will, um, be as amazing as people think it will be." Her voice turned squeaky at the end of her sentence, and she cleared her throat.

There was more silence, which made her nerves hum. But when Mr. Krator spoke again he didn't sound disappointed, or angry, or even bothered.

"Thank you for your honesty, Lynn. I don't think it will be the problem you imagine it to be, though. You are welcome to help craft the interview to ensure the questions are the sorts of things you feel comfortable answering as Larry. And I suspect you get much more into Larry's head when you play WarMonger than even you would admit. Surely you don't need a brand-new quip for every situation? Everybody has pet phrases and familiar idioms they fall back on. We could even do a mock interview beforehand to help you get comfortable in the role."

Lynn hesitated. It wasn't something she *wanted* to do, though a small part of her grinned evilly and rubbed its hands together at the thought of getting to growl cranky threats at the entire gaming community at once, instead of just her opponents in a match. She wondered if the interview would *bleep* out cuss words to keep it family friendly.

"Who would be the interviewer?" she asked, curiosity piqued, despite herself.

"One of the heads of our marketing department," Mr. Krator said. "He's a WarMonger player himself and a huge fan of yours. He was salivating at the idea of interviewing you, and is aware that he will have to stick faithfully to the agreed upon questions so as not to get on the Snake's 'naughty' list."

Lynn laughed. Oh, the joys of mercing.

"I'll...think about it, if that's okay? I'm interested, but I...I don't want to let you down, er, Robert. Maybe we could start with recording virtual ad footage in WarMonger, then I could take a look at the proposed interview questions and we'll go from there?"

"Sounds like a plan, Lynn. Thank you, I am in your debt, truly."

Lynn felt her face heat and she was doubly glad they weren't on a video call.

"You aren't, Robert. *I* should be thanking *you*. TD Hunter is all I've ever wanted—well, minus the sunburn and mosquitos and rabid paparazzi drones. I'm grateful that I can do what I love and what I'm good at to help support my family and, well, build a future for myself. You know?"

"I do, and I'm thrilled Tsunami can provide you that opportunity. But I *am* in your debt. The whole world—well, the whole gaming community, benefits from what you bring to the table. Now, you'll be hearing from my marketing team soon, and they'll be interacting strictly with Larry Coughlin's profile within the WarMonger app, unless you want to give them a different point of contact outside of the app. I've also ensured the details of your location and identity are not accessible through the player profile my employees have access to."

"Thank you, Robert. I appreciate it."

"Don't thank me yet, Lynn. Larry the Snake is going mainstream, and the more attention you draw, the greater the possibility of exposure."

Lynn thought about it for a moment. Though the idea did give her a thrill of dread, she found she wasn't upset by the thought. Ronnie Payne aside—that was a can of worms she had *no* idea how to address—she wasn't the out-of-shape, self-conscious, closet gamer girl she'd been a year ago. She could proudly stand on her own two feet in the real and know that what she'd accomplished was extraordinary. Operation Boss Bash had proven that.

"Either way, I think we'll make it work, Mr. Krator."

"That's the spirit. And it's Robert, Lynn."

Lynn slapped her forehead.

"Sorry, um, Robert." She bit her lip, then spoke before she lost her nerve. "Do you have any idea how hard it is to call your hero by his first name?"

"Hero, eh?" There was a hint of amusement in Mr. Krator's voice.

"Yeah, well, you've designed every single one of my favorite games. You've been in the industry since you were, what, sixteen?"

"Oh, younger than that, just not with tax liability."

Lynn laughed.

"That's exactly what I mean, though. Gaming has... well, I think gaming has saved my life. And probably a bunch of other people's lives, too. And *you* did all that. And I can't imagine the creativity and focus needed to create all these amazing games and build a huge, successful, international company and basically become a game-designing super-star, and—"

"I think I get the picture, Lynn, thank you." Mr. Krator's chuckle was a tad awkward and Lynn realized she'd been gushing. "I will point out, however, that I had an immense amount of help. And the games I've designed only came to fruition through the incredible talent of hundreds of other people working for years to realize our dream. So don't get too starry-eyed. And don't discount your own creativity and efforts."

"I'll try not to. Robert." Lynn grinned. It still felt weird, but she appreciated that Mr. Krator insisted on the familiarity. It confirmed her instincts that he, his games, and his company were worthy endeavors.

"Well, don't let me keep you, Lynn. Thanks for hearing me out. Someone from my team will be in touch soon."

"Okay. Thanks!"

"Good luck with your training, Lynn. You'll need it."

Before she could ask what he meant, the voice call had been ended. She sat in the silence of her room for a minute, mulling over the conversation, until her mother called from the kitchen that she'd better come eat her bacon or there would be none left.

Lynn jumped to her feet and hurried to save her well-deserved bacon from the marauding appetite of her mother.

"It's spring breaaak. Why are we heeere? Why am I even awake right now? It's not even noon!"

"Shut up, Dan," Ronnie said, a growling counterpoint to Dan's pitiful warbling. "At least Edgar didn't threaten *you* with bodily harm if you didn't show up for training."

"Gome on, guys—ifs not *dat* early," Mack said around his last mouthful of *concha* pastry his mother had sent with him for breakfast. Lynn wasn't sure if Mrs. Rios had made the *pan dulche* herself, but it wouldn't have surprised her.

"No self-respecting gamer is seen before high noon if they have a choice in the matter," Dan declared, rolling his shoulders and scratching at his back under the collar of his high-performance athletic wear.

"You know, Dan," Edgar drawled, "you're supposed to wash those things every couple'a uses, no matter what they say about being sweat and odor resistant." Edgar twirled his baton between his fingers. He was the most awake of Lynn's friends since he was used to getting up early to take care of his little siblings and work various jobs.

Dan wiggled and twisted, trying to reach a certain spot on his back while his teammates watched with raised eyebrows.

"Are you—kidding me? I've got—too much to do—to worry about—laundry," Dan said between contortions.

"Don't you all have a maid or something?" Mack asked.

"She's a *cleaning* lady, not a maid, doofus. I've told you that a thousand times. She doesn't do laundry—*will somebody please scratch my freaking back!*"

"There's a tree right there, genius. Help yourself."

Mack took pity on Dan and tried to find the itch while Ronnie spectated and provided scathing peanut gallery commentary.

They were gathered in a little neighborhood park in southeastern Cedar Rapids to try out their new weapons they'd achieved by killing Gyges in Operation Boss Bash, the named boss that had been parked on a utility node just north of their high school. Lynn wanted a practical view of what everyone's new capabilities were before she made any plans for how they were going to achieve the last two Hunter levels and hit max Level 40 before mid-June, a mere ten weeks away, give or take a few days.

Oh, and she had to make sure they left time to pass their senior finals and graduate high school while they were at it.

Fun, fun, fun.

They were blessedly drone-free since they hadn't gone to any of their usual haunts and had gotten very good at losing the little buggers switching back and forth between air buses. As soon as they went into combat mode though and started hunting—and streaming, per Mrs. Pearson's request—the drones' controllers would figure out where they were posthaste.

Once live footage of their hunt started proliferating on the streams, lens junkies—fans obsessed with watching professional TD Hunter players live through the TD Hunter Lens app—would start trying to triangulate their location based on clues in the footage. Guesses would start flying back and forth in the comments, and sometimes they would be right. Then the local lens junkies would start showing up to spectate. Which was why Skadi's Wolves tried not to spend more than an hour in any one location, unless it was particularly remote with no handy landmarks or signs around.

The "civilians," as TD Hunter players called spectators, were annoying and distracting but almost always kept their distance. Lynn had initially been upset that TD Hunter had put out their spectator app, until she realized that people were going to spectate anyway. If they did it through the app, Hugo, as the TD Hunter service AI, could then flash dire warnings at them if they got too close, or even temporarily blind them by blanking out their view if they tried to interfere with the players.

It was a useful solution, simultaneously promoting the game *and* providing crowd control. It enabled Lynn and her team to ignore spectators completely, confident Hugo would handle them.

When Skadi's Wolves didn't livestream, it took drones and civilians much longer to find them, unless some passerby spotted them who cared enough to post about it. But streaming was what brought in the big bucks, and what sponsors were most interested in, so Mrs. Pearson insisted on it several times a week at the very least, if not once a day.

Mrs. Pearson was their extremely no-nonsense PR manager from Global Image Consulting, the company they'd hired to help Skadi's Wolves maintain a positive and *profitable* public image. She and her team took care of all their communication, streaming, and social channels, and vetted all the interview and sponsorship requests. They were a godsend, and working with them had been a good opportunity for Lynn to repair bridges with her middle-school best friend, Kayla Swain, whose stepdad was CEO of the company.

The last time Lynn had heard from Kayla—approximately thirty-three minutes ago in a series of excited texts—the most viral clips from their Boss Bash battle were still trending. Long ago in middle school, Kayla had stabbed Lynn in the back when she'd gotten involved in the cool girls clique at school and chosen to ghost Lynn instead of standing up for friendship over popularity. But last year Kayla had experienced a come-to-Jesus moment and realized how miserable she'd become as part of that crowd. She'd worked hard to regain Lynn's trust, and Lynn was grateful for that. It was still weird having a best friend again after so long on her own. But she was trying to lean into it, despite Kayla's obsession with virtual shopping and her alarmingly excessive use of exclamation points.

It had been Kayla who had suggested Skadi's Wolves hire her father's company when the team was buckling under the stress of invasive and constant attention. Since then, Kayla had installed herself as the unofficial mascot and cheerleader of Skadi's Wolves, as well as a spy to keep an eye on their rival team, the Cedar Rapids Champions. It was Elena, CRC's leader, who had kept Kayla under her thumb for all those years since middle school, cowing and berating her into being an obedient little flunky. Since Kayla had been strong-armed into helping manage Elena's own stream channel—without compensation, of course—she was intimately familiar with Elena's habits and connections. Lynn had no desire whatsoever to know what Elena and her posse of mean girls said about Skadi's Wolves and Lynn herself. But Kayla enjoyed the gossip wars, so she took one for the team and kept an eye on all things CRC so Lynn and the guys could focus on training.

"Whaddya think, boss?" Edgar asked, looming over Lynn. She wasn't short for a girl, but Edgar was six feet and counting, so it was hard for him *not* to loom.

Lynn was busy scrutinizing the different weapon modes of Edgar's new two-handed rifle, Snazzgun of Da Boyz, that he'd achieved in their boss battle.

"This thing is crazy as shit. Have you *seen* this?"

"I know, right?" Edgar said, a bit of crazed glee creeping into his voice. Lynn looked up at him and had to laugh.

"Why do I get the suspicion that someone, somewhere, created this gun just for you?"

"Don't know, chica. But I'd kiss 'em if I could."

The sudden mental image of Edgar kissing someone made Lynn's insides go all hot and squirmy. She shifted and looked back down, hoping Edgar hadn't noticed the flush rising up her neck.

"I'm not sure how this gun is even allowed," she said, focusing on the task at hand. "It has cannon, flamethrower, *and* grenade launcher modes. When did grenade launcher become a thing? That's new. The cannon is above Inferno-level strength, and the flamethrower has a hundred-foot range. The grenade launcher and flamethrower power use is off the charts, though. Not sure how practical they'll be. We'll just have to train with them and see if they're faster or more effective at clearing TDMs without draining your power. You'll run Mack ragged trying to keep up with this power-guzzling beast."

"You know what Mack should have gotten?" Edgar said, turning off his LINC's screen projection.

"What?" Lynn said, eyebrows raised.

"A loot vacuum," Edgar chortled.

Lynn snorted, then got thoughtful.

"Maybe I should poke around the auction site again, see if there's any new rare augments that have some sort of loot collecting mechanic. TD Hunter doesn't have many regular patches, but we might have missed something. I'll bet there's a useful item out there we could buy for Mack. Make his job easier."

"Yeah," Edgar agreed. "I think my ichor use rate gives him ulcers."

"You've got TDMs to explode. I'm sure Mack understands. Hey, guys," she called over her shoulder, shifting her attention. "Quit goofing around and get over here."

By the time they'd gathered around, Dan was still twitchy but no longer dancing like someone had put fire ants down the back of his shirt. They took turns highlighting the notable stats and abilities of their newly acquired weapons. Dan's Ambanese Sniper Rifle had a Splinter Blade bayonet, which meant he would spend less time switching between weapons when he needed to do some emergency melee defense. It also had double the weapon augment slots that most guns had, so Dan was able to load it up with specialty ammo like armor-piercing bullets while still keeping his increased range and stat-boosting weapon augments.

Mack's pair of Croft Desert Eagles were Hell Blaster-level pistols that had insanely efficient power usage. That meant he could use normally high-cost special ammo augments like flechette and incendiary rounds as if they were common rounds, giving him a huge offensive edge while he focused on watching their backs and keeping the team's supplies topped off. They also had a sick ability called Unify that allowed Mack to combine the pistols' firepower into a single baton while using the other for any non-projectile, one-handed weapon like a Blade or a Force Shield. Effectively, it made Mack a lethal flex player with the ability to switch between high-damage ranged offense, melee offense, or straight up defense, whatever the team needed. Lynn added "find Mack a decent shield" to her mental list of things to do.

When they got to Ronnie's sword, Mack snort-laughed at the sight of the name: Zelda's Sword of Mastery.

"What's with that, though?" Edgar asked, seeing that Lynn and Dan were grinning as well.

"Oh, my sweet summer child," Dan said, steepling his fingers, obviously preparing for a long-winded explanation of esoteric game trivia that none of them cared about.

"It's stupid, that's what it is," Ronnie said, forestalling the lecture with a glare at Dan and Mack.

"It's not!" Mack insisted. "It's super clever."

"It's a masterful nod to legacy fandom and geek culture in general," Dan said, wagging a finger in the air. "Its comic irony and subtlety is unsurpassed."

"It's stupid," Ronnie repeated.

"Humor is like food in communism," Dan shot back. "Not everybody gets it."

Ronnie's face flushed, and for a second Lynn thought he was going to go off on Dan. To her surprise, though, he simply let out a scoffing breath.

"Whatever. Let's get this over with."

Lynn hid a smile and mentally gave him a pat on the head, since she couldn't do it in real life. Ronnie's pasty complexion meant even the slightest flush of annoyance, embarrassment, or exertion was impossible to hide. One of the curses of being as pale as a vampire, Lynn supposed, a problem she was *very* grateful she didn't have. But she was impressed by this newfound self-control. If only she could figure out how to give him positive reinforcement without getting on his nerves.

Another problem, another day.

Lynn examined the stats on Ronnie's controversially named weapon. Zelda's Sword of Mastery had all the lethality of a Nitro-class sword on top of multiple stacking DOT—damage over time—auras. The DOTs were aimed at aggressive type TDMs, making the sword particularly ideal for an assault player. The coolest feature, though, was a special ability called Nitro Storm. It was a damage buff that charged up based on strike accuracy. The more skilled and precise you were with your attacks, the faster the ability recharged. Once fully charged, you could activate it to blast an expanding ring of pure damage to everything around you. It would be absolutely epic in situations like those they'd faced in Operation Boss Bash, where they'd been wading through hordes of tightly packed TDMs.

Lynn tried not to be jealous about everybody's shiny new weapons. It wasn't as if she lacked anything in the rare items department. All her Skadi items were overpowered for their level, were stacked with additional buffs, *and* they leveled with her, meaning she would never have to discard them as obsolete. Not only were they likely the most lethal weapons in the game, but keeping the same gear cut down on time wasted adapting new skills and techniques. If she wanted something new to get excited over, she would have to keep her kill-to-damage ratio best in the game and wait until Level 40 for the crowning piece of her Skadi's Avatar set. In the meantime...

"Okay, I know you guys have been busy sleeping for the past forty-eight hours, but between all that snoozing, has anyone read up on the new item icon that showed up on our HUD after we reached Level 38?"

Mack and Edgar exchanged identical clueless looks while Ronnie and Dan shrugged.

"You mean bait?" Ronnie said. "Yeah, I looked it up. Not much tactical chatter on it yet since we're on the leading edge of levelers and it's a new patch, so they didn't have it in beta."

"It looks really interesting though," Dan said, brightening up. "It's basically a detached taunt function. An aggro decoy. We have our own built-in aggro that we manage using globes so we're not constantly mobbed. But with bait we can set it like a mine to activate immediately or with a countdown timer, and it'll draw all aggressive-type TDMs in a specified range until the juice runs out. It stacks like globes, so the more we allocate the stronger the effect is."

Lynn grinned at her teammate.

"Thanks for doing my briefing for me, Dan."

"Uh," Dan looked sheepish, but Lynn just laughed.

"Better you than me. Did you have any thoughts on application?" She had quite a few tricks in mind for this new tool they'd been given, but she wanted to hear everyone else's ideas first.

While Dan chewed his lip and Mack and Edgar read up on how bait functioned in their TD Hunter app's tactical section, Ronnie surprised her by speaking up.

Ever since he'd come back from his "exile" to Elena's Cedar Rapids Champions, he'd been uncharacteristically quiet during tactical discussions. Lynn knew it wasn't from lack of opinions—he had those in spades. Maybe he'd been unsure how to participate collaboratively as a team member instead of simply dictating his opinion as captain. She'd noticed Edgar talking to him a time or two, off on their own, so maybe the others were pitching in to do whatever it was guys did to help each other out. Man to man. That kind of thing.

Whatever it was, she was grateful but still pretty clueless on how to overcome the wall of awkwardness and low-level resentment between them. She still hadn't figured out what Ronnie's problem was, so all she could do in the meantime was be polite and professional, and hope no drama came up that would ruin their fragile team dynamic.

"Supply harvesting," Ronnie said, looking at Dan while he said it.

Dan's eyes lit up.

"Yeah! Set up bait traps, let the buggers come to *us*. Less running around for Mack and better crowd control overall."

"Nice," Lynn said, nodding appreciatively. "Anything else?"

Ronnie didn't look at her as he cocked his head in thought, then shrugged his shoulders.

"Depends on how scarce a resource they are. If TDMs drop lots of them, we can work them into our assault SOPs and team formations to create pockets of enemies we can more easily pick off, increasing our kill-to-damage scores. They'd also be useful in boss fights." He shrugged again and fiddled absently with his batons in the ensuing silence.

"Great insights, thanks Ronnie," Lynn said, then cringed internally. Hopefully she sounded more impressive to her team than she did to herself. She took a deep breath and dove into her own analysis—experience had taught her that obsessing over people's perception of her was a quick and dark path to anxiety and paralysis.

"They'll absolutely be useful in boss fights, but we'll have to train with them to test out various techniques. I'm thinking specifically of using them to break and reform the defensive circles around bosses so we can create functional corridors to the boss instead of fighting back amorphous waves that fill any hole as soon as we make it. But you're right, it'll depend on how effective they are and how many of them we manage to collect day-to-day. They could be a game changer. We'll have to see."

The guys had gathered in a semicircle around her, and they nodded their heads in unison, expressions ranging from focused to determined to eager.

"All right. Why don't we stow the chit-chat and get busy killing stuff?"

"Now you're talkin'." Edgar said with a grin.

"And here I thought I'd get one week—*one week*—to slum around eating cheese puffs and Skittles all day," Dan complained.

"*Skittles*, dude? What are you, *five*?" Edgar asked with a snort.

"Don't you dare judge my choice of fuel," Dan said with mock severity. "My genius requires high quantities of refined sugars to function."

Ronnie's lips twitched upward and he made a scoffing sound.

"Genius? Riiight. Hey, Mack, what's the difference between Dan and a squirrel hopped up on speed?"

Mack's brow wrinkled in thought.

"Uh, what?"

"The squirrel has a girlfriend!"

Everyone laughed but Dan, who made a show of rolling his shoulders and cracking his neck.

"Yeah, yeah, yeah. You're all just jealous of my insane athletic skills."

"Dude," Ronnie said. "you were the only one to fail PE in ninth grade. Even *Edgar* passed—no offense, man."

"None taken," Edgar said, popping a piece of gum in his mouth, then stuffing the wrapper in a pocket. "It was my crowning achievement." He pulled out his other baton and flipped both over the backs of his hands. "So are we gonna start killing stuff or what?"

Lynn grinned. She was happy to see the guys banter; it was good for team morale. It was tough to know if or how to participate, though, so she usually kept quiet. Maybe if she loosened up and tried harder to participate, it would make things less awkward between her and Ronnie? Pithy zingers were her bread and butter as Larry Coughlin, but she prepared most of those ahead of time. Maybe Mr. Krator was right, and she should practice more off the cuff.

Worth a try.

"Just waiting for you yahoos to finish insulting each other," she quipped, and was gratified to see Ronnie snort as a grudging smile pulled at his lips. "Come on, Skadi's Wolves, let's see what this bait function can do."

They broke around noon to switch locations and get some drone-delivered food that they ate while giving their bodies a rest. They no longer worried about little things like travel or food costs. Their sponsorship money more than covered such expenses and every minute mattered if they wanted to reach Level 40 by the championship.

Their experiments with bait had been illuminating, but they needed higher density TDMs to test it on before they could create any battle strategies with it. Drones had gathered throughout the morning, several of them bigger and louder than the tiny paparazzi vultures Lynn was used to, and it got on her nerves. Switching locations was an opportunity to lose their flying fan club and head to a more infrastructure-dense part of the city, and therefore, a more target-rich environment.

Lynn wondered sometimes how players in rural parts of the country fared. True, mesh nodes were ubiquitous, even out in the boondocks. But she didn't see how there could be enough TDM-dense areas to sustain fast leveling. Or did the algorithm use the GPS coordinates of all registered players to generate sufficient TDMs wherever players were located, regardless of what spawn patterns it used in cities?

Those were the sorts of things she pondered during their daily airbus or air taxi rides. That, and even stranger things, like why TDMs never appeared inside buildings—a safety feature?—and why she'd started getting goosebumps and hairs standing up on the back of her neck whenever she passed transformers, nodes, generators, and other places she knew TDMs would be massing in the TD Hunter game.

It wasn't real, so why was she jumpy when she wasn't even in combat mode? Random traffic noises now reminded her of TDM beeps and whistles. She'd catch a whisper of noise behind her and spin, hands coming up automatically to slash at a sneaky ghost. She got some weird looks at school sometimes.

Too much time with her head in the game, probably. She and the guys had been living and breathing TD Hunter for months, it was no wonder she'd started imagining the presence of TDMs all around her. Maybe the team should have taken spring break off after all...

But no, they couldn't afford any down time. She would relax after they'd won the national championship, and not a moment before.

Their afternoon went well despite a rising grumble about working so hard during a school break. Lynn didn't blame them, but she also didn't relent. They needed to spend the rest of the week testing out new weapons and tactics and doing everything they could to inch closer to Level 39.

Mercifully, they had no homework to worry about over break, so once Lynn called it a day in the late afternoon, she knew they were all looking forward to long hot showers and free evenings to unwind. She was hoping to hang out with her mom for a while before Matilda went to work. They'd barely gotten to see each other for months between all of Lynn's obligations and Matilda's night shift schedule. Lynn could tell it was straining things, and it bothered her.

No one understood how precious time with your family was—not until your family was taken away.

Lynn fingered her Helle pocketknife, thoughts far away on her dad's long-ago stories of Norway, while she trudged down the hallway to her apartment door. She was just grabbing the doorknob when she heard a musical peal of laughter from inside the apartment.

She froze.

Was that her mother?

Her mom never laughed. Not like *that*. Not since her dad... no, it must have been some stream playing on the wall-screen.

Except there it was again, quieter this time, but with some gasping, like someone was laughing so hard they were having trouble breathing properly.

Lynn put her ear to the door, listening intently.

"I can*not* believe it. You've got to be pulling my leg... a horde of homeless men? No, you're exaggerating, there's no way... he did *what* to his testicles?... How did you get out of *that*?... yeah right, you just put on an accent and they let you walk away?... Nuh-uh, now I *know* you're lying."

The sound of her mom laughing and giggling riveted Lynn to the door as if someone had screwed bolts through her ear. She didn't move a muscle, just listened as whoever was on the other side of the conversation finished their story, prompting more amusement and accusations of tall tales from her mom.

"Well, I'd better get going, Lynn will be home soon and... yes, yes, I know, eventually. Give it some time. I have dinner to make... uh-huh, I'll bet you would... mm-hmm... bye, now. We'll talk again soon. Bye-bye."

Her mother fell silent, and after a few moments Lynn pulled slowly back from the door and stared at it in utter bewilderment.

Her mom had friends at work, coworkers she gossiped with and such. A few of them were good enough friends that Matilda had them over for dinner once in a blue moon. But none of the voice chats Matilda had with them sounded like *that*. That had sounded like her mom was... flirting with whoever had been on the other end.

Had her mom been talking to a *guy*? A guy she was interested in?

Was her mom *dating*?

Lynn had absolutely no idea what to think about that.

It had been almost nine years since her dad had died. Her mom had never dated, never talked about getting "back into the saddle" or anything like that. Lynn remembered an occasional muttered comment from her grandma in South Dakota about "more grandchildren," but that was it.

What should she do?

Lynn had no idea how long she stood out in the hall, staring blankly while faint sounds filtered through the door of clanking pans and vegetables being chopped on their worn wooden cutting board. Finally, though, her tired muscles and the siren call of the shower broke her from her trance and she gripped the doorknob, still with no clue what to do.

For now, at least, she would do nothing.

Chapter 2

THE FIRST DAY BACK AT SCHOOL WAS HERALDED BY AN ANNOYingly befitting rainy day, considering their grumpy moods and the fact that it was now April. Lynn had mixed feelings about how the day would go, since clips of their Boss Bash battle were *still* making the rounds. Lynn couldn't tell if whoever kept sharing them was trying to do her a favor or give her high blood pressure.

Probably neither, but good luck convincing her brain of that.

It could just as well be Tsunami's doing, Lynn supposed. They obviously had a vested interest in their game trending as much as possible. She just couldn't get over seeing clips of herself pop up in every suggested and trending feed whenever she ventured onto the streams.

It turned out school was a mixed bag: she garnered way more attention than she'd ever wanted or was comfortable with, but at least it was mostly positive. As she and the guys walked from class to class, people tore their unfocused gazes away from their LINC interfaces to stare. The usual suspects booed them, but that was far outweighed by the high fives and "Cool moves, guys!" they got from fellow students they'd never talked to in their lives.

If someone had told her a year ago she'd one day be at the top of the school popularity totem pole, she would have laughed in their face, then asked if they needed to be checked into a mental hospital.

Yet here she was.

At least there were still the CRC groupies who flip-flopped between pretending she didn't exist and acting like she was the scum of the earth.

You couldn't have everything in life, could you?

The publicity was doing exactly what Mr. Krator no doubt wanted it to: make more TD Hunter players. The school was abuzz with talk of the game—apparently a lot of people had started playing over spring break after they'd seen Skadi's Wolves destroy that boss. Lynn didn't care, as long as people left her alone so she could win this freaking championship.

Lynn and the guys always stuck together at school to discourage anybody getting too "friendly," whether fan or hater. Since they were all seniors they had most classes together, and they'd worked out a buddy system for the times their paths diverged. Kayla joined them when she could. It was a hundred times easier facing it all as a team, and it made Lynn understand why Elena always surrounded herself with so many fawning acolytes.

Speaking of useless wastes of space...

"Well, if it isn't the mighty Boss Girl herself."

The familiar, sneering voice made Lynn roll her eyes, and she would have kept walking, if Elena and three of her flunkies hadn't been blocking the door out of the bathroom Lynn was in. She had diverted from her usual path to use the restroom, so the guys were already in class, though thankfully Kayla had held back to go with her.

"You're boring, Elena. Go away," Lynn said, refusing to even grace the bully with a glance as she tried to sidestep around the group.

Once upon a time, the mere sight of Elena would trigger Lynn's fight or flight response, making her body tense and heart rate shoot upward. Lynn had grown since then, and learned that bullies only had as much power over you as you gave them. Her current calm was the result of long months unlearning the automatic fear responses years of bullying had carved into her. She still felt the unwanted anxiety sometimes—would it ever truly disappear?—but at least now she knew how to talk herself out of it.

She'd proven her own strength to herself, and that was something Elena could never take away.

Still, Elena wasn't harmless. A viper's bite was venomous, whether you had an antidote or not. Which was why Lynn watched Elena carefully out of the corner of her eye.

"You know, Elena," Kayla said from behind Lynn, "your superior act would be a lot more convincing if *your* stream had been the one trending for the last..." Kayla mimed counting on her fingers, "*seven* days straight. Haven't you just *loved* watching Lynn's sub count skyrocket?"

Elena's mouth contorted into a sneer.

"Did you hear something, ladies? I think that filthy, whoring traitor tried to speak, but she's too dumb to—"

"*Boor-ing*," Lynn interrupted loudly, eyes rolling hard enough to get stuck in the back of her head. "Elena, you're as smart as a frog with amnesia. Move, or you're gonna get hurt."

"Are you threatening me?" Elena asked in a scandalized voice, and Lynn could tell by the way she blinked her eyes that she was activating something on her visual implants, probably her livestream.

Perfect, Lynn thought, smiling sweetly at Elena as one of Larry's many aphorisms played through her head: *The best ambush is the one your prey walks right into.*

"Nope, just thought you might want to know there's a spider crawling up your leg right now." She glanced down and pointed casually.

Elena screamed like she was auditioning for a horror movie and flailed frantically, trying to jump away, shake her leg, and search for the supposed spider all at the same time. The girls standing with her screamed and backpedaled as well, giving Elena plenty of room to fall gracelessly onto the floor of the hall as she tripped over her own feet.

Lynn nearly missed the opportunity to make a swift exit, she was laughing so hard. But she and Kayla managed to slip out of the bathroom and down the hall before a purple-faced Elena made it back to her feet.

"You—*You*—" Elena spluttered, looking mad enough to commit murder.

"Bye, Elena," Lynn called as she walked away. "I think it's on your shoulder now, by the way."

Another shriek, though smaller this time, followed them down the hall, and Lynn and Kayla laughed shamelessly.

"That was *brilliant*," Kayla said once she'd gotten her breath back.

"Yeah, I guess." Lynn shrugged, still grinning. "It'll only work once, though."

"So what? Maybe it'll teach her to think twice before trying to instigate a fight."

"No way we'd be that lucky." Lynn sighed. They arrived at their classroom, and Lynn glimpsed her teammates inside. "Man, the guys are going to be *so* jealous they missed that. The look on Elena's face... I'm sure she's already deleted whatever footage she started recording."

"Oh, don't you worry, honey," Kayla said, her tone turning downright evil. "I turned on my livestream the second Elena showed up. The *whole world* just saw her make an absolute fool of herself. I could win funniest stream clip of the year with this footage." She broke off giggling, eyes unfocused, obviously rewatching the moment on her AR contacts.

A wicked grin spread across Lynn's face. Maybe these last two months of school wouldn't be so bad after all.

By lunchtime the entire school—and likely half the country— had seen the clip. People were grouped at tables across the cafeteria watching it together, pointing and laughing. Lynn had never seen a clip go so viral, so fast. Not even an hour had passed since Elena had confronted them, and there were already hundreds of remixes, stitches, memes, and more zinging around the mesh web.

Elena, unsurprisingly, was nowhere to be seen. Lynn almost felt sorry for the girl. She hadn't set out to humiliate Elena in front of the world. She was just trying to get to class on time. Besides, if she'd had to physically push past Elena to get out of the bathroom, Elena probably would have gone running to the principal claiming Lynn had assaulted her. Kayla had done the smart thing to protect them both by livestreaming the interaction.

"Kayla, you are *brilliant*," Dan said, still barely able to breathe for laughing, even though he'd seen the clip a dozen times already.

Kayla, sitting opposite Dan at their lunch table, smiled shyly, and Lynn hid a grin of her own at the sight.

"Thanks. I'm just glad I was there to back Lynn up."

"Lynn," Mack said, brow creased, "maybe you should start livestreaming all the time at school, just in case Elena tries something again."

Lynn choked on a mouthful of milk and nearly sprayed it across the table. She swallowed it with difficulty, then aimed a threatening finger at Mack.

"Wash your filthy mouth out and never speak those words again, Maxwell Rios, or I will tell your mother we're dating."

Ronnie and Dan sniggered while Mack shrank back defensively, his warm-toned skin blanching whiter than Ronnie's.

"Geez, Lynn, I was just tryin'a be helpful. She would *kill* me."

"Exactly," Lynn said, adding some Larry growl to the word.

"Mack's right, though," Edgar said around a fry he'd just popped into his mouth. "I think we need to deputize Kayla as your official bathroom wingwoman, just to be safe."

Kayla giggled while Lynn groaned.

"Don't go giving her ideas, Edgar."

"No, I love it!" Kayla said, clapping her hands together. "I could be your official videographer! My stream is going to be hopping after today, I could totally do a Lynn walkalong vlog!"

"Kayla," Lynn said, tamping down a spike of stupid anxiety, "I just got you back as a friend, don't make me murder you now."

Edgar shot Lynn a scandalized look.

"Lynn, don't bite the hand that feeds us. If you touch a hair on Kayla's head, Mrs. Swain will never make us bacon-wrapped steak bites again."

"Yeah!" said the rest of the guys in near perfect unison.

Lynn waved a fork threateningly, encompassing everyone at the table.

"Just stop talking about vlogs and you can all keep your steak bites."

Lynn focused on chewing and breathing deep, slow breaths. She really might resort to homicide if anyone else tried to intrude on her privacy more than she was already enduring. She knew Kayla meant well, though she wondered if her extreme enthusiasm came partly from a place of guilt. Either way, Kayla was fitting in well with their social group and the last thing Lynn wanted was more publicity and drama to mess that up.

"So," Kayla said between bites, "Elena totally tried to cozy up to me in Calculus today and convince me to turn on you—before the bathroom incident, obviously."

Edgar snorted, though Ronnie glared suspiciously at the frizzy-haired girl.

Lynn just raised her eyebrows.

"Let me guess, it didn't go quite the way Elena had hoped?"

"Oh, I told her she could take her slimy, weaselly self and go stick her head in a toilet," Kayla said brightly.

Ronnie looked mollified and went back to watching whatever gaming or political stream he was focused on as he ate. He'd been uncharacteristically subdued ever since rejoining their team. Lynn wouldn't lie, she enjoyed his silence *immensely*. But it also worried her. Had he actually found a modicum of maturity? Or was there something else the matter?

Shaking her head, Lynn grinned at Kayla as she stabbed at the uninspiring grilled chicken on her plate.

"Wish I could've been a fly on the wall for *that* conversation."

"I thought her head might actually explode, she was so outraged. But that's not all. After class two of the other girls she bullies into following her around pinged me and asked me for advice on how to get out from under her thumb." Kayla shrugged and shot a look at Lynn. "I told them what you told me: just ignore her and leave. I even invited them to come eat at our table. I, um, hope that's okay."

Lynn wasn't thrilled at the idea, but she didn't say so.

"That's great, Kayla. You did the right thing. I'm proud of you." Lynn hadn't planned the words, they just felt like the right thing to say. And apparently, they were, because Kayla swallowed, and her eyes got suspiciously shiny.

"Th-that means a lot, Lynn. Thank you."

The guys poked at their food awkwardly and Lynn rolled her eyes. Boys. They had the emotional range of a teaspoon.

"Ya done good, girl," Edgar offered, proving Lynn wrong at least a little bit. "Bullies only have the power you give 'em." He shrugged. "They're mostly cowards. And apparently also afraid of spiders."

Everyone snorted at that and Lynn resisted the urge to watch a replay of Elena's epic fail just one more time.

"Thanks Edgar, you're a sweetie," Kayla said, beaming.

Edgar grinned at the compliment and Lynn felt a weird flash of annoyance. But she was distracted from the thought by Ronnie's abrupt declaration.

"I knew it!"

"What's it this time?" Dan asked, leaning forward eagerly. "Did you find that unlimited ammo code for Missile Command 3000 I told you about?"

"No." Ronnie snorted. "Nobody plays that anymore. Besides,

this is way more important. Reports confirm China has been rationing energy in its largest cities for weeks now. They pretend like everything is fine, but there are widespread blackouts for the poorer sections because the ruling party is shunting all the energy to the business sectors and rich neighborhoods."

Dan leaned back and popped a chip into his mouth.

"Yeah, so what?"

"They've had terrible infrastructure for years now," Mack piped up. "Ever since the pandemics in the '20s caused that worldwide recession and their construction market crashed because they were building all this giant stuff that nobody could pay for."

There was a moment of silence at their table as everyone stared at Mack.

"Oh, come *on*," Dan finally said. "What do *you* know about Chinese infrastructure?"

"Riko and I talk about it sometimes," Mack said with a shrug. "You know China is aggressive and expansionist, so it's a pretty common topic in Japan."

"Oh, so a Japanese love-bot told you some wiki facts about China, big deal," Dan said. "Now you're an expert, huh?"

"Shut up, guys, this is serious," Ronnie said. "This proves that China and the US, or China and *somebody* are conducting cyber warfare in secret, attacking each other's grids."

"Ooor," Mack said, "maybe they just have old equipment and a massive labor shortage because of those idiotic population control policies they had for decades."

"Seriously?" Ronnie said. "When did *you* get a PhD in global politics? Or is that more wiki knowledge from your bot girlfriend."

"Oh, shut up!" Mack snapped. "She's not a bot, and it's not *my* fault you never pay attention in history class. Plus, grid failures are happening all over the world right now. It's a *global* energy crisis, not a US-China thing."

Lynn tuned out her friends as they continued bickering. The mention of energy grids had reminded her of something: she hadn't seen any workmen out behind the school fiddling with its grid equipment that day, she'd checked. They'd been out there nearly every Monday for months. The only thing Lynn could figure was that the increased energy usage every Monday when school resumed tripped whatever error in the system they'd been trying to isolate and fix since the total failure last fall.

But there were no techs today, and no random flickering lights up and down the halls.

Maybe they'd overhauled the entire system during spring break? Or maybe... this was their first day back at school since they'd destroyed that massive Alpha Boss to the north. But that was just a coincidence, right?

Lynn glared at her half-eaten chicken, thoroughly annoyed by her overactive imagination.

Whether it was a coincidence or not, it got her thinking about St. Sebastian's and Lindale Mall, blackouts and conspiracy theories—and she didn't like where her brain was taking her. There had been no catastrophic failures at her mom's hospital since last summer when both the main grid *and* the backup power failed. But she'd heard her mom grumble a time or two about how the things at the hospital still weren't back to normal since that incident. There were electrical crews constantly getting in the way and periodic glitches that kicked in the backup system, which managed to reset at least half the computers and medical devices throughout the hospital.

It sounded too much like what had been going on at her school, at least until today, and Lynn really, *really* didn't like what her brain concluded from that.

She finished her lunch in silence, her earlier elation at Elena's humiliation forgotten as her brain focused on something that seemed much more important than high school drama.

The only silver lining was that she could easily do a bit of solo scouting to see if her suspicions had any merit without having to mention her theory to anyone. And, thankfully, it tied perfectly into figuring out how to get her team to Level 40 by June.

It was raining hard enough that the team had decided to get a head start on homework that evening and work on drills instead of hunting, so Lynn was free to scratch that itch. She sent a message to her mom that she would be extra late getting home, though Matilda wouldn't get it for hours yet, since she was sleeping. Then Lynn refocused on her friends and tried not to dwell on the uneasy feeling in her stomach.

"I am one-hundred-percent certain that this excursion is unwise."

"Just don't say 'I have a bad feeling about this,'" Lynn subvocalized to Hugo. "Then we'd *really* be screwed."

"I am an AI, I do not *have* feelings."

"Exactly. I think we're good."

"No, we are not *good*. It is extremely late and this area would be difficult for emergency services to reach should we need to call them."

"Come on, Hugo. There's a *hospital* a few blocks south. Can't they just fly over here with their helicopter?"

"That is beside the point, young lady—"

"Oh-ho, young lady? What happened to Miss Lynn?"

"I have determined that it is in your best interest to understand the seriousness of the situation, and since you usually ignore me, I am now employing stronger terms of address to ensure your attention."

"Only an AI would think 'young lady' was a 'stronger' form of address," Lynn muttered, hands shoved into the pockets of her rain jacket as she walked down the shadowed gravel road. It wasn't raining quite as hard as the weather app had predicted, but it was still cold and miserable. The rain wasn't a threat to her equipment, of course. Everything from LINCs to earbuds to AR interfaces were necessarily impervious to moisture, since most people never took them off these days. But even with mild rain, the risk of slipping and injury always made her paranoid. They'd had enough minor bruises and sprains over the months that she didn't regret sending the guys home, especially since it was nice to do some scouting on her own every now and then.

The bright lights of downtown Cedar Rapids lit the sky behind her to the south, while the duller lights of the rest of the city created a halo of dimly glowing horizon around her. She was walking through the central rail hub of the city, one she'd discovered had a sizable abandoned lot beside it according to a quick search of EarthMaps. The air smelled of mud, trash, and chemicals, and she had to weave her way around muddy puddles interspersed along the road.

It was the perfect place for a boss TDM to set up camp if it wanted to...she didn't know, maybe siphon off electricity from the surrounding grid? It was a stupid, crazy thought. Absolutely bonkers. Nobody was siphoning off anything, TD Hunter was just an ultra-realistic game and the algorithm obviously had enough geographical data to place TDMs exactly where they needed to be to maintain that realism.

That was it.

"Okay, that's the lot up ahead," Lynn subvocalized, stopping at a fork in the gravel road paralleling the electric rail. She noticed straggling clusters of soggy and disintegrating tents, tarps, boxes, and various other trash along the outside of the lot's chain link fence. An abandoned homeless encampment. She wondered where all the residents had gone. Not that it would have stopped her, but she was grateful she wouldn't have an audience for what she was going to do next.

A memory surfaced from last summer: her mom talking about homeless people dropping dead with no explanation. The hospital had checked for viruses, and finding none had passed it off as some new drug cocktail making the rounds. It had angered Matilda because once the possibility of a new virus mutation had been eliminated—everyone was still jumpy from what had happened in the 2020s—the hospital administration hadn't cared a whit about the victims. It wasn't Matlida's wheelhouse, what with being an ER nurse, but Lynn knew from her mom's comments over the years that being married to a cop had made her much more aware of how much hospitals and local police could work together to help improve their communities, if they chose to. Urban decay affected every city these days, with panhandlers and homeless people wherever you looked. Her mom had told her once that drug cartels often used the homeless as guinea pigs to test out new products before they sold them to their rich repeat clients.

Lynn looked down at her feet, clad in sturdy high-performance, shock-absorbing boots. At least she didn't have to worry about stepping on any old needles.

She could just imagine the look on her mom's face if Matilda could see where she had ventured. Which was why she never told her mom the sorts of places Skadi's Wolves went while hunting TDMs. This was nothing. She was pretty sure they'd interrupted a drug tradeoff once in the industrial district. Nothing had happened because her team had been so focused on fighting the waves of TDMs they'd encountered along the derelict warehouses, the druggies probably thought they were crazy or high with all their leaping and rolling and shouting at each other about Rakshar and Spithragani. The rough-looking men had huddled, then made a quick exit and Lynn had only really thought about who they were or what they'd been doing after the fact.

Lynn pulled her hands out of her pockets and the nippy spring air got to work on her exposed fingers. She flexed them, trying to decide if she should bother rooting through her backpack for her athletic gloves that had kept her fingers warm and safe from frostbite through a winter of hunting. She decided against it and instead slid her twin batons from their stretchy sheaths. The long thin pockets were sewn down along her thighs, built into the high-performance athletic pants TD Hunter had outfitted them with when they'd qualified as a Hunter Strike Team last year. She rotated her wrists and mimed a few basic strikes, warming up her body.

"Hugo, on my mark, drop me into combat mode equipped with Bastion and Wrath, plus full armor and stealth. Hopefully, I won't have to fight too many of the buggers to get a look at what's in that lot."

There was a pause and Lynn wondered if AIs ever sighed.

"If you are absolutely set on this unwise course of action, I recommend at least waiting until your entire team can be here to support you."

Lynn shook her head. It was going to be tricky enough explaining how—and why—she'd found this boss without dragging the guys all the way out on this wild goose chase. *If* she found a boss, of course. Maybe her theory was wrong.

"On my mark—"

"I am officially lodging my protest—"

"Three, two, one, mark!"

Monsters materialized around her, glowing dimly in the night. They might have had impressive reflexes for a game, but Lynn was already moving, slashing and bashing until she'd cleared a twenty-foot circle around her. They were mostly Charlie Class, though there was an inconvenient number of Vargs, Stalkers, and Yaguar, solitary patrol-type TDMs that were more active at night. Most of the monsters didn't stand a chance against Wrath, though, even if they were able to target her past the stealth bonus of her trusty shield, Bastion.

She focused on her work until she had cleared a large enough space to step back and evaluate her surroundings without getting pounced by TDMs.

When she finally did look around, she felt an uneasy sense of triumph.

"Dang."

"I hope that means you intend to immediately retreat and abandon this foolish errand."

"You know, if you weren't an AI, I might mistake you for a pansy. I get that your job is to keep people safe while they're playing TD Hunter, but you gotta break a few eggs to make an omelette."

"As long as that egg is not *you* then I am perfectly fine with the arrangement," Hugo said, his tone just this side of huffy.

"Well, I've seen what I need to see, so you're getting your wish. Let's get out of here."

"With pleasure!"

The glowing ranks of TDMs in the far reaches of Lynn's AR vision faded as the real world reestablished itself. The ominous clicks, roars, screeches, and moans of the TDMs were replaced by the distant hum of airbus engines and the quiet chirp of a cricket nearby braving the chill.

The red dots that had just disappeared from her overhead still glowed in her mind, though, taunting her.

Well, she'd been right. Here was another boss TDM, a made-up monster in a game, hanging around an area that was having very real and very inexplicable electric grid problems.

Coincidence?

It... it *had* to be. Grid problems weren't that uncommon. She heard about them in all sorts of places around the country and around the globe. What she'd witnessed at Lindale Mall and her school could be anecdotal. Correlation wasn't causation and all that. Maybe blackouts had gotten more frequent in the last year, or maybe that was just a skewed perspective. She didn't know enough to make that judgment.

What she *did* know, though, was that Skadi's Wolves needed lots of experience in a short amount of time. So there was no reason not to organize another boss hunt and pound this one into the dirt. What she discovered after that, well... she'd have to wait and see.

Lynn thought back to what her overhead had shown her. Those multi-layered rings in the abandoned lot had looked smaller than the ones that had been around the Alpha Boss Gyges. The distant sparkling mist in her AR sight that had marked the location of the unknown boss had seemed smaller than Gyges, too. That plus the fact that she'd been able get this close and be fighting mostly Charlie Class monsters boded well. If she had to guess, this TDM seemed like a Bravo Class boss, a much more reasonable target that Skadi's Wolves could tackle with a handful of other teams.

Probably. Maybe.

Was she willing to bet on it?

What if not enough teams could make it on short notice and they ended up hurting their rankings instead of defeating the boss?

On the other hand, what if Skadi's Wolves played it slow and cautious? Would they still make Level 40 by mid June?

Making decisions like this had been so much easier in virtual as Larry Coughlin, safely removed from reality. Now there was infinitely more at stake. Infinitely more she could lose. How was she supposed to tell the difference between unhealthy, risk-averse fear and healthy caution that helped her make wise judgments?

And how much of her reluctance came from that uneasy feeling in her gut.

Was she jumping at shadows?

Lynn stood for a long moment in the dark rail yard, considering her options and wavering between fear and determination. Hugo, thankfully, didn't pester her. Finally, she shook her head and turned to trek back toward the lights of downtown where she could hop on the nearest airbus and get home out of the rain.

She was overthinking everything. She needed to focus on two things and two things only: getting to Level 40 and graduating high school. Even if there was... *something* going on, she was just a teenager. A global energy grid war—if Ronnie's theories were to be believed—was way above her pay grade, as Larry would say. Also, not real, because China made way too much money off the US to want to wreck it economically. That was just common sense. The whole conspiracy theory was ludicrous.

Just ludicrous.

The next evening, Lynn got a formal invite on her WarMonger account to participate in a special cross-promotional effort with Tsunami. It offered player "Larry Coughlin" generous compensation to spend an hour or so fighting through various match scenarios in the special TDM-WarMonger crossover mode they'd recently launched. They would record bits and pieces for their advertising campaign, including her voice reading a selection of scripted lines.

That was it. Nice and easy.

Lynn sent them back a counter-offer demanding a long list of special weaponry and armor they would add to her inventory in lieu of payment. Not only was that a believable thing for the "real" Larry Coughlin to do, but she knew for a fact she could make twice as much selling the items in auction than Tsunami had offered to pay her.

She grinned at the thought of Mr. Krator's reaction when he heard of her counter-offer.

Within an hour she'd gotten a response accepting her terms and suggesting several days and times to pick from to do the recordings. At that point Lynn started to feel the nerves. What was she even doing? This whole Larry Coughlin character was a lie. Did she really want to lean into it? Exploit it for her own gain? Okay, so she'd already been doing that for years. But back then she'd been desperate. She'd had no other options. It had been a defense mechanism to survive in virtual gaming. But now...now she could choose to never touch WarMonger again, and still have a bright future in gaming.

TD Hunter had given her that freedom.

And yet, she didn't *want* to abandon Larry Coughlin. He *was* her, even if the skin, the affectations, were a disguise. Plus she'd worked her *tail* off for that success and reputation.

Was it right to keep deceiving her friends, though? How could she tell them now? If they didn't instantly vote her off the team, it would still cause so much tension they'd probably lose the championship.

She couldn't ask her mom for advice, either, or Mr. Thomas. They already knew about Larry Coughlin, but they didn't *get* gaming—or her complex relationship with it. Honesty was preferable in any normal situation, but the whole Lynn-Larry mess was far from normal.

In the end, Lynn gritted her teeth, chose a time, and responded to the message. Once the deed was done, she felt a sort of hollow sorrow. Where was her dad when she needed him? *He* would have known what to do. Rainy day gaming on the couch had been a treasured ritual, smack talking her dad while they competed in all sorts of old racing and street-fighting games—games her father had played as a boy on simulators of consoles that were old even in her grandparents' time. Whether she was dropping banana peels to wipe him out on a track or using punch combos he'd taught her to dominate him in the ring, gaming with him had always been about rising to the challenge, fearlessly fighting with all her heart.

The thought made her chest ache in a way she hadn't felt in years, so she threw herself into homework and shoved the feeling back down under lock and key where it belonged.

Wednesday the rain finally abated, and they got back to putting serious hunting hours in every day, practicing various tactics and squad formations using bait and their new weapon functions.

Between hunting, physical training, and squeezing in the bare minimum of homework, Lynn was back to go, go, go from before dawn to long after dusk. She was glad she and her mom had taken time during spring break to do puzzles together and go out for steaks and ice cream. She barely saw Matilda the rest of the week beyond a wave and a "Hi, Mom, bye, Mom" when she grabbed protein bars to go and raced off to school each morning.

She'd told the guys about wanting to organize another boss hunt and they'd all agreed it was a good idea. Only Edgar had given her a hard look when she casually mentioned she'd already found a boss to destroy. Her other three teammates seemed to take the extra legwork for granted.

To her delight, the far-flung teams of Skadi's Horde jumped on her invite for another boss battle like wolves on a pile of meat. Only about half could make it on short notice, though, which Lynn hoped would be enough. The Lone Gunmen, Monster Control Bureau, Voodoo Girls, Light Brigade, and other familiar faces sent their delighted RSVP, and the "Boss Bash 2.0" was scheduled for the third Saturday in April, rain or shine.

As the days progressed, Lynn picked the brains of the other team captains for how to apply the "bait and destroy" tactics Skadi's Wolves were developing to a large-scale boss battle. Quorra, captain of Voodoo Girls, had a lot of good outside-the-box ideas. Lynn made a mental note to see what the guys thought of making Voodoo Girls their player alternates in case one of them became sick or injured right before the national championship. Picking alternates was a task Lynn had been dragging her feet on, but the success of the first Boss Bash had given her the internal confidence to tackle it.

Derek, AKA DeathShot—or YodaMaster as she'd long known him in WarMonger—was also very helpful as a sounding board for hunting tactics. Derek's insights were so on point, in fact, that Lynn wondered how long he'd really been playing TD Hunter. His current team, Light Brigade, had only been on the books a few months, but he seemed *awfully* well informed on TD Hunter tactics for only having played a little while.

It was none of her business, of course, any more than her Larry Coughlin persona was his. Considering how many times she'd fought with, and against, YodaMaster in WarMonger, interacting with Derek was a tad nerve-racking. But he never acted suspicious, just affable and helpful—as Canadian as a Canadian could be. It made her laugh to herself considering how many times she'd witnessed him cow upstart noobs and pretentious Wall Street types in WarMonger. He could be as deadpan and scary as Larry Coughlin when he wanted to be. She never would have guessed what a chill person he was in the real.

It got her wondering what Derek did for a living. He must have had a flexible job to do so much travel. When she casually probed him for a bit of personal background, he politely brushed her off with a comment about private contracting—though he failed to mention what *kind* of private contracting. She wondered if he was former military, and if he now worked as a *real* mercenary for one of those "global force solutions" military contractors. He seemed too nice for that, but maybe his affability was as much a mask as Larry Coughlin's constant threats.

She tried not to wonder too much about it, though, because she respected his privacy. He was a good gamer, and a reliable team player. That was all she needed to know. After all, it wasn't as if she'd ever be interacting with him beyond occasional TD Hunter or WarMonger gaming.

"You know, chum, it's a good thing Lynn isn't half as ruthless in real life as she pretends to be as Larry Coughlin, or she'd have us all figured out by now."

Steve Riker raised both eyebrows at his friend and fellow Alpha Tester, Derek Peterson, who had joined him for a bite of lunch at Tsunami's headquarters in Texas. Their cafeteria was top-notch. Real food cooked by actual people, none of that

SNAC machine shit. Derek passed through headquarters every now and then between whatever mission CIDER sent him on, and Steve always enjoyed a chance to shoot the shit with the easygoing Canuck.

"That's a pretty bold assumption. I *would* warn you not to underestimate her, but I figure you've been trounced by Larry enough times to know that by now."

They shared a laugh, but once it faded, Derek's expression turned serious again.

"I mean it, Steve. She's a nice young lady. Half the time I'm talking to her, I can't believe she's really that old snake."

"That's because she's putting on a front," Steve said with a shrug. "Lynn is just as much a mask as Larry sometimes. Don't we all put on masks to fit in? The kid's been through the wringer. And she's young. Hell, I'm sure you and me were just as crazy and clueless when we were her age."

A tiny smile curved one side of Derek's mouth.

"You, maybe. I was a right proper little soldier, eh?"

Steve balled up a napkin and threw it at his friend. Derek caught it out of the air and made a show of carefully smoothing it out, then wiping his mouth with it. Steve shook his head.

"She's a tough one. She'll be fine," Steve said, getting back to his steak and potatoes.

"Will she?" Derek said quietly.

Steve stopped with a bite of meat dripping red juices halfway to his mouth. Then he slowly put it back down.

"We don't have a choice, Derek."

Derek looked away out one of the windows that overlooked the Austin landscape.

"We volunteered for this, Steve. We knew the risks. These kids? None of them have a clue."

"We. Don't. Have. A. Choice," Steve repeated slowly.

Derek looked back at him, expression unchanged.

"I know. But I'm glad she's not my daughter."

Steve's gut twisted with guilt, but he didn't let it show on his face.

"Why's that?" he asked.

"Because I wouldn't give a shit about OPSEC," Derek responded even more softly. "I'd ship her off to a desert island until this was all over, somewhere without a shred of infrastructure where she couldn't accidentally wander through an invisible alien entity that could instantly stop her heart and fry her brain."

Steve stared at his friend. Then he realized he was gripping his fork so tightly it had bent. He relaxed his hold, methodically straightened it as best he could, and put it down. His appetite was gone.

"That'd be nice," Steve said quietly, "but there might not *be* any civilization for her to come back to. That's the entire point, *chum*. Do you really think, if you read her in, she'd pick that island over staying exactly where she is right now?"

Derek snorted, though his expression remained grave.

"Exactly," Steve said. "We can't—" His voice caught, and he coughed to clear it before continuing. "We can't play favorites. Everyone in the world is facing the same risks, and the sooner we figure these spooks out—where they're coming from and how to stop them—the sooner *everyone* will be safe again. That's why we need Lynn exactly where she is. She's already running missions, for Pete's sake, and you lucky bastards get to witness it firsthand. Yeah, maybe we can't tell her what's really going on, but that's what *you're* there for."

That finally prompted a ghost of a smile.

"They need to put you in the field on some of these boss fights," Derek said, eyeing his friend. "That waist is starting to look a bit padded, eh?"

Steve straightened and patted his stomach with a look of mock affront.

"Bull. You're just jealous of my abs."

"The ones you drew on, you mean?"

"Don't you dis my artistic skills, Canuck. I'll have you know I got an A+ in my high school art class."

"Yeah? I thought you American types ate your crayons, not drew with them."

"No, no, that's just the Jarheads. Us SPECOP guys pack 'em in with our C4 so we can blow you up with style."

"Cowboys."

"And proud of it! There's a reason people still watch John Wayne movies!"

The Alpha Tester snorted and pushed back from the table, leaving his fish and rice half eaten.

"I should get going. We've got a lot of scouting and prep to finish before Boss Bash 2.0. We need to get on location and scan this boss Lynn found, make sure it's safe enough for all these kids to tackle."

"Don't let her hear you calling her a kid," Steve said, eyeing his own steak. It would be a tragedy to waste such a perfectly delicious cut of meat. But he simply had no more stomach for it, not after what Derek had said.

"Turnabout is fair play, my friend. If she can pretend to be older than both of us, she can take some of her own medicine."

"Well, maybe you can help her tap into her inner Larry while you're at it," Steve said. "I hate seeing what this whole TD Hunter PR stunt is doing to her. I know that's the whole point of the game and the only way we can recruit enough players, but... it would drive anyone insane."

"Being Larry when she games isn't her struggle, Steve. It's carrying those qualities over to the rest of her life. I know how tough it is to keep secrets from the people you love. I think the lies are holding her back. One of these days she's going to have to come clean so she can integrate the two and fully employ all her skills in one united whole."

"Whoo-wee! I can't wait to see that day!" Steve said with a grin. "Jaws are gonna drop. Some people might even need surgery to have them reattached. I almost did."

Derek snorted and held out a hand. Steve gripped it firmly and gave his friend a serious nod.

"Take care, Canuck. These things can kill you too."

"I'll be fine, Cowboy. It's you I'm worried about, you and your blood pressure. Don't forget to hit the gym." He winked and walked away, whistling amiably.

"Cheeky bastard," Steve muttered, eyes falling again on his food. With a sigh, he picked up his plate and headed for the composter. He had a lot to do, and every day ticked them closer and closer to the apocalypse. Time to get back to work.

Chapter 3

THE DATE FOR HER LARRY COUGHLIN PROMO APPROACHED WITH alarming speed, and before she knew it, Lynn was barricading herself in her room with a giant bottle of pop and a polite warning to her mom to not disturb her for any reason. Her mom was used to her doing various recordings and interviews arranged by Mrs. Pearson, so Matilda just wished her luck and put in earbuds to browse the news streams and political podcasts in the living room.

Once Lynn had logged onto WarMonger and gotten into her home screen, she saw the match invite from Sean Dudgeon, Assistant Head of Marketing at Tsunami Entertainment. With a deep breath—and after double checking to make sure her voice modulator was on—she accepted the lobby room invite.

As the match lobby materialized before her, a voice cut in talking in the general lobby chat room.

"—the coolest part is—*oops*! He's here, gotta go!"

Lynn heard a nervous cough, a throat clearing, and then:

"Ah, hello, Mr. Coughlin, sir. Sorry about that, I was just, um, conferring with my marketing team on—"

"I don't care if you were doin' the dirty with a couple a' hookers," Lynn said darkly, her words coming out in perfect gravelly baritone. "Get this show on the road or I'm out. You ain't paying me enough to put up with weaselin' brass."

The voice choked, gulped audibly, and forged onward.

"Of course, sir! I totally understand. You've got important work to do. I'm a bit of a fan. Very honored you could join us today, Mr. Coughlin."

"Don't be. This is a transaction—one I'm not getting paid nearly enough for, based on the last thirty seconds. Give me your name and the mission brief, then shut your yapper before I shut it for you."

"Y-yes, sir. Sean Dudgeon, sir. We, uh, we'd like to start with a basic transport mission in our TD Hunter-themed scenario map. Point A to point B, timed. There's a sliding bonus for number of TDMs and Possessed killed, and stacking penalties for every team member who doesn't make it to the drop-off point."

"Team size?" Lynn barked.

"Five-man team, sir," Sean said. "Myself and three others from our marketing team, plus yourself."

Lynn made a face. She'd been hoping to go at it solo, but she supposed it made sense. Lots of WarMonger players gamed on teams and based on what she'd seen so far of the TD Hunter crossover missions, most players who tackled solo play got drive-piled by TDMs and quickly overwhelmed. She wasn't most players, though, and she'd been interested to see how long she'd survive by herself. It wasn't as if she could hop in and out of combat mode to stay alive like she could when playing TD Hunter in the real.

"Transport?" Lynn continued.

"Uh, on foot, sir."

"Weapons?"

"Well, we've created a Level 20 account for you to use—"

"Make it 35."

"Sir?"

"Don't waste my time with low-level trash, Dudgeon. You're already paying me shit, don't make me fall asleep while you're at it."

"Oookay, right," Sean said, stretching out the words as he likely delegated tasks on his side with furious speed to get the scenario parameters updated.

"Give me the full weapon load out for that level, plus a Vulca Nitron Blade, a pair of Spitfires, a Jiral Gravity Hammer, and a Hexatec Sniper Rifle," Lynn said, naming four rare weapons that weren't as good as her Skadi set, but were better than standard and would give her a tool for whatever ranged or melee situation she found herself in. She could hardly ask for the unique Skadi's

Avatar set, no matter how cool Larry Coughlin would look as a space Viking. It would be like holding a sign over her head with the giant blinking words "LYNN RAVEN" on it.

"Oh, wow, you really know your TD Hunter weaponry, Mr. Coughlin," Sean said, a starry-eyed note creeping into his voice.

Lynn frowned, not liking where this was going. Larry Coughlin usually inspired two reactions: fear or hate. She was fine with either. Sean, though, sounded like he had a fit of fanboy coming on. She was about as comfortable with that as she was with poking out her own eyeballs with a hot iron.

"Focus, fanboy," she growled. "You're making me regret this already. You get two hours from me and not a second more. I've got *real* clients waiting to pay for my expertise."

There were other, much harsher things she could have said. But Sean seemed like a decent guy, and it didn't feel right to be a jerk just because his obvious admiration made her skin crawl. She'd save the scathing stomp-downs for when they were in combat. If he mouthed off then, she'd have no qualms about cowing him into silence.

To her surprise—and chagrin—he was a legitimately good player. She supposed she should have known better than to doubt the sort of people Mr. Krator would hire to help run one of the biggest and most beloved gaming corporations in the world.

Sean and his team—a guy and two girls—took orders well and seemed to genuinely enjoy playing the scenario with her. Of course, they thought they were playing with the great and terrible Larry Coughlin... which *was* her... but not the her everyone thought she was...

The scenario was intense from the get-go, so Lynn let go of her self-conscious second-guessing and eagerly sank into Larry mode. She focused wholly on completing the mission, and let Sean worry about whether or not it looked good enough for his marketing campaign.

As they played, Sean and his team started out cheering and whooping at particularly impressive kills or moves on Lynn's part, which Lynn quickly discovered was worse than any amount of hate-filled trash talk she received from opponents in WarMonger. Trash-talk was part of the game. Cheerleading, on the other hand, made her so violently self-conscious that it yanked her out of Larry mode, threatening their mission on multiple occasions. She finally snapped and went off on her peanut gallery in fine Larry fashion, shocking them into silence with dire threats delivered in the foulest language she could recall from her research. To their credit, they took the hint and for the rest of the scenario kept quiet except for mission-essential communication.

After they'd completed the match and were back in the lobby, though, Sean seemed to forget every single thing "Larry" had told him.

"Oh my *God,* that was *amazing*, Mr. Coughlin. You are just a delight to work with! We recorded some really great footage and I can't believe we got through that mission alive. I was sure we were goners when that swarm of Spithragani came out of nowhere while we were bogged down with the Strikers, and—"

"*Quiet*," Lynn said, low and dangerous.

The sound of Sean's lips smacking together was clearly audible, and Lynn took a deep, calming breath. The gushing praise for Larry Coughlin made her gut squirm with discomfort, and she had no idea why. She'd never felt a bit of guilt playing Larry Coughlin all these years, beating other players at their own game and profiting handsomely from those willing to pay. But this felt different. It felt... dirty.

Why?

The fact that she couldn't explain it even to herself made her grumpy and short while a subdued and nervous Sean had her play a few more abbreviated scenarios to capture specific scenes, then gave her some scripted lines to read for the promo. Of course, her foul mood probably made her Larry performance that much more authentic, but it also left her feeling guilty.

She didn't *want* to be rude to Sean and his team. They seemed like pretty cool people, actually. But something about the whole situation had gotten under her skin, and she counted down the minutes until they were finished.

By the time Sean wrapped things up—five minutes shy of the allotted two hours—Lynn caught herself thinking longingly of *homework*, an alarming sign of how much she wanted the whole thing to be over.

"Well, it's been a pleasure, Mr. Coughlin," Sean said, a note of hesitation in his voice. "Truly, I'm so honored to work with you. I've always wanted to meet you and—er, well, you probably don't want to hear about, um, all that."

"First intelligent thought you've had all evening," Lynn growled.

Sean chuckled nervously, and there was an awkward silence, which made Lynn's insides squirm.

"If I hear any more fanboy sucking up, I'll have to shoot somebody, but...you and your team done good. Thought you'd be a bunch of losers, but you kept your heads, followed orders and got the mission done. That's the name of the game. That and getting paid. Getting the mission done and getting paid are the names of the game. So, make sure the check clears."

"Absolutely, Mr. Coughlin! They'll be so excited to hear it. We all really enjoy watching your match compilations. I swear, your takedowns are pure gold, and—"

"*Fanbooooy!*" Lynn said, her voice modulator making it a threatening rumble.

"Oops! Sorry, sir. Right. Well, we'll get this promotion out ASAP. I'd be happy to send you a link where you can view the finished product before it goes live—"

"I'd rather scrub my balls with sandpaper."

"Oh...right...okay. Got it. No links. Well we'd love to have you back sometime to—"

"You'll see me again just as soon as you quintuple my fee and glue your mouth shut."

"Uhhhh, well I'd have to clear it with Mr. Krator—"

"Get out of here, Fanboy, before I take back my compliments."

"Yes, sir! Of course. Have a nice day, sir!"

"Coughlin, out," Lynn barked, not wanting to cut Sean off abruptly, but also having zero "Foxtrots" left to give.

She peeled off her AR glasses and carefully set them aside, then slumped back into her body mold chair as she rubbed her face vigorously. She topped things off with a good, hearty groan, remembering all the homework she had to do, and feeling much less enthusiastic about it now that she'd escaped Sean's fanboy clutches.

Well, at least she could fortify herself with some coffee and a piece of leftover steak before she tackled the homework. She hated coffee, but it had become a necessary evil over the past few months, since her nurse mother flatly forbade her from relying on energy drinks instead. "Better the devil you know," Matilda said about coffee, being a grudging addict herself with a third shift schedule in a busy ER. Lynn's mother read as much medical research as her life would allow, and often ranted to Lynn about the dangers of believing Big Food and Big Pharma when they said a product was "safe." People had been surviving off coffee for thousands and thousands of years, though, so apparently Matilda figured that was long enough to be certain of the health risks.

Lynn got up and went to her bedroom door, opening it with her mind already turning over which assignments she absolutely had to complete before she went to bed.

She was about to step out of her room when her mom's voice registered.

"Quit it!" Matilda hissed in a tone of badly suppressed amusement. "Lynn is in her bedroom and the absolute *last* thing I need is for her to come out and see me blushing."

Lynn froze.

"Yes, I *know* you do, but you'll just have to wait. Don't make me sing the 'Be Patient' song at you like I used to at Lynn whenever she complained about waiting."

Lynn clamped a hand over her mouth, managing to suppress her snort, but only just. It'd been *years* since she'd thought about that silly song. In fact, Lynn hadn't heard her mom sing it since her dad had died. He'd been even more impatient than Lynn, eating hot cookies right off the baking sheet and getting his fingers and mouth singed for his troubles. They'd both been on the receiving end of Matilda's song more times than Lynn could count.

The memory made Lynn's chest tighten, and she had to force herself to take a deep breath to ease the discomfort. She stayed as quiet as a mouse, though, ears straining and ignoring the guilty pit in her stomach.

"I know, I know. I don't like it either. I just don't know how to tell her...yes, it's been hard for her. For me, too, of course, but I...no, we haven't talked about it. There was never any need, before now, at least."

Lynn swallowed, desperate to step forward and backward at the same time and so locked in place instead.

"Yes, I will, I promise. Thanks, hun. M-hmm. Talk to you later. Bye."

Hun?

Okay, so it was a standard form of address in the Midwest, one her mom used on strangers and family members alike. But still...it felt so weird.

The sound of Matilda standing up from the couch made

Lynn jump, and she leapt backward into her room, yanking the door after her. She stopped just before it smacked into place and gingerly finished closing it with a quiet *snick*. Then she just stood there, heart pounding, emotions in an uproar.

Why was this even a big deal? If her mom had found someone she liked that was great, right? She *wanted* her mom to be happy, right?

Right?

Of course she did, but...

A vision of her dad's cocky grin and twinkling blue eyes hit her so hard she gasped. She snatched desperately at the flash of color and joy, wanting to hold onto it forever. But it faded just as quickly as it had come, disappearing from behind her eyelids like sandy footprints washed away by a rushing wave.

Yet the echo of the memory still ricocheted around in her chest, making her eyes burn.

Footsteps sounded in the hall, then stopped in front of her door, making Lynn's anxiety spike. She bit her lip, using the pain to get a grip on herself.

A ping notification sounded in Lynn's ear, making her jump. It was her mom.

Is your promo over, honey? I'm heading out for work soon. I just wanted to make sure you were set for the evening.

Not trusting her voice, Lynn subvocalized a quick response and sent it.

Yup, just trying to focus on homework now. Thanks for checking in, I'm pretty busy. Have a great shift!

There was a long pause. Lynn didn't dare move a muscle. Her heart pounded in her ears and her stupid eyes kept burning.

Okay, sweetie. Good luck with homework. I'm really, really proud of you, you know that, right?

A lump lodged in Lynn's throat, making it impossible to swallow or subvocalize. She hurriedly projected a keyboard from her LINC and typed out a response.

I know, Mom. Thanks. Have a good night at work.

Okay. Love you, sweetie.

Lynn tried to swallow again, and forced her hand to move.

Love you, too, Mom.

Finally, the sound of footsteps moved away, and she heard her mom's bedroom door open and close.

For a long, long moment, Lynn couldn't move, heart pounding, muscles tingling, something huge and unwanted but familiar welling in her chest.

When she started trembling, she finally stumbled to her bed, crawled under the covers, and pressed her pillow tightly over her head. She didn't know if she was trying to keep something outside herself from getting in, or trying to keep something inside from getting out.

Whichever one it was, it didn't work, because when she finally heard their apartment door open and close as her mom headed off to work, she did something she hadn't done in a long, long time.

She cried.

School the next day was...rough. She'd stayed up to ungodly hours slogging through homework despite puffy eyes and a raging headache. What sleep she'd gotten felt like less than nothing. She'd even skipped her pre-school workout to take an extra long, scalding hot shower in an attempt to feel human again before braving hundreds of curious, prying eyes at school.

Thankfully she was able to slide on a mask of neutrality and more-or-less coast through the day on autopilot, nodding and mm-hmming to her friend's chatter and totally ignoring everyone else. Not even continued gossip about Elena or a hilarious new vid stitch of the pop-girl's epic bullying fail managed to draw Lynn out. A weird grayness blanketed her senses, muffling the world outside.

She wasn't able to claw her way out of it until school was over and they were headed out toward the airbus, the guys all looking at her expectantly to hear the hunting plan for the afternoon. As odd as it might seem, it was a relief having others depend on her. It was the catalyst she needed to shake herself awake, give herself a mental pep talk, and forget about everything but the mission.

She halted in the hallway before the school's front doors and put her hands to her hips, considering. Since she'd had no workout that morning to get her going, she felt sluggish and heavy. But it hadn't rained in a day or two, so it wouldn't be muddy outside. She decided they could all do with a challenge.

"Come on, guys. Let's go kill a mini-boss."

Six months ago, heck even a month ago, before their victory

of Gyges, Lynn's comment would have been met with groans and skepticism. Now, though, the guys just nodded and started checking their gear.

Well, all except Ronnie, who stared at her with furrowed brow, as if he had something to say, but wasn't going to say it without some prodding.

"Go ahead, Ronnie," she said with a careful nod. "We're a team. Everybody's feedback is valuable."

"A mini-boss is too big to tackle while we're still figuring out these new tactics. I mean, just yesterday Mack messed up the timing for the bait sweep and we ended up getting mobbed and had to cut and run."

Out of the corner of her eye Lynn saw Mack's golden skin darken with a flush and he hunched his shoulders, looking away.

Lynn frowned.

"We'll always be learning new tactics, Ronnie. You're right that we're not as cohesive with our attack strategy as I'd like us to be. But the only way to change that is to practice in the conditions we'll be facing at the championship. No amount of dry-runs or training modules is going to prepare us like actual combat will. So, yeah, it's a risk.

"But we've done similar battles before, and I am one-hundred-percent confident in the skills and abilities of everyone on this team." She looked him right in the eye as she spoke, holding his gaze until he nodded grudgingly. Then she caught Mack's eye and said, "Besides, Mack here was just giving us FUBAR practice, right? If we don't face it a few times in the field, how are we going to hold it together if it happens in the championship?"

A little smile quirked Mack's lips, and Ronnie snorted.

"If you want FUBAR conditions, just call in the Cedar Rapids Champions," Ronnie said darkly. "They'll give you all the practice you'll ever need."

There was a moment of silence. Dan and Mack exchanged an odd, almost sympathetic look, as if Ronnie's "exile" to Elena's team last fall had been anything other than the cold hard consequences of his own idiotic actions.

Lynn mentally rolled her eyes.

"You know," Dan said. "I still don't get why in the world they made it to Hunter Strike Team. I mean, Connor's good, I'll give him that. And the other ARS guys are decent I guess.

But Elena is like...like a dumpster fire and a trainwreck had a baby, except pretty, you know?"

The entire team burst into laughter, drawing looks from the few fellow students trickling out the doors. Ronnie mimed a flailing, backwards stagger that had become a meme all on its own on the streams.

"It's ninety-percent Connor," Ronnie said with certainty, once everyone's chuckles had died down. "That and the fact that they were the only ones around for us to team up with when we took out that boss in the qualifiers. *We're* the ones that got them their Strike Team status. Without us, nobody would have made it."

"Without *Lynn*, you mean," Edgar said. His tone was mild, but when Lynn glanced sharply his way, he was eyeing Ronnie with a less than friendly expression. Lynn couldn't be sure, since Edgar was largely a closed book to her, but she'd gotten the impression he hadn't forgiven Ronnie. It warmed her from head to toe to think he was upset on her behalf, but she needed them to all work together as a seamless team. There was no room for resentment.

"Nothing we've accomplished in the past year could have been done alone," she said firmly. "We *all* got us here, Edgar."

He looked at her, registered her raised eyebrow, and shrugged, giving her an innocent look.

"Whatever you say, boss."

Lynn snorted. "If we're done with the theatrical reenactments, let's get going."

She led the way out to the airbus platform even as she fired up the TD Hunter app.

"Good afternoon, Miss Lynn," Hugo greeted her cheerily.

"One of these days I'm gonna go into the settings and customize you to something way less perky," she subvocalized.

"Of course, Miss Lynn, whatever suits your preferences. Though, I will point out that none of the customizable settings negate my built-in directive to be professional and courteous at all times."

"Uh-huh. So what you're saying is, there's no Darth Vader setting?"

"Meaning, can I be broody and mysterious, and threaten you with my force powers to ensure compliance? My apologies, Miss Lynn, but that is not within my programming capabilities."

"Well, that's just lame. You should tell Mr. Krator that's a missed marketing opportunity right there."

"I will be sure to pass on the feedback, Miss Lynn."

"Uh-huh, I bet you will."

Their banter took them onto the airbus, where Lynn plopped down and got busy subvocalizing to her team their destination so they could figure out where they wanted to get off and switch transportation to throw off the vultures.

Lynn thought they'd done a good job at being sneaky, but when they arrived at their destination, she saw a few of those larger, noisier drones she'd been spotting lately loitering in the general vicinity of the power node they were heading towards. Maybe they weren't paparazzi drones after all, maybe they were some kind of new maintenance thing the city was using. Lynn shook her head and firmly ignored them.

"It feels weird to be back here," Mack subvocalized, casting a critical eye over the large grassy field and beyond it the fenced-in node and power substation. With their ever-increasing stream following and therefore ever more determined paparazzi drones, they always subvocalized while out and about. They never knew when some drone might be buzzing around. Even if the buggers didn't have good enough audio equipment to record conversations, there were plenty of AI programs that could "translate" and caption speech based off lip-reading. It was fairly accurate, too.

"Yeah, this is where—" Dan began, then stopped abruptly with a gulp, as if something had gotten stuck in his throat. Lynn raised her eyebrow at him and he busied himself with taking a drink from his hydration pack.

"Why come back here?" Edgar asked quietly, also looking over the field, though his vacant gaze made her think he was examining memories, not the terrain. This field was where Mr. Jerkatude Ronnie had tried to throw her off the team, she'd quit instead, and Edgar had quit with her. They'd walked a long road since then, every one of them.

What was the saying? All's well that ends well?

"Because," Lynn said, "it's the perfect place to test our bait tactics. Lots of open space, no gawkers—yet anyway—and we're already familiar with the terrain."

What she didn't say was that there were also exponentially more TDMs there since the last time they'd cleared the area. She wanted a challenge, and a challenge she would have.

"Okay, but the node has a fenced-in substation around it,"

Ronnie pointed out, shading his eyes to squint at the station in the distance. "We're not going to be able to get to the mini-boss to kill it."

"That's what bait is for, isn't it?" Lynn said with a feral grin.

"What if the boss doesn't go for it?" Edgar asked.

Lynn shrugged. "Then we'll have learned the limitations of bait and killed a whole friggen bunch of TDMs while we're at it."

"Are you sure this is a mini-boss, though?" Dan asked. He, too, was squinting suspiciously at the substation. "The last time we cleared around here, we couldn't get all the way up to the fence to figure out what was inside the rings. We just racked up experience mowing down the easy stuff."

"Uh, easy?" Mack asked, sounding exasperated.

Dan flapped a dismissive hand in Mack's direction.

"Congratulations, Dan," Lynn said cheerily. "You have just pointed out the real reason I picked this spot."

"Yeah, uh, I don't like the sound of that," Mack said, stroking his scraggly beard nervously. He was still trying to get it to fill in all the way. Apparently, Mrs. Rios had finally given up forbidding facial hair and had turned to shoving all kinds of hair growth ointments and beard hygiene products at her son—if she couldn't stop it, at least she could control it some other way.

"Don't worry, Mack," Ronnie said, batons in hand, ready to go. "You focus on your timing. We'll take care of the scary stuff."

Lynn pursed her lips, but didn't say anything. She couldn't force Ronnie to be kind, courteous, or even civil. All she could do was resist the urge to beat the fear of God into him, and set a good example herself.

"It'll be fun, Mack," she teased. "There's some unknown in the center of that circle, that or a TDM we haven't been high enough level to see, yet. I figure now that we're Level 38 we have a shot at it."

"Just what I always wanted." Mack sighed, pulling out his own batons. "Bigger, scarier monsters even better at killing me."

"I don't know what you're complaining about with those sick new pistols you have," Dan said, twirling his batons by the straps like he was some sort of martial artist with a pair of nun-chucks.

"Cut it out, doofus," Ronnie said. "If you bean yourself in the head, I'm not carrying you to the hospital."

"Nah," Dan agreed, spinning his batons even more vigorously, "that's Edgar's job, right, my man?"

Edgar shoved Dan off the sidewalk into the grass, making his friend trip. Instead of falling on his face, though, Dan tucked and rolled, managing to come back up to one knee, though his batons got tangled in the process.

"Dude! *Not cool!*" Dan said. "You threw off my groove!"

"Can dancing cows even *have* a groove?" Ronnie snickered.

Dan hopped to his feet and caught back up with them as they headed closer to the node.

"Duh, of course they can. They call it their mooo-ves."

Everyone groaned, then Lynn got their attention and started going over their battle plan. They were going to go all out, whole hog, pedal to the metal. She wanted to see how much damage they could really wreak with their more powerful weaponry and better crowd control tactics.

Once they got to the edge of the field, Lynn carefully judged the distance, picking a spot to carve out an initial staging point. She wanted to truly clear the area, if possible, not just punch through the TDMs defenses to kill whatever mini-boss was hiding inside. Mostly they'd done sweeps like this for TDMs like Hydras and Bunyips, large, powerful gather types that tended to attract a few smaller rings of aggressive types around them.

Based on their previous battles in the area, she knew whatever was in the center here wasn't a full-on boss. The size of the rings and numbers of TDMs weren't on the scale they'd seen at the qualifiers and north of her school where they'd cleared out Gyges. But they *were* getting up there. The mystery piqued Lynn's curiosity.

"Okay, Skadi's Wolves. You know the plan, you know the objective. Just keep in mind this isn't a do-or-die scenario. We're not livestreaming, there's no one to perform for. Let's take it slow and steady, stress test our new tactics, and keep an eye on our form. No need to get sloppy and let our ranking slide. If we need to blink out, we will. Any last questions?"

There were none.

Everyone lined up, shaking out limbs and doing a few last-minute stretches. Lynn took a deep breath, the scent of grass and spring blossoms on the breeze tickling her nose. It was partly overcast, so the sun played hide and seek behind the clouds. Edgar flashed her a grin a mile wide and winked, which made Lynn snort to herself. She knew for a fact he had entirely too much fun with his new Snazzgun, and enjoyed every opportunity to vaporize TDMs with it.

Dan was hopping from foot to foot, ducking and weaving like he was in a boxing ring and "da da da-ing" along to the old-time video game music he listened to while they were hunting. It was a very Dan thing to do, especially when he randomly yelled out "*mortal combat!*" like it was his theme song.

Mack looked focused and Lynn knew he was going over their formations in his head, doing everything he could to not let his team down. It was one reason he did so well in the support role. He had no ego to speak of, just a big heart and lots of determination.

Ronnie was similarly motionless, holding his batons at the ready so once they joined into his Sword of Mastery he could flow immediately into his first attack sequence. Where Mack's expression was serious, though, Ronnie's was impatient. He didn't comment or look around. Just waited, breathing deeply and evenly.

Lynn smiled to herself and sank into her own ready stance. None of them were perfect, but they were shaping up. If this fight went smoothly and they were able to successfully implement their new tactics, it would go a long way toward easing her worry about the upcoming Boss Bash 2.0.

"Skadi's Wolves, enter combat mode on my mark. Three... two... one... *mark!*"

The vista that materialized around them spun as Lynn pivoted, swinging Wrath in a full circle to clear her immediate area. The initial tsunami of sparks from dozens of TDMs along their line exploding blinded her for a second. Then she could see again, and she glanced out over the sea—yes, the *sea*—of transdimensional monsters between Skadi's Wolves and the power node.

Training kept her limbs moving, gliding seamlessly from strike to strike, even as her mind churned with disquiet.

This many TDMs seemed excessive. Even for a video game. Was it this bad because they'd cleared this area multiple times, and TDMs always came back thicker wherever they'd been attacked before?

She didn't have the time or space to wonder but focused everything she had on the battle in front of her. It sang through her body like fire in her blood, and she felt alive with a joy she would never be able to describe.

As the minutes dragged on and they advanced steadily through the fringe mobs of Delta and Charlie class TDMs, the initial euphoria of battle faded, and Lynn settled into her comfort zone. Her eyes tracked but didn't lock on any one thing; her body became loose and fluid, bending and moving where instinct and thousands of hours of training sent it; her brain registered and reacted to an unending stream of new data, organizing it all in a constantly shifting matrix of master objectives, ongoing strategy, and moment by moment tactics.

It all happened so seamlessly, so second nature to her, that Lynn doubted she could have explained how she did it or why she was so good at it. All she knew was that she loved it and wanted nothing more than to keep doing it.

"Wolves," Lynn said, subvocalization steady despite the jumping, dodging, and rolling she was doing, "one-third objective reached, prepare to implement bait and destroy. Mack, you're up."

"*Choo-hoo-hoo!*" Edgar cheered enthusiastically.

"Copy that," came Ronnie's clipped acknowledgment.

"Time to rock and sock 'em!" Dan said.

"Ready when you are, Lynn," Mack confirmed, sounding determined.

"Everybody drop their bait on my mark. Three...two... one...*mark!*"

Lynn placed her prepared bait marker fifteen yards in front of their advancing line, directly in front of Edgar who was the center spearpoint of their modified V formation. She and Ronnie anchored the right and left flanks, while Dan and Mack stayed about three yards behind the assault line forming a rough pentagon. This formation gave Dan and Mack the freedom to use their ranged weapons to their fullest capacity without having to constantly switch back to melee. It also kept their kill "trail" narrow enough that Mack could gather most dropped resources and items without having to run back and forth across the field.

It wasn't a feasible formation before they'd started using bait, however, because they'd needed to carve a much wider swath through the TDMs to keep the buggers from immediately sweeping around and surrounding them. Now, though, they had a means of crowd control.

Three of their bait markers went front and center to concentrate as many TDMs in their cone of destruction as possible. The other two markers went wide to the left and right, pulling TDMs away from their flanks and rear and giving Dan and Mack time to take them out as they passed without the distraction of fighting for their life in melee.

It only really worked because of the game mechanics of how and why TDMs moved. Every variety had a detection range, and if you were outside of it or invisible to it through heavy globe usage, the TDMs remained in place. So instead of the entire swarm circling the node and sweeping toward Skadi's Wolves like a tidal wave, groups of TDMs broke formation one after another and rushed them as the Hunters moved within detection range. Any time a Hunter engaged in battle, it increased surrounding TDMs' ability to detect them, especially for aggressive types. But when Skadi's Wolves used all their stealth capabilities, three-fifths of the encircling enemies would never react to their presence.

At least, until they attacked the boss.

At that point, all bets were off. It was like the boss was the nucleus, the central nexus of an organism, and damage to the core initiated a system-wide defense response. Which was why they'd only succeeded by the skin of their teeth in their previous encounters.

With their new bait and destroy tactic, though, Lynn was hoping they could employ enough crowd control to advance in a sweeping, sideways route that would take out a good half of the circle before they ever targeted the central boss. *If* they could keep up their ichor and Oneg supplies and *if* their physical stamina held. Those weren't impossible ifs, but Lynn had felt a lot more confident about them before she'd been reminded how freaking many TDMs there were around a boss, even a mini-boss.

If they managed it, they'd have to hit another pizza parlor afterward to carb up and replace an entire day's worth of energy.

She had a fleeting thought that she should ask Mrs. Pearson if they'd gotten any sponsorship offers from energy gel companies, the sort of thing marathon runners used to keep up their glycogen stores. She'd never even heard the word glycogen before she'd started playing TD Hunter, but having a nurse for a mom was darn useful when you were competing in a highly physical sport.

The thought disappeared in a wink as Lynn registered the surrounding TDMs parting in waves as if she and Ronnie were Moses and the TDMs were the Red Sea. Now there was a clustered column of targets in front of them, with space opening up on the left and right, giving their team more room to maneuver.

Edgar whooped and switched from cannon to flamethrower mode. The corner of Lynn's augmented vision lit up as a massive spurt of fire poured into the central column of TDMs, vaporizing the front few ranks instantly. Edgar could only keep the fire going for three to five seconds at a time—its energy use was off the charts. But it was long enough to clear the ten feet in front of him so he could advance and shoot again. Meanwhile, Lynn and Ronnie were taking advantage of the extra elbow room to fight like perfect whirlwinds of destruction and death. Each strike was precise and executed to maximum effect.

On the left side, Lynn took out the successively larger TDMs with a few strikes of Wrath apiece, using Abomination in her left hand to soften up targets and keep the waves from closing in again on the left. On the right side, Ronnie used his Nitro Storm ability to periodically blast a circle of pure destruction around him, keeping the TDMs on the right from building up again as well.

Meanwhile, Dan was sniping targets out of the air and using his armor-piercing bullets on any of the particularly large or tough TDMs that were caught in the aggro of their bait traps. Mack was kept busy stemming the trickle of TDMs that broke free of the bait traps on either side, as well as sweeping up supplies and keeping everybody topped off.

So many things were happening at once, the intensity level would have overwhelmed a normal person in seconds. But years of gaming in high-intensity situations had acclimated their brains to the controlled chaos. All sensory information was automatically filtered, categorized, and reacted to, with Hugo to help manage automated tasks and bring attention to any anomaly the humans' brains had overlooked.

As the team leader, it was Lynn's job to snatch brief moments between tackling TDMs to evaluate the overall situation, redirect anyone who was drifting off course, and recalibrate their overall objective to match the changing tides of battle. Before they started using bait and destroy, that had been increasingly difficult, to the point that she'd had to hold back at times, unable to fight at full capacity and lead at the same time. But this new tactic gave her blessed breathing room, and she felt their overall team efficiency had made a noticeable jump as a result. She'd have to wait and check their scores after this encounter, but she liked what she saw so far.

With their line moving slowly but steadily forward, Lynn kept a close eye on the overhead map and Edgar's direction. He knew their objective was not to charge directly toward the eye of the storm, but to advance at an angle to the left, putting Ronnie's Nitro Storm and Mack's sick pistols closest to the highest-level TDMs, while giving Lynn and Dan a bit more breathing room to perform precision maneuvers. Edgar kept his focus on the twenty feet around him, with the node tower visible above and beyond the TDM lines as a guidepost. Meanwhile Lynn worried about their overhead map and the ebb and flow of red TDM dots.

For a while there, they were rocking and rolling so smoothly through the Charlie and Bravo class TDMs that Lynn followed Dan's example and put on a playlist low in the background. Hugo had helped her find looped, extended versions of her favorite songs so there were no abrupt transitions between them, threatening her concentration. While she'd always have a soft spot for the rock and roll she grew up listening to with her dad, she found the words distracting at times. So for high stake battles like this she stuck with symphonic and synthwave rock.

After thirty minutes of steady progress, they were close enough to the inner rings to execute their pivot. They hadn't managed the maneuver successfully in previous battles, but Lynn was confident they'd get it this time.

The idea was to swing to the right and advance at a steep rightward angle to tackle the inner ring Alpha Class TDMs where they'd already eliminated the lower class TDMs to the outside. If it worked, it promised extra firepower and concentration to focus on the most difficult targets, again increasing their efficiency and effectiveness.

To execute the maneuver, though, they had to time a bait drop perfectly, dumping all five bait markers in a single spot far out to their left flank just as they pivoted and headed right. If they did it correctly, the aggro pull of the bait would create a gap between them and the TDM hordes that would, after their pivot, be behind their left side. If they advanced quickly the other way, the bait's pull would last long enough for them to get out of detection range of the TDMs at their back, keeping their rear clear of enemies.

What made the maneuver complicated, though, was that they *also* had to swap sides, with her and Ronnie, then Dan and Mack switching places. It kept their heaviest hitters on the inside edge. There was an inherent risk to such a maneuver, since all humans had a dominant side and it was incredibly difficult to train yourself to fight with equal precision on both sides. But Lynn had seen the lack of such ambidextrous flexibility bite people in the butt many times in WarMonger. Merc teams who were used to fighting in one specific formation were inevitably broken apart or were boxed in by some terrain feature. She had always sought to be as ambidextrous as possible, and made sure Skadi's Wolves practiced fighting with their off side in the lead as well.

That commitment paid off at times like this when they needed to swap weapon placement, if only they could pull off the maneuver smoothly.

"Prepare to execute bait and switch, boys. Time to head the other way."

"Finally," Ronnie said. "All these Charlie and Bravo class bogies are boring me to death."

The comment made Lynn want to bite back with something snarky, but she resisted the temptation. She was the leader, and unlike Larry Coughlin, she wasn't a lone wolf. She had to lead by example.

"I'll get it right this time, I promise," Mack said.

"Don't worry bro, I got you," Edgar said, switching back to cannon mode on his Snazzgun in anticipation of their maneuver. "If you get mixed up, I'll pick you up and throw you where you need to go!"

"Now that I've *got* to see," Dan giggled.

"Let's save the wrestling moves for training," Lynn said, her lips quirking upward. "Everybody get ready to drop your bait markers and pivot."

Lynn took out one last Rakshar that was lumbering toward her, then gave the command. With a momentary squint, she dropped her marker, danced sideways, and swapped places with Ronnie while she switched Wrath and Abomination to opposite hands. Edgar was the only one who had nothing to do but drop his bait and keep mowing down the TDMs coming at them from the front—something he did with dependable enthusiasm.

In the brief lull of weapon fire, Lynn's eyes flicked upward, drawn by the buzz of drone propellers. Five gray drones, too big to be paparazzi vultures, hovered above the battle, halfway between Skadi's Wolves and the node tower.

Having identified the noise and dismissed it as irrelevant to her current mission, Lynn refocused on forging onward.

The maneuver went even better than Lynn had hoped, and in no time, they were advancing the other way, re-energized by the light at the end of the mission tunnel. The last few inner rings were substantially smaller and had exponentially less TDMs in them, so the heavy lifting was already done. The remainder of the battle would be a test of endurance and precision.

Skadi's Wolves piled into the ranks of Jotnar and Spithragani, carving a path of destruction that made Lynn proud. An unexpected bombardment by half a dozen kamikaze Kongamato slowed them at one point. They had to break formation to dodge the diving, pterodactyl-like monsters that came on too fast for Dan to snipe them all at once. It was a scramble to re-form, but by then they'd collected more bait markers and were able to use them to split a terrifying wave of Spithragani that tried to stampede over them, pouring down acid spray and poison webs. The near massacre of their team had forced Lynn to swap Wrath for Bastion to provide extra defensive stats and take some of the oncoming ranged attacks from the Spithragani. After the stampede split and they were able to pick off the giant crab-spiders, Lynn was about to switch her shield back to her blade when something orange-red and flamelike streaked out from the direction of the node tower and hit Bastion squarely.

She knew it had, because she didn't just see it, she *felt* it.

After fighting TDMs for nine months, Lynn had long ago gotten used to the otherwise odd fact that she was fighting completely insubstantial beings, and so there was nothing but wind to provide resistance to her slashes and strikes, and no force behind the bashes and strikes of the enemy.

Except, of course, those few times ramming the Jotnar and Gyges with Bastion... and the occasional glitches that sent her baton vibrating... and those times her batons had overheated. Heck, there had even been that baton she'd fallen on and snapped way back in beta phase. She'd attributed the resulting sparks and electric fire to the broken internal guts of the baton itself. Except... batons were eighty percent omnipolymer, and as far as she knew it was incapable of spontaneously combusting...

TD Hunter was a cutting-edge game using cutting-edge technology. There were bound to be glitches and weird stuff that happened to the equipment. That was what Lynn had already told herself.

But when that hot, vibrating sensation traveled through Bastion's omnipolymer, through her high-performance glove, and into her hand, a familiar unease settled over her.

Lynn looked up and saw the sparkling mist around the base of the node, extending far enough up it that it was visible over the fencing around the substation.

Well, they'd found the mini-boss, likely a gather type Alpha Class TDM. The tactical forums hypothesized several rarer, high class TDMs not yet discovered, since there were so few players at that level worldwide. Among the Hunter Strike Teams, Skadi's Wolves were in the top fifteen. The only reason they—and likely others—weren't higher was that they had lives and responsibilities they couldn't set aside. Even for those who *could* afford to ignore school, work, or family, the physical stamina required to kill enough TDMs to achieve the higher Hunter levels meant only the most athletic and hardworking players could advance faster than a competitive team like Skadi's Wolves.

"Heads up, guys, I just made contact with whatever's inside that ring. It's ranged, and we are now within its reach."

"Nežinoma rankos spengimo idėja Nežinomos gydytojos motina!" Ronnie shouted.

Ronnie was cursing in Lithuanian again. Did it make sense? Not to Lynn, but then few of Ronnie's actions ever did.

"I don't see it," Edgar yelled, glancing up at the node tower as he methodically torched a line of Jotnar. "Are you sure? Could it have been a Hydra hiding somewhere?"

"I don't see how it could be," Lynn responded, doing her best to clear her immediate surroundings while keeping Bastion up and expecting to catch another bolt of damage. "The TDM mass around it just isn't big enough. Nothing like what we saw at the qualifiers or the Boss Bash. Besides, the ranged attack looked different from a Hydra's plasma bolt. It looked more like fire or something."

"Ooh! Maybe it's a Chimera!" Dan said, sounding entirely too happy about the prospect.

"No," Lynn said, "Chimera are eight feet tall, max. This was angled down from higher up than that."

Her view flashed red again, and while Bastion shrugged off eighty percent of the damage, some of it still leaked through. Lynn knew that the closer she got, the harder it would hit, and the rate of fire might increase as well.

"It just hit me again, is anyone else taking fire?"

Everyone else answered in the negative, which was odd, because Edgar was definitely closer than she was.

"Hugo," she subvocalized, switching to her private channel with her AI, "why am I the only one who can see this unknown? I'm the same level as everyone else."

"Perhaps it has a singular focus, Miss Lynn. It is an unknown, after all, so there is very little I can say about it. Perhaps this is a sign it would be best to retreat and tackle it another day when you are a higher level?"

"Good thing you aren't competing, Hugo. You'd never win so much as a participation ribbon."

"Winning is not my directive. My priorities are the smooth functioning of TD Hunter and the safety of its players."

"Which makes you entirely boring and un-fun," Lynn pointed out, grinning despite her worry.

"As you please," Hugo said. "The fact remains that you are facing an unknown and potentially dangerous situation. I advise you to retreat."

Lynn didn't bother replying because it would only be a waste of time.

"It looks like I'm the only one it's targeting," she told her team. "I'll keep its focus while we advance. Let's do this!"

Two minutes and a dozen shots from the unknown later, Lynn's augmented view flickered. A minute later, it did it again, winking out entirely before coming back online.

"Hugo? What's going on?" Lynn growled.

"Unknown, Miss Lynn. My mesh web connection is entirely normal. Might it be an equipment malfunction?"

Lynn shot furiously at the surrounding TDMs. She focused on headshots since most of the bigger monsters were slow enough and she was close enough for her accuracy to stay incredibly high.

"Anyone's app glitching?" Lynn asked the team.

"Yup," Dan said. "Thought it was just my glasses."

"Mine too," Ronnie said, sounding furious. "I thought they'd patched all the glitch crap that went on early in the game."

Lynn didn't respond right away, remembering the glitches she'd experienced in this same field—though further back—when she'd been merely Level 11. She'd been messing with unorthodox tactics at the time, and Hugo had made a valid point that trying to "game" the system could have unpredictable results.

They weren't doing anything like that now, though. They were wiping the floor with the TDMs exactly as they would have done in a championship. Strictly by the rules.

"Wolves, let's retreat ten yards and switch all weapons to ranged for a few minutes and see if things keep glitching."

Despite some grumbling from Ronnie and Dan, they executed the maneuver and did indeed experience fewer glitches. Lynn had them all retreat another ten yards and found that not only did the glitches go away, but the sparkling mist disappeared and the unknown's attacks vanished along with it. Nobody noticed but her, of course, since she was the only one who could see the unknown for whatever reason.

Well, that was illuminating.

Lynn had suspicions, and she didn't like them at all. She let her team stay there for a bit longer, taking down TDMs at a much slower rate, but still with plenty of targets within their weapon range.

"Hugo," Lynn subvocalized, keeping her voice neutral. "Are you causing glitches in the app to make us stop playing because we're ignoring your safety recommendations?"

There was the tiniest of delays in Hugo's response, small enough that Lynn wasn't sure if she imagined it or not.

"No, Miss Lynn, I am not causing glitches in the app to make you stop playing because you are ignoring my very appropriate and reasonable safety recommendations."

Lynn pursed her lips, aiming at and shooting a Jotnar lumbering toward her. It took a second shot to the head to make it explode, which gave her a little more time to think.

Hugo's answer seemed pretty definitive, but she couldn't shake the feeling there was something fishy going on. She didn't have time to sit around and play word games with an AI—plus she doubted she'd win that battle anyway. She knew the game advertised that it would auto-lock if it detected a player in combat mode entering hazardous locations, such as roads, train tracks, and airfields, and that made perfect sense. She'd tested those boundaries herself early on, just to see how it worked, and it was slightly chilling that mesh web GPS triangulation was so accurate that the app knew where she was to within an inch at all times. The moment she stepped off a curb onto any road big enough to show up on EarthMaps, if she was in combat mode her display was blanked out by the message "Hazardous Location Detected: Please move to a safe location to continue playing."

Whatever this glitching was, though, had nothing to do with the app's built-in safety functions. She suspected if her team engaged in illegal behavior like trespassing on a power substation, Hugo would have something to say about it—like informing the authorities. Otherwise Tsunami might be blamed for their illegal behavior. But they'd hunted around dozens of other substations and similar manmade infrastructure, so what was different now?

"Skadi's Wolves, prepare to advance again. Let's do a bait and destroy formation just like before and see what happens. Hopefully the glitches were a one-off."

Everyone was happy to hear that, and they got back to work, dropping another set of bait markers so they could create lanes to start obliterating the last two rings before the substation. Or at least *this* side of the rings. It was too late in the day to tackle the far side, as satisfying as it would be to make a clean sweep of it.

Once more, though, as soon as they were close enough that Lynn started taking that out-of-nowhere orange-red fire that nobody else could see, their apps started glitching again. Lynn ignored it and ordered everyone to keep pushing forward.

Which was when the apps crashed entirely.

"*What the freaking—*" Ronnie shouted, devolving into Lithuanian as he ripped his AR glasses off his head and glared at them, like he expected to cow them into contrition for interrupting his hunt.

"Okay, that was really weird," Dan said, sheathing his batons and taking off his own glasses to examine them, likely wanting to ensure there was no obvious physical damage—which, of course, there wasn't.

"Does everybody's LINC still work?" Lynn called out, since

they could no longer subvocalize to each other through the TD Hunter app.

After a moment of checking, everyone answered in the affirmative.

"Okay, let's switch to a group voice chat and we'll figure out our next move."

Once the guys had put their AR glasses back on and everyone had switched to their always running team message chat, Lynn subvocalized, "Something like this has happened to me before at this location, back when I was Level 11. Can anyone restart their TD Hunter app?" She'd already tried hers, and it hadn't responded.

"Nope," Edgar subvocalized. "Dead as a doornail."

"Nada," Mack agreed.

Dan and Ronnie couldn't restart their app either, so Lynn motioned for them all to follow her.

"Let's walk back toward the sidewalk and try again. I bet it'll work once we're further away from the substation."

They trudged across the field and tried the app again. Lo and behold, it worked.

"Surprise surprise," Lynn muttered to herself.

"What was that, Miss Lynn?" Hugo asked as the TD Counterforce logo disappeared and the app's home screen filled her AR display.

"Nothing, unless you can tell me why the app just crashed."

"I apologize, Miss Lynn, I am doing a diagnostic as we speak and will open a technical support ticket with Tsunami. All data readings leading up to the error have already been sent to the appropriate technicians and we will do everything we can to ensure the error does not reoccur. For the time being, might I suggest you relocate if you wish to continue hunting?"

"You're welcome to suggest it," Lynn said, suspicions not allayed in the least.

"Okay, so are we going back, now?" Ronnie asked, raising both hands in exasperation.

Lynn looked at the rest of the team, who shrugged.

"Let's try it one more time and see what happens."

Hugo didn't try to talk her out of it, which seemed suspicious in and of itself.

Lynn was wholly unsurprised when the same thing happened again.

"Man! This sucks!" Dan said, kicking a tuft of grass as his no-longer-an-Ambanese-Sniper-Rifle batons sagged sadly in his limp grip.

"Cheer up, Dan my man. Think of all the extra time we get for homework tonight," Edgar said with a good-natured grin.

"Don't remind me," Dan groaned.

"Kas per velnias?!" Ronnie spat, ripping off his backpack to shove his batons violently into it. "This is freaking unacceptable! I'm calling tech support right now."

"I mean, I wish we could have finished the mission," Mack said, "but I am *starving*. Can we go get burgers before we split up?"

Lynn remained silent, staring pensively at the substation, wishing she knew enough technical details about how data transference in the mesh web worked. Then, at least, she might have an inkling about what could be interfering with the TD Hunter app at this specific node. As it stood, she was as clueless about it as Elena was about how to be a competent TD Hunter player.

In the end, they did stop for food, but it was for Happy Joe's pizza, not burgers. GIC had reached out to the local chain after Operation Boss Bash and suggested they offer Skadi's Wolves a sponsorship deal. The owner had been all about it, and Lynn had gotten to chat with him—he was a huge fan of TD Hunter, apparently. His son played it and raved about Skadi's Wolves on a regular basis. The guys had been thrilled to have more excuses to eat delicious pizza. Now Happy Joe's was getting so much business, much of it TD Hunter fans hoping to catch a glimpse of Skadi's Wolves, that the owner was opening two additional locations in new parts of the city, "To make sure Skadi's Wolves always has quality pizza close by," he'd said in his press release about it.

They didn't get much peace and quiet to eat their pizza. Four different groups of people asked for autographs while they were there, which the guys thought was the coolest thing in the world and which Lynn tolerated only because the fans were so polite and apologetic about it. Ronnie even insisted they stream the interactions, which was probably an excellent idea, but which made Lynn want to run screaming from the restaurant. Or maybe hide in the broom closet with her pizza. Since neither of those were options, she forced a smile and played along.

The pizza was *really* good, though, so Lynn supposed it was worth it. The store manager refused to let them pay for it, too, saying it was the boss's orders when Lynn tried to bully her into taking their money. Apparently, Happy Joe's would gladly feed them free pizza, three meals a day every day, with how much publicity it would get them. Not exactly the right diet for high-performing athletes, but Lynn appreciated the thought.

Despite her distaste for the attention, the pizza run ended their hunting day on a high note. Poster girl for Happy Joe's Pizza Emporium had never been on her list of things she'd expected to do in life. But the everyday fans they'd met had reminded Lynn that regular people were a decent bunch, even if all the craziness of stream fame and the insanity of the masses in virtual made her want to puke on a regular basis.

By the time Lynn got back to her apartment, she was sure of two things: their bait and destroy tactics were a resounding success, and hunting followed by pizza was a great distraction from grief.

What she wasn't sure of was what the heck was going on with TD Hunter—and whether or not she dared to dig deeper.

Chapter 4

"DOCTOR," MR. KRATOR SAID, "YOU START."

The briefing for the new US Undersecretary of Defense for Technology and Acquisitions was part of the hand-over of administrations. Given that the reality of TransDimensional Monsters was, thankfully, a surprise, they were taking it rather well. Steve didn't know why he was even at the meeting, since this was above his pay grade. But Mr. Krator knew his background, seemed to value it, and so dragged him along anyway despite his best attempt to avoid it.

"Mr. Secretary, I am Dr. Benjamin Quasnitschka, Chief Scientist for the TD Hunter program," the slightly portly gentleman said. "Just to make sure you're up on the background—"

"Ten years ago a new slew of particles that did not fit the standard model were discovered as a byproduct of research into quantum computing," Secretary John Byerly said. "I've got a PhD in physics, Doctor, I kept up. The particles were quickly assimilated by the computing and IT industry. Anything that makes computers, AI and information transfer better, stronger, faster, cheaper gets used rapidly.

"And there were glitches. Reports indicated that the glitches were randomized because they were location specific. They tended, not always, to occur around power stations but any power system might find them. And since there are power systems virtually everywhere...

"At a certain point though the technology was being used

regularly, most of the information on advancements disappeared, which I was curious about at the time.

"Five years later I find out that a game my grandchildren play is an attempt to kill vast numbers of insubstantial, invisible creatures that are infesting our power systems throughout the world, breaking down our information transfer capabilities and seemingly bent on destroying the world.

"Close enough?" he ended.

"Close enough, Mr. Secretary," Dr. Quasnitschka said. "I did not realize you had a doctorate in physics."

"I found your paper on the most recent advances fascinating," Byerly said. "What I am less happy about is my grandchildren playing a game that could literally kill them. 'We need as many people killing these things as possible' seems... ruthlessly pragmatic. Emphasis on ruthless."

"I think I can answer that one, Mr. Secretary," Steve said. "If I may."

"Go ahead, Mr Riker," the Secretary replied.

"During World War Two we fielded twelve million men under arms," Steve said. "Take an alternative scenario. We take the hit on the chin that we're surrounded by invisible beings whose true purpose and even intellect is unknown. We don't know if they are probes from another world, always here and suddenly blossoming like an algae bloom because we've started using these particles or if they are an actual inimical race from beyond the well of space and time.

"Also, they're going to destroy modern civilization if they aren't stopped and you're all going to die.

"But, we'll ignore the massive social psychosis that would undoubtedly cause. We saw with the respiratory viruses of the 2020s that society does not handle 'it's something invisible that can kill you' well at all at all.

"Assume we went public and went to a full call-up, drafted twelve million men into uniform and put them instead of your grandchildren to killing TDMs. Put every single one into a TDM infantry division.

"Despite numerous attempts to reduce it, the tooth-to-tail ratio of the Army—how many soldiers are in support versus how many actually shoot the enemy—remains stubbornly at ten to one. For every ten soldiers, only one actually sees and engages the enemy.

"Thus, if we make an army of ten million men, we have one point two million actually killing TDMs. Mr. Krator?"

"We currently have sixteen million active players in the US alone, along with about four times that number who are intermittent or dormant."

There was a moment of silence as those gathered seemed to consider the sheer scope of what Mr. Krator's numbers meant.

"Sixteen million, Mr. Secretary," Steve concluded, "is a far larger number than one point two. And we don't have to warn people that the world may or may not end tomorrow. Questions, comments, concerns?"

Lynn welcomed the constant distractions of school and hunting that kept her busy from dawn to dusk as April quickly passed by. She didn't want quiet moments to sit and think. That was when every question, doubt, and insecurity ambushed her. Being perpetually sleep deprived probably wasn't good for her health or her grades, but it meant she fell asleep almost as soon as her head hit the pillow, giving her brain no time to roll out its long list of things she was ignoring. Things like, what awful sabotage were Connor and Elena planning next? What was up with the TD Hunter app and was it connected to power grid wars between the US and China? And last but certainly not least, who was the mystery man who kept making her mom laugh? Were things serious between them? And why, oh why, did the thought make her feel cold and gray inside instead of feeling happy for her mom?

All these questions bothered her, but the last bothered her most of all. Lynn wanted her mom to be happy. Matilda deserved happiness more than anyone after the tragedy they'd both lived through, not to mention how hard her mom worked to provide for them. So why did Lynn feel such a frustrating mix of grief, anger, and defensiveness?

This was the part of being a teenager Lynn hated the most. How dare her stupid brain flop around up there, transfixed by all these confusing, pointless emotions? Why couldn't it be cold and logical about everything, like Larry was? You'd never catch *him* wallowing in emotion.

But then, you'd also never catch him being an understanding, kind, polite, or supportive human being either, so she supposed there were tradeoffs to the "Larry" way of doing things.

She, however, seemed to be stuck in the middle with the worst of both worlds. Her insides were a mess, and that made it hard to ignore the stares and buzzing drones overhead. Shrugging off Ronnie's stupid comments was almost more effort than she had the energy for. Even their slow but steady progress toward Level 39 and their preparation for Boss Bash 2.0 didn't cheer her like it should have. She tried to push through, but her stoic face obviously needed some work, because one evening the week before their planned boss hunt, Edgar pinged her as they sat on the airbus headed home, asking for a voice chat.

Lynn's eyes flicked toward him and he raised both eyebrows. She gave a resigned sigh and accepted.

"What?" she subvocalized, too tired to be polite. Edgar would understand.

"That's what I wanna know," he subvocalized right back, watching her face. "You've been off all this week and last. I just... well, I wanted to ask if everything was okay?"

The words "I'm fine" were already forming on her lips, but something in Edgar's expression stopped her. He seemed genuinely worried, and there was something else there, something she couldn't put her finger on. But it made her want to draw closer, not push away—which was honestly a first. She spent her days avoiding people as much as possible.

"You wanna walk home with me?" she offered, forcing her lips into a little half smile. It was the best she could do.

Edgar's expression smoothed over and his eyes warmed.

"Sure thing, boss."

Lynn kicked his boot halfheartedly.

"Quit it, I'm not your boss."

Edgar grinned.

"That's what *you* think, *Toa Tama'ita'i*."

Lynn rolled her eyes and turned her head to look out the window until they'd arrived at the airbus platform near her apartment complex.

It was evening, as it usually was when they finally returned from hunting four to five days a week. Lynn kept a thin hoodie several sizes too big in her pack to wear whenever she wanted to cover up her conspicuous hunting gear and avoid notice. Edgar had a massive, baggy T-shirt he used for the same reason, and he didn't seem bothered to not have a hood to draw up over his face. Lynn pulled hers closer as they walked down the platform and hurried to her apartment complex. The street lighting wasn't great in that part of town, which Lynn was grateful for because it cut down on the number of paparazzi drones after dusk.

They made it to her apartment building without getting buzzed by any drones. Once inside Lynn could finally relax. They walked in companionable silence up to her apartment, though it turned awkward when they reached her door.

"Um, my mom's probably already left for work, but you can come hang out for a bit... if you want to talk, I mean."

"Yeah, sure. Does that mean you're gonna spill your guts and tell me what's got you all grumpy?"

"I am *not* grumpy," Lynn said, barely caring it was a flat-out lie.

"Yeah, you are, chica. In denial, too."

"Whatever," Lynn muttered and pushed open her apartment door. She scrounged for something snacky and they plopped down on the couch with a bag of beef jerky to share between them—her mom encouraged her to avoid junk foods, so instead she chowed down on pounds of beef jerky, cheese, nuts, and dried fruit for her everyday snacks. It made up for all the Happy Joe's pizza she was eating these days.

Mercifully—or maybe not?—Edgar didn't say a word. He leaned back, propped up by the end cushion of the couch while she sat crosslegged in the middle. He watched her patiently, a little "v" wrinkling the skin between his brows.

Lynn chewed on her beef jerky like her life depended on it, staring at the couch cushion beside Edgar's left elbow.

Stupid brain. Stupid emotions. Stupid life.

"You know my dad died when I was little, right?" she blurted out with no preamble.

"Yeah, you've mentioned it," Edgar said, softly.

"Well... Mom has never... not since... she's never talked about men since then. Like dates and stuff," Lynn said, floundering.

Edgar, curse him, waited in silence, giving her all the space she needed to make a fool of herself.

Lynn sighed and spat it out.

"I think I overheard my mom talking to a guy a few times in the last couple of weeks. And that's fine, I'm not upset at that, right? She deserves to be happy, right? But I just... it feels so weird. And she hasn't said anything to me. And...and...I miss my dad," she finished, voice fading to a mumble.

There was a beat of silence, then a rustle of plastic and the creak of the couch as Edgar put down his bag of beef jerky and leaned forward, bringing him closer. Within arm's reach.

"That's rough, Lynn. I'm sorry."

The kindness in his voice made her brave enough to look up and meet his eyes.

"It's stupid," she mumbled. "He's been gone for so long...I know he would want me to move on...I just don't know how to feel about having...another dad, you know?"

Edgar shook his head gently.

"Ain't nobody ever gonna be your pa but your pa. I'm sure your ma would never try and make it like that, ya know?"

"Yeah, I know," Lynn said, feeling foolish. She loved and trusted her mom. So why was she freaking out?

"Nobody can replace your pa, no way. But maybe...maybe there's room in there"—Edgar leaned forward a little more, pointing at Lynn's chest—"for something else. A friend, yeah? You can be happy for your ma and build a friendship with someone she cares about without having to think of him as your pa, can'tcha? I mean, look at Kayla. She's happy, and Mr. Swain seemed like a cool dude when we met him at that Christmas party."

"Yeah," Lynn said slowly, mesmerized by Edgar's face. His eyes were so soft and kind, she didn't feel the urge to hunch her shoulders or look away or anything. In fact, she felt more relaxed than she'd been all week. His arm on the back of the couch was really close. Close enough to touch.

"Way I see it is, you can miss your pa *and* be happy for your ma at the same time. Maybe it'll feel mixed up and messy, but look around—what family isn't mixed up and messy?"

Lynn smiled sadly, thinking of Edgar's own parents and their rocky relationship. She felt sheepish for bringing all this up when at least *she'd* had a dad who'd loved her to the moon and back. A dad who took care of his family instead of drinking and yelling and hitting.

"Sorry," she said, finally looking away. "I'm sure you don't wanna hear me complain and whine about my problems."

"Actually...I do."

Lynn's brow furrowed, and she looked back at him. His expression seemed unsure, but he gave her a little shrug.

"You're my friend, Lynn. I wanna hear your problems. I want you to know you can tell 'em to me, if you need to. I want... I just want you to know I'm here, ya know? In case you need me." He gave her a gentle smile—not his usual mischievous grin, but something much more genuine and fragile. Suddenly, the gray aching hole in her chest wasn't gray or aching anymore. Her chest felt warm and... full.

"Thanks, Edgar," she said softly. "I... I'm glad you're my friend. Thanks for being here."

"Anytime, boss," he said with a cheeky grin.

Lynn threw a couch cushion at him.

Elena Seville threw her balled-up shirt on the tiled floor of the girls' locker room. She pulled off the rest of her athletic gear in jerky, angry movements as she headed for the showers, not caring about the mess she was making—there was no one there to complain.

Technically, the Cedar Rapids Champions shouldn't have been using the high school's athletic building facilities since they were no longer part of any club or varsity team. But Connor had been captain of the ARS team and she'd been captain of the ARS cheerleaders long enough that they knew the codes to get into the building and everyone who mattered looked the other way.

Besides, she was a student, and this was her school, so anyone who thought she didn't deserve to use the facilities was stupid.

Elena yanked the shower knobs and stood back to let the water get hot, which made her even more pissed off. Why was she even showering here instead of going home where the water was *always* hot? The idea of waiting for hot water was anathema to her mother, and everyone who had ever met Mrs. Seville knew that whatever she wanted, she got.

And there, of course, was the answer: Mrs. Seville.

Mrs. Seville, who thought Elena was a stupid little girl wasting her time chasing after stream fame. Mrs. Seville, who lamented that they didn't live in California where Elena could rub elbows with the right people and where her mother could get her roles that would make her famous. Except Daddy said the traditional acting industry was a corrupt, crumbling house of cards that his daughter would have no part of. Anyone wasting their time becoming an *actor* was a feckless moron because studios could—and did—pay a fraction of what it cost to hire a person and simply used an AI avatar instead.

But Mrs. Seville simply couldn't let go of the glamor and fame of her youth.

Daddy wanted her to get a "normal" education and do something useful with her life. Elena hadn't managed to sell him on the stream celebrity career just yet, but she was *sure* he'd come around if only she had some time to really talk to him about it.

But, of course, she never did. Daddy was always away, meeting investors and managing business assets. He wouldn't have to be if her mother hadn't been such a diva. Mrs. Seville probably thought she didn't notice, but Elena had heard her parents argue about her mother's lavish lifestyle often enough to know where all of Daddy's hard-earned money was going. It was why she didn't go to an elite private school. It was a wonder her parents were still married. Elena had heard them arguing about that too, and knew there was something her mother was holding over Daddy. Somehow, Mrs. Seville had Daddy "by the balls," and he knew it.

That was really why he stayed away. Elena hated him for it. But she forgave him every time he came home, because when Daddy looked at her—the occasions he had enough time to, anyway—his face lit up. His hugs were tight and warm, and she remembered every single one he'd ever given her.

Her mother never looked at her unless she was angry.

The water was finally properly hot, so Elena stepped under the spray and scrubbed herself with furious energy. Fury was the only thing keeping her moving—her limbs were tired and wobbly. But not *as* tired and wobbly as they'd been a few months ago, when she'd decided to actually start trying.

When she'd finally realized she was all alone, and couldn't rely on manipulation or sex appeal to get her what she wanted out of life.

Okay, so Connor telling her she had to shape up or get kicked off the team had been part of it as well. When he'd had that falling out with The Slut in Skadi's Wolves and those lame nerds had sent him packing, he'd come right back to CRC and laid down the law. His stupid former ARS teammates went right along with him, even though *she* was the one who'd hatched this whole plan to become famous and *she* was the one who had put blood, sweat, and tears into gaining them ten million subscribers on their stream channel.

She hated Connor even more than she hated her mother, if that was possible.

They'd had a good thing going at first: she made him famous and took care of his physical needs, and he led the TD Hunter team and made them win. They each had their lanes, and they were good at what they did.

But apparently that hadn't been good enough for Connor.

He'd wanted *real* athletes on his team—which was laughable when The Slut was just some stupid girl that happened to make men crazy with her fatty curves. Elena couldn't fathom why anyone liked that whore. So what if she was good at gaming? Tons of people were good at gaming, and that didn't make them famous. Stream followers didn't care if you were good, they just wanted to be entertained. And no one that fat could possibly be entertaining.

Elena squeezed her bodywash bottle too hard in her pique and sent a massive squirt of soap into the shower wall, adding to the list of things she was angry about.

"Hey, sexy."

Elena jumped with a shriek of surprise and almost slipped on the wet tile. The shower curtain blocked her view of the dressing room, but she knew exactly whose voice that was, and she wasn't having any of it.

"Get out, Connor."

"Aw, come on, Elena. We had such a good thing going, once. You're the hottest girl in the entire school, why shouldn't you be with the hottest guy on offer? It's not like we didn't have fun, all those times we had together. We could have fun again, if you wanted to."

Elena snorted to herself, rinsing off as fast as she could.

She wasn't afraid of Connor—not much, anyway. They used to do all sorts of "fun" things in this very dressing room, once ARS practice was over and everyone else had gone. He'd never crossed the line before, just pushed her right up to it so many times she no longer knew what was normal and what was...not. She'd always given him what he wanted before, because before she'd thought he'd been on her side. They'd made an alliance. There was no reason not to play along.

Now the gloves had come off and she'd seen behind his mask. There was no alliance.

There was only Connor's agenda, and either you advanced it willingly, or you were *used*, whether you liked it or not. He preferred manipulation, but he wasn't above threats.

They loathed each other, and both of them knew it. But they were also the only hope each of them had left of getting some kind of profit out of this TD Hunter scheme. They'd invested too much to let it go to waste.

She'd invested too much.

What would her father think if the one thing she'd assured him again and again would make her famous crashed and burned instead?

No, there was no backing out now. But she was done being Connor's Ponzi.

"Go away, Connor," she said, eyes narrowing at the curtain. "I'm not interested. You wouldn't want my livestream *accidentally* turning on and recording you being a pushy bastard, would you? They'll totally expel you from school if you go viral for sneaking into the girls' locker room and sexually harassing a poor innocent girl."

There was a moment of silence, deepened by her turning off the water so she could grab her towel, dry off, and get out of there.

But her reaching fingers didn't find her towel hanging outside the curtain where it should have been.

"Looking for something?" came that smug voice.

Elena gritted her teeth. He was playing with her, and she didn't have time for that, either. For the first time in her life she had stepped outside her comfort zone and committed to succeeding at something she wasn't naturally good at—not because she wanted to, but because it was the only way to salvage her spiraling life. And now Connor was being a perv and jerking her around when they *should* be focused on winning.

In the end, though, Connor was a man, and she'd been manipulating men since before she was aware of what it meant.

"Connor," she said in a bored tone, "we *used* to have a good thing going, before you got so pushy. You were way sexier when you played hard to get. Winners don't need to be pushy, because winners win, and girls can't resist that. If you have to demand a girl's attention, you've already lost it. Now put the towel back and go be a winner."

There was a tense silence. Elena could just imagine Connor's opaque, unwavering stare through the shower curtain. Her heart pounded in her chest, but she told herself it was just because of how hot her shower had been.

Finally there was a faint shuffle of movement, and a masculine hand slid through the gap between the curtain and tiled wall, towel gripped in its fingers.

"Enjoy your shower, Elena," he said, tone cold and dead as the arctic.

He dropped the towel on the wet floor.

Elena snatched it up before it got too wet and wrapped it around herself as Connor's footsteps faded.

There was no exhale, no relaxing of muscles she hadn't realized were tight. There was none of that because she refused to acknowledge it. She just rubbed dry and got dressed as quickly as possible, ears cocked for any more noise.

Maybe she *would* shower at home from now on. Her mother would be unbearable, but Mrs. Seville's attacks were all mental and emotional. Connor threatened more than that. Men never wanted to hear no, so she'd gotten very good at making men think she was saying maybe. It made for less sulking, and gave her more options later if circumstances changed.

She needed to get Connor obsessing over The Slut again.

Revenge-obsessed Connor was much more bearable than horny Connor, especially since Elena wanted nothing more than to see Lynn Raven crushed and weeping under the brutal boot of failure and humiliation.

Connor had already promised her Skadi's Wolves would never make it to the TD Hunter National Championship, yet despite his efforts, they were still going strong. The Slut had made a fool out of Connor, too, and Elena needed Connor to remember that every single day. She needed to figure out some subtle barbs she could whisper in his ear to get under his skin and keep him up at night, stewing. Maybe then he'd finally get rid of those idiots.

There was supposed to be only *one* champion team in Cedar Rapids. *One* local celebrity to get all the attention. That stupid Raven girl had manipulated a clueless group of loser gamers to do the work for her, stealing all of Elena's rightly earned limelight. It was sickening to watch. The Slut was obviously sleeping with all four of them—just look how they went everywhere together like some sort of weirdo cult.

That was the only explanation as to why Skadi's Wolves had such a huge following. Everyone was dying to know what was really going on. If she thought she could have replicated it with Connor and his three bozo ARS teammates, she would have held her nose and done it. But The Slut had done it first, so copying it now would have looked lame.

No, the only way to reach her goal was to show the world she could do it all: be a gorgeous, glamorous stream celebrity *and* a competitive winner. Guys seemed to go crazy over the whole "gamer girl" mystique, and she was making steady progress with her subscriber count as she learned how to emulate that trend.

It was all its own kind of game. A much more complex and difficult game than something as simple as TD Hunter. Becoming a stream celebrity was *hard*, and she would show the whole world how competent and desirable she was—Connor, and her teammates, and her feckless fair-weather "friends" at school be damned. Then even her daddy couldn't deny her. He would realize she was worth sticking around for.

She would show them all.

"Nice day for a bit of exercise, eh?"

Lynn cast a dubious look at Derek Peterson, AKA DeathShot13, who just shrugged, a faint smile curling his lips.

"You're the one who said rain or shine," he pointed out.

"Yeah, and I'm regretting it," Lynn sighed, wiping at the moisture that had collected on her eyebrows and was threatening to run into her eyes.

"Come on, boss, it's barely a sprinkle," Edgar said, his big shoulders damp on the top, but the rest of him dry, shielded by his top-heavy bulk.

"Yeah, this is nothing compared to hunting in the snow," Dan said, a disgustingly chipper bounce to his movements.

"Y'all are adorable," said Bradley Hayek, AKA HoldMyBeer, who had informed Lynn when they'd shared first names after the last Boss Bash that he preferred being called literally anything over Bradley, including "dipshit," "Mr. Studly," and "hey you!"

They'd settled on Hayek, to avoid the potential confusion of using an abbreviated version of his gaming handle that was the same word as his favorite alcoholic drink.

"Kids these days," he continued, shaking his head, "just try fighting in a sandstorm lugging eighty pounds of body armor and gear. The worst part is when the sand gets in your pants and it's hours before you can get to the shower."

"Days, in a combat situation," said Crispus DeLeon, AKA Operation_Stinkbug, with a leering grin. "By that time you're rubbed raw and you beg your mates to put you out of your misery."

"Stop scaring the kids," said Gregg Santoro, AKA MrE_006, giving Lynn and her team a reassuring smile. "Don't mind him, Crispy was dropped on his head as a baby."

"Hey, don't leave out the rest," Crispy protested, "I was dropped on my head as a baby *and then* did a headspin! It was the start of an epic breakdancing career."

Lynn had no idea if she should take Crispy seriously—she assumed not—so she didn't reply. Mack and Ronnie seemed equally unsure of how to take the gregarious and ridiculous members of Team Light Brigade. It was Dan, the master of smack talk, who took to them like fish to water. Soon after they'd arrived at the access road that led to the abandoned lot Lynn had scouted, Hayek and Crispy were already teaching him lewd insults. Sonia Peterson, AKA Sonia388Lapua, AKA Derek's wife, caught them at it and shut them down with several quiet but scarily cold comments about "minors" and "professional conduct." Dan tried to protest that he was only a minor for another month, but Sonia's arch expression silenced him as quickly as it had Crispy and Hayek.

Team Light Brigade had been the first to show up at their designated meeting place, but the rest of the ten teams who had accepted Lynn's invite soon followed. She'd given them all tips on how to avoid drone notice, and Skadi's Wolves had been particularly sneaky making their way downtown that morning. So far Lynn hadn't seen a single paparazzi drone, though there were the normal scattering of delivery and service drones buzzing around the city center, including more of those small gray drones—too small for deliveries, but too big to be paparazzi vultures.

Since they were borderline trespassing on the nearby rail yard, Lynn had made the executive decision to not livestream Boss Bash 2.0, a choice she'd made sure all other teams agreed to before she'd shared the location. Hunters were welcome to record it, though, and share appropriately edited clips after the fact on their various streams. Lynn had to trust people not to be idiots about it—a potentially unwise amount of trust, but she also knew better than to insist on a rule people were going to ignore anyway.

They were gamers, after all. Rules were not their forte.

Fortunately, the abandoned lot had construction fabric along the chain link fence surrounding it—albeit tattered and old. But it would be enough to obscure their location.

Neither Kayla, Ronnie, nor Mrs. Pearson were fans of Lynn's decision—livestreams garnered exponentially more engagement. Lynn politely noted their protests, then ignored them. Any excuse to hunt without livestreaming was a good day in her book.

She supposed it was too much to expect good weather on top of it.

"Visibility is still fair," Derek noted, surveying the battleground, "and the forecast doesn't call for anything heavier. We'll be fine."

Lynn scanned her surroundings too, looking for any hazards she might have missed. Most of the lot was weed-overgrown gravel, though it turned to dirt in some places. The grass was long, but not impassable, and she couldn't see any obstacles beyond a few thorn bushes. Turning back to the assembled Hunter teams, Lynn caught Ronnie staring down the access road.

She hid a smile.

There was only one team yet to arrive, Team Voodoo Girls. Their captain, Quorra, was a striking brunette with a pixie cut that went perfectly with the cyberpunk-ninja aesthetics of their TD Hunter augmented reality armor. Lynn had noticed Ronnie staring at the young woman more than once during their last operation, but so far had resisted the urge to call him on it. The Lynn side of her wanted to build trust and rapport with Ronnie. The Larry side wanted to embarrass the heck out of him.

Decisions, decisions.

The guys regularly gave Mack grief over Riko, but it wasn't because of the romance aspect. It was because they were all convinced his "internet girlfriend" was really a scam bot that would one day fleece him for his entire net worth. The scammer was probably playing the long game and waiting until Mack was uber rich. But the guys hadn't started in on Dan about his obvious crush on Kayla yet, nor had anyone mentioned Ronnie's eyes for Quorra. So, she decided to keep her mouth shut.

Out of the corner of her eye Lynn noticed Ronnie straighten, and she turned toward the head of the access road to see a group of five girls jogging toward them. Their matching athletic gear was black with neon pink and blue highlights, and all the girls had added matching color streaks to their hair. It gave them as impressive a look in the real as in augmented reality.

"Sorry we're late," Quorra said when they arrived, barely breathing hard at all. "Airbus had a malfunction on the way here. There was an emergency landing, and we had to wait for another one to come pick us up."

"No worries," Lynn said, shaking the young woman's hand. "Nice getup, by the way," she said with a little smile, deliberately *not* looking at Ronnie.

"Thanks!" Quorra said with a grin. "We had a huge audience jump after Operation Boss Bash, thanks to you, and even picked up our first sponsorship. We could finally afford to do a team makeover, and man, the fans *love* it."

"That's so cool," Lynn said, smile widening. "I wish I could figure out how to get gear that looked like our team's skin in game."

"Oh my gosh, that would be *so* epic!" Quorra said, her eyes lighting up. "I bet you could find someone to custom program it for you. All your stuff is smart fabric, right?"

"Yeah," Lynn said, "but we have so many sponsorships it would look ridiculous to have those on top."

"Good point," Quorra agreed, eyeing Skadi's Wolves gathered around. Her gaze lingered on Ronnie, whose once-gangly frame had filled out impressively, though he would never be as bulky as Edgar. Ronnie noticed her attention, went flaming red, and looked away.

Lynn pressed her lips tightly together. Who was smiling? Not her.

"You guys are, like, one of the top Hunter Strike Teams in the *entire world* though," Quorra pointed out. "Surely you could negotiate different terms for your sponsorships, right?"

"Ooh, that's a great idea," Dan said, holding up a finger.

"We'll bring it up with our agent *later*," Lynn said firmly before Dan could derail the conversation. "For now, let's get this show on the road. I told Happy Joe's to expect a mob of hungry gamers this afternoon, so the clock's ticking!"

Their pre-battle huddle felt more like a reunion than an op briefing, and Lynn had to put on her Larry face and yell at a few people before everyone got serious. Despite that, seeing everyone together gave her a level of warm fuzzies she would never have admitted out loud.

The plan Lynn outlined took into account the smaller area, smaller group size, and improved tactics Skadi's Wolves had test run. She'd been hesitant to share their bait and destroy tactics, especially on the TD Hunter tactical forum. Skadi's Wolves had worked long and hard on their new strategies and it felt unfair that others would get a leg up in the competition without lifting a finger of their own. At the same time, it went against the spirit of the game to hoard the information. After all, Skadi's Wolves had benefitted immensely from the training and tactics provided by TD Hunter and its many players around the world.

Her compromise was to wait until after they'd posted their Boss Bash 2.0 footage before sharing a comprehensive overview. Sunday she would have time to write a post on the forum. She'd even throw in instructions on how players could implement the new moves in their own hunting missions, either as teams or solo. She honestly enjoyed discussing tactics, so it would be something to look forward to in between writing essays and filling out calculus worksheets.

Lynn was pleased to find most of the other teams had been working on their own bait tactics, though no other team had tested and refined their tactics as thoroughly as Skadi's Wolves had. With the combined input of all ten teams, Lynn was able to modify her initial plan into something she was confident would work. At the end of the day, her goal was to make a clean sweep of the entire TDM "infestation" in the empty lot—both the boss and its surrounding rings. They had the manpower for it. As long as they didn't run into any surprises, it was doable. Then they could relax and enjoy some top-notch pizza.

Of course, she should have known better.

Lynn was disabused of her cocky feelings almost as soon as they dropped into combat mode. Most of the TDMs might have *only* been Bravo Class and lower, but that didn't make their sheer numbers any less overwhelming. The combined teams of Skadi's

Horde mowed them down by the hundreds, but hundreds more just took their place. There was a strangely high number of electrovores stacked in with all the others, especially bunyips and hydras, as if they'd decided to abandon their standard behavior and crowd into this one space to feast on whatever invisible currents criss-crossed the abandoned lot—Lynn had counted at least five node towers within sight of their current position.

Complicating matters further was the high chain-link fence. Unlike TDMs, Hunters were at the whim of the physical world, and the fence restricted their lateral movement and lanes of retreat. Skadi's Horde improvised, adapted, and overcame. The bait mechanic made a world of difference. With it they were able to influence the ebb and flow of TDMs to keep from being flanked by monsters they'd been unable to target past the fencing on either wing of their formation.

Then they got within range of the boss, and all bets were off.

They discovered with unpleasant swiftness that the towering column of sparkling mist was ranged. Lynn and the few other shield-bearers rushed to the front, drawing its fire and burning through armor plates like they were paper. The fire must have been coming from more than one place, though, because players started dying far sooner than Lynn had anticipated. Despite the feeling she had something to prove, Lynn ordered everyone to retreat to the edge of its range. She pulled those with Force Shields from their teams and advanced in line with them while Skadi's Wolves fended off any opportunistic TDMs. This allowed them to get just close enough to interact with the unknown boss, firing their ranged weapons into the mist and enduring its returning attacks long enough for Hugo to identify it.

Thankfully, Hugo was particularly efficient in identifying the boss. In what felt like record time the mist solidified into a hideous, monstrous plant that Hugo designated as Ya-Te-Veo. It was rooted to the ground but had a dozen flailing, toothed branches that looked ready to lift a human into the air and stuff it into the jagged maw at the center of the thing. It was those sinuous branches that were flicking out, throwing spikes or giant thorns or something at the gathered Hunters. The ranged attacks had a DOT element, like a poison, and between all dozen branches the rate of fire was overwhelming. Thus their armor plates being about as effective as paper.

Lynn pulled everyone back again to figure out how to kill it. Seeing its lethal appendages swaying and snapping hungrily, Lynn was doubly grateful she'd kept her people a healthy distance away, relying on ranged fire only. Just because St. Sebastian's was barely a half a mile south didn't mean she wanted to find out what would happen if a branch touched one of them.

Which was a ridiculous thing to think, because this was a *game*.

The sane part of her rolled its eyes.

The Larry part of her spat on the ground and bared its teeth at the boss.

Nine months ago, she would have discounted her gut and charged in headlong. But she felt the responsibility of leadership like a physical thing weighing on her shoulders, and it made her hesitate. She was used to disengaging all emotion from the stakes of a game, analyzing the patterns, and exploiting them to win, and win, and win again. It was the cold logic that made her so efficient in WarMonger. She never got caught up in the heat of battle, it was all just a game. Just patterns.

But now her instincts were whispering formless, indistinct warnings in the back of her brain, and for the first time a trickle of fear invaded her emotionless focus.

What would Larry do?

Lynn's thoughts raced, looking at the situation from all sides and searching for the logic in it. Larry wouldn't let fear drive him, that was certain. But he also wouldn't discount it as unimportant. It was all a part of the pattern. So what did the fear mean? How did she integrate it?

The answer came with the lunging thrash of Ya-Te-Veo's branches, reaching toward her as if it could still perceive the threat, even if she were out of range.

Duh.

Treat the game as if it *were* real.

In a moment Lynn's perspective shifted, and everything seemed to click into place. All she had to do was recalibrate her parameters to account for the additional risk. Take TD Hunter at its word instead of trying to "break" the pattern and game the system, like she'd done at the qualifiers.

A thought flitted across her brain, too quick to nail down: Hugo and Steve treated the game like it was real, too, didn't they? Why would they do that?

There was no time to mull it over. She had a boss to kill and a horde of Hunters to lead to victory. She scanned the battleground again, sharp eyes calculating ranges as her brain flipped through possible strategies that achieved all her goals: destroy the boss, avoid physical contact, and maintain the most competitive stats for her people as if this were the National Championship and she were being scored.

"Listen up, Skadi's Horde! The ranged attacks and bunch of arms makes killing Ya-Te-Veo tricky. Direct contact with the boss gets you some seriously nasty debuffs. We've got to avoid it at all costs. I want everyone to come out of this with fantastic scores, so here's how it's gonna go. We're gonna split and sweep up as much of these rings on either side as we can while staying out of the boss's range. I want max efficiency, and pick up every scrap of ichor and Oneg you can find. Once we've got plenty of space, we're gonna form three squads, two wings to concentrate bait and a squad in the middle with all our highest damage dealers—plasma cannons, flame throwers, you name it. Wings will draw fire so the spear can close and skewer this ugly bastard. We'll need to mix and match teams to make it work, so everybody leave your drama at the door and get ready to work together like you've never done before. Let's do this!"

She started rattling off group assignments, calling out teams and individual Hunters from memory based on the updated weaponry profiles they'd all sent her in the last few weeks.

In no time they'd reorganized and pulled back, splitting into two groups to sweep through the multitudinous but vulnerable masses of TDMs that formed the rings around Ya-Te-Veo. The next thirty minutes were a slog, but Lynn kept everyone sharp by staying on top of each team's progress vis-a-vis her group leader display that was fed data from each team captain. By the time they'd regrouped at their original starting point, everyone was raring to get at the boss and end the fight. They had pizza to get to, after all.

"Hey, Edgar, you ready to be my point man?" Lynn subvocalized in a private voice chat.

Edgar turned away from Ya-Te-Veo and grinned at her, eyes alight.

"Are you kidding me, boss? I was *made* for this shit."

"Don't call me... never mind." She shook her head. "Just get out there and give it hell. And...try really hard to avoid direct contact, okay? Take my word for it that the debuff is bad. *Really* bad."

"Can do, boss." He gave her a two-fingered salute and hefted his Snazzgun formed out of his two omnipolymer electric blue batons. In her augmented sight, it was a ludicrously massive thing with too many barrels to be real, patched together from a dozen different weapons like Frankenstein's monster in gun form. It had massive, rough-toothed jaws fashioned from metal plates that framed the business ends of the barrels, looking for all the world like a hungry mouth ready to eat everything it could reach.

Lynn rolled her eyes and switched back to the group chat.

"Everybody split into your assigned groups. Maui_You'reWelcome is the spear tip. RonnieDarko is leading the melee element of the spear: keep those cannons safe, or we'll never kill this thing. I'm leading the right wing and DeathShot13 is leading the left. Make sure everybody drops their bait markers together and be ready to dodge. *Nobody* is allowed to get hit with that debuff, got it?"

All the teams chorused their acknowledgements and Skadi's Horde got to work. To Lynn's relief, the plan actually worked. She hadn't been sure the bait would be enough to distract Ya-Te-Veo away from the closer, more damaging threat that closed to rip into its ugly, twisted trunk.

But it worked—perhaps a little too well. Ya-Te-Veo seemed especially interested in her, as though it could pick her out as the leader and instigator of the threat it faced. The TDM boss ignored the ranged fighters shooting it to swipe at Bastion with singular focus. Facing it was like dancing with death. She kept moving, close enough to keep it engaged but far enough away that she could still dodge. Mack kept her alive, shoving Oneg at her while she was too busy avoiding hits to let her attention waver for even a moment. She had no idea how Derek's wing was holding out and had no reprieve to find out. Something about Derek's team, though, made her confident they would pull through. Team Light Brigade oozed competence, despite Hayek and Crispy's antics. Maybe it was their military air.

She didn't need to look to know how the tip of the spear was doing. Edgar kept up an almost constant stream of whoops and ululating war cries that made her grin even while she dodged tree branches with teeth trying to rip her head off.

Fire pounded through her veins, and she rode the battle high long after it should have ebbed, knowing she couldn't slow until the objective was won. When the battle high was gone, iron resolve and cold, hard spite kept her at it.

There was no way Larry the Snake was going to get beaten by a tree. Not even one with teeth.

Ya-Te-Veo might have been a Bravo Class boss, but their victory was still a very, very close thing. By the time it finally exploded, blinding them all temporarily, they were so low on supplies Lynn didn't even let them take advantage of the TDMs' strange paralysis in those brief moments after the boss's defeat. Everyone just scooped up what loot was in reach and got out of there.

The abrupt silence and eerie calm after several hours spent in combat mode was disorienting. But then Edgar's deep laugh broke the silence, and he whooped, fist in the air.

"Take that, you big ugly bush!" he yelled.

Other people broke out laughing and soon everyone was hugging, shaking hands, or animatedly recounting their near misses. Quorra and her VooDoo Girls came over and gave Lynn double high fives, while the members of the Monster Control Bureau came to congratulate Ronnie, who had led several of them in their successful melee fight against the last, toughest ring of TDMs to get their cannons into range of Ya-Te-Veo. From their grins and gestures, Lynn guessed they were comparing weapon stats and blade lengths. It was good to see Ronnie smile. He didn't seem to do it much these days.

"Congratulations, Miss Raven, you have achieved Level 39!" said Hugo in her ear. "Your leveling details, achievement bonuses, and reward items have been minimized for later perusal, as per usual. Additionally, you and the members of your hunting group have been attributed credit for the discovery, analysis, and defeat of Bravo Class Boss Ya-Te-Veo. A list of your loot and experience rewards can be found in your leveling history."

"Awesome, thanks, Hugo," Lynn subvocalized, scanning the triumphant members of Skadi's Horde to make sure no one looked hurt, dizzy, dehydrated, or otherwise in need of help.

"Excellent work, RavenStriker."

Lynn turned to see Derek's genial smile, his wife Sonia close by his elbow.

"It was quite the ride, Ms. Raven," Sonia said with a respectful nod. "Most fun I've had in...well since the last time we killed monsters together." She chuckled.

"Oh, yeah, thanks," Lynn said, shaking the hand Derek held out to her, though only because of the manners her mother had drilled into her. The knowing look on Derek's face made her nervous. Like he was sizing her up. And what was a group of grown, obviously competent adults doing playing TD Hunter on this level anyway? There was no way this was just a hobby for them, they were too good. They weren't treating it like a relaxing escape on their day off.

They were treating it like a job.

"Really glad you could make it," Lynn continued, smiling with only a bit of effort. "I'm surprised you could get time off work, really. I know you travel a lot, right?"

Derek *didn't* glance at Sonia, but Sonia glanced at him.

"A fair bit, yeah. Our schedules are pretty flexible, though."

"Cool," Lynn said. "What is it you do again?"

"Consulting," Derek said easily, not missing a beat.

"Oh, wow. What kind of consulting?" Lynn had no idea why she was prying. Something was just...off.

"Large-scale pest control, actually," Derek said with a flash of a smile. "We mostly do government contracts, US and Canada. But we consult with a few big corporations too."

"Wow," Lynn said again, this time legitimately impressed. She wondered what sorts of pests needed large scale control. Rats? Ants? Roaches? She was about to ask when Hayek and Crispy appeared, flanking Derek and Sonia and slapping their teammates on the back. From the Canadian couple's expressions, it was an annoying familiarity that they tolerated with long-suffering good humor.

"Good job, kid," Crispy said. "Ya nailed it." He squinted one eye and made a shooting gesture at her with one hand. "Next time, though, could you pick a boss with no arms? I'm gettin' too old for all this jumping around."

"Shut up, Crispy," Hayek drawled. "You love it, and you know it."

Gregg, the last member of Team Light Brigade, ambled over, stretching out his arms and shoulders as he came.

"We like it when he gets tuckered out, Ms. Raven," Gregg said, eyes twinkling. "That way he sleeps at night instead of keeping us all up with his whining."

"Please, call me Lynn. Or Raven, I guess, if you want to go with handles."

"Raven it is, then," Gregg said with a respectful nod.

They were interrupted by an enthusiastic Dan, who somehow looked like he had *more* energy now than he'd had when they'd started the boss fight.

"Are we going or what? I'm *starving*. I could eat a whole cow if it was made out of pizza! Plus the Voodoo Girls want to sit with me and it's rude to keep the ladies waiting!"

"*Us*, Dan," Ronnie growled, coming up behind his friend. "They want to sit with *us*. Now stop being a spazz. You're embarrassing everyone."

Dan shoved him and said something rude, which got Ronnie all fired up, looking like he would gladly sock Dan in the face. But then the ladies from Team Voodoo Girls walked over, Quorra at their head, at which point the boys calmed down, though later Lynn caught them kicking each other's shins when they thought no one was looking.

In the end, all ten teams made time to partake of Happy Joe's pizza, and it turned into more of a spectacle than she'd intended. She hadn't wanted to clean out their kitchen the way they'd done last time, but apparently Happy Joe's had ordered extra supplies—and not kept quiet about the fact that patrons might catch a glimpse of Skadi's Wolves if they came around that afternoon.

With a deep breath for calm and control, Lynn fixed a polite smile on her face and resigned herself to signing hats and shirts and napkins. Drones were never allowed inside buildings, but there were several local streamers who livestreamed the whole thing—at least until the manager kicked out everyone but paying patrons so the Hunter teams could sit down and eat. GIC had received all the footage from Skadi's Wolves in real time, so Mrs. Pearson's team had already started putting up clips and getting the algorithms churning before they posted the full play-through. Kayla, like clockwork, pinged Lynn with the latest stream stats and juicy gossip from the "Team CRC" fan circles, where the prevailing complaint seemed to be that nobody on Team CRC looked like they were actually having *fun* while they hunted.

Even Steve pinged her with a little congrats.

"*Saw the news, kid. Congrats on bagging another one. Pretty soon Mr. Krator is going to make you the TD Hunter mascot. You'll never get rid of us, then.*" Steve included a smart image of a cheeky smiley face sticking its tongue out whenever her eyes got to that point in the message. It made Lynn snort. It also made her create a mental note: *never let Mr. Krator talk me into being a mascot.*

That should be pretty easy, right?

After all the pizza was gone—literally every last piece, mainly due to Edgar and Dan—the various teams split up to head home, exhausted but happy. Lynn was determined to go straight back to her apartment, shower, and sleep. For a long time. Oh, and hopefully hang out with her mom somewhere in there, because she'd barely seen Matilda for weeks.

When Lynn opened her apartment door, the first thing she saw was her mother sitting on their living room couch, arm raised in the flicking motion that turned off their wall screen, a guilty look plastered across her face.

"Mooom?" Lynn said slowly, closing the door behind her. "What are you doing?"

Matilda laughed, a little flush rising on her tawny cheeks.

"Oops, you caught me!" She pushed herself up and held her arms out for a hug. "I know watching you on the streams makes you feel weird, but I can't help it. Congratulations on your successful hunt! GIC hasn't posted the whole thing yet, but the clips so far look amazing. You look like you're having the time of your life."

Warmth suffused Lynn's tired limbs and a smile snuck its way onto her face. She dropped her backpack with attached hydration pack and took four big steps to get into her mother's arms. Even though she was almost the same height as Matilda, she went low while her mom went high, and they fit together seamlessly. Matilda's grip was tight and warm, and Lynn sort of melted, not realizing how tense she'd been all day, weighed down by her responsibilities and the stress of all the public attention.

"Thanks, Mom," she said, cheek pressed against her mother's shoulder.

"You're welcome, honey. I'm so proud of you."

They stood that way long enough for Lynn to notice her

mom's heartbeat, strong and steady. Matilda didn't let her grip slacken until Lynn shifted.

"Go take a nice hot shower, sweetie. You deserve it."

"Do I really smell that bad?"

Matilda made a comical face. "You kinda do, yeah."

Lynn laughed and trudged off toward the bathroom.

"Oh, by the way, good news!"

"Yeah?"

"My friend Karen pinged me just before you got home. She's on the weekend shift at St. Sebastian's and said she overheard the electrical repair crew talking about how they'd finally gotten the hospital grid to stabilize and stop throwing off all these weird surges they think have been causing the blackouts. She figures management will *finally* reduce our shift hours so we're not overlapping as much to be on hand whenever there's a problem. That means we can eat dinner together again in the evenings!"

Lynn's stomach dropped like an anvil thrown off an airplane at thirty thousand feet. She swallowed, feeling cold goosebumps break out on her arms.

"Oh... that's good. I'm really glad." The smile she forced onto her face must not have been convincing, because Matilda's brow furrowed.

"What's the matter, honey? I thought you'd be excited."

"I am!" Lynn insisted. "I'm just really tired and sore. Sorry."

"It's okay. Go take your shower and get some rest."

"That's the plan," Lynn said weakly, turning back toward the bathroom. Only then did she let her face contort into the grim frown that mirrored her thoughts.

What are the odds, Lynn?

What are the odds?

She didn't know the answer, but she *did* know what "The Snake" always said whenever his fellow mercs complained about his successes, as if being at the right place at the right time was a coincidence:

"Idiots and lazy people believe in coincidence. I believe in patterns."

Maybe it was time to find the pattern... and see where it led.

Chapter 5

LYNN WAS PREOCCUPIED ALL WEEKEND, THOUGH SHE TRIED TO put everything TD Hunter from her mind so she could enjoy time on Sunday with her mom.

Matilda surprised her with an afternoon out. They ate steak—Lynn would *never* say no to a nice bloody steak—got matching chocolate sprinkle ice cream cones and enjoyed a glorious hour exploring the world at a VR cafe. There were rooms you could rent decked out with all the latest VR equipment, from goggles, to haptic gloves, to scent sprays. There was even one super expensive room with a full-body rig—a haptic harness on a three-sixty treadmill that let you run, jump, fall, do flips, and more, all while enjoying seamless virtual reality. One day, Lynn promised herself she'd try that beast out. With her mom, though, they donned goggles and haptic gloves and hop-skipped together across the globe. They visited the Great Wall of China, Machu Picchu, and the pyramids at Giza. They strolled down Champs-Élysées, popped into the Louvre, and finished off their hour at Redwood National State Park gaping at trees taller than the biggest skyscraper in Cedar Rapids.

As fun as Sunday was, though, it was almost a relief to dive back into real life and let her brain return to gnawing on all the bones it had been collecting.

Homework assignments.

Paranoia about Elena and Connor.

Patterns... suspicions and patterns...

She was so preoccupied that on Monday when they were all loitering in the hall before class, it took Edgar's nudge and Mack's hushed "whoah," before she finally looked up and saw what had shocked them: Ronnie coming toward them, shoulders hunched, AR glasses firmly in place and fully opaque. Except the glasses couldn't hide the purple and blue spreading from his left eye.

"Dude," Dan said, voice hushed, "What happened?"

"None of your business," Ronnie growled, trying to push past them into the classroom. Edgar stepped in his way, though.

"Bro, come on," he said quietly. "That's not how we roll. Who did that to you?"

"Was it Connor?" Lynn asked, clenching and unclenching her fists.

Ronnie gave a derisive snort.

"That pretty boy? He's a stinking coward. Sends other people to do his dirty work."

"Okay," Edgar rumbled, voice calm. Very, *very* calm. "So, who did he send? Who did it?"

"It has nothing to do with Connor. Now get out of my face!" Ronnie snapped, trying to push past Edgar's bulk.

Of course, trying to push past Edgar was like trying to push past a multi-ton block of solid granite.

Edgar didn't budge.

"Who. Did. It?" he asked again, so low Lynn felt more than heard the rumble of his voice.

"Forget about it, okay! It's none of your business. Now get your fat ugly mug out of my way!"

Edgar still didn't move, despite the gathering fury on Ronnie's face. Mack stepped closer, hovering anxiously.

"Come on, Ronnie, calm down, people are starting to stare."

Lynn looked around, seeing that Mack was right. The problem was, they weren't staring at Ronnie. They were staring at *her*.

"Hey, Lynn!" a tall, dark-haired guy called, someone Lynn recognized as a fellow senior, but not one she'd met before. "Nice vid! When are you going to make it a movie? I'd buy it!" His friends standing with him hooted and made lewd gestures at her.

Lynn's blood ran cold.

"Shut your stupid pieholes before we shut them for you!" Dan yelled back.

But other people in the hall were starting to react too, obviously watching something on their various AR feeds. Their reactions swung wildly in all directions, from wide-eyed horror to incredulous glee.

"What did Connor do this time?" Edgar groaned quietly.

Lynn's heart was racing too fast for her breath to keep up. Out of instinct more than any deliberate choice, she blindly felt for Edgar's arm and gave it a reassuring squeeze.

"I'm sure it's nothing you did, Edgar," she said, keeping her voice steady. Just a few months ago, Connor had been involved in disseminating a selectively edited vid of their confrontation with him at St. Sebastian's after Mack had been hurt. Connor's callous attitude and immediate attempt to replace Mack had been the straw that broke the camel's back. Lynn had led the rest of her friends in booting Connor out of Skadi's Wolves, at which point he'd laid hands on her and set Edgar off, causing a fistfight between the two young men.

Though he'd never admit it, Lynn was sure Connor had cut a deal with the sleazebag paparazzi streamer who'd posted the video. No doubt Connor had provided the footage and directed the streamer how to edit it to make it look like Edgar had assaulted Connor unprovoked. Connor's effort to get Edgar kicked out of school and arrested for assault had gone nowhere. TD Hunter's legal team had stepped in—since it had involved a team-related matter—and pointed out the obvious ways it had been edited, plus provided the original video that Hugo had made sure to record. Connor dropped the matter like it was a rotting, slimy fish, but Lynn knew they hadn't seen the last of Connor's tricks.

What had he done this time?

People were forming huddles in the hall now, those in the know whispering to those who crowded in to hear the latest gossip. No doubt links and vid clips of whatever it was were swirling back and forth like leaves in an autumn storm. Some people glanced at her with pity in their eyes. Others with leering expressions not fit for polite company.

Ronnie, his fury at Edgar forgotten, glared around at everyone in the hall, as if one of them would be intimidated by his expression into confessing whatever secret they were all in on.

When nothing happened beyond more sideways looks and

mean snickers, Ronnie stomped over to one of his casual friends Lynn had seen him talking to on occasion. The guy's eyes were unfocused and his expression was frozen in a sort of horrified fascination, like he couldn't have looked away if he'd wanted to.

"Hey, Eddie! What's going on?"

Eddie jumped and looked over, guilt washing over his slack-jawed expression.

"Uhhhh..." Nothing more came from his mouth and his eyes flicked from Ronnie to Edgar, who had followed and was now a silent, looming presence at Ronnie's back.

"Well? What's going around?"

Eddie's mouth opened and closed soundlessly like a suffocating fish.

"Hey, I'll send it to you, Ronnie boy!" yelled a jeering voice from down the hall, one Lynn didn't recognize. "You're gonna *love* it."

Lynn was frozen. She wanted to run, to hide. But she wouldn't do that, not anymore. Yet the looks she was getting had triggered deep, ugly trauma she'd worked so hard to bury. Dread paralyzed her and all she could do was stare at Edgar's back, as if there were answers to be found written across his broad shoulders.

Out of the corner of her eye she saw Ronnie stiffen for one horrible moment. Then he violently yanked his AR glasses off and threw them across the hall, yelling incoherently and flailing like he was having a seizure.

"Ronnie! What the heck? What's going on?" Edgar said, his voice no longer calm.

"Gaaah! Oh my God! Get it out of my brain! I can't—I didn't mean—I didn't want—" Ronnie slapped his face and rubbed his eyes, shaking his head like a wet dog shaking off water.

Other students were drawing back, retreating down the hall, leaving Skadi's Wolves alone like they had some sort of gruesome communicable disease. Edgar and Ronnie weren't helping.

"Get a grip and tell me what's going on!" Edgar yelled at Ronnie, grabbing him by the back of his shirt and shaking him.

The unhinged fear and anger in Edgar's voice broke through Lynn's paralysis and she stumbled forward toward the two.

Edgar needed help. She had to do something. But then Ronnie finally stopped his hysterics and went limp in Edgar's grip. He opened his eyes, and the first thing they landed on was her. He flinched back, all color draining from his face until everything but his black eye was white.

"Principal," Ronnie croaked, turning to Edgar. "We need to go see the principal, *now*. N-nobody look at anything anyone sends you. Just—it's not worth it. *Don't look.*"

"A faketime *what*?" Principal Charles asked, looking dumbfounded, as if Ronnie had just told him the Moon was crashing into Earth.

All five of them had stumbled straight to the principal's office, avoiding eye contact with everyone they passed. Lynn wasn't sure if Ronnie had been leading them or running away from her. She also couldn't have said if she'd been clutching Edgar's hand to support herself, or to hold him back from lunging at people they passed. Guys were wolf whistling and making lewd motions with their hands, and girls were openly laughing and shaking their heads. Lynn couldn't hear any of them because, after the first few comments, she'd set "I Am the Fire" to play in her earbuds and left it on repeat until they got to their destination.

Now they were lined up inside the relative quiet of the principal's office. Ronnie, Dan, *and* Mack had already explained the situation to the vice principal—twice, because they kept talking over each other—before she'd finally understood, gone white-faced, and banged on the principal's door.

"A faketime..." Ronnie hesitated, then mumbled the last word quietly to the principal, as if he couldn't stand to hear himself say it again.

"A faketime *porno*?" Principal Charles said loudly.

Lynn flinched. She kept her eyes fixed straight ahead, seeing nothing.

"Y-yes," Ronnie said, breath leaving his lungs shakily.

"And it's being shared around the school?" the principal asked.

"*Yes!*" Dan, Mack, and Ronnie said together.

"You need to tell the IT department to shut the school net down," Dan said, sounding authoritative.

"But, those sorts of...*things* are blocked by our firewall, aren't they?" the principal asked.

In the stunned silence that followed, Lynn could almost hear the eyeballs falling out of their respective eye sockets because her friends were rolling them so hard.

The administration *tried* to enforce strict firewall filtering on all mesh web activity on the school network. By school policy, all student LINCs were programmed to exclusively use the school network while on school grounds. But there were myriad ways around it. The poor, overworked tech department played whack-a-mole with the perpetrators. For every exploit they patched, three more were sussed out by the resident nerds and disseminated through the student body. Lynn had never been sure why they'd bothered trying to control a bunch of tech-savvy teenagers.

Now she knew.

"Your firewalls are about as effective as Swiss cheese," Dan said grimly. "Every student in the school who wants to...to... know what's going on can find out."

"But we can't shut down the school network," the principal said. "Classes are about to start."

Lynn felt Edgar twitch forward, and she tightened her hold on his hand. The last thing they needed was Edgar taking a swing at the principal. She could feel him trembling, though. He needed to hit something.

"Who cares!" Mack yelled, and Dan and Ronnie started yelling too.

"All right, you three, calm down. I don't appreciate your tones, and—"

"*Po velnių!* Who cares about our freaking tone!" Ronnie said, voice going all high-pitched, "You're aiding and abetting *sexual exploitation*, you *atsilupėlis*! You *can't unsee*—" Ronnie choked, but rallied himself. "You can't *unsee* that shit. Shut it down before more people see it!"

The argument continued, washing over Lynn without touching her. She was in a gray fog, disconnected from everything, trying to think of nothing. But memories and thoughts wormed through anyway.

Hey, dude, look at her chest! Do you think she uses those things?
If she doesn't, it'd be a crying shame.
I'll use them for her!

It was middle school all over again.

She felt the impulse to cross her arms over her chest, to hunch her shoulders. To hide.

A faketime porno. Her. In a—

Her mind shied away from the idea. She couldn't think about

it. She couldn't wonder what was in it. She couldn't imagine how people were reacting at that moment, what they were saying, watching an AI-generated video that looked like her, doing... doing... *things.*

You can't unsee that shit.

Lynn squeezed her eyes shut and shook her head, wishing desperately she could wash out her brain with bleach—burn even the morbid imaginings right out of her head.

She became vaguely aware that Principal Charles was on a call with the IT department and Dan, Mack, and Ronnie had come back over, forming a semicircle around her and Edgar. All three of them seemed incapable of looking her in the face.

"Should we ping her mom?" Mack asked quietly.

"She's not going back to class, that's for sure, you idiot," Ronnie spat.

"Y-yeah," Edgar said shakily, then took a deep breath. "I'll ping her ma. Dan, you call Mrs. Pearson and tell her—"

There was a tone in Lynn's ear of an incoming call, and the guys all stiffened as if they'd received the notification as well.

Lynn couldn't make her lips move, so she blinked twice to accept the call.

"Good morning, Skadi's Wolves," Mrs. Pearson said, her voice brisk and businesslike. "Considering you answered my call, I assume you are *not* in class, and are aware of the... illegal video that has surfaced?"

Nobody said anything for a moment, then Mack mumbled, "Yeah. It's, um... it's all over the school."

They heard a short, bracing sigh.

"I am sorry, Ms. Raven. First of all, you should know GIC has already issued an immediate takedown order to the originating site, and we are scanning the mesh web for any other iteration or clip of the video that might crop up. We caught it early, and this sort of content is already banned from the streams and any sort of social media site, so their filters should prevent it from going viral via those avenues.

"Unfortunately, people can still talk about it, and screen captures embedded inside otherwise innocuous videos will likely slip past the filters. We will do everything we can, I promise. We have lawyers on staff and Mr. Swain has already authorized us to begin paperwork to sue the hosting site, based on the authority you granted us as your public representatives. Law enforcement has been notified so that an investigation can be launched to find the creator. We are also prepared to threaten lawsuits against any site or individual who knowingly disseminates this content. But...well, you can't stop people from talking about it, my dear."

"Can you find out who shared it at our school?" Edgar asked, his voice hoarse.

"Unfortunately, only the internal administrators of your school's network would be able to track down that data. If you would like, we could send an investigation request to the school, to use as part of the lawsuit. Since Ms. Raven is a minor, this falls under child trafficking and exploitation laws, which gives us much more legal authority to demand certain measures be taken."

"Every single person who watches that, that *thing* is breaking the law, right?" Edgar asked. Ronnie shifted, shoulders hunching, turning even further away from Lynn.

"Yes, technically," Mrs. Pearson said. "Though to prosecute, you would have to prove the person had knowingly solicited the content. No judge would accept a case against foolish teenagers participating in a viral event at their school. However, we will inform your principal of the applicable laws, and make sure he notifies the student body and staff that anyone caught disseminating the illegal content could face criminal charges.

"Now, gentlemen, I need to speak to Ms. Raven privately. You ought to inform your parents or legal guardians of what happened as soon as possible. You will all likely be called as witnesses in the eventual lawsuit against the hosting site, and the prosecution of the creator if he or she is ever caught."

"I bet it was Connor," Dan growled. "He should be locked up for this. He already tried to smear us once. Tell the cops to investigate *him*!"

"We should not speculate on the responsible party," Mrs. Pearson said firmly. "I will be sure that Mr. Bancroft's past involvement with, and accusations against, Skadi's Wolves is relayed to the proper authorities."

"Thank you, Mrs. Pearson," Mack said.

"Just doing my job, Mr. Rios. But...I am very sorry you've been targeted. This is the worst part of fame, a situation I would never wish on anyone. The good news is that it will be forgotten in time. The best course of action is to put it from your minds and act as if it never happened. Any attention brought to it will only fan the flames. Scandal begets attention, and attention drives algorithms. Do not say *anything* on your respective streams, and do not talk about it with *anyone* but your legal guardians. We will prepare a statement to post on all of your accounts. It is a delicate balance, as we do not want to contribute to the furor or incentivize people to go looking for the video.

"Now, go home and read a book, all of you. Stay off the web. We will keep you updated about any developments. Goodbye, gentlemen. Ms. Raven, if you would stay."

There was a pause, then Mrs. Pearson spoke again, her tone much gentler now that it was just the two of them.

"I am so sorry, dear. Are you all right?"

"I—" Lynn's words stuck in her throat. She had to blink several times, fighting back a burning in her eyes as she cleared her throat and found her voice. "I'm... okay. Well... not really. But... you know..." She couldn't think of anything else to say, so she didn't.

"Do you have someone to accompany you home? Your mother works third shift, does she not? So she is already at home?"

"Um... yeah. She's home. I, uh, I'll hang with the guys, I guess."

"Good. As long as you are not alone."

Silence.

"It is much to take in, I know," Mrs. Pearson said. "Do not feel ashamed for being overwhelmed, Ms. Raven. Anyone would be. A crime has been committed against you. It is completely normal that you would feel confused, hurt, even violated, right now. The social-gossip factor will only compound those feelings, so... please take care of yourself. Find a good therapist, if you need one. We can recommend several, if you want a referral. I am sure your mother, being a nurse, will have resources to tap as well. Do not hesitate to reach out if you need assistance, all right?"

It took a moment for Lynn to realize she'd been asked a question.

"Um, yeah. I will."

"Good. Well, we have much work ahead of us, so I will bid you good morning. My team will continue posting content from your recent boss fight to keep the content flowing on your streams.

We have a few old interviews as well that we had been holding back for a rainy day. There is nothing you need to do for the next few days. Stay off the web, I implore you. Everything will be better once this becomes old news."

"Okay," Lynn said faintly.

"Goodbye, Ms. Raven."

Lynn couldn't bring herself to open her mouth again, and the call ended with a soft tone.

She didn't move or speak. She just stared at the wall. Eventually, Edgar squeezed her hand.

"You done talking to Mrs. Pearson?" Edgar asked.

Lynn jerked her head in affirmation.

"Okay. Come on, guys. Let's take her home."

Principal Charles, who was still on a call with someone, put up a hand.

"One second, Dave—you kids need to go back to class. Except Ms. Raven, of course. You are, uh, excused for the day. I'll let your teachers know."

"We're going with her," Edgar said, his words rumbling ominously.

The principal swallowed, which wasn't an unreasonable reaction. It had taken *four* male teachers to pull Edgar off that kid who'd assaulted Lynn in *middle school*. Edgar was five years older, a foot taller, and covered in muscle—a fact not lost on Lynn, though she felt guilty ogling her friend, so she tried not to. At this point, if Edgar lost control, there was likely nothing short of lethal force that could stop him.

"O-of course, Ms. Raven shouldn't be alone. One of you can be excused from class. But the others need to go back. None of the rest of you were depicted in the...erm...content?" The principal asked delicately.

Out of the corners of her vision, Lynn could see the guys looking at each other.

"Uh, none of us watched it, so we don't really know," Dan said.

"But if we had been, Mrs. Pearson would have mentioned it," Mack pointed out.

"Yeah, probably." Dan shrugged.

"In that case," the principal continued, "one of you—"

"I'm staying with Lynn," Edgar said in a tone that brooked no argument.

"We should all go together," Mack said, looking determined.

"Now, kids—no, Dave, I'm not done, just wait a minute—your education is important, and—"

"Go," Lynn croaked.

Everyone's eyes locked on her. Ronnie looked away immediately.

"Dan, Mack, Ronnie, go back to class," Lynn said, forcing herself to look at them. "I'll...I'll be fine with Edgar. I refuse to let any of you get in trouble over this." A bit of warmth seeped into her limbs. She stood up straighter.

"That's what they want. They *want* our team to fall apart. They want us to give up. But we won't. Not on school, not on TD Hunter, not on anything. Go back to class and ignore *everyone*. Stand up tall and don't react to a single comment. Do you hear me?" Fire was stirring in her veins again, enough to steady her voice and give her the strength to keep talking. "We won't give them a *shred* of satisfaction."

The guys' expressions hardened, and they nodded, even Ronnie, though he still couldn't meet her eyes. He stared just over her shoulder, jaw clenched.

You can't unsee that shit.

Lynn shuddered, trying not to think about it. She knew what he'd seen wasn't his fault. He didn't do anything wrong. In fact, he'd stood up for her. For the first time.

He'd defended *her*. Not just the team. *Her*.

Lynn's brow furrowed.

"Thank you, Ronnie."

His eyes flicked to hers in surprise.

"What?"

"Thank you," Lynn said slowly, holding his gaze. "Thank you for...being angry...for being disgusted, instead of..." She couldn't finish the sentence, so she just nodded gravely at him, then looked up at Edgar.

She felt beaten. Pummeled. Stripped bare. Violated.

But she was still standing.

"Let's go home."

Edgar squeezed her hand. He still hadn't let go.

"Yeah. Let's."

Lynn didn't want to interrupt her mom's much-needed sleep, so Edgar stayed with her all morning and afternoon until Matilda woke up for her usual shift. They spent the time playing old-fashioned, non-mesh-connected games on Lynn's wall-screen, cleaning the kitchen, and even getting some homework done based on notes Mack sent them from class. Anything to stay focused, to keep her mind from wandering to dark places.

Edgar tried to cheer her up with hilarious fail vids that he was always posting in their ongoing team chat—vids she never watched. You never knew what other vids the algorithm might shove in your face, and she hated accidentally stumbling across a vid about *her*. But with Edgar there to vet them, she didn't mind indulging him, and honestly some of them were pretty hilarious, especially the ones with creative voiceovers. Edgar's favorite usually involved crazy traffic fails in Russia where electric and automated vehicles were scarce due to how poorly they operated in cold and snow. Then there were the amateur stunt fails that always got him snort-laughing. One vid he showed her was some drone operator trying to catch his falling drone, not watching where he were going, tumbling straight into a canal, and landing on top of an alligator that almost ate him then and there.

They both lost it at that one.

"Ah, Florida man. He always gets me." Edgar sighed theatrically, wiping his eyes.

"What was with that drone, though?" Lynn asked. She'd seen weird reports lately of drones mysteriously dropping out of the sky, but she'd never seen it happen before.

"Who knows? Maybe it ran outa juice."

"I don't know about that," Lynn said.

Edgar just shrugged. "Either way, it was funny as heck. Did you see the size of that alligator? Oooh, man, it almost took off his arm!"

Lynn shook her head at Edgar's bloodthirsty streak and distracted him from vids by showing him her speed puzzle hobby she did with her mom. He was game to give it a try, so Lynn dumped the puzzles out and got started on hers. Five minutes in, though, she looked over at Edgar and laughed.

He'd put together only a few dozen pieces, and was scratching his head, staring at the mess.

"You have to look at the pattern, Edgar."

"What pattern?" he asked, raising his hands helplessly.

That only made Lynn laugh harder. She tried to show him

what she meant, but he punched her arm good-naturedly and told her he'd rather be out in the woods. That got them talking about the woodland craft book he'd given her, which led to an adorable moment when he admitted he wanted to be a farmer one day. Lynn thought he was joking, but his eyes were earnest, not mischievous, when he talked about the peace he found digging in the soil.

"I realized I loved dirt and growing stuff the summer I turned thirteen and got my first job landscaping," he told her. "The next time we visited my Nana and Papa's farm in Utah, I paid attention to what they showed us and asked to help out. It was amazing. The work was just chores to my kid brothers and sisters. But to me... it was sorta magic."

Lynn cocked her head, a smile lifting one corner of her mouth.

"The outside, all the plants and stuff, seems super chaotic to me," she said. "It's all so messy—and itchy."

Edgar laughed.

"Yeah, it can be. But it's rewarding bringing order to the chaos, ya know? Don't tease me, but I play cultivator games sometimes."

"Really? Like FarmSims?" Lynn snorted. "Don't let Ronnie find out. He thinks life isn't worth living unless you're shooting someone."

"I mean, I like that too." Edgar shrugged, giving her a crooked grin. "Blowing things up is pretty sweet."

Lynn squinted at him.

"So, what you're saying is you want to be a... grenade farmer when you grow up? If you don't water the baby grenades, they explode?"

This time Edgar guffawed, slapping his knee. He nearly fell over on his forgotten puzzle.

Lynn shushed him furiously. Her mom was trying to sleep.

When Matilda did eventually wake up, it was a good thing Edgar was there, because Lynn found she literally could not tell her mom what had happened. She just couldn't get the words out. Saying it out loud made the mental images come back and it was like reliving it all over again.

It was a struggle for Edgar to spit it out too, but he finally got the point across.

Then, of course, they had Hulk Mom on their hands. Edgar had to physically hold her back from marching out of their apartment—in her pajamas, no less—to go string Principal Charles up by his balls for allowing such content to be disseminated on *his* school's network.

Edgar managed to sit her on the couch while Lynn made coffee at mach speed. They shoved it into her hands and retreated to wait until she was slightly less murderous. Matilda gulped it down, scalding hot, muttering darkly between swallows. Lynn caught phrases like "criminally negligent" and "castrate the filthy coward."

Seeing her mom so angry healed an old wound in Lynn's heart she hadn't even realized was still there. Matilda was so upset, it gave her permission to be upset, too. And that was something she'd never let herself do. Every bit of hurt, embarrassment, and fear she'd endured in middle school, she'd suppressed, mostly through gaming. She couldn't stop the bullies. Most teachers thought she was overreacting. Those that cared couldn't be everywhere at once, and it was often her word against the bullies. If she went home and whined to her mom about it, it would just stress her mom out when Matilda was already exhausted from working overtime and night shift.

So Lynn had stayed silent.

She'd crafted Larry Coughlin—to escape being scared and weak and *prey*. She'd become the predator, and no one could touch her while she was The Snake.

But now it was happening all over again, and she had to choose how to react to it.

By the time Matilda finished her coffee, she'd fallen silent. Her expression was still filled with fury, but now when she looked at Lynn, Lynn could see the sorrow carving deep lines across her mother's still beautiful face.

Matilda put her mug down, stood, and opened her arms with a softly spoken, "Come here, sweetie."

Part of Lynn didn't want to move. It would be easier to keep suppressing it, keep toughing it out. But most of her knew she needed to mourn, or she'd never heal.

She looked at Edgar.

"Thanks..." Her throat closed and she could say no more. But she knew she didn't need to. Not with Edgar.

He hugged her tightly around the shoulders and said, "Ping me if you need anything. Promise?"

Lynn nodded against his chest. He smelled of cedar wood and beef jerky, and she breathed it in, enjoying it.

He pulled back and gave her one last, searching look. Then he turned, grabbed his backpack, and left the apartment.

Finally, Lynn went to her mom and let herself be wrapped up in warmth, love, and safety. They sank down on the couch, and Lynn let go of her grip on control.

She was nine again, and her father had just died.

She was eleven, and her best friend had ghosted her.

She was thirteen, and she'd been pinched and groped at school.

She was fifteen, and she was alone, finding sanity through killing people in virtual.

She was seventeen, and she'd been sexually trafficked in virtual for revenge and profit.

She cried for it all, heavy with the weight of it.

After a while, the heaviness grew a little lighter, as if the process of lamentation had a cleansing quality of its own. Despite the pain, for the first time in as long as she could remember, she truly believed that, someday, things would be all right.

That week Lynn did school from home. Her school had all the technology needed for Lynn to watch her classes live and submit her homework remotely. Normally you had to have a doctor's note proving some communicable disease or other mitigating factor. Lynn? She had her mother. She was pretty sure Matilda threatened the principal with dismemberment if he didn't let Lynn remote in. GIC's formal inquiry into the illegal vid was another factor. Principal Charles was probably happy to keep Lynn away from the general student population for a while.

Lynn felt guilty about it, like she'd abandoned her team to weather the social storm alone. But when she brought it up, they all told her to stop being a martyr and stay home. Even Ronnie agreed, though Lynn suspected he had other reasons for wanting to see less of her.

They still hunted in the afternoons, though. Lynn put her foot down and flatly refused to deviate from their planned hunting schedule. The guys had tried calling her bluff the first day, so she'd simply gone out and started killing TDMs by herself at their agreed-upon meeting place. They'd eventually showed up, looking sheepish, and after that everything TD Hunter-related went back to normal.

Well, except for the droves of paparazzi drones. But those were no surprise. Lynn simply turned her music up a little louder and kept her eyes on the earth. Dan with his sniper rifle had the skies covered. GIC was doing their best to handle the legal aspects quietly and get the furor to die down as quickly as possible, but in gaming forums and streams, the scandal was too juicy to pass up and miss out on the algorithmic boost. The saving grace was that she was a minor, and so GIC was able to bring much bigger threats to bear against various platforms that would normally not have lifted a finger to seek out and remove the vid itself.

But people still talked.

So, Lynn became a digital hermit. She disconnected from the mesh web as much as she possibly could and still function. GIC took care of all web content and interaction with the outside world on her behalf, and Mrs. Pearson checked on her regularly. Lynn didn't even log onto WarMonger, though nobody there knew who she was or what had happened. She was too afraid of hearing chatter about the scandal.

She definitely didn't do the research about TD Hunter, grid systems, and international politics she'd been intending to do, looking for patterns. Too much risk she'd be slapped in the face with something she could never unsee.

It surprised Lynn how much extra time and brain space was freed up forsaking the mesh-web. She figured she became the most studious and dedicated senior of her entire school with how hard she focused on homework. She studied harder, exercised harder, and hunted harder than ever before, just so she didn't have a moment of freedom or energy to let her mind wander.

It was refreshing but isolating. Her lifeline was ongoing text conversations with the guys in their Skadi's Wolves message group, plus Kayla and Edgar checked in on her regularly. Her mom spent what time with her she could—they got together with Mr. Thomas for dinner several times, and he entertained them with stories from his youth.

By the end of the week, Lynn felt almost normal again in her isolated little bubble. She started to linger outside now that the weather was turning warm, enjoying the feel of the grass and catching sight of sunsets after a few hard hours of hunting. It made her understand Edgar better and what he saw in the peace and quiet of nature, where trolls and cliques and the gossip of billions of people couldn't touch you.

Friday evening after clearing several miles' worth of electric rail, Lynn and the guys were huddled under one of the many bridges that passed over the rail, taking care of some admin discussion while it was on Lynn's mind. She'd finally gotten around to proposing Voodoo Girls as their alternates for the championship, and after the excellent time they'd had fighting Ya-Te-Veo together, everyone but Ronnie was all for it. Ronnie's problem—or at least the one he was willing to say out loud—was that they weren't ranked high enough on the team leaderboard.

"Fair point," Lynn conceded. "But we'd have to take time to vet some other team we approached simply based on their ranking. Plus, we'd have to find one close enough to come train with us at least a couple times to make sure they could integrate smoothly. But we already know the Voodoo Girls, we know they're a solid team with experience taking out bosses, and we know they live in this area. Besides, if Mack breaks his leg or something, that means you would get to hang out with Quorra."

"Hey!" Mack protested. "I'm not gonna break my leg. If anyone was going to injure themselves it'd be Dan. *He's* the one who thinks he's some reincarnated kung-fu master."

While Dan and Mack fell to arguing, Lynn noted the rosy tinge of Ronnie's cheeks and ears as he stared intently at the underside of the bridge.

After that, there were no more objections to Lynn's proposal, so she made a mental note to reach out to Quorra and see if the Voodoo Girls were even interested in the offer. They turned to making plans for where to hunt on Saturday but were interrupted by a group call request from Mrs. Pearson.

"Ms. Raven, gentlemen, I apologize for interrupting your evening, but there is an important matter I need to bring to your attention. I was hesitant to bring it up and further upset Ms. Raven, but Mr. Swain believes it is wisest to inform you of the situation."

Lynn's heart rate spiked. She felt that familiar pressure of anxiety building in her chest, and she gritted her teeth.

"Because of the recent illegal video that was created, Ms. Raven's accounts have been receiving a large volume of messages not fit for polite company. However, we have also received multiple contacts from, as best as we can determine, the same individual, directed not only to Ms. Raven's accounts, but to the rest of the team's accounts as well. The messages indicate this person has developed an obsession with Ms. Raven."

A chill swept through Lynn, and her tired leg muscles seemed to decide it was an excellent time to give out all together. She didn't know if Edgar sensed her distress or just wanted to be supportive, but he moved closer and reached out just when she needed something to steady herself. She clutched his arm for a moment as she shifted from leg to leg, informing her body on no uncertain terms that it was fine and had better quit being dramatic.

"Are you sure they're real?" Ronnie subvocalized, tone dark. "That's just the sort of thing Connor would do: send creepy messages to freak Lynn out and make her quit."

"While it is certainly *possible* they could be a hoax, I've run them by our law enforcement consultant. He believes they are not a hoax, and that they do represent a credible concern. Enough, at least, to inform the victim."

"Wait a minute," Lynn subvocalized, drawing everyone's eye. "Back up. You said my accounts *and* the guys' accounts were getting threatening messages? Is this person stalking all of us?"

"No, Ms. Raven, the messages make it clear that you are the object of their obsession. However, your teammates closely associate with you and are with you on a regular basis. They are also, well, male," Mrs. Pearson said, "so the stalker seems to feel the need to... scare off the competition, so to speak."

Lynn's fists clenched and she blinked slowly one, two, three times.

"So, you're telling me," she said as calmly as she could, "that some sicko is threatening *my* friends just because we're on the same team?"

"I'm afraid so, Ms. Raven, but we are more concerned about y—"

"Forget about me! They're threatening my friends!" Lynn snapped out loud, too agitated to keep it to subvocalization.

"No, we're not forgetting about you," burst out Edgar, who obviously had the same problem. "*You're* the one being targeted here—"

"Mrs. Pearson said we're *all* being targeted," Lynn subvocalized, forcing herself to be calm. There was no telling if some sneaky paparazzi drone was eavesdropping, and she would be damned if she let a gossip column get a whiff of her private business.

"Yeah, but you're the famous one," Ronnie subvocalized, glaring at a spot over her shoulder. "You're the one someone made a...a vid of."

Lynn couldn't tell if the tinge of venom in Ronnie's words was aimed at her, or the shadowy perpetrators making their life hell. Maybe Ronnie didn't even know himself.

She opened her mouth to argue, but Mrs. Pearson's firm voice cut her off.

"This individual could be anywhere in the world. Many people say unhinged things in virtual, and there is no indication that this obsession has escalated past harassing messages. We would tell you right away if we received any evidence that there was a credible physical danger for you to worry about. However, it would be unwise to dismiss the possibility entirely. I respectfully request, if you are not already doing so, to stay together, in pairs if not as a team. Do not play TD Hunter alone and use exclusively private transportation from now on."

They'd already been using a mix of private and public transportation and had stuck pretty close together since their falling out with Connor, so that wouldn't be a huge change. But the next thing Mrs. Pearson said made Lynn wince.

"By law, we have informed Mrs. Raven and Mr. And Mrs. Nguyen of the situation, since Lynn and Dan are still minors. Mr. Johnston, Mr. Payne, Mr. Rios, I strongly encourage you to inform your parents of the situation, though it is your decision to do so or not. It is possible this individual may attempt to threaten you or your families in some way, so it would be wise for them to be on the lookout for harassing or threatening contact from any source. If any of your parents would like to talk to me about the situation and what actions they should take, please encourage them to reach out. It is what I am here for."

Oh, boy. Her mom was going to F.R.E.A.K.

"Do any of you have any questions?"

Dan slowly raised a hand, as if he'd forgotten Mrs. Pearson couldn't see them.

"Uh, are we going to keep livestreaming? There are plenty of geo-analysis apps out there that can pinpoint our location based on the background in our vids. It's what the paparazzi stooges use to sic their drones on us, once they get enough footage to analyze."

"Good point, Mr. Nguyen. For the time being, we will stick to posting recordings and see what happens. If things calm down and there are no more attempts to contact, it will likely be safe to continue livestreaming."

Well, that was a small relief, at least.

"What about Happy Joe's Pizza?" Mack subvocalized.

"Hmm," Mrs. Pearson said. "It would likely be best to order out for the time being, rather than dining in."

Dan's face fell like his favorite kung fu film stream had been cancelled, and Ronnie snorted in dark amusement.

"Anything else you can tell us Mrs. Pearson," Edgar said, calm enough to subvocalize again. "Anything about who this person is or what to watch out for?"

"I am afraid not, Mr. Johnston. The threats were general, not specific, and whoever it is has at least some knowledge of how to remain anonymous in virtual. Our people are working on it."

"Well that's good," Dan piped up. "It means they're probably some lame wannabe hacker still living in their mom's basement and having wet dreams about Ly—" Edgar smacked Dan on the back of the head so hard Dan lurched forward. He straightened, rubbing his head and looking mortified. "Llamas! I meant llamas!"

Lynn shook her head, wanting, but not quite able, to smile over Dan's attempt to lighten the mood. She stared sightlessly at the rail line behind the guys, and the brush, fence-line, and industrial area beyond it. She still had a tight weight in her chest and a sick feeling in her stomach, but mostly she was pissed. This last year had been a journey the likes of which she never could have foreseen. But part of it had been finding the best humanity had to offer...and the worst.

She supposed it was naive to expect the one without the other.

"Thanks, Mrs. Pearson," she subvocalized, realizing Mrs. Pearson was waiting to see if she had any questions. "We already stick together, but we'll be extra careful. We'll keep a lookout for anything suspicious."

"Very well, Ms. Raven. I am sorry for this added stress, but let us know if there is anything at all we can do to help."

"We're all really grateful for your help. GIC has been amazing."

"I am grateful you gave us the opportunity to partner with you," Mrs. Pearson said, her tone warming. "You have been one of our most enjoyable clients to work with. You would not believe some of the divas I have had to cater to in the past."

Lynn snorted, eyes flicking to Ronnie, who was glaring at the ground as if a rock down there had personally offended him.

"Well, we need to get going, so have a nice evening, Mrs. Pearson."

"You as well Ms. Raven, gentlemen."

There was a long silence after the call ended. Lynn stared around the group, her own mix of anger and worry reflected in everyone's eyes. She finally opened her mouth to speak, but Edgar beat her to it.

"Okay, we need to work out a buddy system."

"Yeah." Lynn sighed and rubbed her forehead. "I wish Mrs. Pearson had let me tell my mom later, in person. I bet she's freaking out right now at the hospital. I'm surprised she hasn't already pinged me."

"I wouldn't blame her for freaking out," Edgar muttered, prompting Lynn to give him a raised eyebrow. His face got a little darker, but he held her gaze levelly, and she sighed again and shrugged.

"Dan and Ronnie," he subvocalized, not taking his eyes off her, "you all live pretty close together, so you can buddy up. Lynn, Mack and I live closest to you, so one or both of us will buddy up with you. We'll always make sure you have someone with you once you step outside your apartment building."

She rolled her eyes.

"That's not necessary and you know it."

"Mrs. Pearson said—"

"That there's no credible threat right now."

"But—"

"I'm a big girl, Edgar, I can take care of myself."

Ronnie snorted, but turned it into a cough, angling away from them. Lynn glared at him and stood straighter.

"You're strong and brave, Lynn," Edgar said, expression dead serious. "Everyone knows that. But you shouldn't *have* to go it alone. Nobody should. We're your team. What kind of people would we be if we didn't have your back?"

Mack was nodding, and Dan puffed out his chest, though at

full height he was an inch or two shorter than her. Lynn looked at Ronnie, who was now staring fixedly at Edgar's feet.

"What about you, Ronnie? What do you think?" Lynn subvocalized, probably more aggressively than she should have. Ronnie stiffened and his jaw worked, but after a few tense moments, he looked her in the eye and said:

"I think friends don't let friends do stupid shit."

He shrugged and looked back at the ground, scuffing at the gravel with his foot.

Lynn breathed in deep, then let it out slowly. That was possibly the wisest thing to ever come out of Ronnie's mouth. And she kind of hated him for it. But she couldn't let her frustration at the situation hurt her team. They needed unity now more than ever.

"Fine," she said, shaking her head.

Was it just her, or did Edgar's big shoulders relax a fraction?

"All these private air taxis are going to cost an arm and a leg," Lynn pointed out in one last feeble attempt, more for the sake of appearance than anything else.

"That's what they pay us the big bucks for, right?" Edgar said with a big grin, his teeth white against his dark skin.

"But I could be spending that money on steak," Lynn grumbled, hitching her shoulders and feeling grumpy.

Dan giggled. Actually giggled.

"You're like a werewolf or something, Lynn. You've got golden eyes, you're obsessed with meat, and you named our team Skadi's Wolves. It's epic." His goofy smile was as brilliant as the sun, and Lynn couldn't help smiling back.

"Yup, that's me, internationally famous gamer by day, bloodthirsty werewolf by night. Maybe I should just let the stalker come. I'll eat him for supper." Lynn bared her teeth, and all the guys guffawed.

Chapter 6

LYNN GOT REAL INTIMATE WITH HER BUILDING'S FLOOR PLAN and the exact time of sunrise and sunset over the next week. There was a back door out to the HVAC units that only maintenance could access from the outside. Edgar took to meeting her there, and they'd sneak out to the strip of woods between Lynn's apartment complex and the next, woods they were already familiar with from hours of hunting TDMs. They would take a circuitous route out to the main road to meet their already reserved air taxi that would take them to school, stopping on the way to pick up Mack at his house.

It was all very cloak and dagger—more so than usual, anyway. But it was the compromise between what Lynn could tolerate, and what kept Matilda from tying her up and locking her in her room for the rest of her life. Lynn could tell her mom was trying, really *trying*, not to smother her. But the look of muted terror on her mom's face when Lynn had arrived home after Mrs. Pearson had broken the news...that look had pierced Lynn to the core.

Imagine having your husband killed by a mugger, and then someone started stalking your only child? Your only child that spent hours at a time wandering around the city...

All Lynn could do was give her mom extra-tight hugs, and sincerely do her best to be careful. It made Edgar happy, anyway, and Lynn did enjoy walking to school with him. Sometimes they chatted, sometimes they quizzed each other on their next test at school, and sometimes they walked in silence, content to keep their peace.

Matilda let the school know about the new arrangement, as well as the reason for it. Lynn hadn't wanted her to, but knew there was no point protesting. At least Matilda didn't threaten the principal's manhood this time.

School was...a challenge. But it wasn't the hell Lynn had expected.

She wasn't in middle school anymore.

She wasn't alone anymore.

She wasn't helpless anymore.

For the most part, there was no direct harassment. The students must have taken the principal's disciplinary threats seriously. Of course, having a six-foot-something muscle-bound shadow at her back didn't hurt either. Kayla nearly tackled her with a hug outside their first class, and after that stuck to her side like a limpet. When their class times coordinated, all four of the guys would form a phalanx around her as they walked the halls, glaring at everyone they passed. Lynn sighed and rolled her eyes, but didn't protest.

Plenty of students giggled, whispered, and pointed surreptitiously as she moved through the school. But to Lynn's surprise, many others approached, braving the glares, and asked how she was doing. One of the guys from her senior year science class—a tall guy named Elliot with glasses and at least five perpetual cowlicks—stopped her and said what had happened was a disgrace to humanity. He even offered to help track the culprit down and make his life a living hell. Ronnie and Dan perked up at that and exchanged glances, but Lynn just gave Elliot a grateful smile and thanked him.

The few times she had to face harassment directly, she simply cocked her head, stared at her tormentor, and considered what Larry would do to them if given half a chance. Apparently, the mental exercise made her look like a sadistic psychopath—according to several members of the ARS team anyway. Lynn just shrugged and went about her day.

After school, Skadi's Wolves caught a private air taxi to wherever they were going to hunt, then called another when it was too dark to hunt anymore. Lynn made an effort to ping her mom every hour or so, quipping something lighthearted about what they were doing, just to help take the edge off her anxiety.

By Wednesday, Matilda seemed to have calmed down, though her grip was still abnormally tight every time they hugged. Skadi's Wolves didn't hunt that evening since it was pouring down rain. They were used to taking a day off for heavy storms and cramming on school so they could hunt every evening it was moderately clear. Lynn enjoyed a rare suppertime with her mom, puttering around the kitchen and helping cook some good old Iowa steak—AKA stuffed pork chops. Matilda seemed happy to be spending time together, but there was something off. She kept staring at Lynn, lost in thought, or fiddling with whatever was in her hands, as if nervous about something. Once they tucked in to supper, Lynn demolished her chops in record time, then noticed her mom had barely touched her food.

Lynn put her fork down and took a long drink of water, thinking about what to say.

"Okay, Mom. What's up?" Lynn lifted an eyebrow at her mother's suddenly guilty look. "You're twitchy and not eating. If I were *your* mother, I would think you were hiding something from me." Lynn couldn't help grinning impishly when she said it, and Matilda gave a choking laugh.

"I guess that's what I get for being such a great mom, hm? You've learned all my techniques?"

"Yeah, though I still haven't figured out that mom death-stare you use on people to make them instantly grovel and beg for forgiveness."

"Oh, you won't perfect that one until you've raised a child to teenage-hood," Matilda said, one side of her mouth twitching upward. "It's an acquired skill."

"I'll take your word for it, and also, stop deflecting. What's going on, Mom, really?"

Lynn's eyebrows slanted outward and she reached forward to gently touch her mom's hand on the table.

Matilda closed her eyes and let go of a deep sigh. When she opened them, the guilt was back, but it wasn't tinged with shame or sadness. It was more of a sheepish look than anything else.

"I have something I should have told you a while ago, but... well it never seemed like the right time. And now things... well things are happening and it still seems like the worst time in the world to put *more* stress and change in your life."

Matilda kept talking, dancing around the point, and Lynn finally decided to be merciful and put her mom out of her misery.

"Mom, are you dating someone?"

Matilda froze, mouth hanging open. Then she snapped it shut and looked downward, the gold tone on her cheekbones and the tops of her ears becoming rosy.

"Mom, is that...a blush? Are you blushing?" Lynn crowed.

"Oh hush, you! You don't get to tease me about a man when you haven't even kissed Edgar yet!"

"What!?" Lynn said, completely thrown off track.

Matilda's eyes flew wide, and she slapped a hand over her mouth.

"What do you mean, 'haven't even kissed Edgar yet'?" Lynn said, brow furrowed, barely believing what she was saying.

Her mom scoffed.

"Oh, come on, sweetie. He is so obviously over the moon for you. I keep waiting for him to say something. It is pure *torture* watching the two of you!"

Lynn leaned back in her chair, stunned.

"I—I mean...he's a friend...he's a good friend...but...he's never...not like *that*..."

"I know," Matilda sighed. "I think he's worried he'll scare you off, after everything you endured in middle school."

Lynn stared at her mom without really seeing or hearing her, eyebrows scrunched together so hard they were in danger of sticking that way.

Edgar? Over the moon? For *her*?

The past nine months raced through her thoughts, and she remembered how he'd encouraged her before their first Operation Boss Bash when she'd been so nervous she could have thrown up.

You're beautiful, for one. And smart. And talented... And you inspire people, Lynn. You see people... people no one else sees. And you don't give up on them.

He'd been close enough to kiss her...she thought he might have...thought maybe she wanted him to. But then he hadn't. He'd simply caressed her cheek. So she'd put it out of her mind, assuming he was just trying to be a good friend.

I think he's worried he'll scare you off, after everything you endured in middle school.

No... there was no way. Edgar was *nothing* like those bullies. He had never done anything to make her feel unsafe or uncomfortable. He fought for her, he had her back...

He fought for her...

Lynn thought hard, trying to remember every time Edgar's fuse as long as Florida had run out. The pattern she was forced to acknowledge was that it only ever happened when *she* was involved. Sure, he got upset and pushed back sometimes when his other friends were being picked on. But it was never blind rage so severe he put another kid in the hospital.

Lynn's eyes finally refocused and she found her mom smiling with a smug little curl to her lips.

"Mom!" Lynn snapped, "wipe that look off your face. We're talking about *you* here, not me." Lynn mentally shelved her mother's shocking claim to ponder another time and put on her sternest face. "Out with it. I overheard you talking to someone a couple times. I didn't mean to overhear, so... well, I didn't want to bring it up... it's your life and all..." She petered off lamely, her stern expression slipping as uncertainty and confusion bubbled up.

"Oh, honey, I'm sorry." Matilda shifted her hand to lay it on Lynn's and give it a comforting squeeze. "You're right. I'm... well, not dating exactly, but I've been talking to someone. Someone wonderful. And we... well, we'd like to *go* on a date, but I wasn't willing until I'd talked to you. So I've been putting it off for a while. And then all the horrible things at school happened and..." Matilda smiled apologetically, her eyes searching Lynn's.

For what? Approval? Permission?

Lynn took a deep breath.

"I want you to be happy, Mom. I want that so much. You deserve it. I... I miss Dad, but..." She swiped angrily at her eyes, annoyed at the moisture that welled up there. "It'll probably be weird at first, but a—a friend helped me realize Dad will always be Dad. You're not trying to replace him, just... trying to be happy."

"Oh, honey." Matilda now gripped Lynn's hand in both of hers, her own eyes shining. "I'm so sorry this hurts you. That's the last thing I want. And you're right, I would never—could never—replace your father. He will always be—" she paused and swallowed, "he will always be my one true love. I've spent a long time ignoring the part of me that wanted more because I thought I should focus only on you. To be there for you. But someone"—she smiled sheepishly—"pointed out that it's a disservice to you to isolate myself out of fear, and maybe... maybe I was causing you to miss out on a healthy, family relationship." More moisture welled, and a single drop spilled over to run down Matilda's cheek.

"Oh no, Mom! You haven't done anything wrong. You're all I ever needed, I promise."

Matilda shook her head, chuckling wetly.

"Thank you so much for saying that, sweetie. But I think he is right. I think I've been holding both of us back because... because I'm so afraid of going through loss again. It's just been easier to keep my head down and stick to what was safe."

Lynn felt a stab of guilt in her heart. Why had she never encouraged her mom to get out there and find love again?

Matilda narrowed her eyes suspiciously at Lynn.

"Don't you even start, missy. I can see that guilt you're trying to hide. You are *not* allowed to feel guilty. I'm a grown woman and responsible for my own choices. Besides, you know very well how strong-willed I am when it comes to taking care of my family." Matilda shrugged and Lynn grinned. Her school principal certainly knew how "strong-willed" her mom was. That was for sure. "So, do you really think anything, even you, could have stopped me from dating again if I thought it was the right thing for our family?"

Lynn was forced to shake her head.

"See? So stop feeling responsible, okay, honey?" Matilda gave her hand another squeeze, and Lynn nodded.

"So, um," Lynn said, voice scratchy from emotion, "who's the lucky guy?"

Her mom swallowed and looked away, color rising in her cheeks again.

"A good man, Lynn. But... I'm not sure yet if I can do this. If I'm really ready to... let someone else into our safe haven. So, I thought, and he's agreed, that we should do one in-person date, and then if everything feels right and we decide we want to keep seeing each other, then I promise I'll tell you everything. We can even make our second date a family event, so you can get to know him too. Is...is that all right?"

Lynn smiled and turned her hand over to squeeze her mom's fingers reassuringly.

"Yeah, it's all right." A thought occurred to her, and she narrowed her eyes. "But he'd better treat you right, or I'll track him down and give him a taste of ol' Larry the Snake."

Matilda snorted, and Lynn's brow furrowed.

"What's so funny? You think I couldn't do it?"

Her mother untangled their hands and raised hers to wave back and forth in negation, all the while smothering obvious amusement.

"No, no, honey. I'm sure you would make him regret the day he was born. It's nothing. Just...wait until you meet him, okay?"

"Wait until I meet him, huh? You sound pretty sure this first date will go well," Lynn pointed out, picking up her fork to finish the scraps of her pork chops and cheese-covered broccoli.

"Well, I am, at least where *he's* concerned. It's me I'm worried about."

"But why, Mom?"

"I..." Matilda swallowed. "I keep waiting for my heart to throw on the brakes and tell me I'm betraying your dad's memory."

"Oh, Mom." Lynn couldn't stand to see the sorrow and guilt in her mother's eyes, and she realized then how silly she'd been to tie herself up in knots over the thought of "another man" coming in to replace her dad. Her mom had obviously been struggling with the exact same tangle of emotions. "Dad would want you to be happy. He wouldn't want you to be alone, not if you were longing for companionship."

"I know," Matilda said, sniffing and swiping at another line of moisture that had trailed down her cheek. She took a deep breath. "That's why, when this man asked if it was all right to woo me—"

"He asked you *what?*" Lynn's jaw dropped.

Matilda laughed. "I know, so romantic, isn't it?"

Lynn gave her mother a horrified look. She didn't get the appeal, but her mom sure did seem to like it, so she guessed it was okay.

"Anyway, when he asked to woo me, I said yes. I know in my head it's what your dad would have wanted. But my heart... well, you know."

They exchanged a sad smile.

"That's why we decided on one sit-down date before I tangle you up in it and risk your heart too. I just don't know what my heart will do once we're sitting face to face, holding hands, kissing—"

"Okay, okay, Mom, stop!" Lynn leaned back, holding up her hands in self defense. "I do *not* want to hear about your, er, *adventures* with your new boyfriend, okay? You'll scar me for life."

Matilda gave her a mischievous grin, but picked up her own fork and started eating her neglected dinner. Lynn could guess by the sparkle in her eyes and the curve of her mouth all the comments her mother was holding in, and she was grateful. She did *not* need more on her plate, or more thoughts to clutter up her brain, than she was already dealing with.

"So, when is this first date going to be?" Lynn asked before her mother gave in to temptation and started making comments about wanting grandchildren.

"Oh, he is ready to drop literally everything and meet me on a moment's notice. His exact words," Matilda said with a grin.

"Wow. Good job, Mom. You really hooked a good one, didn't you?"

Matilda snorted and muttered something like, "You have no idea."

"So how long have you two been talking?"

Her mother got a shifty look, and Lynn raised an eyebrow.

"Well, we met a little over six months ago, but he took things very slow at first. All gentlemanly and professional. We've only been exploring the possibility of a relationship for about four months."

"'Exploring the possibility'? Come on, Mom, do you like this guy or not?"

Her mother pursed her lips.

"That's a very forward question, young lady, but...well... yes." Her severe expression morphed into a grin.

"Okay," Lynn said, waving her fork, "so go ping him right now and tell him you'll meet him tomorrow."

Matilda raised both eyebrows.

"That's awfully short notice."

"Not for him, per his own words, right?"

"Well, yes, but... my shift at the hospital—"

"You *never* take sick or family days, Mom. You are the most hardworking, dependable nurse in that entire ER. So call in, and go tell your beau you'll meet him tomorrow. Go on!" Lynn waved her fork again, more commandingly this time, and her mom shook her head, grinning ear to ear.

"I'd better watch it. If you and him team up against me, I'll be in for some serious trouble."

Lynn grinned right back. "All the more reason for you to hurry up and go on a date so *I* can meet him, too."

Matilda gave out a mock sigh and put her fork down.

"All right, young lady. You can have your way, *this* time."

Her mom stood and went off into her bedroom, closing the door with a soft click. Lynn snorted and got back to finishing her dinner.

Yes, things in their life were absolutely bat-shit crazy right now. But all the more reason for them to have something to look forward to. Something to bring smiles and goodness into their lives.

Lynn mentally crossed her fingers and hoped with everything she had that this guy, whoever he was, turned out to be the real deal and not some schmuck who was going to break her mom's heart.

Because if he did, then Lynn would have to graduate high school, win the TD Hunter National Championship, *and* track down a douchebag conman to show him exactly what Larry the Snake thought of liars and perverts.

And she did *not* have time for that.

The next day at school, Lynn used the thought of her mom happy and in love to ignore the usual harassment. It must have been pretty effective, because Edgar asked if she was all right, she was smiling so much.

Lynn assured him she was fine but said nothing more. It was her mom's news to share or not whenever she was ready.

It must have been fate, then, that Thursday was the first time she had to go within earshot of Elena Seville and her clique.

The few times they might have encountered one another, Lynn had turned right around and walked the other way, not trusting herself. But this time the pop-girl and her fawning sycophants were blocking the door to the cafeteria, and all the guys were hungry, so Lynn just took a deep breath and kept walking forward, hoping to slide around without engaging. Interestingly, Connor and his ARS stooges were nowhere to be seen. Lynn wondered at that, since Team CRC was still on the leaderboards and still in the running for the National Championship, so Elena and Connor were obviously still working together. Was there trouble in paradise?

Predictably, Elena had no intention of passing up a chance to be petty and vile. As soon as she spotted Skadi's Wolves, a smug smile slithered across her face and she shifted to cross her arms, the position conveniently shoving her breasts up to greater prominence. Lynn couldn't help but notice the difference in the pop-girl's demeanor from several weeks ago. Her expression was confident and her posture was relaxed, as if she thought her social standing, not the TD Hunter leaderboard, determined her ultimate success. Her clothes looked like she was a walking billboard for most fashionable athlete—and maybe she was, if she'd gotten sponsorships for elite celebrity-brand athletic wear.

"Well, well, look who it is," Elena drawled. "The Slut and her gang of pimps."

Lynn gritted her teeth so hard pain shot through her jaw. It was one thing to insult her. She could take that. But to attack her friends, too? To insinuate they were abusers and criminals?

"I *told* you she's been banging those loser nerds this whole time, but no one believed me—until now." As if on cue, all the girls flanking Elena tittered, their giggles like fingernails on a chalkboard to Lynn's frayed nerves. She refused to look over at them, refused to acknowledge their vile words. But she could see Elena's leering grin in the corner of her eye as she tried to hurry past.

"I wonder which one of them made that juicy, juicy vid."

Lynn saw red.

Before she knew what she was doing, she'd pivoted and taken three quick, sure strides, closing on Elena like a prowling wolf. Elena's vindictive sneer morphed into a look of alarm, then sheer terror. The girls on either side of her scattered like sheep while Elena stumbled backward toward the wall.

"W-what are you doing? Get away from me, you freak! Help!"

Lynn saw only one thing: her target. Her fingers flexed, yearning for a weapon to grip, a stock and barrel to hoist, a bead to draw on her target. In the absence of anything else, she balled her fists and raised them in front of her as her mind calculated attack vectors, weighing the pros and cons of each.

"Lynn, stop! *Lynn!!*"

The noises around her were noted but filtered out as meaningless. Only her target mattered.

She decided on a weak spot—Elena's perfectly straight, fashionable nose—and prepared to strike. No hesitation. Attack into the ambush. Complete the mission.

A huge hand descended onto her shoulder and yanked her back. She stumbled, almost falling, and thumped into a solid object that was warm against her back. She immediately surged forward again, but thick arms wrapped around her shoulders and held her close.

She struggled.

"Lynn! Calm down! Stop it!"

Voices yelled—Mack, Dan, Ronnie—but she didn't care.

That harpy. That evil, *evil*—

"Hey, *uce*," a deep, soothing voice rumbled somewhere above her head, breaking through her tunnel vision. "I got you, girl. I got you."

Lynn finally relaxed, knowing resistance was pointless. She closed her eyes and let her head tip back to lean against Edgar's chest, trying to shut out the commotion and find her equilibrium. Find her sanity.

"You done good, *Toa Tama'ita'i*. But friends don't let friends do stupid shit, right?"

Lynn snorted softly, not opening her eyes.

The shouting finally quieted, though there was still a low murmur of many voices. Lynn could just imagine the crowd of eager onlookers, hoping for a fight.

"Come on, *uce*, let's go eat lunch," Edgar said, loosening his grip to turn Lynn gently and tuck her against his side so he could lead them both into the cafeteria. Lynn let him, and didn't open her eyes until she'd tilted her head forward to lock her gaze on the floor. It was safer that way. All her happiness had vanished, replaced with cold, hard anger. Better to keep anyone else from stumbling into her sights.

She couldn't help overhearing the chatter, though.

"Did you see that?"

"That was *sick*, man."

"Elena squealed like a pig. I've never seen her move so fast."

"I hope someone got that on vid, I can't *wait* to stitch it."

Lynn's lips twitched, just a fraction. Then Edgar steered her to a seat, and she dutifully sank down while he swiped her meal card and went off to get them both food.

As satisfying as scaring the living daylights out of Elena had been, Lynn knew no good would come of it. She'd never set out to humiliate Elena. Not the first time and not this one either. But Elena wouldn't see it that way. And there was no one in the whole school who held a grudge better than Elena. Well, maybe Connor, but he was a lot sneakier about it.

Mrs. Pearson had updated them just yesterday that there was still no concrete evidence of who had made the illegal vid. Dan and Ronnie were convinced it was Connor, and Lynn agreed it was plausible. But it could have been a lot of other people as well. The world was filled with degenerate scumbags, and the more she succeeded, the more effective GIC was in their promotion efforts, the bigger a target it painted on her back.

Mr. Swain's warning echoed in her head:

Once you breach the barrier, it's a permanent thing... the Alpha always gets picked on. It's a test to see if they're still worthy to be the Alpha. So, people will denigrate you, cut you down.

TD Hunter and GIC had made her the Alpha of a global monkey troop. She'd heard Mr. Swain's words when he'd warned her what would happen, back in the fall. But she'd had no idea... she didn't know if she was capable of handling it, not after what had been done to her. And what *she'd* almost done.

Lynn and Larry. Larry and Lynn.

Was Larry a guardian angel? Or a corrupting demon? Was he really a part of her? Or had she grafted him onto her psyche as a coping mechanism—a mechanism that had now dug in roots too deep to weed out?

What sort of person was all of this craziness turning her into?

The smell of cocoa butter and floral perfume tickled Lynn's nostrils a few seconds before Kayla plopped down into the seat next to her. Her friend's slender arm wrapped around her shoulder for a squeeze, and Kayla's soft, tight coils of hair brushed her cheek as Kayla tilted her head onto Lynn's shoulder. Then Kayla let go and said:

"Are you okay, Lynn? Elena *totally* had it coming, but I'm glad Edgar stopped you. It would be *so* unfair, but you'd definitely get in trouble, and you do *not* need that drama in your life right now!"

Lynn's heart squeezed in gratitude, but she couldn't bring herself to open her mouth. So she just nodded and let Kayla chatter on.

Edgar returned shortly with food, and everyone sat and dug in. Lynn let the usual lunchtime chatter wash over her as she forced herself to eat at least some of her lunch. She needed her strength for hunting that evening.

She would not let Elena win. She would keep her head about her. She would be smart, and focused, no matter how much she longed to break Elena's face into a thousand pieces. Lynn's mom had her date that evening, so Lynn had plenty to think about to keep her occupied. Plus, there was all that research she kept meaning to do, those patterns that tickled the edges of her suspicion. And then there was Edgar...

Lynn ducked her head and focused on her food.

"And I don't know who she's working with now, but they're a lot better than that shoddy outfit she went with after she lost my free labor," Kayla said.

Lynn's ears perked.

Most of the guys were done with their food, and Kayla was still talking, apparently having enough gossip on CRC's activities to keep the guys riveted through all of lunch.

"Her stream has picked up a lot of subscribers—nowhere near Skadi's Wolves, of course—and she's got fairly quality content, if you're watching for pop-girl nonsense and lots of cleavage, not legitimate gaming know-how. And Connor? I don't know *what* he thinks he's doing. He might be pretty on camera, but his stream content is as soulless as a dead fish, I'm telling you."

"That's because he *is* a soulless, dead fish," Dan quipped, and everybody but Lynn laughed. Lynn's lips did twitch, though.

"You said it, not me," Kayla said, her voice rich with amusement. Lynn glanced at her and caught her friend fluttering her eyelashes at Dan, which made Lynn's lips twitch more.

"Anyway, Connor might be a skilled gamer, but he's about as authentic and likable on stream as a serial killer—wait, that might not be a good comparison," Kayla said, brow furrowed. "I know at least three serial killers in jail for life who have *huge* stream followings." She shook her head and got back to her main point.

"I hate to say it, but Queen Harpy seems like she's reached her stride on the streams. She's not floundering as much with the gaming lingo—and did you see how toned her legs are getting on that fitness promo she did last week?" Kayla spoke as if she legitimately thought the guys followed Elena's content. She was met with blank, horrified stares.

"I would rather watch Lynn play Kim's Diva Princess than *anything* remotely related to Elena," Ronnie said into the silence.

There was a splutter of laughter from Dan and Mack, and Lynn raised both eyebrows at Ronnie, whose face flushed. Belatedly, Lynn realized Ronnie had not been trying to make a joke. In fact, he'd sort of, kind of been complimenting her.

Would wonders never cease.

"Okay, that's fair," Kayla said, tossing her bouncy curls, then opening her mouth to continue full steam ahead.

"You know, I never actually played that game," Lynn said quietly. Everyone heard it, though.

Ronnie's brow furrowed.

"Then why did you say you did?" he asked, almost sounding offended.

Lynn rolled her eyes.

"Because it's what you expected me to be playing. Because it got on your nerves. Because it got you to shut up. Take your pick."

Careful, she thought to herself. She hadn't meant to speak up, and she was dancing perilously close to the truth.

"Well, that's stupid," Ronnie grumbled.

"Not as stupid as your idiotic 'girls got no game' mantra," Lynn said stiffly. "Did it ever occur to you that I never told you about my gaming skills because it was easier to lie than argue with a raging jerk about his moronic bigoted ideas?"

Ronnie's jaw dropped, as did everyone else's at the table but Edgar's. He just looked at Lynn with a sad sort of resignation.

"I—not—that's—" Ronnie's face got redder and redder, and Lynn sighed, regretting her words. Yes, they were true, but they weren't really true anymore, at least not that Ronnie had openly shown. She was just so upset about Elena, she'd let her tongue get away from her. But what was she supposed to do now? Apologize? She'd only spoken the truth, and Ronnie needed to hear it eventually. But now he was going to blow up and stomp away from the table and their team dynamic would suffer and their scores—

"I'm sorry, Lynn."

Lynn's gaze flew to Mack, who had a deep V of concern between his thick dark eyebrows.

"You are totally right," he continued, slowly. "I never even thought about that. And now here you are, the most badass player in all of TD Hunter. I... I'm sorry for not, well..." He glanced at Ronnie, who was still red, but no longer gaping. Rather, his jaw was locked tight. Mack swallowed and sat up straighter in his chair. "I'm sorry for not speaking up. I considered myself your friend, but I didn't act like it. Sorry," he finished, shrugging stiffly, eyes sad.

"Thanks, Mack. It's all good," Lynn managed to get out, trying very hard not to let on that her eyes were burning with unexpected emotion.

"Yeah, uh, guess I'd better say the same," Dan said, shoulders slumped but willing, at least, to meet her eyes. "I should'a known better, honestly, what with my mom and my older sister. They are scaaary smart." He grimaced. "Big sis would probably slap me silly if she were here. Sorry, Lynn."

Lynn snorted at that, but couldn't stop her lips from twitching.

"I'll forgive you if you promise to stop stealing the last piece of pizza *every time*. I swear, you have to be hiding it in your pants or something. No way you can eat that much."

"Hey! I am a calorie-burning machine!" Dan protested, holding up both arms to flex his biceps. "Do you see these guns? They need fuel!"

Kayla burst out giggling and couldn't stop, and then the bell for class rang loud and rudely over their heads.

By the time Lynn had grabbed her backpack and looked up, Ronnie had vanished. She sighed internally.

Well, he hadn't exploded, claimed to be innocent, or stomped off like a petulant child.

Baby steps.

Matilda wasn't back yet when Lynn returned from hunting that evening, which Lynn took as a good sign. She'd sent Lynn a ping a few hours ago saying she'd arrived at the restaurant and would let Lynn know when she headed home.

Lynn took her usual scalding shower, scarfed down leftovers, and forced herself to work on homework, even though her mind was distracted checking her messages and the time at regular intervals.

Late in the evening, almost the time Lynn would be going to bed, she was surprised by the front door lock clicking and the sound of someone coming in.

"Mom?" she called.

"Oh, hi, honey!"

"I thought you said you'd ping me when you were headed back?"

"Oops! Sorry. I guess I was pretty distracted."

Lynn grinned. That sounded promising.

Matilda came around the corner into the kitchen, face flushed and eyes sparkling. She wore dark jeans and a pretty blouse whose V-neck dipped lower than Lynn would ever dare to wear. Without a word she dumped her purse on the table, pulled back the second chair, and plopped down.

"Well?" Lynn asked.

Matilda looked like she was fighting a huge grin. She bit her bottom lip in a vain attempt at composure, but then apparently gave up and let the smile take over her face.

"He's...he's..." Words seemed to escape her.

"Okay, Mom, I don't need you to write a love song or anything," Lynn said, holding up her hands. "Just...did he treat you okay?"

Matilda's expression softened.

"Yes, dear. Very much so. He was incredibly understanding and sweet. No need to castrate anyone today."

Lynn snickered.

"Yeah, he's gonna need those soon, isn't he?" she pointed out.

Her mom gasped, eyes going wide, then she swatted Lynn's arm, grinning like a fool.

"You watch your mouth, young lady, or you and I will be having an in-depth discussion about the female reproductive system, monthly ovulation cycle, and foundational principles of safe—"

"Okay, okay!" Lynn shouted, putting her hands over her ears. "I'll be good, I promise! You already made me memorize that in, like, sixth grade. I still remember."

"I'm sure you could use a refresher," Matilda said sweetly.

"No, I'm good, I promise."

There was a brief silence when they stared at each other, feeling out this novel situation together.

"So, when do I get to meet him?" Lynn asked. She felt a trickle of uncertainty, but was genuinely excited for her mom. Her mom had lived through a lot, and had treated every sort of person under the sun in her ER. She was one of the best judges of character around. If Matilda approved of him, this guy must be the real deal.

Matilda's excitement cooled a little and she leaned back in her chair, picking at the strap of her purse.

"Well, I know you're so busy with school and getting ready for the championship, and I don't want to put any more stress on you, so..."

Lynn raised an eyebrow.

"That sounds a lot like stalling, Mom. Do you not *want* me to meet him?"

"No! It's not that, honey. It's just...a complicated situation and I worry about all the stress you're already under."

"And you're worried I won't like him?" Lynn guessed.

Matilda chuckled softly. "No, I know you'll like him. We'll get together soon, I *promise*. For now, though, it's past your bedtime and you have school tomorrow."

"Uh-huh," Lynn said, knowing better than to push. Her mom was right, she *was* under a lot of stress. "Just promise me you won't hold off because you think I'm too busy. If—no, *when*—we win this competition, I'll be *more* busy, not less. So no procrastinating, okay?"

"Promise," Matilda said, smiling.

Friday Ronnie didn't show up for school.

They all low-level panicked, until Dan got a ping from him saying his dad was sick and he had to stay home to take care of him.

Lynn tried not to spend the morning paranoid about what was *really* going on. Probably Ronnie's dad *was* sick. All totally normal. Not in any way related to yesterday. Why was her brain so paranoid?

When they sat down for lunch, her paranoid brain was vindicated.

"Uh-oh," Kayla said halfway through her salad, eyes unfocused as she read or watched something on her AR display.

"What now?" Dan grumbled, glaring around the room as if he expected an ambush.

"Oh my *God*," Kayla gasped indignantly, still enthralled by something none of them could hear or see.

"What is it?" Edgar demanded, an ominous rumble in his voice.

Kayla's eyes refocused and she looked around at the table, her gaze stopping on Lynn.

"They doxxed you!" she said, outrage all over her face. "Those low-life creeps actually *doxxed* you!"

"Who?" Mack asked, leaning forward. "Elena?"

"No, she's not *that* stupid," Kayla scoffed.

"Connor?" Dan asked, sounding hopeful.

"No, no, nothing like that. It's a TD Hunter fan stream that talks about CRC like they're gods or something. I'd swear one of Elena's flunkies runs it, except her flunkies don't know a thing about TD Hunter, and this streamer knows her stuff. But she's a total tool and talks trash about Skadi's Wolves all the time. She showed the clip of Lynn going after Elena yesterday and claimed Lynn assaulted Elena! And then she doxxed Lynn! She says Lynn is a public menace and should be behind bars! Can you *believe* it?"

Lynn took a deep breath to calm herself. Her hands were clenched into fists beneath the table, but she tried to keep her expression neutral. Edgar was watching her, a worried look on his face. She gave her head a tiny shake and lowered her eyes to the table so she wouldn't have to engage with anyone.

It wasn't good, but it wasn't as bad as...as the vid. Honestly, Lynn wasn't sure it was a big deal at all except for the insult of it. After all, paparazzi drones regularly followed her around, and her real name was all over the mesh web. It wasn't that hard to find someone's address from publicly available information, not if they weren't actively trying to hide it.

And she hadn't been.

"That creep!" Kayla said, back to watching her AR display.

"What now?" Dan asked.

"That little punk is telling her followers to spread Lynn's address around so people can harass her for being a *bully*. To *Elena*." Kayla looked around at them again, her expression now too incredulous to have room left for outrage. "That's—that's—that's *ridiculous!*"

"Maybe, but I bet people still lap it up," Mack said gloomily.

"That's it," Kayla said, expression hardening. "I'm doing a rebuttal vid."

Lynn's eyebrows rose.

"Are you sure that's smart?" Mack asked.

"Probably not, but I'm tired of this! I can't just sit around and let people tell ridiculous *lies* about my friend! I mean, people have been doing that for months already, but this is taking it too far. These asinine, brainless cretins in the comments are joking about how someone should show up at your apartment and teach you a lesson." Kayla's worried gaze turned to Lynn.

"You should talk to Mrs. Pearson," Edgar rumbled. "See what she thinks. There might be something you can do, but you gotta be smart about it."

"Good idea," Kayla said, looking determined.

After school, with Ronnie still MIA, they decided to stick close to familiar territory and hunt around the woods north of the school. Lynn was curious to see what sort of activity they'd find around the power node where they'd destroyed Gyges, though if the TDM numbers had repopulated they wouldn't be getting too close, not without a full team of five to fight with.

Being unable to do their usual aggressive sweeps for maximum loot and experience points, Lynn had them work on herding groups of TDMs into a kill zone so Edgar could practice his aim with his grenade launcher. They were still trying to get a handle on the best way to integrate grenades into their overall strategy. Like the flamethrower, they weren't often worth the energy expenditure without tightly packed groups of high class TDMs.

It was a strange hunt. The energy on the team was different without Ronnie there. Everyone seemed less focused. Mack and Dan kept getting sidetracked, arguing about technique, and Edgar wasn't his usual, kill-everything-that-moves-and-cackle-gleefully-while-he-did-it self without Ronnie there to charge with him. Even she struggled a little. Ronnie and Dan usually held the right flank and needed little supervision or direction, which left her more brain space to coordinate with Mack and keep an eye on the big picture.

It felt weird to realize it, but Ronnie played a vital role on their team—beyond being a skilled player, of course. He made them all better, and they needed him back. Lynn tried not to worry that they still hadn't heard from him besides his ping to Dan that morning.

They didn't find out much about the power node except that the TDMs had definitely repopulated. They weren't able to get close enough to get a good picture of what was immediately around the node.

By the time it got dark they were all tired and subdued. Mack split off to ride home with Dan, since Ronnie wasn't there, and Lynn and Edgar took a separate air taxi back to her apartment. Everything that had happened over lunch came rushing back to Lynn, and she wondered if there would be mobs of angry CRC fans outside her apartment building's door.

Edgar walked a little closer to her than normal on their way to the back utility entrance. The late April evening was mild and beautiful, with the chirping of a few brave night creatures in the woodland beside Lynn's apartment complex.

Since Mr. Thomas was elderly and long ago retired, he was almost always around to let them in their "secret" entrance, they just had to give him plenty of heads up. He didn't miss their long faces, and Lynn quietly explained what doxxing was while they walked him back to his apartment. He shook his head sadly, but promised to keep an eye out on things, since he was closer to the building's front entrance than she was.

After that, since there were no crowds with signs or pitchforks—in fact, the area was as deserted and quiet as always—Edgar gave her a tight side hug, then headed back out the utility entrance to retrace his steps. He could have ordered another air taxi that would have shown up right outside her building's front door. But Lynn got the impression he relished the walk through the woods, even at night. Plus, there still might have been drones hanging around, looking for juicy footage.

Lynn was tired, but they hadn't fought as long or hard as they usually did without Ronnie there, so she decided to take the stairs and give her legs a workout. She slowly climbed and then trudged down the hall toward her apartment, eyes on the ground in front of her, thoughts swirling back and forth. Should she be worried about Ronnie? The mental image of Ronnie's black eye peeking out from behind his AR glasses was forefront in her mind. Dan, Mack, and Edgar had all promised to reach out to him tonight and check on him. If they didn't hear from him by tomorrow... she wasn't sure what she would do.

On a sudden whim, she relaunched the TD Hunter app.

"Hey, Hugo, I don't suppose you can tell me if someone on my team is actively, or has recently been playing TD Hunter, can you?" Had Ronnie simply been too embarrassed by their confrontation yesterday and decided to play hooky? Was he hunting right now?

"Good evening, Miss Lynn. Unfortunately, I am not at liberty to disclose the activities of other TD Hunter players. However, if you recall, members of your group *do* appear on your navigational map whenever they are in combat mode. So, if this team member were currently playing, you *would* be able to see their location."

Lynn stopped abruptly and pulled up her TD Hunter navigational map. Then she let out a sigh. No blue dot. She remembered last summer how Elena had tricked Mack into joining a bogus group and then CRC had used the function to follow Skadi's Wolves around to all the best hunting grounds. But wherever Ronnie was now and whatever he was doing, he wasn't playing TD Hunter.

"Um, Hugo... if it were an emergency, could you tell me where Ronnie was? Like, if he went missing?"

"If a player's app is running on their LINC, whether in active use or in the background, then yes, our system would be able to ascertain their geographical location. However, per the terms every player must agree to before using the app, only certain members of TD Hunter support as well as uniformed law enforcement and emergency personnel can request that information."

Lynn made a face, drifting forward again toward her apartment door while her eyes still searched the navigational map, zooming it out to encompass all of Cedar Rapids.

"Y-you came. You're finally here!"

Lynn's head jerked up and she stopped, the navigational map minimizing automatically to one corner of her display.

A man in rumpled shorts and baggy T-shirt stood by her apartment door, wringing his hands and staring at her, wide-eyed, like she was the newest incarnation of the Dalai Lama. If she hadn't been so distracted by her thoughts and her display, she would have seen him far sooner. As it was, they were barely ten feet apart. He looked older, maybe in his fifties, with unkempt hair, red baggy eyes, and stubble all over his chin. His skin was deathly pale, like someone who spent all their time in virtual, probably getting meals delivered and wearing the same clothes for days on end.

Speaking of clothes, Lynn caught a sour whiff of body odor and wrinkled her nose.

"Who are you?" she said, eyeing her door. The weirdo wasn't blocking it, but to reach it she would have to come within arm's reach of him. Every nerve of her body was on high alert, and she mentally cursed herself five ways to Sunday for not being more aware of her surroundings.

"I-it's me. Mr. Vulvx829. I came as soon as I could. I knew they were keeping you from me. I knew you gave out your address as a call for help. I just knew it!"

Alarm bells were going off like Handel's Hallelujah chorus in Lynn's head, and she backed up a step.

"Don't go!" the man said desperately, reaching forward with a hand as if to stop her.

"I don't know who you are or what you think you're doing, but you're in my way and I'm trying to go home," Lynn said calmly, even though she was anything but calm.

"Miss Lynn, should I call for assistance?"

Hugo's voice in her ear almost gave her a heart attack—she'd completely forgotten about having TD Hunter open—but the shock was immediately followed by a wave of relief.

"Y-yes," she subvocalized. "Wait, can you ping Edgar? He left just a little while ago, he should be close." Mr. Thomas was downstairs, but he walked with a cane and Lynn wasn't about to put him in danger. Her neighbors on this floor were virtual strangers. Lynn might have nodded politely to a few of them, but she didn't know their names or their schedules. Many of them hadn't lived there long. She and her mom were the only ones on their floor who'd stuck around more than five years, as far as Lynn knew.

"O-of course you don't know," the man said, giving her what he probably thought was a reassuring smile, but was really more of a grimace. "They kept it from you, didn't they? They said you never got my messages, those fu-fu-fu—" His head twitched several times to the side and he bit out an angry stream of vulgarities, though his eyes never left her. "They poisoned you against me, didn't they? H-how could you let them come between us?"

Lynn's eyes were wide as saucers now, and her heart was racing like a rabbit in flight. Time to get out of there. She would take refuge in Mr. Thomas' apartment until the police arrived and removed this obviously deranged person.

She took another careful step backward, but the man's eyes flew wide and he put his hands together in front of him in a pleading gesture.

"Don't go, don't go, don't go. I just found you. All my life I've been searching. When I saw your beautiful video I knew it was you. It was you all along. You're the one they promised me."

Lynn froze again as the guy kept rambling, going on and on about his delusions. Now he was waving his hands in the air as he worked himself up. Lynn tried to push down her panic, but her endocrine system was having none of it. Where was her Larry calm and focus when she needed it? This was no game, this was the real deal, and her body was flooding her with all the fight or flight hormones it was designed to, scrambling her attempt at a calm response.

The guy didn't look like he had a weapon. He hadn't threatened her—yet. Did she dare stay put and wait for Edgar or the police? She could probably outrun him if she bolted, as long as he didn't get his hands on her first. He was so close.

She'd almost decided to stay frozen, keep the guy talking so the authorities could grab him up, when his ranting shifted from "disturbed creep" to "psychotic perv." At his graphic descriptions of the "things" they would do together, Lynn gagged, a surge of nausea nearly bending her double.

"Don't laugh at me!" the wacko yelled, as if she'd just guffawed instead of choked. "You want it, I know you do! Why else would you have sent me that video!"

Lynn stumbled back, trying to run and not throw up at

the same time. She *knew* she should have bolted as soon as she saw the guy. But it was too late, now, and her moment of indecision cost her. The creep lunged for her and managed to grab hold of her backpack as she turned to flee. His scrabbling fingers found purchase and yanked backward hard enough to make her stumble and careen into the wall. He was on her in an instant, clawing at her backpack, grabbing her arm, trying to find purchase in her hair—though she'd been braiding it tightly to her head for months now, so there was nothing there for him to yank.

"Get off me!" she screamed at the top of her lungs, panic and fury rising in an adrenaline-fueled storm. She threw an elbow backward and tried to wrench herself free, but her feet got tangled with his and they both toppled to the ground, him on top. He tried to straddle her but she bucked furiously and rolled, managing to get her legs free. She couldn't roll away and get to her feet because he had a death grip on her backpack straps and was using them to hold onto her. His breath stank of stale curry as he ranted in her face, words she completely blocked out as she kept screaming and yelling. With her arms trapped by her sides, she didn't have enough room to get in a good punch or jab. But in her struggle her hand brushed her thigh and she felt a familiar lump in her pocket.

Still kicking, writhing, and yelling, she managed to get her dad's pocketknife out and flick the blade open one-handed, a move she'd practiced many times.

Then she stabbed the freak in his side and twisted the blade with all her might.

He screamed, the sound high-pitched and wailing, and jerked away. She almost lost hold of her knife, but her grip was firm as her attacker let go and rolled away, cursing and sobbing out a litany of vulgar epithets.

Lynn scooted backward on her butt, shedding her backpack as she went, and scrambled to her feet. She held the knife out in front of her, its small blade shining with blood.

"Get the *hell* away from me!" she shouted as the man stumbled to his feet, holding his side, still cursing her. He looked undecided, despite the blood leaking from between his fingers.

But then the stairwell door behind her banged open so loud it sounded like an explosion.

"*LYNN!*"

The roar—half desperate call, half promised threat—decided things for "Mr. Vulvx829." He turned and fled, stumbling a few times in his pain and haste, toward the stairwell at the opposite end of the hall.

Edgar pounded down the hall toward her, his thunderous approach vibrating the floor and the walls and the very air. Lynn expected him to shoot past, making a beeline for the bleeding perv getting closer and closer to the stairwell and escape.

But he screeched to a halt next to her instead and put his body between her and the fleeing man, big hands on her shoulders, wild-eyed face bent to meet her eye.

"Lynn! Lynn! Are you okay! What happened? What's hurt?"

Lynn tried to duck around him, to keep that creep in sight, but Edgar's grip was firm.

"What are you doing?" she yelled, finally meeting Edgar's eyes. "Go get him! He's getting away!"

"Lynn, you're covered in blood, I'm not leaving you!"

"It's *his* blood, you idiot! I'm fine!"

"I'm still not leaving you!"

Lynn realized she was shaking. Her scalp burned where the man had ripped at her tight braid, trying to find a grip. Her body ached from falling hard to the floor and being mashed and yanked by her attacker.

The fight or flight adrenaline high, its job now done, peaked, and plummeted. Her grip on her knife slackened, and it thumped to the floor, just as her legs buckled.

Before she could crash to the floor Edgar caught her, one arm sliding around her back, the other hooking under her legs so he could lift her up and hold her close to his chest. His arms were strong, his body warm and rock solid, unaffected by the post-adrenaline shakes that were now making her teeth clack together.

"I got you, *manamea*, I got you. You're safe. I got you."

Edgar was murmuring nonsense into her hair, the same thing over and over like a mantra. Or a prayer. She didn't mind, it was a soothing alternative to the chaos of shock and nausea and screaming obscenities in her head.

"The authorities are almost here, Miss Lynn," Hugo said

in her ear. "I updated them on your status and the probable location of the assailant. All will be well, Miss Lynn. All will be well."

Lynn wasn't sure if that was the AI's attempt at being comforting, or if it was simply stating fact. But she quickly forgot about it as the shakes got worse and her brain vacillated between hysterics and hyperventilation, clearly unsure what the best response was to the shit that had just gone down. She wanted to ask Edgar where her pocketknife had gone, to make sure it didn't get lost, but she couldn't form words, so she gave up thinking about it. Instead, she turned her head into his chest, pressing deeper into that temporary haven, and let the gasping sobs come.

Chapter 7

POLICE SHOWED UP, QUESTIONS WERE ASKED, AN INITIAL STATEment was taken, the building was searched. All of it was tedious and frustrating because Lynn just wanted to go to sleep, forget everything that had happened, and move on with her life.

Edgar was there for her through it all. He didn't let go of her until EMS insisted she uncurl from his lap and sit up so they could examine her and make sure she didn't need any medical attention. She thought about telling them to shove it, but her mother had taught her to respect medical personnel, so she kept her mouth shut and did as she was told.

Her pocketknife was bagged as evidence. She watched them take it away with a helpless sort of sadness, knowing she'd probably never see it again, since the creep that had attacked her had disappeared handily. The police said they would check local cams and drone footage and be in touch with ERs in the city, but there was no guarantee they'd ever catch him.

At least her knife had served her well, with distinction and honor. Her dad would have been proud.

By the time her mom arrived, most of the poking and prodding and questions were done. Which was good, because Matilda would have clocked anyone who got between her and her daughter.

They hugged desperately, and Lynn had to fight off a second round of hysterics that tried to bubble to the surface.

Matilda insisted on doing her own examination, and by that

point Lynn just leaned against Edgar and let her do whatever she wanted.

She was so tired.

But she had enough strength to do one important thing: send a ping to Mrs. Pearson, copied to her team.

I think I found my stalker. Goes by Mr. Vulvx829. 5' 9", average build, 50s, scruffy stubble, short graying hair, baggy red eyes, looks like he lives in virtual. Hope that helps.

After that, she put her LINC in dark mode and let Edgar and her mom worry about everything else.

Eventually, all the cops and their entourage left.

Matilda made her a mug of warm, sweetened and spiced milk, something Lynn hadn't had since she was in middle school. Her dad used to make it for her when she was little, calling it "Grandma's Favorite Recipe" because it was his Norwegian grandmother's favorite late-night treat. It was his go-to solution any time she was sick, afraid of the dark, or simply couldn't fall asleep.

Lynn drank it gratefully, still leaning on Edgar, who she could tell from his occasional stillnesses and distracted, vacant look, was having subvocalized conversations with someone. Or multiple someones. Probably the team. She hoped he told them not to come rushing over, she didn't want them to see her like this—exhausted, disheveled, fragile.

The thought made her lift her head and peer up at Edgar.

"Is Ronnie okay? Have you heard from him?"

"He's...okay. Nothing you need to worry about."

"Worrying about my team is my job," she mumbled, head drooping once again.

Her mom took the mostly empty mug from her slack hands and disappeared into the kitchen. When she came back, she took Lynn's hands and helped her up.

"Come on, sweetie. Let's get you in bed. You need to rest."

With a slight detour to shower—scalding water and her pine-scented body wash helped scour the memory of sour BO and stale curry from her nostrils—Lynn finally tumbled into bed. Matilda tucked her in. Lynn noticed a slight tremor in her mom's hands as she did it. Sleep pulled at her, but she untangled one arm enough to find her mom's hand in the dark and hold it tight for a moment. Her strong, unflappable-in-a-crisis, no-nonsense mom, now with no crisis left to stand up to, had to contend with the haunting "almosts" and "what-ifs" of nearly losing her daughter.

Her mom squeezed her hand gratefully, then firmly finished tucking her in and left her to sleep. Lynn heard voices as she drifted off, and wondered how long Edgar would stick around before her mom finally shooed him off.

The answer was: all night.

When she emerged from her bedroom late the next morning, sore but more rested than she'd been in months, Edgar lifted his head from where he was camped out on the couch.

Lynn stared at him. He grinned sheepishly.

"Your ma was pretty upset last night. I didn't want to leave her alone, you know?"

Emotion thickened in Lynn's throat, and she nodded.

"Did you—" Lynn croaked, then shook her head and went to the kitchen to get a long drink of water before coming back. Now Edgar was sitting up, and running a hand over his chin, as if checking for stubble.

"Did you get any sleep?" she tried asking again.

"Yeah. Few hours. Then I convinced your ma to take a turn."

"Good," Lynn said, feeling oddly numb and at loose ends without her usual morning routine to follow. She drifted over to the couch to lower herself down gingerly beside Edgar.

"You get something to eat?"

"Your ma made bacon and eggs before she turned in. Left you a covered plate in the microwave."

God bless mothers. Lynn heaved herself up with a groan and went back to the kitchen to warm up her plate and eat. Edgar joined her in the kitchen while she ate in silence. It was strangely relaxing having him around. Normally being in the presence of others was nerve-wracking. Silences were awkward and she was constantly watching for cues that they were upset or she'd done something wrong.

But Edgar was so chill. He just sat, relaxed, and slowly masticated a piece of gum like some giant beast content in its den. If there were thoughts churning in his head, he gave no outward indication. When he was ready to speak, he would speak, and not a moment before.

She, in contrast, had plenty of thoughts churning around, but no desire to voice them. Her mother's words kept poking her, and she couldn't help watching Edgar from under her lashes, looking for any sign he was "over the moon" for her.

Well...he *had* rushed to defend her, and had stuck around for hours to make sure she and her mom were okay. But friends did that sort of thing, too. Right? What did it even mean to be over the moon for someone?

Lynn had no idea, and would rather hunt TDMs than think about it. As long as Edgar was content to be there, she was happy to have him. He was loyal, hardworking, funny, and he didn't expect her to talk all the time or keep him entertained.

He was a breath of fresh air, in other words.

"Okay," Lynn finally said, once she'd put her dirty dishes in the sink and sat back down at the kitchen table, "How soon can we get the guys together? The weather outside is perfect for hunting, and we're wasting daylight."

"Whoah, *uce*. Hold on there. Hunting? You just got jumped. You need to rest."

"I'm not hurt, just a little sore. And I already got plenty of sleep."

"Nah, nah, girl," Edgar said, shaking his head. "We ain't huntin' today."

Lynn narrowed her eyes. "Oh yeah? Try to stop me. I'm not sitting around this apartment, moping like a sad little victim. We've got a championship to win, and I'm not letting anyone—not Elena, not Connor, and not some random creep—stop us from winning it."

Edgar held up his hands in a placating gesture.

"I get it, boss. We got stuff to do. But you're not some machine, right? Last time I checked, oh"—he mimed turning his wrist over to glance at a watch that didn't exist—"five minutes ago when we was sittin' on the couch, you could'a passed for a war zone refugee." He gestured at the rat's nest in Lynn's hair and at her face, which she could only assume looked as haggard as she felt inside.

"Psh," Lynn said, gathering herself and sitting up straighter. "I've had some protein. I'm fine now."

Edgar's lips twitched, but he still shook his head.

"Your ma—"

"Is not awake, so it's a moot point. If you don't want to join me, fine, but I need to do *something*, or I'll go crazy. And don't say homework, or I might stab you."

Edgar chuckled softly, then rubbed the back of his neck.

"Well... if all you need to do is *something*, I'm sure there's a few *somethings* I could come up with."

Lynn's brows scrunched together and she stared at Edgar, trying to figure out what he was implying. Did he just...?

The sound of a door and the soft pad of footsteps on the apartment rug made both of them turn toward the hall to see Matilda emerge, eyes puffy and red but with a look of iron-clad determination on her face.

"Oh no, I'm sorry for waking you up, Mom," Lynn said. "I didn't realize how loud we were talking. We can go somewhere else so you can sleep."

"No." Matilda shook her head and went to stand behind the third chair at the table, gripping the back with both hands as if to hold herself up. "I was already awake. Couldn't sleep." She turned her baleful eyes on Lynn. "You, young lady, will *not* be hunting today."

"But—"

"You will *not* be hunting," Matilda continued doggedly, "because I will be helping you buy a house today."

Stunned silence filled the room.

"A...house?" Lynn said, leaning back. "Me? T-today?"

"Well, we won't be closing the sale today, I'm sure. But we can go house hunting, and by Sunday night we'll pick one out. Sale can be on Monday, once banks are open."

"I—that's—Mom, are you out of your mind?"

Matilda looked directly into Lynn's eyes, her expression firm.

"No, Lynn. I've finally found it. We have both been working ourselves to the bone for *years*, and for what? A brighter future? Well, we need change right now. I thought about it for hours and hours last night, and I cannot in good conscience insist that you drop out of this competition and give up the very thing that gives you purpose. Besides, much of the damage has already been done."

Lynn winced, then winced again when the movement pressed on the sore spot on her hip where she'd fallen yesterday.

"Therefore, as your parent and legal guardian, I am advising you to buy a house using the money you've been saving up from your gaming m—"

Lynn's eyes flew wide and her eyes darted to Edgar and back as she made a furious negation gesture under the table where her mom could see her but Edgar couldn't.

"—mmm sponsorships," Matilda pivoted smoothly. "I looked over all your accounts last night, and I think it will be enough. We'll offer to buy cash in hand, and that's sure to get us a better deal. I've already done all the research. The housing market in Cedar Rapids has been in a slump the past year, and prices are quite reasonable."

"Okaaay," Lynn said, giving her head a little shake. "But... why a house? We don't need much space, and we live in an okay part of town already."

"Honey," Matilda said, raising an eyebrow. "Yesterday you were attacked on our doorstep by an insane stalker who found you because petulant, foolish, fame-crazed imbeciles online shared your address with the world. Not only is real estate a secure and wise investment for money that is otherwise just sitting around, but as your mother it is my job to keep you as safe as I'm reasonably able. Based on how insanely well you're doing with TD Hunter and your partnership with Tsunami, I doubt you'll have trouble getting into a wonderful game development program, if you don't just go straight to game testing for Tsunami after this TD Hunter competition. You need better quality of life right now, for your own safety and well-being. So," Matilda paused and took a deep, cleansing breath, "you are going to buy a house in a gated community, and GIC is going to help you do it with as much anonymity as possible. I've already scheduled a meeting with Mrs. Pearson at eleven. They have helped other clients do similar things to protect their safety and privacy."

Lynn sat there, stunned, trying to wrap her mind around it all.

A house? Buy a house? Leave this dingy, lame apartment she'd spent a third of her life in?

A tiny smile quirked one side of her mouth. It *would* be nice to finally do something with all the money she'd earned. Besides buy copious amounts of steak and top-of-the-line athletic gear, anyway. She'd been paying extra on her mom's old medical debts too, from when the doctors used experimental stem-cell therapy to try and save her dad's life after he got shot in the head. But her mom was right. All her hard-earned money from mercing as Larry Coughlin had just been sitting around, doing nothing, for years now. Add that to the sponsorship money pouring in since GIC had started managing her affairs, and yeah, it *was* pretty silly to just sit on it against a vague possibility she'd need it for college someday.

Lynn took a deep breath and spread her hands. "Okay. I'm in. What do we do first?"

Matilda looked at Edgar.

"First, Edgar needs to get safely home so his mother doesn't think I've kidnapped him."

"Oh, no, Mrs. Raven. I'm good. My ma knows what's up. If I went home, she'd prolly kick me right back out and ask why I wasn't over here taking care of my—um, my friend." He shifted in his chair and gave Lynn a sideways look, as if he expected her to protest.

"Don't worry, I know better than to get on your mom's bad side. You can hide over here and pretend to take care of me so she won't get mad."

Edgar swiped at his brow and blew out an exaggerated sigh of relief, which made Matilda laugh too.

"Come on, you two jokers. Let me show you the houses I had in mind, and you all can do your own searches to see if you can find anything better. We can do in virtual walkthroughs of our top picks until our meeting with Mrs. Pearson. Then after lunch we can go check out the physical locations. Sound like a plan?"

"As long as you make more bacon, Mrs. Raven, I don't care what you want me to do, I'll do it," Edgar said solemnly.

Lynn snorted. "Make that steak and I'll second it."

"Why not both?" Matilda asked, arms open wide. "I'll go pull some nice cuts out of the freezer to grill for lunch and we can get started."

Mrs. Pearson was on board with everything Matilda had in mind, and she went over the additional measures and protections GIC could help them with. She did, though, advise against Lynn attempting to purchase a house so quickly without an agent.

It was all very precipitous, but Andrew Underwood, the agent Mrs. Pearson connected them with, was the height of professional, and didn't seem at all surprised at the pace her mom wanted to move. It wouldn't have been possible purchasing with a mortgage, he explained, since banks had legally regulated timelines they worked on for approving and implementing mortgages. But, if Lynn found a house she liked over the weekend and the seller accepted her cash offer right away, there was no reason they couldn't be moving in by the middle of the week.

Drew, as he insisted they call him, got them dozens of house options within an hour of their call with Mrs. Pearson. Besides their must-have of being within a gated community, Lynn didn't really care what the house looked like, as long as it was a good investment.

Her mom convinced her to care a little more than that and assiduously consulted her on her preferences every time she tried to throw up her hands. After all, it was *her* money. At Drew's recommendation, they would be purchasing the house through a trust to protect Lynn's identity and address. Once Lynn turned eighteen, the ownership would be transferred to her. The entire idea made Lynn feel weird—she would have happily left the ownership of the house to Matilda, but her mom wouldn't hear of it.

"You worked hard for this money, and you will use it to set up a secure life for yourself, young lady. So, no more protests!"

Of course, Matilda got her way. It was her prerogative as a mother, she said.

Based on the virtual walkthroughs, they winnowed their options down to five, and gave Drew the go-ahead to contact the sellers and see if they were open to a cash offer. Three of them were, so that afternoon Lynn, Matilda, and Edgar—who, it had become clear, would not be leaving Lynn's side until she ordered him away, much to Lynn's chagrin—caught an air taxi to go look at the houses in person.

The first house was nice, but on the upper limit of their price range and also in the very front of the neighborhood on a prominent corner. Gated the community might be, but it wasn't Lynn and Matilda's idea of keeping a low profile. They also needed additional funds to outfit the house and worry about all sorts of home-ownership costs like insurance, taxes, and the like.

House number two was a solid contender, but it was a condo. That made it much more affordable, but low on privacy, and without as much space as Lynn had been hoping for. It was also the furthest of the three from St. Sebastian's, and since Matilda would be the one living there long-term, Lynn decided it wasn't a good choice unless they could find nothing else.

They hit the jackpot with the third house. Drew had suggested they visit it last, since it was their top pick, so they had a better sense of what other options they were comparing it to, and Lynn had to agree he'd been right.

It wasn't a mansion by any means, not like Mr. Swain's house in his swanky neighborhood. But it had enough bedrooms to give them space for friends, as well as extra rooms to convert into other sorts of spaces, such as a home gym, something Matilda was almost salivating over.

Lynn, not so much.

She had to admit, though, it would be convenient not to have to sneak around like a criminal just to get to the gym in the morning. And, best of all, the house had an enormous, open basement. It was minimally finished, but Edgar took one look and immediately declared it their new Skadi's Wolves Den. His hands danced as he pointed this way and that, painting a picture of where they would put the mini fridge and snack bar, the titan-size flex screen, the sectional couch and body mold chairs, and even a thing called a foosball table. Lynn had seen them in pictures but never touched one before. It was an entirely analog game with tiny men on rotating sticks that "kicked" a ball back and forth toward goals on either end, reminiscent of an old-style soccer match. Edgar said such tables used to be popular in bars and youth centers. He had good memories of playing it with his dad when he was little.

In addition to the interior benefits, the house had several spreading trees surrounding it, which would help with privacy, and it was at the end of a cul-de-sac. Behind it was the high wall that went around the whole community, and right past the wall the ground dropped away down a sheer cliff to one of the major highways that went through Cedar Rapids. The location was the main reason they could afford the price: not many people wanted to live around the noise of a highway. Apparently, the house had been built before the expansion of the road, so it had lost value over time as things became more urbanized and traffic increased. But Lynn couldn't care less about the noise, and Matilda loved how inaccessible the house was.

Anyone who wanted to get to Lynn now would be instantly obvious, and of course Matilda had already promised—or rather threatened—to have a top-of-the-line security system installed that would include cameras focused on the cul-de-sac and anyone who dared drive up it. Matilda even floated the idea of adopting a guard dog, but Lynn shot that down quickly. It wasn't that she didn't like dogs. The idea of a loyal, four-footed shadow delighted her. She and her mom simply wouldn't be around enough to give it the care and training it deserved. Maybe in a few months once they were settled in and she'd graduated high school.

The stray thought occurred to her that she already *had* a loyal shadow, though he had two feet, not four. But she batted away the idea, reminding herself that Edgar had his own life and his own problems, and had better things to do than babysit her.

They let Drew know about their house choice and he got to work on all the paperwork for a formal offer to the seller. Meanwhile, Kayla had heard about what had happened through her dad, who of course was kept abreast by Mrs. Pearson. Kayla immediately contacted Lynn to inform her in no uncertain terms that she and her mom would be staying at Kayla's house until their new place was ready to move into. Lynn attempted a feeble protest, but Kayla threatened to tell her dad Lynn needed a total wardrobe overhaul to match her rising fame, and Lynn knew Mrs. Pearson would jump on the suggestion like a cat on a mouse, so she had no choice but to accept Kayla's hospitality.

Which, of course, was a relief, even if she couldn't bring herself to admit it out loud.

That night she and her mom spent an hour packing up their personal possessions, mostly clothes, but also pictures, treasured objects, and all Lynn's gaming paraphernalia. They stashed their boxes in Mr. Thomas' apartment so they could pay a service later to collect them and take them to the new house without anyone the wiser that they were moving.

Mr. Thomas was, of course, devastated to hear about what had happened. He gave Lynn a long hug, his weathered, bony hands trembling when he pulled back and grasped both her hands in his. He looked her right in the eye and said:

"Don't you let them win, Lynn. Do you hear me? Never let the world intimidate you into giving up on what you know is right. Trials hurt, surely they do. But they also mold us, if we let them, into stronger people. Strong enough to take on the world, and win."

"Don't worry," Lynn said, smiling. "Me giving up is about

as likely as Edgar here voluntarily giving away bacon-wrapped steak bites."

"Hey, now," Edgar said, putting a hand to his chest, "I'd give them away to *you*... a few, anyway."

"Uh-huh. I'll be sure to remind you of that the next time Mrs. Nguyen makes them," Lynn threatened.

Mr. Thomas chuckled.

"I will miss you sorely, Lynn, and you too, of course, Matilda. You have been such a blessing in my life. But I know there are good things in your future, and with such friends as young Edgar here to stand by your side, I doubt there is anything you will not accomplish, if you put your mind to it."

Matilda came in for a hug, too, and Lynn blinked back a burning tingle in her eyes.

"Hey, don't think you get off that easy," she said, wagging a finger at her neighbor. "You still have to come over for dinner sometimes. We'll call an air taxi to pick you up and everything."

"I would expect no less," Mr. Thomas said with a flash of white teeth and a twinkle in his eye. "After all, your mother makes the finest homemade taco pizza in the city."

Matilda rolled her eyes but smiled. "Yes, yes, butter me up, Jerald. I won't forget about you. Maybe I can arrange some homemade dinner deliveries once we're settled in."

"Goodness, no, I was only paying you a compliment," Mr. Thomas protested. "I would not dream of imposing on your time in such a way."

"Don't be silly, Jerald," Matilda said. "It's not an imposition. It's a gift. *You* are a gift."

Mr. Thomas choked up—actually choked up, with tears and all—and Lynn's mom pulled him aside, patting his back and speaking quietly to him while Lynn and Edgar looked the other way.

Lynn leaked a tear or two of her own as they got into their air taxi to head over to Kayla's house for the night with backpacks and duffle bags full of clothes. It was already deep night, so there were only a few drones hanging around in the light of the parking lot illuminators, their operators obviously hoping their persistence would result in something juicy and valuable for the gossip streams. Lynn didn't care. Even if they tried to follow the air taxi, Lynn and the members of Skadi's Wolves had gotten used to programming circuitous routes into their air taxis to take them along the main interstate artery, where speeds upwards of eighty miles an hour shook off most drones, as well as routing through several tunnels. It extended travel time, but they'd gotten used to it.

Miraculously, word of the assault hadn't broken on the streams yet—and GIC intended to keep it that way, at least until they were prepared to release whatever carefully worded statement would actually do Lynn some good while not hampering the criminal investigation underway. Cedar Rapids' police department *had* put out a BOLO on the perv, but none of that information indicated Lynn as the victim.

Once at the Swains' house, Edgar helped them carry all their stuff inside, then endured Kayla's loud, grateful gushing over his heroic rescue of her best friend. Lynn couldn't help smiling at the picture of Kayla's enthusiastic thank-you hug, her petite arms barely reaching around Edgar's trunklike middle with his muscle-bound arms trapped under her slender ones. What really made the moment, though, was the panicked look Edgar shot Lynn, as if being hugged by the bubbly Kayla was the equivalent of a full-blown press conference and medal-awarding ceremony. He seemed much more comfortable with Mr. Swain's firm handshake and quiet murmur of thanks, after which he started reluctantly toward the front door, moving about as fast as molasses in winter.

By the time Edgar was gone, and Lynn and Matilda had been installed in the Swains' guest room, it was past midnight of what had been a very long, but productive day.

Showers were quick and they both collapsed into the queen bed with grateful sighs.

"When do you go back to work, Mom?" Lynn mumbled, staring at the fancy texture patterns on the ceiling.

"I don't know yet, honey. When I got the call on Friday, my supervisor said to go and don't worry about coming back until you were okay. I'll talk to her on Monday and see how long they can manage without me. Maybe a week. There will be a lot to do at the new place, fixing a few things and getting it all furnished."

"Okay," Lynn said, glad her mom hadn't made it sound like she was taking time off to hover and worry about her. "You know you can go back to work whenever you feel like it. There's no rush on getting the house fixed up. I'm fine sleeping on a mattress on the floor. You know I don't need much."

"I know, sweetie." The mattress shifted as Matilda turned on her side to face Lynn. "I've been thinking..."

"Yeah?" Lynn asked, turning on her side, too, so she could see her mom's face. Matilda's expression was serious.

"I think I'm ready for a change at work."

Lynn's eyebrows rose.

"I've been working nights so I could be there when you left in the morning and got back in the afternoon, and because night shift paid better, which we needed. But now that you're spending so much time outside the house, my schedule doesn't make sense. What if... what if I'd *been* there, waiting for you, when you got home Friday night? None of this would have happened—"

"No, Mom!" Lynn said, reaching out to touch her mother's hand. "It wasn't your fault. Don't ever think that."

"I know, honey. But... if I'd been there, it might have helped. And I want to be there. I want to be home when you're home. I have so little time left with you, sweetie, you're growing up so fast. I want to make the most of the few weeks we have left before you graduate and go off to do great and wonderful things."

Matilda smiled, but there was a sadness in her eyes that no amount of bravery could hide. She reached out and tucked a strand of Lynn's thick black hair behind her ear.

"Come on, Mom," Lynn said. "I'm not leaving any time soon. Where else am I supposed to get homemade taco pizza and stuffed pork chops every day? And who else is going to almost beat me at speed puzzles?"

Matilda chuckled. "Now you're just being cheeky. Regardless, I think it's time for a change at St. Sebastian's. There's an opening for the day shift Charge Nurse, and I'm going to apply for it."

"I'm sure you'll get it. You're the best nurse in the ER."

Her mom smiled. "Day shift is a whole other animal. We'll see."

A thought occurred to Lynn.

"Hey, do you think returning to the 'land of the living' will make it easier to date Mr. Wonderful?" Lynn asked, trying and failing to hide her grin.

"Mmm, probably," Matilda said, also failing to hide her smile.

That made Lynn happy. She wanted her mom to have a good life that didn't revolve around Lynn and her problems—of which there seemed to be many. The fact that she would likely get a job or go away to college soon hadn't really sunk in, she'd been so focused on leveling and keeping up with homework. Now that she was thinking about it, she didn't like it one bit. Obviously, she wanted to grow up and "do great things" as her mom had said. But the thought of leaving her mom alone to come back to an empty house every day made her heart ache.

Maybe this whole dating thing was serendipitous. If Mr. Wonderful turned out to be as amazing as Matilda seemed to think he was, maybe Lynn wouldn't have to worry about leaving her mom all alone.

"Go to sleep, honey. You need it."

"So do—you," Lynn pointed out, her attempt at sternness interrupted by a massive yawn. "I know you're used to being up right now, but you've barely slept in twenty-four hours. Promise me you'll try to sleep."

"I promise," Matilda said, smiling and squeezing Lynn's hand. "Will you promise me something, too?" she asked, a little hesitant.

Lynn's brow furrowed. "Sure."

"If you're...struggling. If everything inside your head gets to be too much...please promise me you'll ask for help? Sometimes the deepest wounds are where we can't see them. Pretending they don't exist doesn't make them go away. It just makes them fester and affect our lives in more subtle ways. I—I know. I've lived through it. So...please promise me you'll take care of yourself, sweetie?"

Emotion thickened her voice, but Lynn got the words out anyway.

"I promise, Mom."

Matilda nodded in thanks, rolled over halfway without letting go of Lynn's hand, and turned off the bedside light. She returned to her place and settled down for the night, her grip loose but warm, inviting Lynn to stay for as long as she needed and pull away whenever she wanted.

Lynn fell asleep holding her mom's hand.

Sunday was disgustingly sunny, with endless blue skies and birds chirping all over the place. A year ago Lynn would have lamented the fact that it was getting too warm for the baggy, formless hoodies she used to wear to hide her body from judgmental eyes.

Now, though, she stared up at the sky, grateful for the perfect weather and rather enjoying the warmth of the sun on her face. She only let herself revel in it for a moment, though, because a vulture drone might buzz by overhead at any moment, and she'd rather hunt in peace for as long as possible before the gossip mongers spied her.

She stepped back under the maple tree that was exploding with newly budded leaves. Edgar was sitting at the base leaning against the trunk, waiting with her for Dan, Mack, and hopefully Ronnie to show up. They were back at the node and substation where app glitches had prevented them from doing a clean sweep a few weeks ago. They had leveled since then, and the nagging itch of unanswered questions and amorphous suspicions had drawn her back to the location. They had unfinished business there, and today they were going to finish it.

Besides, after everything that had happened recently, she was itching for a victory, and she *would* have her satisfaction. With all the craziness that had been going on, she'd struggled to keep things together on the TD Hunter front, both mentally and organizationally.

Today was all about getting back on track.

She'd already spent part of the morning messaging with Quorra from Team Voodoo Girls—thankfully, they were thrilled at the opportunity to be alternates. They'd gotten the admin stuff out of the way, registering the necessary information with TD Hunter, then had discussed getting together a few times before the championship to hunt as a group and make sure everyone was on the same page.

With those tasks completed, Lynn was feeling optimistic and motivated. The sunshine was just icing on the cake.

Lynn went to stand by Edgar. One of his legs was propped up, the other straight, and he was picking at the fat, green blades of grass. He kept plucking particularly large blades and folding them together between his hands, then putting his lips to his folded hands and blowing. Lynn watched him go through half a dozen before she finally caved and asked:

"What in the world are you doing?"

"Makin' a whistle."

"Out of grass?" Lynn raised an eyebrow.

"Yup. Read about it in a book."

"Okay..." She watched him try a few more times, then

couldn't help speaking up again. "You know you could search 'grass whistle' on the streams and instantly find hundreds of vids on how to do it. Watch a few of those and you'll probably figure out what you're doing wrong."

"Yup, probably."

He kept plucking grass.

"So...why don't you?"

"Cuz I wanna see if I can figure it out myself."

"But...why?"

Edgar shrugged.

"Dunno. Challenge of it, I guess. Papa showed me how to do it years ago. If folks could figure it out before the streams and mesh web, I prolly can too."

Lynn shook her head but plunked down beside him anyway to hunt for especially fat blades of grass for him to use. He was incredibly patient about it, far more so than she could have been. His slow, deliberate movements were weirdly calming, as if they proved there was no rush, nothing in the world to be worried about. Soon she was far more invested in the process than she'd thought possible, and was asking him about the theory behind it and his technique. He nearly had it once, too, but only managed a few feeble squeaks before they both broke down laughing.

"Hey, guys, whatcha doing?"

Dan's voice surprised them both, and Lynn looked up to find Dan and Mack peering at them in confusion like they couldn't fathom why anyone would be rolling around in the grass—or at least could only fathom one reason, but that reason was impossible with clothes on.

"Whistling with grass," Lynn said hurriedly before either of them could contribute their own comments or theories. She sat up and leveraged herself to her feet in one smooth motion, then hastily brushed herself clean of discarded grass blades. That was when she belatedly realized it was *only* Dan and Mack staring at her.

"Um, where's Ronnie?" she asked, looking at Dan.

Dan shrugged helplessly.

"No idea. He hasn't responded to any of my messages since Friday."

Lynn's jaw firmed and her brows drew together. "All right, that's it. We're going to his house to make sure he's okay."

Dan made a face.

"What?" Lynn said.

"That's...probably a bad idea."

Lynn's eyes narrowed. "Why?"

"Well...you know Ronnie. If he's ignoring us, it's probably because he wants to be left alone. We should just give him space."

Lynn's nostrils flared, but she emotionally stepped back from the situation and tried to think like Lynn the Team Captain, not Lynn the paranoid friend. What would Larry do if a team member went MIA?

"Did Ronnie commit to being a reliable member of this team?" Lynn asked, voice level, neutral.

"Uh," Dan said, looking at Mack, then Edgar, who had gotten up and was now standing in their little circle. "Yeah?"

"Is Ronnie's radio silence normal?"

Dan shrugged. "Uh, kinda? I mean, he gets upset sometimes, but he doesn't usually go silent, not with me."

"If it were anyone else but Ronnie, would you think twice about doing a wellness check, considering all the craziness that's been happening recently?" Lynn asked, still businesslike.

"Uhhhh."

"No," Mack answered for him, expression determined.

"Right then," Lynn said, "we're going—"

"Hey, guys! Sorry it took forever to get here, the stupid air taxi had some kind of malfunction and—"

Everyone spun toward the approaching voice to see Ronnie jogging toward them down the sidewalk, hunting gear on and batons ready to go in their sheaths along his thighs. As Ronnie registered their expressions, he slowed, then came to a stop a few yards away from their now open circle.

"Why are you all staring at me like that?" he said, defensiveness tingeing his voice.

Lynn's eyes raked him from head to toe, noting his fading black eye, and the fact that there were no new bruises—at least not visible ones. Their athletic gear covered them from the neck down, protecting their skin from sunburn, bug bites, and various cuts and scrapes from rolling, jumping, and dodging across all sorts of terrain.

They also conveniently covered up bruises pretty much anywhere but on the face.

"Why are we staring?" Dan finally said once he'd gotten over his surprise. "You didn't respond to any of my messages, dude! We thought you—"

"Might have had some trouble with CRC," Lynn inserted smoothly, schooling her expression. "Considering what happened to me on Friday, our team has legitimate safety concerns. We need to stick together and look after each other."

Ronnie's brows drew together and he stared at her—actually looked her in the face for the first time in a while. He glanced at the other guys, but then his eyes went back to her. He started forward again slowly and closed the distance between them, completing their circle.

"Are you...okay?" he said quietly, brows still deeply furrowed. His gaze bounced around, like he was now checking *her* for injury, then returned to her face.

It was ridiculous—and extremely inconvenient—how choked up that simple question made her. She didn't know how to handle it after so long being angry, frustrated, and finally forgiving of Ronnie's deep flaws. So she retreated deeper into Larry mode, figuring it was for the best since Ronnie seemed allergic to "girly" things like emotion.

"I'm as good as I need to be to win this competition. Glad you could make it. We have a lot of work to do."

"Yeah," he said, gaze finally dropping. "Sorry I've been...busy."

Not, *"sorry I've been a jerkwad for years,"* or, *"sorry I let egotism nearly destroy our team."*

Was it normal to feel grateful and angry at the same time? She had no idea.

"Shit happens," she said in a carefully neutral tone, shoving back the urge to pin him down on it. Not the time, not the place.

"Tell me about it," he muttered, glancing at her again, this time with a spark of anger in his gaze. "If CRC pulls *one* more stunt, I swear—"

"You'll do nothing," Lynn said firmly, though she was gratified at his anger. "There's no proof they've done anything at all, and claiming otherwise is a waste of time. Let GIC and law enforcement do their job. Connor's worst nightmare is losing. So, let's get busy serving that up to him on a golden platter."

Ronnie looked mulish, but Lynn caught and held his eye with a hard gaze, and he finally huffed out a breath and rolled his eyes.

"Fine. Whatever. But if they put a single toe out of line, I'm not taking it lying down." He lifted his chin, eyes defiant.

Lynn simply smiled.

Not a normal smile. A Larry smile.

"Sure thing, Ronnie. But you'll have to get in line."

Ronnie smiled back. Actually *smiled* at her.

"Good," he said, then reached down to pull out his batons. "Can we kill stuff now?"

"Thought you'd never ask," Lynn said dryly, turning back to look at her whole team. She took a cleansing breath. "Okay, guys. We've been here before. Things didn't work last time, but I'm going to assume TD Hunter is competent enough to have fixed the glitches we pointed out to them a few weeks ago, and since we're already familiar with the terrain and strategy, we can devote our focus and energy on wracking up as much experience as possible today. There's no reason we can't annihilate every single TDM on this field and inside the substation. It's not so big that line of sight will be affected, and our ranged weapons will reach. So let's get to work and prove we're a lean, mean, killing machine."

Dan pumped his fist and Edgar made his whooping *"chee-HOO"* sound as everyone got out their batons and Lynn went over starting positions. She wanted to be able to give the center TDM their undivided attention when it came to it, so they were going to try and clear the closer side, then swing around back where the wood line came much closer to the station and clear as much as they could there as well before circling back around. It would likely take them several hours to do, but if they worked quickly and efficiently, she thought it was doable.

To up their speed, she was going to try a modified form of their bait and destroy formation. Instead of spreading out and moving slowly to clean up the far-flung masses of Delta and Charlie class TDMs before they tackled the inner rings, Lynn wanted to simply cut a generous swath in toward the center, then once they pivoted to sweep around the circle, have Mack with his double pistol insane rate of fire focus outward on all Delta and Charlie class TDMs close enough to be drawn in by their bait. It would leave a distant scattered ring of the lowest class TDMs still loitering around, but they'd be too far away and weak to bother Skadi's Wolves.

At least, that was the theory.

It would also give Mack high-pressure accuracy practice, which he needed despite his griping. He liked to take his time, but Lynn knew time was a luxury none of them had, and Mack needed to start trusting his instincts. His pistols had to be an extension of his brain, his whole body operating as a seamless unit. He was good, but not there yet, and it was her job to push him to the brink if they wanted any hope of winning.

Predictably, Mack griped up a storm once he heard the plan—"how am I supposed to keep you all supplied *and* focus on killing TDMs?"—but Lynn was having none of it.

"Did you think this would be easy, Mack?" she asked, giving him a raised eyebrow. "We're competing against the best players *in the world*. We've reached the top ten internationally and are jockeying for top spot in the US. We might not end up winning this thing, but if we don't, it darn sure won't be because we failed to push ourselves past what we thought possible.

"So, stop *looking* for stuff to pick up. It's all over the place. You don't need to mentally acknowledge everything you grab, that's giving it too much attention. I know you haven't had that Lute of Looting augment we bought you on the auction sites for very long, but you have to remember that it increases your loot radius enough that you shouldn't have to actively *look* for anything unless we're low on a specific supply. Talk to Hugo about how else you can automate loot pickup. Also, stop looking for loot during the heat of battle, only go after essential supplies. All our top-notch gear is from boss fights—we won't find anything better dropped by regular TDMs.

"Focus on those for now. Any improvement, no matter how small, could be the difference between winning and losing in a competition this fierce."

Mack nodded smartly.

"You're right. Riko says I worry too much, that I need to focus on what I can improve and forget about everything else."

"Great," Dan said, slapping his forehead. "Now he's taking life advice from a love bot."

"She is *not* a bot!" Mack snarled.

"*Children*," Lynn said ominously, and they quieted, though everyone but Mack was now smirking.

"You all can tease Mack on your own time," she said. "Everybody line up and let's do this."

Though Mrs. Pearson had been skeptical about it, Lynn had insisted they livestream at least part of this fight. Anyone who thought they could sabotage Skadi's Wolves or hold them back was in for a rude awakening, and Lynn intended to make that abundantly clear.

There was nothing she or her teammates needed to do to facilitate the livestream, either. With the precipitous rise in high-level gamers streaming their battles, TD Hunter had released a "support team" patch that enabled players like Lynn to invite her PR team to have "support" access to her app. It was view only, so all they could do was navigate around the app and see what Lynn was seeing through her AR interface. But the function made it infinitely easier for PR teams to manage a gamer's livestream feed and switch views between members of a team, all the while adding various graphics or additional content without the gamers themselves having to waste an iota of thought on it. It did up viewership whenever Lynn or the guys had their mics hot and bantered while livestreaming. At this point, though, TD Hunter had become a legitimate spectator sport, so subscribers didn't expect constant commentary. Lynn had seen some top-tier players in Germany and the UK hire actual AR sports commentators knowledgeable about the game to give a live play-by-play. Other players would go back and record their own commentary overtop their livestreams.

Lynn pinged Mrs. Pearson and let her know they were going into combat mode. And then it was time to rock and roll.

It felt so good to be back in the saddle. Lynn had some minor aches and pains, but they vanished under the rush of adrenaline and endorphins from launching into the augmented world she'd come to know and love.

It was an odd thought, "loving" TD Hunter. But there was no other way to describe the satisfaction and sense of "this is where I belong" that came over her when she could let go of all her earthly worries and focus exclusively on doing what she did best: gaming.

WarMonger didn't even come close. It was like a whole other world, that cold, sterile separation between game and gamer where she sat, immobile, with only her fingers and brain engaged in the fight.

TD Hunter was next level, more real even than being in a

VR harness. The intense physical investment and healthy chemical feedback from the exercise, combined with the highly realistic visual and audio stimulation, was frankly addictive. Lynn didn't mind hunting 5-6 days a week anymore. In fact, if she missed a day, she got antsy. She'd read about marathon runners, competitive bodybuilders, and other such athletes feeling the same way.

Who knew gaming would become the new face of health and wellness.

The first part of their mission went smoothly. They advanced like a well-oiled machine, sweeping up TDMs by the hundreds. They had gotten so efficient that Lynn had suggested weapon rotations for each of them so that they wouldn't injure certain muscles and ligaments through highly repetitive movements. For her that meant swapping Wrath and Abomination from hand to hand every five to ten minutes. For the guys that meant sometimes switching to a melee or ranged weapon they didn't normally use, but that was perfectly serviceable for anything but the toughest fights. As a side benefit, it made them all flawlessly ambidextrous.

They subvocalized back and forth on their team channel as needed while they fought. Mrs. Pearson would let them know if she wanted to record any audio, so they didn't have to worry about watching their words.

As was her habit when she got a second of breathing space, Lynn checked the skies about thirty minutes in, and was surprised to see how many drones had already gathered. Not just paparazzi drones either. There was a handful of those larger gray drones hovering higher up in the zone reserved for delivery and utility drones, just below the airbus lanes. Lynn didn't have the spare attention to wonder who they belonged to or why they were there. She simply noted their presence and kept on fighting.

An hour in they'd cleared the open-field half of the TDMs rings around the substation. The other side was going to be trickier, but strategic use of bait markers would help them control the flow of enemies so they could cut through the circles longwise without being mobbed from every side at once. If they'd had four or five other teams with them, they could have easily made the sweep without bait. But Lynn knew they couldn't depend on other teams to help them out on short notice.

She needed to know what they were capable of accomplishing

by themselves. And if she was a tad overconfident, well, that was the price of pushing yourself in a competitive sport.

The second phase of their battle went surprisingly smoothly. Too smoothly, in fact.

Even using bait to draw TDMs away from their team long enough to get out of range and prevent cumulative pileups, the TDMs seemed unusually apathetic. Her team had no trouble at all cutting a swath through the higher-level rings and luring the lower level TDMs away until they'd passed by. A part of her yearned, almost *needed* to stop and consider this deviation from the pattern, but she couldn't afford to. The best she could come up with on the fly was that protective rings around mini-bosses or high-class gatherers like Bunyips simply weren't as aggressive as the rings that formed around the bosses. Perhaps bosses like Mishipeshu, Gyges, and Ya-Te-Veo increased the surrounding TDMs' range of aggression, exhorting their minions to converge on whatever pesky hunters were attacking.

Like an immune response.

Whatever the case, Lynn and her team were tired, but determined, once they'd made it back around to the field side of the substation. There they had a chance to breathe, hydrate, and gulp down some energy gel before they advanced for the final attack. The fine spring day wasn't hot, but the cloudless sky meant full sun, and with how hard they were working sweat poured down their foreheads and into the collars of their athletic wear. Fortunately, the specially made fabric was up to the task of wicking away body moisture and staying dry so that they didn't come away from a day of hunting with massive, full-body rashes.

Lynn eyed the substation. It was only about the size of a tennis court, with a see-through chain link fence and little within it that would block line of sight. Also, based on her experience, most Alpha Class TDMs were large enough to rise above the level of the fence. All Skadi's Wolves had to do was advance to the fence and bait all the remaining TDMs around whatever electrovore was in the middle feeding. Then the final mini-boss could be easily defeated with ranged fire from outside the fence.

All very simple and easy.

Which, of course, made Lynn suspicious.

The entire point of gaming was to enjoy overcoming challenges, so player enjoyment often hinged on a game designer's ability to prevent a game from becoming too boring or easy. One way game designers did that was by lulling players into complacency just before an enemy attacked or a trap was sprung.

That was what this felt like.

Or maybe she was just crazy paranoid from playing WarMonger for too long, which involved fighting human players almost exclusively. TDMs, by and large, were a predictable bunch.

Which made Lynn even *more* suspicious.

"Well, what are we waiting for?" Ronnie asked, batons out and at the ready.

Lynn pursed her lips, staring hard at the substation as if she could see something in the real that would clue her in on what awaited them in combat mode.

"Nothing," she finally muttered, and signaled the guys to get ready to go back in.

"Hugo," she subvocalized, "we're not going to have any trouble this time, are we?"

"I can assure you that our technical support team has and always will do everything they can to ensure the proper functioning of the game. I took careful note of all processing data available from your last incident here and if there was a problem to be fixed, you can be sure it was fixed."

"Meaning, if the problem was caused by some kind of outside electromagnetic spectrum interference, there's nothing we can do, and there's no telling if it'll glitch again."

"I *was* trying to couch it more optimistically than that, but yes."

"Uh-huh." Lynn's lips quirked, and she switched to the team channel to give the guys a heads up before they got started.

Once they were lined up and ready, Lynn muttered, "Well, here goes nothing," and signaled the advance.

They had one last ring to deal with, TDMs that stood virtually *in* the fence line, which they'd left to deal with later last time so as not to get too close to the substation and trigger more glitches. Now those TDMs were the only targets left, so Skadi's Wolves advanced steadily. Lynn let them come within the natural aggression range of the protective Alpha Class TDMs, saving their bait markers in case they needed to lure out any stubborn nonaggressive types from inside the substation.

The line of mostly Jotnar, with a smattering of Spithragani, lumbered toward them. But between Edgar's Snazzgun, Lynn's Abomination, and Dan's Ambanese rifle, they killed almost all of them before they were in melee range. Lynn let Ronnie finish off the remaining Jotnar, just to give him something to do. Sometimes he still grumbled about the ranged fighters getting all the glory, but today he was unusually subdued. Or should she simply say focused on the mission? They circled the fenced in area, cleaning up every last red dot on their overhead that was within the area of the substation.

And then... nothing.

The hair on the back of Lynn's neck prickled as she gingerly walked right up to the substation fence and peered through the links, eyes searching for the telltale sparkling mist that would indicate an unknown TDM—something that would not show up on her overhead.

No Bunyips. No Hydras. Not even some sneaky Lectas or Lectors. No glitches, either.

Lynn pursed her lips. Then she sent a ping to Mrs. Pearson. *Are we still livestreaming?*

Asking her was easier than navigating out of the TD Hunter app to check her stream channel.

Yes, came back the answer.

Well, okay, then. So she couldn't give up just because her Larry senses were screaming at her that this was an ambush and she should get out of there now. Yes, Ghasts and Phasmas liked to sneak up on you, but Skadi's Wolves had advanced so much that those low class TDMs barely made them blink. Plus you could usually hear them coming.

"So, it's empty?" Edgar asked, coming up to stand beside her.

"No," Lynn said, chewing on her lip. "Something's up. I just haven't figured out what to do about it yet."

"Is there an unknown in there?" Dan asked, coming up on her other side and squinting hard, raising a hand to shade his eyes from the sun. "I don't see any mist."

"Want me to nuke it with some grenades?" Edgar asked, raising his Snazzgun.

"No," Lynn said absently, "let's not waste ammo, in case we need it soon."

"Okay, so what are we going to do, sit here and count daisies?" Ronnie asked, impatience creeping into his voice.

Lynn felt a weird sense of relief. *There* he was, good old annoying, rude Ronnie. At least if he was being a jerk he was okay, right?

"Line up, normal battle formation, ten feet from the fence," Lynn ordered, rather than respond directly to Ronnie's comment. She matched actions with words and backed up from the fence.

"Everyone ready?" she asked, looking both directions down their line.

"I'm ready for *pizza*!" Dan half shouted, half complained.

"Come on, Lynn, do it already," Ronnie yelled. "Why are we pussyfooting around?"

He's right, she told herself. She took a deep breath, aimed Abomination, and let loose a stream of fire right into the center of the substation.

A sound like a hundred shrieking Phasmas and roaring Rakshar nearly blew out her eardrums. And that's when all hell broke loose.

Chapter 8

ALL FIVE OF THEM FLASHED RED WITH DAMAGE AND LYNN'S health bar plummeted.

"Back up, back up *now*!!" Lynn yelled, forgetting to subvocalize.

She wasn't the only one. Ronnie was shouting incoherently in Lithuanian, probably cursing the fathers and forefathers of whatever was attacking them. All the noise nearly drowned out her command, but the guys were already stumbling back, and they quickly got themselves together and copied her quick backward trot to put some space between them and whatever-it-was in the substation.

Lynn swapped out Wrath for Bastion, and not a moment too soon.

The roar came again and *still* they all flashed with damage, all at once, which seemed impossible. But with Bastion's defensive buffs in play, the damage was survivable. That first hit had taken out over a third of her health in one massive blow.

What the heck was this thing?

Finally, *finally*, Lynn spotted something. The sparkling mist rose above the substation fence, faintly visible against the solid intense blue of the sky.

And then it kept rising.

"Holy shit!" Mack yelled. "It can fly!"

"Fire, for heaven's sake!" Lynn yelled. "Fire!"

She was already firing, and in her augmented vision the air

filled with streaks of blue, green, and yellow bolts, based on the type of ammunition everyone was using. Without any kind of visual, Lynn had no way of knowing if their shots were even hitting the thing.

"Hugo! How close does it have to be for you to start identifying it? We won't survive long enough to kill this thing if we can't see it!"

"Already working on it, Miss Lynn, but I will not be able to complete my analysis at this range."

Lynn didn't even have time to wonder if they would need to use bait to lure it close out of the sky when the mist started rushing toward them.

Fast.

"It's diving, everybody scatter!" Lynn yelled, raising Bastion above her head and staying exactly where she was. That *was* her job, after all.

"Miss Lynn! It is extremely unadvisable to—"

"Shut up, Hugo!" Lynn subvocalized, teeth gritted, still firing. "Wolves, hold your fire! As soon as it lands, hit it with everything you've got!"

She was taking a steady stream of damage, but Mack was already on it, funneling her Oneg. And it looked like none of the guys were taking damage anymore. Good. It was focusing on her.

She tensed, eyes locked on the mist rushing ominously toward her, bait at the ready. Just before it reached her, she dropped every bait marker she had right where she was standing and dove sideways, rolled to her feet, and sprinted away.

Damage hit her back, instantly slicing her health in half, and she felt a weird surge of nausea, as if her nerves were getting the better of her.

Keep it together, Lynn, she told herself, spinning to put Bastion between her and the TDM.

Shit, it didn't go for the bait, or at least it wasn't enough of a distraction to keep it from firing on her.

"Hugo! I need a visual, *stat.*"

Her augmented vision was full of flashes and explosions as Edgar, Dan, Mack, and Ronnie were bombarding the monster with everything they had. But still the mist kept coming in *her* direction.

"Lynn! Watch out!" Mack yelled.

Lynn rolled to the side as a Spithra filled the air where she'd just been with poison spit. The green sticky stuff covered the grass and gave off a billow of smoke that was so lifelike Lynn expected to smell the acidic stench burning her nostrils.

"Where the *shit* did that thing come from?" Lynn yelled, scrambling to her feet and trying to keep Bastion between her and the mist. Between blasting away three more Spithra that tried to rush her from behind, she glanced at her overhead and was horrified to see it full of red dots converging on their lonely little group.

"*Šūdas!*" Ronnie yelled, summing up Lynn's thoughts exactly.

Either new TDMs were *already* spawning in the area they'd cleared, *or* the whatever-it-was could somehow summon TDMs far outside the normal aggression range to come to its defense.

Both possibilities were bad.

Now they had a gathering mob of TDMs at their back *and* something trying its very best to incinerate them from their front. The low-level TDMs at their back wouldn't normally be a problem, but they could hardly turn around and deal with them.

Shit, shit, shit.

"HUGO!"

"Analysis complete, Miss Lynn!"

Never were sweeter words spoken.

Not that they made her feel any better as the mist surging toward her transformed in her augmented vision into the serpentine neck, spreading wings, and hulking body of a freaking *dragon*.

"Craaaaaap!" Dan yelled.

"*Chee-hooo*," Edgar hollered, probably just happy to have something to aim at. "Take *that*, you beastie!" He switched from plasma blast to flame thrower—did fire even *work* against dragons?—and went to town.

"Draca, Sierra Class 1 electrovore," Hugo rattled off, speaking fast and abbreviating his usual rundown of a newly discovered monster. "Attacks are firestorm, rending bite, tail pummel, and stomp. Full body armor. Stealth +20. Detection Level 40."

"But we're not Level 40," Mack wailed, struggling to keep up with Edgar guzzling ammo and Lynn guzzling Oneg.

"I told you it was unwise to approach the substation," Hugo said, his calm voice at odds with the chaotic situation.

"Later!" Lynn yelled, putting aside her own confusion at Sierra

Class 1. So, was it a boss? But it wasn't unique, so were there now Sierra class TDMs that weren't bosses? That was new, but then TD Hunter rarely announced updates and patches—*shit!*

Lynn lunged to the side to avoid the huge, roaring stream of orange fire that shot toward her. The Draca's mouth was open wide, gleaming teeth as long as Lynn's arm curving down into the open maw. It looked disturbingly similar to the dragon-headed muzzle of Abomination, which was currently pointed at the Draca and pouring fire into its eyeballs.

The damage didn't seem to faze it. Its body did flash with each hit, a visual indicator in the hunters' displays that it was, indeed, taking damage, even if they had no way of knowing how much damage each attack inflicted.

TDMs were amassing at Lynn's back and she had to turn sideways, Bastion held up between her and the Draca, Abomination pointed the opposite direction to take out some Rakshar that were getting dangerously close.

What in the freaking hell were they going to do?

"Afternoon, Skadi's Wolves. Lovely day for a hunt. Need an assist?"

"Derek?" Lynn croaked out loud in her shock. The greeting that sounded in her ear popped up a label at the edge of her display stating it was from the old Boss Bash 2.0 hunting group she'd created—and thought she'd deleted. Maybe she'd forgotten?

Sounds of shock and cheering were filling the group channel, coming from her guys who were understandably thrilled to not try and defeat this crazy new TDM by themselves.

"Yes!" Lynn subvocalized, risking a moment of inattention to scan her surroundings. There it was. An air taxi parked by the street curb at the edge of the field, currently disgorging the fully geared-up members of Team Light Brigade.

"Also, what in the *world* are you doing here?" She lost sight of them as she rolled to avoid another gout of flame from the Draca that was still pursuing her relentlessly, even though she was doing a fraction of the damage to it that Edgar and the others were.

"Oh, we were in town for something else when Crispy—I think he's a fan of yours, by the way—

"Ew! No, I'm not! I just can't figure out how to turn off these stupid stream notifications!" Crispy's whiny voice joined Derek's in the group channel, and Lynn grinned.

"Anyway, we saw you all go live, finished up our business, and thought we'd come over to say hello before we left town again."

"I told him it was the polite thing to do," Sonia's cool, smooth voice added.

"And here you are, having fun without us!" Hayek butted in, sounding genuinely scandalized.

"You are *welcome* to it, you freak of nature," Lynn subvocalized.

"Awww, she knows your real name," Santoro said, a grin audible in his voice.

"DeathShot," Lynn subvocalized, remembering this time to use Derek's handle, "we need Oneg, stat."

"Headed your way, RavenStriker," Derek replied.

"Dan, quit staring and kill these Phasmas mobbing me!" Ronnie snapped.

"Thanks, guys," Mack said. "We were almost out of Oneg."

"Team Light Brigade," Lynn said, backing up further as the Draca kept stomping toward her, "pair up with Skadi's Wolves and assist as needed. DeathShot, with me. Keep the Draca surrounded. Keep moving. Hopefully we can confuse it."

The giant dragon, its body festooned with alien-looking spines and darkly patterned armor plates, moved with heavy steps that she could almost feel vibrating the ground between them. Or was that Bastion vibrating in her hand from gush after gush of rushing flame? The augmented reality was so intense now she was imagining things, her brain creating stimuli to match what she expected.

Team Light Brigade was booking it across the field, and before she knew it, Derek was at her back, blazing away at the lower class TDMs surrounding them. Her overhead map on her display told her they weren't that thick, yet. But more were appearing at the far edges of her sensory range.

They needed to wrap this battle up and exit combat mode or their scores were going to take a nosedive. Or, at least, even more of a nosedive than they already had with that ambush from the Draca. Hopefully defeating the TDM, along with the bonus for discovering another unknown, would bump their scores back up.

High risk, high reward.

"Mack," Lynn said, "forget the Draca, focus on supplies, Edgar's using ichor like a hog. Ronnie, this bastard is fixated on me. Slice it and see if it reacts. If not, use your power up ability on it for max damage. And *be careful*. A direct hit from it might kill."

She was worried, sending Ronnie within feet of the huge beast. Mack's inexplicable seizure when they tried to kill Gyges under Connor's leadership was fresh on her mind. But the Draca wasn't a boss, and it really *was* fixated on her. Abnormally so.

The Draca kept advancing and Lynn kept falling back, moving in a wide circle, Derek keeping just ahead of her as he cleared the TDMs in their path. Much like with proper bosses, no TDMs got anywhere near the Draca, leaving Lynn free to focus on not dying.

"Edgar, switch to grenades! We don't have the ichor for flame and the Draca's armor might be immune to it."

"Can do, boss, *chee-hoo!*"

Well, at least Edgar was having a fun time.

The Snazzgun started making a rhythmic *clunk-pop* sound as Edgar launched grenade after grenade at the Draca.

It didn't even look at him.

Instead, it lunged forward and tried to bite Lynn's head off.

Lynn threw herself to the side, landing hard on the grass, Bastion still between her and the expected gout of flame that would soon follow. But no flame came toward her, just teeth. Really, really long teeth. Lynn ducked and shoved Bastion upward, deflecting the huge snout away from her face.

Then Derek was there, shooting the Draca point-blank in the eye and yelling at her to get up and get her precious "fanny" out of melee range.

The Draca didn't even glance Derek's way.

Lynn rolled away from another lunging bite, losing hold of Bastion and Abomination in the process. With her hands free, she popped to her feet and, since its head was now between her and her batons, ran toward the Draca's chest, figuring it would have to back up to reach her.

"*What in the everliving hell are you doing?*" Derek yelled out loud. Lynn thought she might have just given him a heart attack, based on his strangled tone.

"Trying to stay out of its sight line," Lynn subvocalized. "Quick, throw me my batons." She kept her gaze angled up, skipping back and forth to keep directly under the Draca's neck. If she ran out from under it now, it would flame or bite her before she could get out of range, and this close the damage would end her.

Derek deactivated one of his weapons, stowed the baton in its sheath, scooped hers up, and threw them to her one at a time, all while the Draca ignored him like he didn't exist.

"Hugo, what the freaking heck is wrong with this thing?" Lynn subvocalized. "Is this a game glitch?"

"I do not have sufficient data to make that determination, Miss Lynn. Might I suggest you focus on killing it?"

"Genius-level advice, Hugo. Really brilliant."

"I aim to please, Miss Lynn."

"DeathShot, get back before it changes its mind," Lynn subvocalized. Then she activated her weapons, this time Bastion and Wrath, and began stabbing the big ugly thing in the chest.

That, apparently, was too much for the Draca. It bent its neck nearly double trying to bite her, but she stuck close to its chest, Bastion held behind her head just in case, and kept stabbing. It abruptly stomped forward, perhaps trying to trample her with its big stumpy feet. It wasn't so quick, however, that she couldn't keep pace with it. Finally it gave a roar of frustration, crouched, and took flight.

"Everyone target the Draca, *now*! Kill it before it turns and flames us!"

Ten guns of varying size—twelve if you counted Mack's twin Desert Eagles and the two sweet Uzi-shaped pistols Santoro had—belched destruction at the fleeing Draca, which flapped giant wings as it rose. No backwash of air buffeted Lynn's face, but she could imagine it alongside the very real-sounding *thump-thump-thump* of its heavy wings. She'd switched Wrath to Abomination, keeping Bastion at the ready just in case, and was pouring fire into the Draca's belly. Any moment now, it would curl its head down and bathe them all in flame.

Except then it exploded into a Fourth-of-July-worthy display of sparks that rained down on them like falling stars.

Something small and hard smacked Lynn right in the forehead, and she went down on one knee, clutching her head, eyes squeezed tightly shut.

"Owowow!"

Hugo's voice filled her ears. "Taking you out of combat mode, Miss Lynn. Are you all right? Are you injured?"

"Something fell on me. What the heck *was* that?"

"Nothing connected to TD Hunter, I can assure you," Hugo said, as if offended that she might even think it.

"Lynn, are you okay?" Edgar's voice rang out across the field and soon she heard multiple people running through the ankle-high grass toward her.

Lynn slowly opened her eyes and gave her head a little shake, now that the initial wave of pain had passed. Edgar was kneeling in front of her, looking concerned, and the rest of the two teams were gathering around too.

"I'm probably going to have a headache, but other than that, I think I'm fine. Is my forehead bleeding?"

"No," Edgar said with a frown, "But you've got a mark on it, like something hit you. What happened?"

Lynn looked around her on the ground, finally spotting the culprit.

"There," she pointed, and Mack, who was closest, bent and picked it up.

"A drone?"

"A paparazzi drone, specifically," Lynn said grimly, glaring at it. "If it had been any other kind of drone I might have more than a headache."

The drone fit neatly in Mack's palm, the propellers on one side broken off, probably from hitting Lynn's head.

"What the heck!" Ronnie said. "Is someone trying to off you with a drone or something?"

The guys looked at each other, faces scrunched in varying expressions of confusion or disgust. Derek and his team, though, looked nonplussed. Maybe they hadn't heard what had been happening to Skadi's Wolves—well, mostly Lynn—over the past few weeks.

Lynn stood slowly, gaze casting further afield.

"Everybody spread out," she said. "Look for more drones."

The guys gave her funny looks, but the members of Light Brigade obeyed without a word.

They found eight more dead drones, all of them the small, palm-sized ones used by streamers everywhere. Lynn looked up, noting only one or two little drones still hovering off in the distance, no doubt capturing the bizarre display for the streams.

The larger, gray drones were nowhere to be seen.

"That is sooo weird," Mack said, nudging the pile of drones they'd made with a booted foot. "What do you think made them all malfunction like that, all at once?"

"A surge from the substation, probably," Dan said, shrugging.

Ronnie, though, didn't look convinced. He met Lynn's eyes with a dark expression, and she wondered if his wild theories were as insane as hers.

That Draca killed these drones. Or the TD Hunter game did.

The TDM dragon had been directly overhead. The drones had been directly overhead. Drones in the area that had *not* been directly overhead were still functioning just fine.

It couldn't be a coincidence.

Derek didn't seem interested in the strange phenomenon, or at least not as interested in it as he was in something else behind Lynn, in the direction of the road.

Lynn turned.

"Great," Hayek grumbled, *"civilians."*

"We *have* been streaming for a while," Mack pointed out, his grin contrasting with Hayek's sour expression. "Come on, they probably want our autographs."

"You guys go," Lynn said. "I'll call an air taxi so we can leave as soon as it gets here."

"I'll stay with you," Edgar rumbled, looking as suspicious as Hayek looked sour.

"You do that, buddy boy," Crispy said, slapping Edgar on the back as he passed, headed after Dan, Mack, and Ronnie. "I just *love* messing with their heads. Don't get to do it often enough."

"Crispus," Derek said, warning in his tone.

"Don't worry, boss. I'll be good, I promise," the man called over his shoulder. "I won't bite *anybody*, not unless they ask *real* nice."

"Sonia," Derek said.

"On it," his wife replied, and Lynn got the hilarious impression of a mom and dad with three unruly boys. Well, mostly unruly. Santoro seemed pretty level-headed. Maybe he was the oldest child. Which made Hayek and Crispy the middle and youngest, respectively.

"Is he usually like this?" Lynn asked Derek, watching Crispy greet the dozen or so spectators—mostly teens—who had gathered on the sidewalk to gape at the two teams of fully geared-up TD Hunter players.

"Hm. Worse, actually. We keep him in a box under the stairs when we're not working. Helps minimize the crazy, eh?"

Lynn's eyes widened and she looked sideways at Derek, only to realize his eyes were twinkling and one corner of his mouth was twitching. The snort from Santoro would have clued her in, too, and the way Hayek had one arm across his chest, his other arm propped on it with a hand over his mouth, hiding whatever expression was there.

She went back to watching her friends enjoy some well-earned fame. It wasn't her thing, but she didn't begrudge them the attention. Most likely the group of spectators had caught the tail end of their fight, watching through the Hunter Lens App. At least the app had done its job and no lens junkies had wandered right into the middle of the battle like oblivious, entitled idiots. Lynn had heard that some people who spent nearly all their time in virtual lost their sense of social awareness because they spent their waking days interacting with AIs and computer-generated environments that molded themselves around their users, never criticizing or correcting their behavior. After all, the customer was *always* right.

"So..." she began again, "you just *happened* to be in town, huh?"

"No, yeah, for sure. We have a contract with GForce Utilities. You wouldn't believe the number of outage incidents caused by pests chewing on things. We go all over, helping root out the problem. Cedar Rapids has been having its fair share of issues lately, so we've been back and forth."

Lynn raised her eyebrows, though she didn't comment. Derek seemed totally at ease, unfazed by her question.

"Well, thanks for the help. You really saved our bacon."

"Our pleasure," Derek said with a warm smile.

"We'd be even *more* pleased if there was *actual* bacon," Hayek commented more loudly than necessary.

"Our friend's ma makes amazing bacon-wrapped steak bites," Edgar said.

"Whaaat?" Hayek's eyes got round as saucers and he turned pleadingly to Derek. "We *have* to go meet their friend's ma."

"Not a chance," Derek said, not even looking at his teammate.

"Come on, boss," Santoro piped up. "Bacon-wrapped steak bites? We've got the time, don't we?"

"No, we don't," Derek said firmly, glancing at Lynn as he said it. "Apologies, I've tried to civilize them, but I think it's a lost cause, eh?"

"Don't look at me," Lynn said with a grin. "I've got my own circus to run. You should see Dan and Ronnie when they really get going."

"Maybe you need to invest in boxes for them, too," Derek said, completely deadpan.

Lynn burst out laughing, and even Edgar cracked a smile.

"Come on, you lot," Derek said, "Looks like the air taxis have arrived."

It took a combined effort to peel Dan, Mack, and Ronnie away from their fans, though said fans seemed ready to *run* away from Crispy, who was grinning like a crazy person. Which he very well might have been.

Skadi's Wolves and Light Brigade exchanged handshakes and heartfelt farewells, though the farewells were subvocalized in a group chat, since the dozen spectators were still standing there, staring at them—at Lynn, mostly, which made her skin crawl.

Lynn finally breathed a sigh of relief once they were in their taxi and headed out. Her mind was crowded with thoughts all clamoring for attention, but she had no chance to mull them over yet because Dan wanted to talk about their "amazeballs" fight, and it was as good a time as any to debrief. Normally they would descend on Happy Joe's after a battle, but they all agreed, while not explicitly saying so, to lay low for now, which Lynn appreciated. Kayla had said she was happy to host the team if they wanted to come over, so they decided to head to her place. Lynn was sure that Dan's badly hidden crush on Kayla had nothing to do with the decision.

Nor did bacon-wrapped steak bites.

"Why was it focusing on Lynn?" Mr. Krator asked.

The guy never slept and kept up constantly not only with TD Hunter but with all his other games, too. If Steve hadn't been former SPECOPS he'd have wondered how Mr. Krator did it. But Steve was quite familiar with the drive that enabled humans to push beyond their mental and physical limitations. Mr. Krator had that drive. So did Lynn.

"That's an interesting question, sir," Steve said. "We've seen it often enough that it's not an anomaly. TDMs tend to focus on her, and when we understand what TDMs are or their motivations, maybe we'll understand better, sir."

"Why the simple weapons?" Secretary Byerly asked, his voice coming from the holo screen at the head of the conference table. The vid of the newly identified Draca was interesting to several parties, though all Steve could think about was how Lynn had run straight toward danger *again*. That kid was going to get herself killed, and there was nothing he could do about it. "We can already fire dispersed TD particles. Why not just bombard the nodalities with drones?"

"Simplest answer, Mr. Secretary: humans survive better," Krator replied. "Longer answer... You have a physics degree. Discuss it with Dr. Quasnitschka.

"If we *could* go public, we'd have millions of very smart people all over the world working on advancing our weaponry. If for no other reason than self preservation, but since our research into weaponry has, oddly, positively influenced the advancement of computer technology, also for that.

"Since we cannot go public—everyone agrees the public reaction would be less than optimum—we are faced with a limited number of researchers trying to improve the weapons. They are doing well. The weapons we have now are frighteningly more powerful than what we started with. But..."

"We're finding bosses that require cannons, sir," Steve said. "And we're past pop-guns but not by much. And that's another reason we have to use humans. The range is just that short."

"So we put children's lives in danger to save the world," Secretary Byerly said, dyspeptically. "I wasn't expecting a dystopian novel as my main project."

"You want dystopia, sir?" Steve said. "Go play the TD Hunter-Warmonger crossover. That's what we face if we fail."

Monday morning Lynn rode to school with Kayla. Edgar wanted to meet them at Kayla's place and personally "escort" them. But Lynn told him that Matilda had bought her *and* Kayla mace to carry, so his "escort services" were unnecessary. Kayla giggled at that, and even Lynn managed to crack a smile. Edgar agreed, if grumpily.

They rode on Kayla's normal school air bus. They could have gotten an air taxi, but Lynn had thought long and hard about it the night before and decided she would rather live with possible harassment than with anxiety *about* harassment. The past year had taught her that facing her fears head on—from bullies to public opinion to team drama—gave her the confidence to overcome any obstacle life threw at her.

She'd done the hiding thing ever since she'd moved to Cedar Rapids, and she was done with that.

The ride to school was both nerve-wracking and oddly gratifying. She definitely got some mean looks, and one guy made a suggestive gesture at her, which she ignored completely.

Kayla didn't, though.

Kayla slapped him.

He was so shocked that, between the physical assault and Kayla's quiet threat to report him for sexual harassment, he did nothing but glare at her as she walked away.

The air bus monitor likely saw the whole thing, both the gesture and the slap, but said nothing. Lynn wasn't sure if that was good or bad but figured if the guy got written up then Kayla probably would too, so she kept her mouth shut.

Kayla led her to a back corner of the bus where she introduced Lynn to two other girls, both former Elena groupies she'd talked into walking away from Elena's clique. They were shy at first, but with Kayla there to grease the wheels, both were soon laughing and giggling about various school gossip. Lynn just smiled politely and stared out the window.

She let Kayla lead the way off the bus and to where they usually met up with the guys before class. It was hilarious how Kayla, petite and several inches shorter than Lynn, parted the masses of students with her confident stride and withering glare. Edgar spotted them coming first, probably because he was half a head taller than even Ronnie, who was the second tallest of their group. His dark face broke out into a wide smile when their eyes met, and Lynn's heart did a weird sort of flip-flop in her chest.

She ducked her head under the guise of rubbing her nose and hoped her face didn't look as pink as it felt.

"Here you go, boys," Kayla declared when they reached the guys. "Your captain safely delivered, just like I promised."

"What do you mean 'promised'?" Lynn asked, raising an eyebrow. "Do you guys have some sort of secret chat going or something?"

Her friends exchanged guilty looks.

Lynn rolled her eyes.

"You know I can walk myself to school like a big girl, thanks. I'm not five."

"Can't be too careful," Edgar said quietly, stepping in to close their little circle. "That stalker is still out there."

Lynn's skin felt clammy at the memory, but she took a deep breath and showed Edgar all her teeth.

"That's what the mace is for."

"Yeah," Edgar agreed, "but it would be better if you didn't have to use it."

"Would solve a lot of our problems, though, wouldn't it," Ronnie muttered. He glared at everyone who passed, as if humanity's mere existence was a personal insult.

That was pretty normal for Ronnie. He was *not* a morning person.

"What do you mean?" Mack said, pulling at his little goatee. It was starting to fill out a bit. Maybe. Or maybe that was just her brain looking for something nice to say about Mack's poor excuse for facial hair.

"I mean," Ronnie said, lowering his voice, "that if he was stupid enough to try and jump Lynn again and she maced the *shiknaskyle kalakutpisa* in his ugly little face, the cops could come haul him off to prison where he belongs."

"Good point," Dan said, looking thoughtful.

"No, *not* good point!" Kayla protested. "We're not putting Lynn in danger just to catch some creep. Shame on all of you!"

The class bell tone echoed through the hall, cutting off any further debate.

Lynn kept thinking about it, though, all day long.

After school, Lynn and Kayla headed back to Kayla's house instead of Lynn going off hunting. Matilda had spent the day with Drew, arranging things with the house's seller and the bank so that as soon as Lynn got home and changed clothes, they could head off to the real estate attorney's office. Edgar had wanted to tag along, and honestly Lynn would have loved to have him. But they had barely three weeks left until finals, and Lynn refused to monopolize Edgar's time when he should have been studying.

It was surreal, watching her mom sign page after page of legal documents that, after her eighteenth birthday, would make her an official homeowner. It was also pretty boring, and she was very glad to have her mom there to worry about it all so she could focus on school and hunting.

When the last form was signed and the check handed over to the seller, they all shook hands and Drew proudly presented them with their new house keys.

Then the real work began.

The seller had left some large pieces of furniture that were too much trouble to move and not nice enough to sell, like a large, well-loved sectional couch upstairs and another one in the den, a scuffed dinner table with chairs that had definitely seen better days, and a few wobbly bookcases. The appliances had also stayed with the house, though on closer inspection, it wasn't clear how much more life was in them.

Still, all in all, they only needed to make a few large purchases to make the house baseline livable, such as beds, dressers, some lamps and shelves, and the like. Matilda would scour the discount stores tomorrow for those items. Most of the furniture from their old apartment was old and beat up, and it was safer to stay away from their former home anyway because of the doxxing.

That evening, Kayla, along with Mr. and Mrs. Swain, went to Mr. Thomas' apartment in an extra-large air taxi to pick up all the Ravens' boxes and move them to the new house. Lynn was shocked at their willingness to help—she'd spent so long assuming she had no one to rely on but herself and her mom. But as Mrs. Swain put it, they'd been neighbors once, and she wasn't going to let a silly thing like distance keep them from being neighbors again. Lynn was pretty sure her mom teared up at that, though she hid it well.

Reluctantly Lynn let her mom unpack their essentials while she rushed through her most pressing homework. Then they both passed out, Lynn on the couch and her mom on a folding camp cot they'd borrowed from the Swains.

The next morning Lynn woke up late, did a modified workout in the mostly empty basement, and rushed to shower and get out the door. She didn't even have time for her usual "Back in Black" singalong in the shower to hype herself up to face the day. Her mom shoved a bag full of breakfast burritos at her, kissed her on the forehead, and sent her off.

When Lynn opened her front door—now *that* was a weird

feeling—she was greeted by the sight of Edgar sitting on her front porch.

"Edgar!" Lynn said, throwing up her hands.

He stood and gave her an apologetic little shrug, not really looking sorry.

"Better to ask forgiveness an' all that, yeah?" he said, badly hiding a smile.

Lynn made a face, wondering how likely it was that he would simply ignore her if she told him to chill out and stop being so protective. He'd probably pretend to try. He might even actually try.

But deep down, Lynn knew it wasn't in him to not stand by the people he loved.

Belatedly, Lynn realized what it was she'd just thought.

He stands by the people he loves.

That was swiftly followed by the memory of her mother's comment, leaping to the forefront of her brain like it had been lying in wait for another chance to be noticed.

Oh, come on, sweetie. He is so obviously over the moon for you.

"Uhhh, Lynn?" Edgar said, waving a hand slowly in front of her face. "You okay?"

Lynn shook her head, realizing she'd been standing there, frozen, staring at Edgar like he'd grown three heads.

Or maybe he'd had three heads all along and she'd just now realized it.

"You gonna yell at me some more, boss?" he asked in his best languid drawl, obviously trying to make her smile.

And darn it, she did.

"Nope, not this morning, because we're late for school. But *tomorrow*, when we're not late, I promise I'll yell at you extra to make up for it."

"Sounds like a plan," he said, grinning crookedly. He jerked his head toward the road. "C'mon. Air taxi's waiting."

Lynn shook her head but hurried down the steps anyway, letting Edgar fall in behind her.

Yeah, no way would he listen if she told him to stay home. And once she realized that she realized something else too: she didn't really want him to.

Go figure.

Lynn was distracted at school that day because her mom kept sending her pictures of her thrift store finds. The pings wouldn't come through during class—the school's mesh connections policed all traffic in and out and only allowed non-emergency contact between classes. In addition to basic furniture, Matilda found a weight rack missing only a few weights and a treadmill that looked like a New Year's optimism purchase—used a few times, collected dust for years, then finally shuffled off to a discount store.

Edgar continued to show up on Lynn's doorstep every morning that week. Between him, her friends at school, her team after school, and her mom at home, she was never alone. Lynn was not a fan of this new development, but she knew why everyone was hovering and tried not to be grumpy about it.
She coped by doing some extracurricular work in the evenings between bouts of homework. Drones falling from the sky onto their heads was *concrete*. It was an actual physical thing that everyone had seen. It wasn't in her head. But *why* had it happened? Why had *any* of the weird stuff connected to TD Hunter happened?
She had no idea and was afraid to go the Ronnie route and start making up theories. So instead, she did some of that research she kept telling herself she would do. There was no time for a true deep dive, but she puttered around on various military forums she'd been a part of for years doing research for her Larry Coughlin persona. She also cautiously sought out some less reliable but far more fertile sources of information in various conspiracy theory groups she always heard Ronnie talk about. It wasn't that she expected to find answers there, but she was curious what people's theories were.
On the military forums, things were pretty muted but telling if you knew what to look for. Units called up, but not overseas. Equipment and assets disappearing. Temporary reassignments with no explanation. There wasn't much theorizing as to why, at least not by active-duty members. They knew better than to run their mouths. But some retired guys who loved to hear themselves talk went on about a secret energy war with China. They claimed the US was beefing up its infrastructure assets and deploying troops to protect critical choke points. With all the military intel personnel getting moved around they figured there were secret hacking units or spy cells being deployed to keep tabs on what China was doing.

The civilian groups were going on and on about energy grid warfare too, but talked more widely about all the usual suspects: Russia, Iran, North Korea, etc. People were divided on whether there would be any physical war with boots on the ground, or if it would turn into the second Cold War where the threat was crashing critical infrastructure from afar rather than launching nuclear missiles.

And then, of course, there were the crazies ranting about alien invasions, which was standard. It was *always* about the alien invasion.

Lynn tried to poke around on news sites for other countries, curious what was going on elsewhere besides the US. What she found was confusing. If the US and China were in an energy or technological Cold War, why were *all* other countries around the globe seeing increasing problems and failures in systems that used to be reliable? Was there anything to the theory of some anarchist combining malware with AI to create an intelligent virus that was strategically spreading across the globe, attacking all countries indiscriminately?

Some of the talking heads theorized about source code, and how most AI around the world had been developed by a few select mega tech corporations. So, if there was some flaw in the source code, maybe that could cause a large array of problems across scattered systems and locales. That didn't account for everything, though, like drones dropping out of the sky. Even if their AI had gotten scrambled, they'd still have power. Ditto with some of the airbus crashes and power outages she'd heard about. Was it *just* a coding problem? Or were there bad actors out there using EMP guns?

Or maybe it was absolutely nothing but blowing smoke. Maybe there had always been problems with infrastructure, and the intense, 24-7 news cycle and streams were amplifying people's fears, causing a self-fulfilling prophecy. Maybe humanity was simply growing too energy hungry too fast, causing a pesky blackout here or a grid failure there in every country around the world.

Whatever it was, it did nothing to allay Lynn's fears beyond convincing her there was no way she'd be able to figure out what was going on in her small corner of the world. So instead of letting it keep her up at night, she firmly put the strange coincidences from her mind and focused on the responsibilities in front of her.

On Thursday morning when she came downstairs from her shower, she found Edgar sitting at the kitchen island eating bacon and scrambled eggs that Matilda kept piling on his plate like he was a starving waif she was desperate to fatten up.

Lynn stopped dead and glared at the two of them.

"Mom!"

"Yes, dear?" Matilda said, all innocence and sweetness.

Lynn gestured helplessly at Edgar, but Matilda simply shrugged.

"What was I supposed to do, sweetie? Let him keep sitting on our doorstep like a wayward orphan? What would the neighbors think?"

"That he was a friend waiting to go to school with me," Lynn said, but there was no real bite to her words. She sighed, rubbed her temples, and went to sit beside Edgar at the island where her mother had already placed a second plate piled high with bacon and eggs.

A few minutes later, when Edgar slid off his chair to go put his dishes in the sink and had his back turned, Matilda locked eyes with Lynn, jerked her head in Edgar's direction, and mouthed "*grandchildren.*"

Lynn choked on her eggs, spraying a mouthful of half-chewed yellow bits across the entire island.

Needless to say, she was once again distracted at school, though for entirely different reasons this time. In fact, it took her math teacher three times saying her name before it registered, and Lynn looked up at him near the end of her calculus class.

"I just got a ping from the principal. He would like to see you in his office right away."

Whispers broke out between the other students and a sliver of fear cut its way along the inside of her chest. She stamped down on it with furious determination.

"Why, what's wrong?" Lynn asked with forced calm.

"Nothing to worry about, Miss Raven, he would just like to speak to you. Go ahead, all your assignments will be in the class portal."

Lynn gathered up her things and her bag and left at a measured, confident pace, even though she could feel every eye in the room drilling a hole in her back. Most of them were fueled by curiosity, but she knew at least three of them were full of worry.

"Principal Charles wanted to see me?" Lynn said when she made it to the central offices and approached the vice principal's desk.

The vice principal was quiet for a moment as she pinged her superior, then Principal Charles came out of his office holding a nondescript bubble mailer with a printed label.

He held it up, his expression tense.

"This was just delivered by courier. The courier was instructed to put it directly into your hands. I sent him away, obviously, and considering, erm, recent events, I called the police. They're on their way to come pick it up, and I felt it was incumbent on me to, well, inform you of the situation."

Fear niggled at her composure like a predator clawing at a turtle hiding in its shell. So she stood up straighter, held out her hand, and said, "Give it to me."

The principal hesitated, but at Lynn's firm look he finally held it out.

"It's evidence, Ms. Raven, so I don't think you should—"

Lynn shoved a finger under one flap and tore.

"—open it."

"The police can have it after I see what's inside. This is my safety at stake. I'm not going to bury my head in the sand."

She opened the envelope gingerly, in case it was booby-trapped in revenge for the hole she'd stabbed in her stalker's side. Instead, she caught sight of something strappy and lacy.

She nearly threw up in her mouth.

Taking a deep breath, she peeked again, and the only other thing she saw were some crumpled silk rose petals and a folded piece of paper. Though disgust pulled her mouth into a grimace, she reached in gingerly and pulled out the letter. Printed text crowded both sides of the page like the author had no idea what proper font size and spacing was.

If it really was from Mr. Vulvx829, it was possible he'd never printed a thing on paper in his life, not if he lived in virtual all the time. Lynn steeled herself and skimmed the letter, her eyes skittishly jumping over entire sentences, actively *not* reading it aloud in her head and trying not to absorb a single word of it. She was looking for names, addresses, any clue that might shed light on her stalker's identity. When she turned the page over, the sight of numbers caught her eye and she didn't bother skimming the rest of the letter, focusing instead on the bottom of the page.

You sick, stupid bastard, she thought.

The moron had included several means of contact over the mesh web, apparently delusional enough to still think Lynn wanted to talk to him if only he could get past her evil, oppressive gatekeepers.

She quickly memorized the information and returned the paper to the package, then laid the package gingerly on the vice principal's desk.

Curiosity burned in the principal's eyes, but he was smart, or at least professional, and kept his mouth shut.

"The police can take it. I hope it leads them right to the bastard's front door."

"We can all hope that," Principal Charles said, nodding a little too eagerly. He was probably worried Matilda was going to call him again and chew him out for something he'd done, or failed to do, when it came to protecting her daughter. Lynn almost pitied him.

"We will, of course, inform school security to be on guard for trespassers and loiterers, and have them personally escort any non-employee adults who need to enter the school. Our students' safety is our top priority."

Lynn smiled to herself, knowing the principal hoped she would pass that tidbit on to her mother. Matilda certainly left an impression when she wanted to be remembered.

"Thank you, Principal. Can I go back to class now?"

Principal Charles nodded in dismissal and she headed back toward her math class in a daze, feeling the whole situation was surreal.

Was this really happening to her? How had her life changed so quickly? She had a house, now, for goodness' sake. Her mom was moving to day shift—she'd told Lynn last night that she was being fast tracked to become the Charge Nurse. Apparently the higher ups had been wanting her to accept a promotion for a while, but she'd always preferred working directly with incoming patients. Lynn was happy for her, but it was a big change for both of them. Not to mention Lynn's precipitous fame, the fact that she'd regained her best friend, and Edgar...well...

The bell rang just as she was getting back to her classroom, and her teammates were the first people out the door.

"Lynn!" Edgar said, hurrying over. His eyes looked her over from head to toe as if he expected her to have been jumped on her journey to the principal's office. "Are you okay? What happened?"

Lynn shook her head at him and the other guys as they crowded around.

"Not now," she said, eyes darting toward the stream of students coming their way. She didn't want to tell them about the package at all—they would all freak out, of course. But she knew they would push until she told, so she was going to wait until lunchtime at least when they could get a table in the corner and have some privacy.

At lunch, just as she had predicted, they all freaked out. For a minute there she was afraid Edgar was going to flip the entire table. Ronnie got even darker and more angry-looking, and Dan and Mack exchanged worried looks. Dan recovered the fastest, and managed to wheedle the details of the letter out of her—the contact details, of course. Not the... other stuff.

Kayla joined them a little later, and once she noticed the grim, silent faces around the table, she threatened to strangle every one of them unless they told her what was going on. Lynn gave her an extremely abbreviated version, but even that made Kayla slap her hands over her wide-open mouth as if to hold in a scream.

"We should all just forget about it," Lynn said, resolutely starting on her boring salad with extra chicken and hard-boiled eggs on top. "The police will find him, I'm sure, and we can forget any of this ever happened." She dreaded telling her mom, but knew she had to, for her own safety. She also needed to update Mrs. Pearson. Swallowing her reluctance, she sent them each separate pings. She included a bit more detail in her message to Mrs. Pearson, including the contact information she'd memorized. If anyone could light a fire under the police department's rear to find the stalker, it was GIC and their threat of legal action. To her mother she only said the stalker had mailed her something to the school, so the school was going to beef up security, and she promised to stay with the guys at all times so that her mom wouldn't worry. Well, any more than she was already worrying, at least.

The weather turned overcast and rainy in the afternoon, and Lynn reluctantly called off hunting. They were close to hitting Level 40—quite close after their bonuses for discovering and killing the Draca. But she would stay nervous until they'd all reached max level. In the meantime, they had mountains of homework to do.

When school let out, Matilda surprised them with a ping inviting the guys over to the new house for snacks and study time, since they couldn't hunt. They piled into an air taxi which Lynn directed to the new place instead of a prime hunting location. When they arrived, Matilda led them down to the basement, acting entirely too casual as she went.

They found out what she'd been up to when they reached the bottom: somehow she'd managed to outfit the basement den as a mostly functional rec room in a single day. There was no snack bar, of course—that would take some custom work by a building contractor. But there was a fold-out table with pop and snacks, an honest-to-God foosball table, and a few old, first-generation body-mold chairs in front of the crown jewel of the basement: a giant wall screen that spanned half the room.

Lynn was speechless.

"I figured you all needed somewhere to relax and study for finals," Matilda said, before shooting each of them a stern look. "And *no* gaming until your homework is done!"

The guys stared around with jaws hanging almost to the floor. Then Mack turned to Lynn's mom and seized her in a spontaneous hug that surprised a soft "oof" out of her. Dan was close behind, though he was more polite about it and stuck to a side hug, before moving over so Edgar could do the same. Ronnie didn't move in for a hug, but he shoved his hands into his pockets and gave her an awkward thank you, eyes wandering the room instead of looking at her as he spoke. Matilda received it all graciously, then shooed the boys off to the snack table.

"Mom...I—"

"Oh, don't thank me, honey," Matilda said, gathering her into a dignified side hug instead of her usual enveloping embrace. "It was *your* money that paid for it."

Lynn snorted and shook her head. She appreciated that Matilda hadn't brought up the stalker's package at school—everything that could be done was being done, so she didn't even want to *think* about it. But she also suspected that this den project was her mom's way of coping. Plus it gave her mom leverage to keep Lynn safely inside and with people at all times.

"While I've got you here, though," Matilda said, "I do want to make sure we're on the same page as far as, ahem, physical contact goes."

Lynn's brow scrunched down and she pulled far enough away to give her mom a sideways look.

"Uh, come again?"

"We don't need to have 'The Talk' again, do we?" Matilda asked, eyebrows rising.

"Ew! No!" Lynn hissed, glancing nervously at the snack table where the guys were busy fighting over who got which party-sized bag of chips, because apparently sharing wasn't a thing. "Are you implying...oh, Mom, that's gross! They're my *teammates*. And this is one big open room! What do you think we could possibly *do*?"

Matilda shook her head, chuckling.

"There's a bathroom down here, too, missy, so I don't want to hear it. I'm a nurse. I know *exactly* what sorts of things teenagers get up to if given half a chance."

"That's *dumb* teenagers, Mom. I'm not *dumb*," Lynn said with such fervor that her mom laughed.

"That's what they all say, isn't it? My point is that as long as you are a minor, the same rules apply here as we've always had at our apartment."

"Okay, Mom, I *get* it. Please stop talking now!"

"All right, all right," Matilda said, holding up her hands. "I'm done. Pretty soon you'll be an adult and I won't even be able to pull the 'my house, my rules' card anymore, seeing as how *you* will be the homeowner. Maybe I'll retire and sit around watching K-pop and eating fudge all day and *you* can be the breadwinner."

Lynn shook her head, grinning, and gave her mom a playful shove.

"Yeah, yeah. Get out of here, Mom. We've got studying to do."

"Have fun," Matilda called as she headed for the stairs. "I've only got a few more days off until they put me to work *supervising*, ugh." She shook her head sadly, as if she couldn't believe the depths to which she had stooped. "I've still got holes to spackle, showers to re-caulk, a ceiling fan to replace, and a lot of painting to do. I'll be upstairs if you need me!"

"Uh, do you need any help?" Lynn called after her, feeling a twinge of guilt.

Her mother's voice drifted down the stairs.

"Are you serious, child? Please graduate high school *first*, *then* you can worry about helping me do home renovations."

Lynn snorted again and muttered, "Yes, ma'am."

"Hey, your ma need some help?" Edgar asked, coming up to Lynn holding an open bag of kimchi kettle corn and popping pieces into his mouth whenever it wasn't occupied with talking.

"No, she says we have to graduate high school before we're allowed to worry about her."

"You know," Edgar said, "my ma has a whole work party of free labor in our house, I'm sure she'd be happy to lend them to your ma for a day or two as long as your ma feeds 'em."

Lynn made a face and shook her head.

"Edgar, I've *met* your siblings. They're like a pack of wolf pups: incredibly cute and infinitely destructive. I'm pretty sure they'd cause more problems than they'd solve."

"Eh, probably," Edgar agreed, then tossed a piece of kettle corn into the air and caught it in his mouth.

With some concerted effort, they got down to business and started chipping away at homework. Dan was prone to being distractible, but they all had their own earbuds and AR displays to link to their school portal, so they were able to spread out and get their work done without distracting each other. Lynn suspected that Dan, Mack, and Ronnie were likely sharing answers in their own private chat, based on the subtle body cues she knew indicated someone was subvocalizing. Humans were used to talking with their voice *and* their body, and you had to specifically concentrate on *not* moving to subvocalize to someone you could see without unconsciously using body language as well.

Regardless, they were big boys, and would do whatever-it-was regardless of her opinion. Plus they'd likely been doing the same thing since middle school anyway, Dan and Ronnie since their elementary days.

Edgar was different. He sat apart from the other guys and seemed completely focused on his work. Lynn sat near him—but not too close. He'd asked her for help with school in the past, not because he lacked intelligence, but because he conceptualized things differently than most people and she seemed able to explain sticking points in a way that made sense to him. She hoped her presence sent the right mix of encouraging signals without being insulting.

Or looking like she was trying to come on to him, which she didn't know how to do even if she'd wanted to.

Friday was a repeat of Thursday, minus the package and call to the principal's office. Lynn couldn't help wondering if her stalker was watching the school. Did he have a way of tracking private air taxis? The rain stuck around so they focused on homework again after school since the weekend was supposed to be clear.

The guys huddled even closer this time, and Edgar eventually joined them, making Lynn suspicious they were doing something other than school. But she kept her nose out of it and focused on writing halfway intelligent essay answers for her global studies class.

Near the evening, though, with Matilda puttering around upstairs fixing supper, Ronnie abruptly stood up and cleared his throat.

Lynn looked over at him and raised an eyebrow.

"Uh...Lynn. Could we, um, talk to you?"

Lynn's eyebrow rose higher.

"Sure. Go for it."

When she didn't move, Ronnie cleared his throat again and motioned for her to join the guys' little powwow on the couch.

She looked at Edgar, wondering what in the world was going on.

"Come on, boss," he said, motioning as well. "We all took baths this morning, we don't smell too bad."

Lynn choked on a laugh and reluctantly went over to the sectional, though she didn't sit down. She crossed her arms and eyed her four friends who, to a man, looked as fishy as an ocean trawler full of tuna.

Chapter 9

"All right. Spill," she said. "What's going on?"

The other three guys looked at Ronnie, who was still standing. Ronnie, caught in the spotlight, fingered the hem of his T-shirt, as if he didn't know what to do with his hands, and he kept meeting her eyes and glancing away. There was a pink tinge to his cheeks and the tops of his ears, which would have been adorable if Ronnie's personality hadn't been the polar opposite of all synonyms even remotely related to adorable. Eventually he cleared his throat again and straightened his shoulders, steeling himself for something.

Lynn wasn't sure if she was more curious or terrified to find out what it was.

"So, uh, we've talked about it, and we've decided that it's time to take matters into our own hands."

Lynn's eyebrows rose into her hairline, but she kept her mouth shut, fascinated to see where this was going.

Ronnie faltered and glanced at Edgar, who shook his head.

"Uh-uh, bro. This was *your* idea. You tell her."

Ronnie's idea? That sure boded well...

"Yeah, so," Ronnie began again, rubbing the back of his neck, "with the contact information you got from that rat bastard, we figure we can send him a message pretending you want to meet him, pick somewhere easy to surprise him and box him in, and then citizen's arrest the freak so the police can throw him in jail where he belongs and we can stop worrying you're going to get assaul—"

"Shut up, moron," Edgar snapped. "She doesn't need you to bring up that shit."

Lynn thought she might have permanently lost her eyebrows in the wilderness of her hair; they'd been up there so long and didn't seem like they were inclined to come down any time soon. She stared at each of the guys, in turn, completely speechless.

Message? Surprise? Citizen's arrest?

All of the guys were staring back now, their expressions ranging from Mack's half determined, half terrified lip-gnawing to Edgar's calm but dead serious look he got whenever he made up his mind about something. Dan seemed oddly hyped, as if excited at the thought of finally getting to use the kung fu moves he'd been watching obsessively all his life. And Ronnie? Ronnie was angry. But not, for once, at her. There was also a gaunt, haunted look lurking in his eyes that Lynn could only wonder about.

"Okaaay," she said, propping her hands on her hips. "First off, you're all crazy. Batshit crazy."

Edgar smiled dangerously, no doubt noting that her first words had not been *"no, absolutely not."*

"Second of all, why the heck would we do something so stupid? The police have the same info we have. I'm sure they'll figure out this guy's real name and address and arrest him in a couple of days."

Ronnie shook his head.

"I've been looking for this guy since GIC first mentioned the stalker-y messages you were getting."

"*What?*" Lynn said, a dangerous note in her voice.

Ronnie put up his hands.

"I didn't read any of the messages, I promise. I mean, not really. I didn't dwell on the details, just skimmed stuff for clues. I swear I didn't look at *anything* else in your message accounts, cross my heart and hope to die."

Lynn's adrenaline spiked through the roof until she remembered that GIC had no idea about her Larry Coughlin alter ego and had no access to any of her WarMonger or related accounts. So what had Ronnie done? *Hacked* her stream messages?

Should she strangle Ronnie? Maybe. She would wait to hear the rest of what he had to say before deciding for sure.

"So, you hacked into my personal messages—"

"No!" Ronnie shook his head. "I mean... not really. I got Mrs. Pearson to give me remote access to her workstation one evening so I could show her something 'important' I wanted her to do with my stream channel, and then I just, um, authorized my stream profile to access the profiles GIC manages for us, including yours. You can revoke access any time, I promise. I didn't really hack anything."

Lynn tried to relax her jaw, which she'd clenched so hard her teeth were beginning to ache. She must have had her dead-eyed Larry face on, because Ronnie swallowed hard and it looked like a bit of sweat was breaking out on his forehead.

"Dan helped," he croaked, as if that made the situation any better.

"Hey, it was *your* idea!" Dan protested. "I just lent my hacking expertise—I mean, not to hack *your* stuff, Lynn. Just the creep's stuff," Dan hurried to add, stumbling over his words. "And we couldn't have done it without Elliot from science class. He has *maaad* skills, I'm telling you. I'll bet you a 1972 mint condition copy of *Fist of Fury* that GIC and the cops have no one who can do what we can do. I mean, come on, they're *adults*. We've been doing this stuff since we were, like, three."

Lynn pursed her lips, but jerked her chin at Ronnie, silently granting him permission to continue making a case as to why she shouldn't strangle him.

"So, uh," Ronnie said, then swallowed again before getting back into stride. "This creep is good. He's left no crumb trail, and we haven't been able to back trace any of his messages. They all lead to dead ends, and we were trying to, uh, avoid committing any serious felonies ourselves, haha." He laughed weakly, saw Lynn fail to smile, and hurried on.

"Anyway, the police *might* be able to pressure data companies to hand over this guy's identifying information, but it'll take them weeks or months to cut through the red tape, and there is *no way* we're going to sit by that long and give this creep another chance to jump you. That's insane. I mean, if he'd knocked you out or tased you or something, he might have done... *things*, and—"

Lynn waved her hand sharply, cutting Ronnie off.

"Don't," she said quietly, knowing better than to even *think* about that sort of possibility. "So why the *hell* do you think it's a good idea for me to make *contact* with that sick bastard and meet him *face to face?*"

"*Us*," Ronnie said, slapping his chest with both hands then gesturing at the rest of the guys. "Not *you*. Good grief, Lynn, we're not suicidal. Your mom would *literally* skin us alive if we put you in any danger. Thanks, but I'll take my chances with deranged stalkers."

Lynn blinked, shocked speechless.

"You... *you* want to track down an insane attempted kidnapper and citizen's arrest him... for *me*?"

She stared at him, trying to bore into his brain with her eyes and figure out what in the world was going on in there. She knew why Edgar would go off the handles and attack any threat to her well-being. But why would *Ronnie* of all people put himself in danger for *her*?

Ronnie's words from last year rang in her ears:

...you're an emotional girl who couldn't keep it together. You got scared and pulled out! You have no idea how to be on a team...

...you're just a noob wannabe we let tag along because we needed another player! You're not even a real gamer!

She's a liability and I won't play with someone we can't trust. I want her off the team!

Those words had been seared into her memory, though she did her best to keep the memories buried for her own mental well-being.

Maybe her long-suppressed anger and righteous accusation showed in her face, because Ronnie swallowed even harder. But instead of dropping his eyes and muttering some excuse, he stood up taller and held her gaze.

"Why? Because we're a team, and I won't abandon my team."

Again.

The unspoken word hovered in the air between them, burning them both with its heat.

So, this was all about shedding guilt? Make this grand gesture, and then he'd consider himself off the hook for all the shit he'd ever pulled?

No, she didn't think so—

"We're not asking your permission," Ronnie said, perhaps in response to the way Lynn's expression had hardened. "We're doing this because it's the right thing to do. That creep assaulted you, is obviously planning to do it again, and we're not gonna stand for it. I might not be able to pound Connor's face into the dirt because he's too smart to get his hands dirty, but Edgar witnessed this guy assault you, so by law we're allowed to make a citizen's arrest. Believe me, I've done all the research. We're not breaking the law and we won't get in trouble. This is the right thing to do."

Lynn raised an eyebrow, wondering if the allowances around citizen's arrests included luring the perpetrator out on false pretenses. And if "won't get in trouble" included parental trouble, or just legal trouble. She could already imagine what the "adults" would say. And the list of a thousand reasons why this was foolish, dangerous, and irresponsible.

She glanced at Edgar.

"Why not just tell the police all this so *they* can lay in wait for him once you've dangled the bait?"

Ronnie shook his head, mouth twisting into something bitter and brittle.

"There's no telling what they'll do. I don't trust the police as far as I can throw them, not with—well..." He trailed off, glancing at Edgar, and Lynn wondered how many times Edgar had called the police on his dad. And what about Ronnie and that black eye? Where had he gotten it? A klutzy accident? Or had someone given it to him?

"Whoever lays the trap, us or the police, we only have one shot at this," Ronnie said doggedly, expression dead serious. "Once this creep figures out we're on to him, he could disappear for months, *years*, stalking you from the mesh web only to come out of the woodwork when you least expect it. There's *no way* we're letting that happen. Not when we can do something to stop it."

"That sounds like a pretty good argument to let the police handle it," Lynn said dryly. "They have more experience and better resources. Unless—" She put up a finger as Ronnie opened his mouth, cutting off whatever hot retort he'd prepared. "*Unless* you agree to use *me* as the bait."

"*No*," Edgar snapped, the sound rumbling like a feral growl in his chest.

Lynn crossed her arms again.

"Then I'm marching upstairs right now and telling Mom about this whole moronic plan. She'll tell the police *and* all your parents, and that will be that. She'll probably put a tracker anklet on me, too, knowing her."

Edgar and Ronnie glared daggers at her, and she glared right back.

"If this is the only chance we have," she said quietly, "then the *only* smart thing to do is for me to be there personally to make sure he's lulled into a false sense of security and doesn't sniff it out as a trap. You can arrange everything, I don't care. Find the perfect spot, somewhere Edgar can hide right behind me so he can jump out and beat that bastard to a bloody pulp if the creep so much as lays a finger on me. Do whatever you want. But *I'm* going to be there. I'm going to look that freak in the face, smile, and burn his eyes out with *this*."

She flicked the canister of mace out of her pocket and held it up, pointing it threateningly at each of the guys in turn.

They flinched back, then looked at each other. Dan and Mack seemed undecided and kept their mouths shut. Ronnie and Edgar, the obvious ringleaders, locked eyes for a long moment. Then Edgar nodded.

"Deal," he said, grinning at her like a wolf who'd just caught scent of its prey.

Ronnie and Dan did all the prep work. "Mr. Vulvx829" responded almost immediately to their initial dangle of bait from a new, anonymous account that "Lynn" said she'd created to "escape the clutches of her jailers." But it took him longer to respond when "Lynn" suggested they meet. Surprisingly, it was Ronnie who cautioned patience. They had their target in their sights, and if he'd learned anything from gaming it was that people who jumped the gun never won.

The stalker finally replied in the middle of that next week, sending her an address to come to. Lynn was initially excited, hoping he'd been stupid enough to send them his home address. Nope, it was a seedy hotel. Based on how rundown and grimy the place looked, she wouldn't have been surprised if it was a prostitution hotspot. Ew.

"Lynn" countered with the suggestion of a bar in downtown Cedar Rapids. It was a nice enough area, but there were distinctly dark alleys to the side and behind the bar, and "Lynn" suggested they meet in one of those to have some "privacy."

The tension of waiting for a response frayed everyone's nerves, but Skadi's Wolves went on hunting as much as they could while focusing mainly on school. The guys stayed occupied by arguing constantly over the merits of various weapons, augments, and attack strategies, not to mention their obsession with the leaderboards. Players' ranks changed constantly, sometimes minute-to-minute, since TD Hunter was played all around the world in every time zone, and every battle influenced a person's scores. Dan and Ronnie had notifications set up on their LINCs so they'd see as soon as so-and-so had passed what's-his-name, or so they could imagecapture their display if they broke the top one hundred on an obscure stat they'd been working to advance on.

Lynn tried to limit how often she checked the leaderboards, for her own sanity. Beyond overall team score, overall individual score, and her kill-to-damage ratio, she rarely checked her ranking, unless she was trying to gauge the effectiveness of a new move or team tactic she was testing. She had found that the less time she spent hunting, the more she was tempted to waste precious energy obsessing over her scores. Their current de-emphasis on hunting made Lynn antsy, but finals were in just a few weeks, whereas the TD Hunter National Championship wasn't until the middle of June. They had time. Not much, but some.

Meanwhile, Matilda was settling into her new day shift. She drank entirely too much coffee to be healthy—by her own admission—but she was adapting. Thankfully, Lynn's school schedule meant she left about the same time as her mom, and she had the guys to hang out with until her mom got off shift every evening. It was sort of a moot point anyway, since their den had become the unofficial Skadi's Wolves hangout. Lynn didn't miss the fact that her mom kept it stocked with copious amounts of beef jerky, bananas, nut mixes, granola bars, energy drinks, and pop. Enough for five hungry teenagers, to be exact.

Nobody complained, of course.

When they finally got a reply from Mr. Vulvx829, it was equally relieving and nerve-wracking. He'd agreed to the meeting place, though he insisted on a later time—*after* the sun had set and when underage teens hanging around a bar would likely raise eyebrows. Fortunately, there was a coffee shop across the street with big glass windows.

Dan sent the final "acceptance" message, and they all got down to business discussing their attack plan and exactly what each person would do in various contingencies if things went sideways.

Saturday night arrived.

They wore their TD Hunter gear—all skintight, tough fabric

that would give no purchase and would protect them from minor scrapes and bruises. No backpacks. No batons. There was a fine line between a citizen's arrest and a lynching.

Lynn braided her hair into a tight coil around her head, tucking in the ends and using liberal amounts of her mom's hairspray to make things stiff and secure. She slid a palm-sized canister of mace into each of her thigh sheaths that normally held her batons.

They met at Lynn's house beforehand to make sure Matilda saw them all dressed up to go hunting and wouldn't think anything of them staying out later than usual—the championship was weeks away, after all.

Everybody switched their smart fabric TD Hunter uniforms to their default settings of boring black with red and blue piping, and they all wore baggy jackets and hoodies to further obscure them. With the ubiquitousness of AR and even VR interfaces in public, nobody would look twice at a bunch of teenagers with tinted AR glasses ignoring everything around them.

Ronnie and Edgar had scoped out the bar and alley earlier in the week and Edgar found a place to wedge himself between the wall of the alley and the dumpster where nobody would see him in the dimness after night had fallen. They all took the same air taxi to an AR/VR arcade a few streets down from the bar. From there, Edgar peeled off from the group. With several hours still left before the appointed meeting, he was going to casually walk to the bar, slip into the alley, and hunker down in his hiding place. An hour before the meeting, Lynn and the rest of the guys took an air taxi to the coffee shop across the street, where Ronnie, Dan, and Mack got out and went to find a corner table where they could see the alley across the street but couldn't easily be seen from the outside.

Lynn stayed in the air taxi and sent it off to a random destination just to kill time. She'd wanted to wait at the arcade, but Edgar flatly refused to let her wait around anywhere by herself.

The next thirty minutes, alone, were some of the most nerve-wracking of her life. Her stomach was tied up in painful knots and she had to do *something* to keep her mind from reliving the terrifying memories of her assault, not to mention the horrifying mental images that sick man's ranting had seeded in her brain.

But she was alone in body only. The guys kept up a constant

stream of subvocalized chatter in their usual group chat, and everyone had emergency apps installed on their LINCs with trigger words preprogrammed to connect directly with the city's police and emergency services.

Lynn wished she could work on homework or think about something unrelated, but her Larry brain wouldn't let her do anything less than obsessively review their plan, poking it every which way looking for flaws. When she'd done that half a dozen times, she started going through the self defense moves she'd been studying for the past week, mentally walking herself through each escape move and defensive strike again and again and again.

The guys occasionally checked in on her, forcing her to say something so they knew she was still there. Otherwise she would have stayed completely silent.

Thirty minutes until the designated meeting time, Lynn had the air taxi drop her off at the bar. She went straight into the alley and took up a casual position leaning against the brick wall mere feet from the ally's dumpster. She'd left her ratty hoodie in the air taxi—it was disposable, and she didn't want to give her stalker an easy handle to grab her—so her heart was in her throat, hoping someone passing twenty feet away at the alley entrance wouldn't look down the alley and recognize her. After a few minutes when no one so much as looked her way, she began to relax.

"Is your entire body numb, yet, Edgar?" she subvocalized.

"Nah, I found a good position back here, and I can shift a bit."

"Keep that blood circulating," Dan chimed in, like he was some sort of sports coach. "It'd be hilarious if you tried to rush to the rescue and fell flat on your face because your legs were asleep."

"Come on, Dan, don't jinx it," Mack said, sounding the most worried out of all of them. He was their lookout up the street, while Ronnie kept his eyes peeled the opposite direction, and Dan kept his eye on their anonymous message account in case the stalker pinged them last minute.

"Shut up, everyone," Ronnie said. "Let Lynn concentrate."

Night had fallen. Ronnie and Mack started by calling out every time they saw someone coming down the street the same age or build as the stalker. But Lynn quickly put an end to that. It ratcheted up her anxiety to insane levels.

"He'll probably show up fifteen minutes early," she subvocalized. "He'll probably be too eager to wait until the meeting time.

He'll also probably come in an air taxi. If I were him, I'd have the air taxi wait and convince my target to get into it with me."

Maybe it was morbid, going through endless scenarios in her head, but as long as she kept everything clinical, examining strategies and probable reactions, it gave her a sense of preparedness and calm.

This creep was delusional, but he was still human, and humans were predictable.

Almost as if she'd been able to see into his head, an air taxi pulled up nearly fifteen minutes early on the dot. The figure that climbed out had a light jacket on with the hood pulled up, but his stature, rumpled clothes, and the twitchy way he moved were instantly familiar.

Lynn's stomach surged. She fought the feeling down, forcing her limbs to stay still. Relaxed. Ready.

"It's him," she subvocalized, almost too nervous to get the words across in a way her sensors would pick up. She swallowed and started narrating the man's movements. "Black jacket, green pants, hands in his pockets. He's looking both ways up and down the street. Now he's looking down the alley. I think he's seen me. The air taxi is staying there. He's walking toward me."

Adrenaline rushed through her limbs and fear roared up into her head out of nowhere, screaming at her to *run*.

"You got this, Lynn," Edgar said. "I'm right here."

"We're coming," Ronnie said, and Lynn could hear the scrape of chairs as the guys rushed to spring their trap.

She breathed in. Out. In. Out.

He was getting closer, face shadowed in the dim alley, his figure turned into some frightening boogieman simply because of the darkness that cloaked him. Then he passed the dim bulb hanging over the back entrance of the bar, and the light momentarily illuminated his face.

Lynn glimpsed sunken eyes, a weak stubbled chin, and a tongue darting out to wet chapped lips. Her mouth twisted in disgust, though she quickly smoothed her expression to neutrality.

This was no frightening, mysterious stalker. This was a weak, craven, pathetic loser who had barreled down the rabbit hole of delusion and contemptible lechery. He'd exchanged his humanity for hedonistic demons, and she was about to put an end to the harm he did in the world.

Lynn pushed off the wall and walked forward several steps, giving herself plenty of room to move. She already had her two mace canisters secreted in her palms, hidden from the view of her approaching target.

The creep was already muttering as he approached. She caught words like "beautiful angel" and "she's here, she's mine, she's here." It was a struggle not to bare her teeth at the man, a warning to stay back. She settled on the balls of her feet, ready for anything.

"Steady, *Toa Tama'ita'i*. Wait till you see the whites of his eyes." Edgar's smooth, calming voice filled her head. She knew he was right there, at her back, ready to fight.

"Mr. Vulvx829," Lynn said out loud, affecting the girly, airheaded tone she'd always used to annoy Ronnie with talk of Kim's Diva Princess. "Is that really you? I can't see your face, and I just *have* to see your face. Come closer, honey, and pull back your hood."

Saying the words made her shudder in disgust, but she was desperate to get a clear shot at his eyes. Her mace was a special gel formula so she didn't have to worry about spray blowing back into her face. But her effective range was about fifteen feet, and she wanted him at ten, with his hood down, before she acted.

Her girly affectation seemed to put him off his guard, though. He took his hands out of his jacket pockets and pulled back his hood, walking faster toward her. His unkempt face was slack in a sort of rapturous disbelief and his eyes shone with feverish obsession.

"My beautiful, beautiful—my beautiful—it's me, I swear. I'm here. Come here. I'll—"

Lynn wasn't listening, she wasn't even home. Larry was watching the distance close, waiting for the target to pass the mark, muscles tense and ready.

Three steps.

Two.

One.

Lynn whipped her hands up, aiming and firing her mace canisters with the same smooth ease she fired Abomination. Two streams of gel arced out and hit the man square in the face, getting into his open eyes and mouth. His hands jerked upward far too slowly to block the spray.

Mr. Vulvx829's insane rambling changed to shrieks of agony

and he stumbled back, hands frantically scrabbling at his face, trying to wipe the gel away.

"Hang on, Lynn! We're coming!"

The guys' words and the pounding sound of feet on concrete were distant echoes in her mind, barely registering. She stalked forward, still firing her mace at the wailing, flailing form, coating the stalker's face, neck, hands, and every bit of exposed skin she could find in the viscous, burning substance. She could feel her face transform into a feral snarl as she spat words at her would-be attacker and likely rapist, if he'd had his way.

"Burn in *hell*, you disgusting. Pathetic. *Monster.*"

"You got him, Lynn. You got him."

Strong hands grabbed her shoulders, pulling her back, but she wasn't done. She threw the canisters with all the fury in her, one after another, hitting the man square in the stomach. He doubled over and crumpled to the ground like a marionette whose strings had been cut.

Ronnie was on him in an instant, with Dan close behind. They flipped the still-thrashing man onto his stomach and fought to grab his hands and bend them behind his back so they could zip tie them. Edgar hesitated, then hurried over to help subdue the man while Ronnie yelled about a citizen's arrest, reciting some sort of legal jargon he'd no doubt memorized for the occasion.

A handful of passersby had gathered from the street. A few looked like they were about to try and intervene, but Ronnie just kept repeating his citizen's arrest spiel as Edgar held the man's arms down and Dan helped him zip tie his wrists, then his ankles. Lynn was intensely grateful she'd insisted they all wear the high-performance gloves they normally used when hunting in the cold. She'd sprayed *a lot* of gel on the stalker and the guys were getting it smeared on their gloves and sleeves. They would have to wash their clothes in special formula to remove the oleoresin capsicum oils before they'd be safe to use again.

By the time Ronnie, Dan, and Edgar got up, backing away from their trussed-up arrestee, a crowd of people had gathered and Lynn knew with absolute certainty that most of what had happened had been recorded, if not livestreamed then and there.

Well, so much for keeping a low profile.

It was probably a waste of effort at this point, but Lynn still ducked her head and moved to the far wall, putting Edgar's bulk between her and the crowd. He noticed her and turned, putting his back to the stares, and gently pulled her into a protective hug.

It was only then that she realized she was shaking.

The stalker's screams had subsided into pitiful moaning, and when a few people in the crowd yelled that someone should help the man, Ronnie repeated his citizen's arrest spiel again. Dan added that the guy was a stalker who had sexually assaulted a woman, so he probably deserved to enjoy the mace aftereffects. After that, no one else complained.

The police arrived and took over the scene. Vulvx829was bundled off in one of the squad cars, the crowd was dispersed, and a perimeter was set up. One cop helped the guys wipe off most of the gel with decontaminating wipes all cops carried in case they were accidentally exposed to pepper spray. Another started taking statements from everybody.

It was grueling and tedious, but Ronnie had prepared them well, and they all knew what to say and how to explain the situation. It didn't take the cops long to confirm the BOLO out for the suspect and corroborate their story with the report filed from Lynn's initial assault.

Once Lynn had said what she needed to say, she shut down and zoned out. She was tired and soul weary, and this wasn't TD Hunter. She wasn't the captain, and she didn't want to be in charge. She just wanted to disappear back to her room and sleep.

She didn't consciously think it, but instinctually Lynn knew her team had her back, and she didn't have to be strong anymore. Edgar was never further than arm's reach from her, and Ronnie seemed to handle being in the spotlight just fine.

She'd never been more happy to let him have it.

There was significant fallout.

She ended up in the news. The official outlets didn't mention her name, since she was a minor, but the entire incident was eternally memorialized on the streams. Within a day, hundreds of hours' worth of commentary on the exciting events had been generated by dozens of streamers.

Thank the heavens Lynn had GIC to manage it all.

The guys were there in the news, too, of course. Ronnie especially stole the limelight—much to Lynn's relief—because GIC arranged an interview with the city's biggest local news stream, and Ronnie rocked it. Even Lynn was impressed. Yeah, he was kinda cocky. But he *had* masterminded the whole operation, so credit where credit was due. Thankfully, he had enough sense to not incriminate himself by confessing to questionable mesh web activity, and he kept everything involving her vague. He and his friends were just concerned citizens who had witnessed a crime and had stumbled on a chance to apprehend the criminal.

Even so, it only took forty-eight hours for someone to sniff out the existence of the faketime vid and make the connection between it, the doxxing, and the stalker. The stream waters frothed with wild speculation, conspiracy theories, and hungry gossip sharks desperate for an inside scoop.

Lynn wouldn't have survived it with her sanity intact if they'd still been back at her apartment. But because of Drew's help and her mother's wisdom, nothing anywhere connected her name to her new home.

At home, she was safe.

Lynn avoided the streams like the plague, forbade her friends from telling her anything, and only grudgingly let Mrs. Pearson keep her up to date with developments she needed to know about for her own safety and well-being.

The fallout went further than that, though.

Matilda was furious at all of them. She almost banned Ronnie from ever darkening their door again until Lynn calmed her down enough to explain *she* had insisted on being involved.

The guys' parents were no happier. Fortunately, Mack had turned eighteen earlier in the spring, or else Mrs. Rios might have literally locked him in their house to keep him "safe" from "all that gaming drama."

Edgar managed to avoid most of the limelight, so his family wasn't badly affected, and his mother seemed to really trust his judgment.

Mrs. Nguyen, being a lawyer, took the entire incident more calmly than the other parents. Even so, Lynn heard her mom talking hotly several times in the evenings with Mrs. Nguyen about Skadi's Wolves and their ability to make their own decisions. Dan turned eighteen at the end of May, so maybe his mother knew she couldn't get away with anything too drastic, at least legally. That didn't mean Dan didn't get an earful at home, but he seemed to take it in good humor.

Ronnie's dad... Lynn had no clue what he thought or if he even found out about the incident. Ronnie never said a word, and coldly changed the topic if anyone tried to bring it up.

The furor was good for stream revenue, though. Lynn had always been pretty disparaging of stream celebrities making a living off of notoriety.

Now, being unwillingly catapulted into the same situation, she was intensely grateful for the ability to monetize the attention.

If she was going to be crushed by the opinions of the entire world, at the very least she could afford to own a house, feed her family, and save for her future education in the process.

GIC turned down dozens of interview offers, to the point that Mrs. Pearson told Lynn she should pick one to do if she wanted the frenzy to die down. GIC had already released official statements, but the denizens of the mesh web seemed to want it from the horse's mouth.

Mrs. Pearson picked out a reputable stream, vetted all the questions, and Lynn endured the interview with gritted teeth—internally gritted, anyway. She smiled for the interview because she knew Mrs. Pearson would nag her endlessly if she didn't.

By the weekend, even Ronnie was sick of the whole thing.

With finals barely a week away, they decided to hole up at Lynn's house for the weekend to cram and finish final reports. It killed two birds with one stone: avoiding the public *and* their parents at the same time. Matilda allowed it, but for once told them they were on their own for meals, since they were now "adults capable of putting themselves in danger and arresting people," they could make their own supper.

Yup. She was that pissed.

Lynn called the guys together in the den before they started studying for the weekend and passed out little dixie cups, then poured everyone some of her mom's Pinot Noir that Matilda kept for that rare evening when she needed a little something extra to relax.

Lynn held her cup out and looked around at her friends. Her heart was full of a lot of things, much of it tangled together and confusing. But transcending all that mess was the unmistakable warmth of gratitude.

"You all know I hate people," she started.

"Geez, thanks, Lynn," Dan said.

"Bro, let her finish," Edgar growled.

"As I was saying, I'm not a fan of people. I'd rather be gaming than doing anything else. But if there was anyone in the world I wanted to spend time with...it would be you guys."

"Hear, hear!" Mack said, grinning.

Ronnie rolled his eyes, though the slant of his mouth might have been described as a begrudging smile. Or at least not a frown.

"So, here's to friendship, teamwork, and having each others' backs," Lynn finished, raising her cup and catching Ronnie's eye. He snorted, but downed his dixie cup of wine anyway, then coughed and thumped his chest.

"Ug, that stuff is gross," Dan whined after recovering from his own coughing fit. He fled to the snack table where he could wash it down with a nice swig of pop.

Lynn noticed that Edgar didn't drink his wine, but she was pretty sure she knew why, and didn't mind one bit.

"And, uh, guys," she said, motioning for Dan to bring the pop over so they could all find some relief, "next time we decide to arrest someone, can we do it in secret, please? I'd almost rather deal with a stalker than this circus."

"Deal," Edgar rumbled.

"*Yes,*" Ronnie agreed fervently.

Watching the guys fill up their cups with pop and start fighting over snacks, Lynn wondered: was it all worth it? Was TD Hunter and the prize they hoped for worth the way their lives had been turned upside-down? Mr. Swain's words came to mind, back when they'd chatted at Kayla's Christmas party.

I've wondered, at times, if operating a PR company was even the right thing to do. But fame is just a tool to achieve worthy goals.

Was this insanity the way it would always be? Hiding from the world and afraid to look at even a single stream?

Did she even have a choice at this point?

Lynn's jaw firmed and she threw back her cup of pop to wash away the sour bite of wine—they would definitely pick something *else* to toast with next time.

In the end, they were already here, so close to their goal that Lynn could taste it. She wasn't going to let other people's opinions control how she lived her life. No matter what anybody said, she wouldn't back down. She wouldn't give up.

And if she had to endure the trial of notoriety, then at least she'd find a way to use that fame for a worthy goal.

Chapter 10

SCHOOL WAS ALMOST MIND-NUMBINGLY BORING COMPARED TO the roller coaster of adrenaline highs and depressive lows she'd lived the past few months—okay, the past *year*. But she knew completing high school was important, regardless of whatever career she was lining up for herself.

So, she tried to focus.

It was like pulling teeth.

That was why, one late evening mid-week when she saw a message to Larry's WarMonger profile from Sean Dudgeon asking for a good date to do a paid interview, she responded with:

"*Now*."

She got a polite, but confused response asking for clarification. So she wrote back:

"Right now, you idiot. I'm sitting here killing morons in virtual, no reason I can't answer stupid questions at the same time. If you say no, I can't guarantee when I'll be available again. Things are... heating up."

She wasn't actually killing morons in virtual, but it was a fabulous idea. So when Sean replied that he would be happy to do the interview right away, just give him a few minutes to set up a recording session, Lynn gleefully closed all her homework apps, logged onto WarMonger, and hopped into a random lobby.

Half the people in it left as soon as they saw who had joined.

Lynn cackled, left the lobby, and tried another one. Eventually, she would find one filled with either fools or people unaware of "the Snake's" reputation, and then the fun would begin. By the time Sean connected with her on voice chat, she *was* killing morons in virtual. That part was glorious, but as Sean gave the usual pleasantries and started briefing her on the interview, she regretted her hastiness.

Did she want to do school?

No.

Did she want to be interviewed?

Absofreakinglutely no.

Could she submerse herself totally into Larry mode, be grumpy, and throw out some good one-liners?

Probably. She was desperate enough to try, anyway.

A few of Sean's questions she nixed on the get-go, but Sean didn't seem surprised. He hadn't lined up anything intrusive or surprising—probably because he was too terrified of Larry's reputation, rightly so. The ones she grudgingly agreed to answer were more fluff than anything else, but they were certainly fertile ground for some nice, grumpy Larry rants.

"Ya know," Lynn growled, her voice modulator translating her grumpy tone into a deliciously threatening rumble as she tracked across the dystopian landscape with a sniper rifle, "I'm one of those people just hates stupid skins."

The rifle bounced as he shot a moron in a giant purple rabbit skin in the head.

"First skins were fine. Military gear. Things you'd wear in my kind of world. World of nothing but war, war, war and carnage. How the world should be."

"You really think the world should be like...WarMonger?" Sean asked.

"Be a better place. World's too soft. Look at this moron! He's wearing a panda suit!"

Crack!

"Can you believe this idiocy? He looks like a talking marshmallow! Makes me dumber just lookin' at him."

Sean coughed in a way that might have been covering a laugh. "The value of the skins, though..."

"Oh, I get it," Lynn said, getting into stride. "Games are expensive to build and maintain. Selling skins of...a now *dead* voluptuous elf maiden helps *me* have *fun*! Not to mention increasing their hit box. Good target practice.

"Do I think the world should be more like WarMonger? Hell, yeah! We're overrun by weaklings and morons. Just look at this furry wannabe running around in a wolf costume... who is now *dead*! Tough luck, wolfie. With situational awareness like that, you deserve to die! You wouldn't last three seconds in an actual world like WarMonger. Survival takes strength and smarts, two things totally absent in this pathetic bunch of weaklings, morons, and Ronnie Darko."

"Ah, yes," Sean said. "It's somewhat of an open secret that you... frequently have killed Mr. Darko..."

"Ran into him in an early lobby," Lynn replied. "Kid thought I didn't know Lithuanian! I knew Lithuanian before I banged his gramma! Say those words to Larry Coughlin and I'll wash your mouth out with CLP! Or just occasionally kill you before you know I'm there.

"Should the world be more like WarMonger?" Lynn said, tone going serious. "Of course not. I've been to the places that make WarMonger look tame. It's no place to raise a family, make a life. But would it clear out a bunch of the weaklings and furry wannabes? Damn straight. And, in conclusion, Ronnie Darko *delenda est*!

"Now, gotta go find... Look at *this* asinine excuse for a monkey's balls! Cover is materials which will stop a twelve point seven millimeter round! THAT! WALL! IS NOT! COVER! As you just discovered by dying. Also, quit wearing a stupid Warhammer Ork skin! It may be green but it *does not blend in with houses*! Only real Orks can pull that shit off! What a numbskull. Can you believe they let these chuckleheads onto the servers? Also, Ronnie Darko *delenda est*. That is all."

"Well," Sean said, "this has been a very, erm, informative interview, thank you, Mr. Coughlin. Before we go, do you have any thoughts to share on the new AR game, TransDimensional Hunter, that's been taking the world by storm?"

Lynn knew what Sean was fishing for, and was happy to give it to him.

"My thoughts, Fanboy? Get off your fat, lazy hineys and go kill some monsters. You know what women like? Strong, fit, competent men. You know what men like? Strong, fit, competent women. Win-win."

Sean laughed.

"Quite an endorsement, thanks, Mr. Coughlin. We at TD Hunter have worked hard to create a next-level gaming experience that also makes our players happier, healthier people. There's really no downside!"

Lynn almost snorted but managed to hold in the reaction. She could think of a good dozen downsides to TD Hunter, but most of them didn't apply to people who were not named Lynn Raven, so she kept her mouth shut.

Sean fan-boyed a little more but finally ended the interview. Lynn took the opportunity to grunt an almost civil goodbye and disconnect before Sean could ambush her with more worshipful chitchat. She leaned back in her body-mold chair and rubbed her face.

Wow. Sean had done the impossible: made her want to do homework again. If only she could figure out some way to harness the feeling to zip through the rest of her final reports and finish reading through four years' worth of class notes to prep for her exams.

Mr. Krator had touched base a few weeks ago, revisiting the whole stunt work for a Larry Coughlin promo idea, but she'd told him there was no way she could spare the time, no matter how much he offered to compensate her. She didn't know if he would decide to go forward with the promo using some other stunt actor, but she didn't have the energy to worry about it.

To put off homework just a little bit longer, Lynn opened up her TD Hunter app and began poking around aimlessly. She wandered over to the TDM lists and scrolled down to the boss section, which spanned the end of Bravo Class, part of Alpha Class, and the Sierra Class section.

Lynn remembered the first time she'd ever seen these lists as a beta tester last June. Then, many more entries had been grayed out than filled in. Over time, most of the Delta, Charlie, Bravo, and Alpha entries had been populated by a menagerie of monsters, the majority of which she'd encountered herself. She even spotted a few familiar names like Gyges and Ya-Te-Veo, with RavenStriker listed in the "discovered by" section.

Sierra Class, though, was almost entirely unchanged from what she'd seen when she was a beta tester. There were still dozens of unique bosses, each with individualized names. And every one still said "RESTRICTED INTELLIGENCE" in large block letters.

"Hey, Hugo," Lynn subvocalized. "When I reach Level 40, will this 'restricted intelligence' message finally go away on all these Sierra Class bosses?"

"Yes, it will disappear once you have reached the appropriate level to warrant access."

"Uh-huh," Lynn said, noting the oddly specific way the AI had replied. That happened often when she asked questions, as if Hugo was particularly concerned with ensuring players understood the exact parameters of every answer.

Not a bad thing, overall. But Lynn had the growing suspicion the AI had been using it to avoid telling her the information she was actually looking for. Or maybe she was just being paranoid again. There wasn't enough of a pattern for her to pinpoint what was going on yet.

Well, she could always get to Level 40 and find out. It wasn't as if the game hadn't changed since she'd beta tested it. That was absolutely normal. Games weren't static things. Developers were constantly releasing patches to fix known issues and vulnerabilities, implement updates, and release new features, some of which were designed and put out there responding to specific user demand. Good game designers kept a close eye on their fan community, and Lynn knew Tsunami had an entire department devoted to staying plugged into the various fan communities of its many games. They took a genuine interest in what gamers wanted, though she was sure it was a headache trying to balance all the differing preferences of their worldwide gamer base.

But the effort they put into trying was undoubtedly one reason why Tsunami was so successful.

So, small changes in TD Hunter didn't surprise Lynn, like the appearance of the Draca entry in the Sierra Class section. It was the only Sierra Class TDM that wasn't listed as a boss. Did that mean there would be more non-boss Sierra Class monsters? Lynn shivered at the thought. Bosses were unique, and relatively rare. Regular TDMs were not.

The idea of facing multiple Dracas at once was bone-chilling.

Her eyes went back to the Draca entry, and she mulled over why they'd even been able to see the thing, much less kill it—a question she hadn't been able to revisit since their battle with the

Draca. Technically, they shouldn't have encountered the Draca until they'd reached Level 40. So was this an update to TD Hunter's patterns? Or was it an algorithmic aberration—something Lynn was certain she'd experienced before, but couldn't prove. She'd always had a gut-level feeling the TD Hunter algorithm was out to get her. Steve had said it was simply responding to her aggressive play style by creating challenges commensurate to her level of skill. It was supposed to be the most advanced, dynamic, and responsive game AI ever created, after all.

Hugo was a perfect example of the success Mr. Krator and his design team had achieved. When service AIs had been on the rise, companies the world over had discovered that most customers *hated* not being able to tell if they were interacting with a human or a computer. Most service AIs were designed to be inhumanly perfect, or purposefully rough around the edges, making it obvious either way that they were not human.

Hugo was unique among service AIs, and it was one reason, Lynn suspected, that TD Hunter was *so* popular. The AI had frighteningly realistic human idiosyncrasies, and could easily have pretended to be a real person. But because the AI so unerringly and deliberately leaned into its self-identification as a game control system, it made Hugo fun and engaging instead of creepy.

All of which begged the question: What was *really* going on with TD Hunter and all the crazy glitches, odd TDM behavior, and grid-related things she'd seen? Drones falling from the sky? It was insane, and Lynn was honestly afraid to speculate, because then she might find some logical explanation that she had no way of knowing was accurate. And she couldn't afford to be distracted by conspiracy theories, no matter how logical they were.

A tone in her ear reminded her how late it was getting, and she heaved a sigh and started getting ready for tomorrow.

Whatever was going on, she was *almost* an official high school graduate. Things would get much easier on the other side of finals, surely.

Surely.

The last week of Lynn's high school career was less eventful than she'd imagined, considering the years she'd spent anticipating it. Or maybe it just felt uneventful because it was one long blur: go to school, take exams all day, go home to study, collapse into bed, rinse and repeat. She barely had time to eat, and would have skipped meals entirely if her mother hadn't intervened. In the evenings, dishes of steaming, hearty brain food appeared at her and Edgar's elbow as they studied.

Edgar kept coming over after school because he said his house was raucous chaos and he couldn't get a shred of studying done. Neither Lynn nor Matilda complained, so he kept coming around like that stray cat you made the mistake of feeding once, and forever after it decided your house was the place to be.

They spent hours sitting within feet of each other, yet Lynn felt like she barely saw him all day, much less talked to him. In a way he was distracting to be near. She kept wondering if he was going to try to reach out and hold her hand, or caress her cheek again, or... she had no idea. She couldn't forget what her mom had said, and yet Edgar was a perfect gentleman: protective and attentive without getting into her personal space. Yet the way he smiled at her... like nothing in the world made him happier than just being in her presence. It was so confusing. How did he actually feel? Was there something there? Or was she imagining things? She had no idea how to tell, and she was too busy to waste time agonizing over it.

She didn't even have time to be tired. So she wasn't, except during those rare moments of stillness between transitions. Then fatigue hit like a sledgehammer, so deep her bones ached with it, and she found she could sleep *anywhere*. Even standing up.

The guys looked like they had it just as bad. The stress made Ronnie unbearably grumpy, while Mack went on and on about how sad Riko was that he had to skip their usual late-night chats. Dan went around looking like a hamster who'd fallen in an espresso machine, complete with dilated eyes and hair sticking up in all directions. They were pretty sure he was taking some sort of brain-enhancing drug, but had screwed up the dosage because he was smaller than the average guy.

The only time any of them acted fully conscious was when someone at school made the mistake of picking on a member of Skadi's Wolves. Between Edgar's bulk and Ronnie's glare, the usual suspects gave up their snide comments and insulting gestures. Word had spread through the school about what "those crazies" had done to Lynn Raven's stalker. There was no telling how far they'd go. The guys seemed to revel in their newfound status as edgy tough guys. Lynn tried not to roll her eyes and snort at the idea. Having a "security detail" of "crazies" had cut the bullying down to virtually zero, which was a relief. The few brave enough to still try got loomed over by a knuckle-cracking Edgar while Ronnie eviscerated them with his razor-sharp tongue.

They were mere days away from graduating and leaving the insane cliques of high school behind forever, so they had all stopped caring about getting into trouble. Principal Charles seemed equally eager for them to no longer be his problem.

How she got through finals Lynn had no clue. She was pretty sure it was only due to the brain's ability to operate on autopilot, and energy drinks. If Connor had wanted revenge and had figured out some way to catch her away from her teammates, he could have beaten her till she passed out and Lynn would have just been grateful for a chance to close her eyes. Fortunately, the CRC seemed just as weighed down under the workload. The few times she spotted Connor and Elena from afar, both looked tense and tired.

After the last test on Friday, Lynn went home, collapsed into bed, and slept for almost twenty-four hours.

When she woke up on Saturday, Matilda pointed her at a nice pair of slacks and blouse hanging on her door and told her to get dressed and come eat something. When Lynn appeared in the kitchen, dressed but still bleary-eyed, her mom had a steaming breakfast burrito waiting for her, despite the fact that it was several hours after lunch.

Breakfast burritos were appropriate no matter what time of day.

"Okay, Mom, what's up?" Lynn asked after making the burrito disappear in record time.

"We're going on a tiny vacation," she said, a bit of a sly smile tucked into the corners of her mouth.

"Mom, come on. You know I don't have time for that! We've got to hit Level 40—"

"You can spare *one* afternoon, dear. And besides, I already told the guys you wouldn't be hunting today, so they're all still asleep and likely won't wake up until after sundown."

Lynn sighed.

"Okay, so where are we going?"

"Des Moines."

"Uhhh, what's in Des Moines? Besides corn and insurance companies, I mean?"

Matilda laughed, her eyes sparkling.

"You'll see."

Lynn was still too groggy to argue, so she grabbed her things and followed her mom out the door.

A mini airbus awaited them on the curb. It was basically just a long-range air taxi that people could reserve when they wanted to travel between cities in privacy. It was a bit roomier than the typical air taxi, and had a minuscule bathroom in addition to a tiny bar of for-pay snacks and drinks.

Lynn took the opportunity to nap more on the hour ride to Des Moines. She and her mom also chatted about low-key things, like outfitting Lynn's workout room with more equipment and how finals had gone. Lynn was confident she'd passed all her classes, but she certainly wouldn't be valedictorian.

Once they were approaching Des Moines, Lynn enjoyed peering out the window at the scenery. The air lanes for buses and taxis were low enough you could really enjoy the details of everything that passed below. The countryside was a riot of spring green turning to full summer. As they passed over the outskirts of Des Moines itself, there were all sorts of interesting bits of city infrastructure to see, from electric rails running like arteries through the city, to the massive warehouse district next to blocks of power stations and the tall power nodes reaching for the sky so they could manage the flow of electricity beamed back and forth across the city.

Lynn was trying to count how many power nodes she could see from the airbus window when she heard a high-pitched, painful whine of machinery that cut off abruptly along with every light in the vehicle. Then her stomach wrenched upward as the entire craft listed and began a sharp nosedive. Her scream mingled with her mother's for an endless, heart-stopping moment before the lights came back on and the airbus came to life again, swiftly righting itself and slowing to a normal descending pace.

Both Lynn and Matilda had been thrown from their seats, but were otherwise fine. The cabin lights flickered once and a calm, feminine voice stated: "Due to safety concerns, this airbus will be conducting an immediate emergency landing. Please buckle in and remain seated. An air taxi has already been dispatched to your location to transport you to your final destination. If any of your party is injured, please call 911 and inform the proper authorities. Thank you."

Lynn helped her mom up and they both strapped in. Matilda's eyes were round as saucers, her mouth pressed together so tightly her lips were blanched white. She reached out blindly and found Lynn's hand, gripping it painfully tight. Lynn didn't protest.

The airbus landed safely on a street corner in Des Moines' northeast warehouse district. The cool voice came on again to politely request they exit the vehicle with their belongings and wait on the street to be picked up by their air taxi. They did as requested, and as soon as they were clear and the door closed behind them, the airbus seemed to shut down, all lights switching off as it settled heavily onto the pavement.

Lynn and Matilda looked at each other.

"Come on," Lynn muttered, grabbing her mom's hand and guiding her down the street, away from the airbus. "We'll wait over here at this corner."

The day was fair and the weather was pleasantly warm, so the five-minute wait for the replacement air taxi gave Lynn a chance to take some deep breaths, slow her racing heart, and be reassured by the solid ground beneath her feet. When she checked in with her mom, Matilda still seemed shaken, but better. They both hesitated before getting into the air taxi, but what else were they supposed to do? Air taxis and airbuses were incredibly safe forms of transportation compared to manually driven vehicles, regardless if they were electric or old gas-guzzlers. They might call an automated ground taxi, but what were the chances of a freak failure like they'd just witnessed happening again in one person's lifetime? After all, the backup batteries *had* kicked in. There was no telling what had caused the complete system crash, but a fresh air taxi was likely the safest way to continue their journey.

Still, they stayed buckled in, and Matilda's grip on her seat's armrests was firm. Lynn wanted to break the tension with conversation to wipe away the fear she knew her mom was struggling with, but she couldn't stop thinking about the airbus crashes she'd heard about in the last few months.

The air taxi deposited them safely in downtown Des Moines,

right among its proud cluster of skyscrapers housing the city's wealthiest and most important businesses.

Lynn stared up at the buildings, then looked at her mom. "Come on, Mom. Spill. What's going on?"

Matilda cracked a smile for the first time in half an hour.

"You'll see. Come on." She reached out and took Lynn's hand and guided her down the street toward the large glass doors of one of the skyscrapers.

"Mooom," Lynn complained.

"Oh, stop whining. I never get to surprise you. So hush and enjoy the ride."

Lynn obeyed and switched her attention to her surroundings, peering carefully at everyone and everything they passed, trying to guess what in the world was going on. It wasn't until they'd entered the skyscraper and were approaching the information desk—manned by an actual person, instead of being a simple kiosk—before Lynn finally spotted the familiar logo decorating the wall high above their heads.

"GIC? Mom, why in the *world* are we at GIC's headquarters? Wait a minute," she slowed, pulling against her mom's grip, "we're not going to some kind of ambush interview, are we?"

Matilda stopped and gave her a concerned look.

"Honey, *please*. Do you really have so little faith in me? I promise this has nothing to do with GIC itself or any publicity. We're here because Mr. Swain was kind enough to let us use one of his empty offices as a private and neutral meeting place. You're much less likely to be recognized in Des Moines, and there won't be any drones hanging around looking for you."

"Meeting place? Who are we meeting?"

But her mom had turned back around and approached the desk, where she asked politely for directions to GIC's front office. The woman manning the desk gave Matilda directions, and Matilda marched off to the elevators, leaving Lynn to trot after her in an effort to catch up.

"Mom, *who* are we meeting?"

But Matilda would only smile mysteriously.

Lynn thought about it the whole way up dozens of floors. Then she gasped.

"It's *him* isn't it? Is this a date? Are we meeting Mr. Wonderful?"

Matilda laughed, a full-throated, gorgeous sound full of delight.

"It took you long enough to figure it out," Matilda teased.

"Hey, I just finished a week of finals with no sleep! I'm *definitely* not firing on all cylinders."

"I know, sweetie," Matilda said with a warm smile. "You're normally far too smart for me. It's been fun watching you glare at everything we pass like some sort of grumpy noir detective." Before Lynn could protest the comparison, her mom went on. "With everything going on, I kept waiting to bring up the second date idea we talked about, until I was running out of time—"

"Running out of time? What do you mean?"

"You'll find out soon. Anyway, I planned everything for today so we could get it done promptly and not distract you from finals *or* hunting."

The elevator doors opened, revealing an airy foyer of polished steel and glass with tasteful accents in blue and white. Front and center was a chest-high semicircle desk manned by a beautiful and professional-looking secretary who gave them a welcoming smile. A tall, muscular man was leaning on one end of the desk, his back to them, talking to an older woman standing nearby dressed in an iron gray skirt suit. The man wore slacks and a polo shirt that only barely fit around the muscles bulging in his arms, and the edges of tattoos peeked out from below his polo sleeves. His graying high-cut seemed weirdly familiar, but Lynn didn't give it a second glance because she recognized the older woman.

"Hi, Mrs. Pearson," Lynn called out, giving her PR manager a little wave.

"Good afternoon, Miss Raven," Mrs. Pearson said, her stern face softening into a smile.

The tall man straightened and turned around, and Lynn stopped dead in her tracks.

"*Steve*? What in the world are *you* doing here? Does GIC manage Tsunami's PR, too? Or Mr. Krator's?"

Steve's strong, square face broke into an awkward grin and he reached up to rub the back of his neck. He gave Lynn a welcoming nod, but the person his eyes locked on to was...

Matilda.

"Wait...no...*no*..." Lynn muttered, staring at Steve Riker, TD Hunter tactical support specialist for Tsunami, her occasional mentor and, she thought, sort-of-kind-of friend.

"No. No way. You? *You're* Mr. Wonderful? *You're* dating... my *mom*?!"

"Honey!" Matilda exclaimed, making a shushing motion with her hand. "Not so loud. I know GIC's employees are unfailingly discreet, but would you mind *not* shouting our personal business across the entire building?"

Lynn didn't really hear her. She was still staring, slack-jawed, at Steve, whose face was becoming distinctly pink.

"Why don't we move this scintillating discussion to a private meeting room," Mrs. Pearson suggested dryly.

She herded the three of them toward one branching hallway like an extremely severe sheepdog. Lynn moved in a daze, mouth still open, brain absolutely destroyed. It tried to reboot several times, and failed.

Steve?

Mrs. Pearson led them to a smallish office with a window, an empty desk and three comfortable-looking waiting chairs. A side table bore a selection of bottled drinks and a tastefully arranged charcuterie board. The elder woman ushered them inside, paused a moment to tell Matilda to ping her if they needed anything at all, and left the room, closing the door quietly behind her.

Silence fell, and stayed.

Steve?

Lynn couldn't even wrap her mind around it, and while she was trying, her emotions kept morphing and thrashing around between wild extremes.

Was she angry? Happy? Betrayed? Excited? Shocked? All of the above?

Matilda took pity on her, gently grasped her arm, and led her to one of the chairs where Lynn sank slowly down, mouth *still* open, unable to stop looking between her mom and Steve.

"Honey," Matilda said, finally breaking the silence, "you're going to catch an entire swarm of flies in that mouth of yours if you don't shut it soon."

Lynn snapped her jaw closed.

"*Steve?*" she asked again, her voice more than slightly strangled.

Steve chuckled, a definite edge of nerves beneath the sound.

"Surprise, kid. Before you stab me, let Tilly explain, okay?"

"*Tilly?*" Lynn said, her strangled voice rising an entire octave as she swung her disbelieving gaze on her mom.

Matilda had no hope of hiding her grin, which was roughly the size of Texas, so she didn't try as she explained, "I'm allowed to have a nickname, if I want. Just be happy I vetoed Snookums and Honeybun."

Lynn's jaw dropped open again and her eyes swung back to Steve.

"To clarify, Tilly here likes to joke," Steve said, raising one eyebrow. "I value my man parts, thank you very much. I would never call her something that would put them in imminent danger."

Matilda gave Steve a wicked look while Lynn tried not to flop over and die from embarrassment.

"This is *sooo* weird," she said faintly. "I think my brain might explode."

"Oh, honey, I'm sorry," Matilda said, dragging one of the other chairs over to sit close and put a hand on Lynn's knee. "I know this is a lot to take in. It's the main reason I kept putting this off. You're already dealing with so much."

Lynn gave her head a little shake to clear it and gave Steve a proper look over. Her brow was still scrunched, but she wasn't angry, just...searching.

Steve did her the courtesy of meeting her gaze unflinchingly—though of course she'd expect no less. He was an upstanding man, and though there was still a little sheepishness to the way one corner of his mouth crooked upward, his expression was open and unapologetic.

"Okay," Lynn said slowly, and swung her gaze to her mom. "Explain."

Matilda smiled. She seemed to be having a hard time *not* smiling, which was different, but good.

"Well, if you recall, you went and gave yourself a concussion at the end of the qualifiers—"

"Hey! It wasn't on purpose."

"Yes, so you say, sweetie. But that is where we first met. I was pretty focused on your health at the time, but it didn't escape my notice how genuinely concerned Steve was, too. And, well, it would be pretty hard to not notice his, ahem, manly physique."

Steve grinned at Matilda.

"I knew there was a reason I still hit the gym every day."

"What can I say," Matilda said, returning the smile and

adding a sappy little sigh, "I'm a nurse, I have a thing for guys who take their health seriously."

Lynn rolled her eyes. "*Anyway,*" she said pointedly, giving her mom a poke.

"Yes, anyway, we had a chance to chat a little bit that day and it turned out we were both very big fans of, well, *you*, dear."

"Ummm, okay?" Lynn scrunched her face in confusion.

Matilda laughed. "Don't read into it, honey. You'll understand better when you're grown and have children of your own. Steve followed up with me a few times over the next month to check on you and make sure you didn't have any lingering aftereffects from the concussion. We talked about other things, too. Just friendly chit chat. And, well... it was *fun*, you know?"

Lynn didn't, not really. But she wondered if it was something like how she never minded talking to Edgar, even though anyone else trying to chat with her ended up being annoying or boring or both.

"One day sometime mid-fall, he called and said he knew his 'Lynn concussion' excuse had run out, but did I mind if he kept calling me anyway? Aaand, I said sure." Matilda's face broke out into a smile again and she glanced at Steve, who was half leaning, half sitting on the desk, hands palm down on its surface, propping himself up as he listened. "After that we kept in touch," she continued, "chatting via message or call a few times a week, just getting to know each other, enjoying each other's company. Being friends, I guess."

Lynn's gaze swung to Steve and she raised an eyebrow.

"So, while you were giving me advice and tactical support for TD Hunter, you were cozying up to my mom behind my back?" Her tone wasn't accusatory. Not on purpose, anyway. She just needed to understand.

Steve took a deep breath and faced the question head on.

"Your mom and I are adults and have the right to privacy in our personal lives, especially considering we were just talking to each other as friends, nothing more. I'll admit our... connection was as much a surprise to me as it was to Tilly, though it didn't hurt that your mom is smokin' hot."

"*Steve!*" both Lynn and Matilda said at once.

He snickered, unrepentant, and continued. "We discovered we had a lot in common. We've both lost spouses—mine was a decade ago, breast cancer, no kids. We're both passionate about what we do. And we both care about an amazing, reckless, moody teenager who gives us gray hairs."

It took a second for Lynn to realize he was talking about her.

"Moody?" she said, incensed. "I am *not* moody."

Steve put up his hands. "Don't look at me, Tilly's words, not mine."

Lynn swung her baleful gaze on her mom, who didn't look even a tiny bit sorry.

"Just wait till you have a teenager, honey."

"You keep saying that," Lynn muttered.

"Because it's true," Matilda cackled.

"The point is," Steve calmly continued, "there wasn't much to tell, and neither of us wanted to distract you. Plus, there was a conflict of interests."

Lynn raised both eyebrows this time, having already thought of this and curious what Steve was going to do about it.

"The TD Hunter Championship stipulates that children, spouses, significant others, etc, of Tsunami employees are not eligible to compete. Now, considering we weren't in any way connected when you qualified for Hunter Strike Team, there's no issue. But it *is* one reason we've taken things slow and kept it on the down low. You've got enough media attention on you that *any* hint of cheating or scandal will get instantly blown out of proportion and probably used against you, even though we're not even officially dating."

"Oh, you're not?" Lynn asked, looking at her mom. That wasn't the impression she'd gotten.

"We've met once, just a casual dinner between friends. And this isn't a date. It's a family meeting." Matilda gave an innocent smile.

"Casual dinner between friends, huh?" Lynn said. "Like any gossip streamer in the universe will believe that."

"Which is why," Steve said, "I will be giving Mr. Krator my two-week notice as soon as we finish this 'family meeting.' The TD Hunter National Championship will be my last day on the job. I've had a good run with Tsunami, I have a lot of respect for Mr. Krator and what he's doing, but I'm ready for a change. I've got another prospect lined up."

Lynn looked back and forth between her mom and Steve, once again reeling from the surprises that just kept coming.

Quit his job at Tsunami? For *her mom*? That seemed... intense. Could he really care about her mom that much?

"But—but—your job. Tsunami. It's, like, the premier gaming company in the entire world! Why would you give that up for... for..."

Steve raised his eyebrows.

"For a chance?" he finished for her.

Lynn nodded mutely.

Steve's expression softened and one side of his mouth quirked.

"I know it's hard to have perspective when you've only been around for seventeen years—"

"Almost eighteen," Lynn muttered.

"Almost eighteen years," Steve conceded. "You've been working harder than any teenager I've ever witnessed for a chance at a life that involves Tsunami. I respect that, but that's you. Me? I've been around the block. Several times. When you get to be my age, you realize the only thing that matters in life is people. A job is just a job. But family..." He trailed off and shrugged his shoulders. "That's all assuming, of course, you want me," he finished simply and fell silent, watching Lynn with a carefully neutral expression.

"Want you?" she asked, not directed at anyone in particular. More like questioning reality itself.

Steve, though, took it as a request for clarification.

"In your life. If you don't, Tilly and I will still explore having a relationship, but we'll wait until you're out of the house, to respect your wishes. I'm not here to butt in and destabilize your life. Your future is too important to me. But I would be—" He paused and swallowed. "I would be *honored* if you were willing to let me be a part of your life, in whatever capacity you're comfortable with. Friend, mentor, whatever."

A tiny smile quirked Lynn's lips.

"Whatever? So eloquent."

Steve mock-scowled at her.

"I knew there was a reason your mother warned me about your smart mouth."

Lynn snorted. "Are you kidding me? You've *heard* Larry speak more than three words strung together. That should have been warning enough."

"Yeah," Steve said, frowning slightly. "Moving in with Larry the Snake... that's going to take some getting used to."

Now it was Lynn's turn to grin evilly.

"I'll keep you humble, old man. It'll be good for you."

Steve scoffed, but it was around a smile.

"You seem to be forgetting the *other* half of the time when I've put you in the ground before you even knew I was there."

Lynn adopted a superior look. "I was just letting you win to protect your fragile ego."

This time Steve spluttered in laughter and shook his head.

"Whatever you need to tell yourself, kid. And on the topic of wargaming, I need to put it out there that I used to be Army Ranger, so there are things about my life I won't ever be able to share, secrets I have to take to my grave. Matilda and I have already talked about it, but I wanted to make sure you knew what you were getting into."

Lynn scoffed, surprised at how apprehensive Steve looked.

"Come on, Fallu. You think I hadn't already guessed that? You've always dropped hints, and I'm pretty sure there's some rule somewhere that you can't have guns that big without the United States military owning them." She gestured at Steve's impressive arms, expecting him to laugh.

But he just shrugged and looked down, still seeming uncomfortable.

"Sooo..." Matilda said, looking between them.

Lynn made a show of crossing an arm and propping her elbow on it to stroke her chin thoughtfully. Really she was trying to sort through what the heck to think or feel. Change was scary. Caring about people made you vulnerable. But it also made you stronger. All she had to do was look at Skadi's Wolves and how far they'd come. Her mom was clearly head-over-heels, and Lynn had always liked Steve. He was calm, competent, a hard worker, and had a good sense of humor. Mr. Krator seemed to trust him. He'd had Lynn's back, had looked out for her in ways she hadn't even been aware of until after the fact. There had been times he'd... well, he'd almost reminded her of her dad. Not in looks or mannerisms. Just the way he called her "kid" and had been there when she'd needed someone to turn to.

And that, in the end, was all that mattered.

"I dunno, Mom. He seems pretty feisty," Lynn finally said into the increasingly tense silence. "You sure you can house-train him?"

Matilda gave Steve a sideways look, still unable to completely suppress her smile. It kept popping out at the corners when she tried to look serious.

"Oh, I think he'll do just fine. I managed to civilize *you*, after all."

Lynn rolled her eyes but didn't take the bait. Instead, she pointed imperiously at the third chair.

"Sit," she declared. "Interview time."

Steve raised his brows, but pushed off the desk and relocated to the chair so that he was facing Lynn and her mom.

"Chicken or steak?" Lynn said, looking stern.

"Steak, obviously. Come on, that's an amateur question. Give me the real stuff." He made a "come at me" gesture, eyes twinkling, and Lynn maintained her serious scowl only through sheer willpower.

"Early bird or night owl?"

"Former military, remember. I run on coffee. Time of day is irrelevant."

"Cardio or weightlifting?"

"Cardio is a necessary evil. You have to embrace the suck, kid."

"Wrong answer." Lynn scowled harder.

Steve grinned. "Hate the truth all you want. Doesn't change a thing."

"Hmph. Watch it, or you might flunk your interview."

"If I do, I can always fall back on my Adonis-like figure and my supernatural ability to crack walnuts with my glutes."

Lynn and Matilda lost it. Lynn almost fell out of her chair, she was laughing so hard. It was the mental imagery. Every time she calmed down, a vision of Steve in a bodybuilder pose, all oiled up with a walnut in his butt crack had her dissolving into giggles again.

A long drink of water and several bouts of resurgent giggles later, Lynn finally regained enough composure to say, "Okay, Mom. We can keep him."

For the first time in a while, Lynn felt truly relaxed. Steve pulled the small table of food and drink to the center of the room so they could sit around it, snack, and talk.

It was mesmerizing, seeing her mom light up, laughter and joy written all over her face. They laughed more in the next hour than Lynn thought she'd laughed since her dad had died. Steve didn't even seem like he meant to do it, he just slid in these deadpanned one-liners that had Lynn and Matilda rolling. And he was at the top of his banter game, something Lynn was already familiar with from playing WarMonger with him.

They did eventually calm down and talk of more serious things, like how they were handling the publicity stress and security measures at their new house—Steve was very intent on that topic, and made several suggestions that Lynn promised they'd implement as soon as possible. Matilda had kept him updated in general terms about the craziness with the faketime vid and Lynn's stalker. They were two things Lynn had no desire to expound on, except that Matilda was still obviously shaken and upset that Lynn and the guys had taken her safety into their own hands, so Lynn felt the need to walk Steve through their plan and defend their decision.

By his closed-off expression, Lynn suspected he had little desire to step into a topic of contention between her and her mom, but Lynn needed to know what he would say. Would he take her mom's side, or hers? How was he going to deal with the craziness that had invaded their lives? He seemed trustworthy and loyal, but did he really understand the baggage they came with? Would he balk at the difficulty?

"Lynn, what you did took a lot of guts, and I'm proud of you for that. You didn't lie down and let someone else's evil and harm control your life. You took charge, faced your demons, and protected yourself."

Matilda opened her mouth, expression furious, but Steve held up a hand.

"At the same time, what you and your teammates did was extremely reckless. I'm amazed someone wasn't seriously injured or killed. It sounds like your stalker likely had some kind of mental illness, which would make him unpredictable and dangerous. He might have had a gun or a knife. He might have tried to kill you. He might have succeeded. I'm sure you can understand how incredibly upsetting it was for your mom to find out you'd put yourself in that kind of danger, especially after..." He paused and grimaced, but kept talking very gently, "especially after how your dad died. Hopefully you can give each other some grace. What's done is done. But Lynn, never forget that trust is a privilege, not a right. It is hard-won and easily broken." He took a deep breath, expression growing even more serious. "Sometimes life requires secrets. I'm no exception considering my military background.

It was one of the roughest parts of my marriage, the things we couldn't talk about. But there's a difference between those kinds of secrets and deliberately sneaking around behind your mom's back when your safety and well-being are still her responsibility."

The full impact of her actions weighed heavy on Lynn's shoulders, and she looked at her mom, who was no longer scowling. She just looked tired. And haunted.

"I'm sorry, Mom," Lynn mumbled, twitching one hand to brush her mom's fingers hesitantly. "I had to do it. I...I *had* to."

Matilda swallowed, hard, but turned her hand over to take Lynn's hand in hers, squeezing gently.

"I probably would have done the same, sweetie. Just...just take care of yourself. Please?"

Steve leaned back and crossed his massive arms, a dark look on his face, though it seemed to be directed at the situation, not at either of them.

"You know, kid...I guess it wouldn't hurt to tell you that after you got attacked, I reached out to some of my old unit buddies who work in personal protection now to track down your stalker. We planned to make him quietly disappear. But, well, you got to him first." He bared his teeth in an approving smile.

"Steve! Don't encourage her."

Steve shrugged. "Credit where credit is due, Tilly. Those kids planned and executed a pretty flawless operation. Coulda gone sideways, but it didn't. Not bad for a bunch of teenagers. Payne masterminded it, you say?" he asked Lynn.

Lynn nodded. "We all pitched in with feedback and stuff, but it was his idea and he made it happen."

Steve pursed his lips thoughtfully.

"Huh. Good to know. That Payne kid has really come along. I gave him a bit of a nudge back in the fall, offered some professional development advice, so to speak. Sounds like he took some of it to heart."

"You did?" Lynn said, cocking her head. She'd assumed the trauma of being on the same team as Elena was what had shocked some sense into Ronnie. But maybe that hadn't been the only thing.

"You and your friends had a good thing going at the qualifiers. Didn't feel right when it broke up. Payne needed help pulling his head out of his, um, posterior," Steve said delicately, glancing at Matilda. "You needed him to be a functional teammate, so I did what I could, hoping things would work out once Connor got kicked to the curb."

"Thanks, Steve," Lynn said after an awkward little silence. "You didn't have to do that."

"Eh, it wasn't much." He shrugged. "You make it easy to root for you."

Things fell quiet again as they each were absorbed in their own thoughts.

"So, you think your guys are ready for the championship?" Steve asked.

Lynn pursed her lips, but nodded slowly.

"We're almost to Level 40. I'm sure we can make it by mid June as long as we don't slack off. And the guys...they're good. You're right, we've come a long way. They're...they're good guys. I think we have every chance of winning. We just have to stay focused."

"Magically getting rid of all the publicity would help too, I'll bet," Steve commented.

"Yeah, like that's ever going to happen."

"At least you've got Mrs. Pearson, right?"

"Oh my gosh, she's *amazing*."

"You're telling me. If she was Army enlisted, she'd be a Master Sergeant and every battalion commander would fight over her."

They fell to extolling Mrs. Pearson's virtues, which Steve knew more about than Lynn would have guessed. Apparently they'd had quite a bit of back and forth, what with the legal trouble Connor had threatened earlier in the year and the vid-slash-stalker problem.

"Mom, you'd better be careful," Lynn said at one point. "I think Steve has a secret crush on Mrs. Pearson."

Steve's horrified expression sent them both into another fit of giggles.

By then it was starting to get late. They'd cleared out the charcuterie board and drinks, and Matilda said Lynn needed to go to bed early and catch up more on her sleep if she was going to survive two weeks of hardcore hunting. Mrs. Pearson magically appeared as they headed for the door, as if she'd been hovering, waiting for them to need her. She walked them to the elevator and shook each of their hands before striding purposefully off to whatever her next task was.

"Well," Matilda said, not moving toward the elevator call button.

Steve's mouth quirked and he shot a glance at Lynn.

"Cover your eyes, kid," he said in a joking tone, then gently towed Matilda toward him by her elbow.

Lynn made an exaggerated expression of disgust, but couldn't help peeking out of the corner of her eye as Steve gave her mom a warm hug, then paused and whispered something in her ear that made Matilda blush furiously. Then he dropped a kiss on her mom's cheek before stepping back and pushing the elevator button Matilda had been avoiding.

"Good luck the next two weeks, Lynn. You've got this, I have no doubt. I'll see you at the championship. Safe travels," he said to them both.

"Oh!" Matilda said, as if suddenly remembering. "Our airbus had a malfunction on the way here. It dropped out of the sky for a second before the backup system kicked in. It was *terrifying*. I think we might take a ground taxi home, even though it'll add an hour to our trip." She made a face.

Steve's gaze sharpened and he glanced at Lynn, then back at Matilda.

"I'm really glad to hear it all worked out. That ground taxi is probably a good idea. I've been hearing about more and more malfunctions in the airbuses lately. Could be some sort of firmware issue going on. There's been a few really high-profile accidents. No sense pushing your luck."

"What about you?" Matilda asked, brow creasing as she reached out to lay a hand on his arm. "Surely you're taking an airbus to get back to Texas in time for bed?"

"Oh, don't worry about me." He laid his opposite hand on hers and squeezed gently. "Mr. Krator sent me in one of Tsunami's corporate fleet cars. They're top of the line, custom software. Not the same as these mass-produced airbuses that have been having problems."

Matilda visibly relaxed. "Good." She leaned in for a quick peck on his cheek, returning his earlier gesture of affection. "Come on, sweetie, elevator's here."

Lynn gave Steve a grin and a wave, and he clapped her shoulder and gave it a squeeze.

"Keep your head on a swivel, kid. Truth is stranger than fiction, and it'll kill you a whole lot faster."

"Yessir," she said, miming a two-fingered salute.

"Hey, don't you start. I worked for a living."

Lynn snorted. "Isn't it weird that I know exactly what you're talking about even though I've never served? It's crazy the stuff you pick up from hundreds of hours of crawling forums and hanging out in chat groups."

"Don't let it go to your head, kid."

"Tell that to Larry the Snake."

"Uh-huh. Get out of here, or that elevator's going to leave you behind."

She threw one last wave at him as she hurried after her mom, feeling optimistic for the first time in a long while.

Steve hadn't felt this shitty since the worst days of his marriage, when the weight of what he'd seen and done crushed him, his wife could see it, yet the wall of silence between them still had to be maintained.

No, actually. This was worse.

He'd never been forced to keep his silence at the expense of his wife's safety.

Steve lifted the beer he was nursing to his lips and took a long sip, then resumed leaning against the balcony of his modest apartment, staring out over the twinkling lights of Austin.

Just two more weeks.

Not that it would make anything better. It would probably make things worse, if Lynn did what everybody hoped she would do.

A ping in his ear interrupted his depressing train of thought. A message from a contact he'd labeled "The Canuck" popped up in the corner of his vision, splashed across his LINC interface contacts.

How did the big reveal go, eh? Did she stab you?

Steve snorted softly. Leave it to Derek to be politely nosey. Their days of Alpha testing TD Hunter together were behind them, but their shared love of gaming and mercing adventures in WarMonger helped their bond of friendship weather the high-stress, uncertain, and ever-changing environment of CIDER. Between Derek getting assigned to go undercover and back Lynn up physically, and Mr. Krator unofficially sanctioning Steve to watch out for Lynn from a distance, their coordinating efforts had led Steve to confide more in Derek than he'd expected.

She thought about it, Steve responded, subvocalizing the text. *But I convinced her mom my face was too pretty to disfigure.*

Steve could imagine the Canadian's muted amusement, though the thought only briefly lifted his mood. Soon he was back to brooding about the convoluted situation life had thrown him into.

Stop brooding, Cowboy. It'll work out. Derek's message blinked annoyingly across Steve's vision. Damn Canuck. He wasn't YodaMaster for nothing. The guy could read people like nobody's business.

You can't talk, Steve responded, deflecting. *You married your battle buddy.*

Derek's answer was almost immediate.

Yeah, after engaging in a secret romance in virtual while we were still in the same chain of command. Count all the ways that could have gone wrong. Don't be fatalistic, eh? It'll work out.

Steve took another sip of his beer before subvocalizing his response.

It's not just that. Their airbus malfunctioned on the way to Des Moines. Almost crashed. I don't know if I can do this. To Lynn. To Tilly. They deserve to know what risks to avoid.

The words were one side of the argument his brain had been having with itself for months now. An argument that would never, could never, get in the way of OPSEC. Because the other half of the equation was that this was war. There would be casualties. Everybody was at risk, and none of them could play favorites. The whole world was counting on them, even if the world didn't know it.

Derek took a long time in replying. Maybe he was trying to think of something useful to say. There wasn't much *to* be said. The Lynn that Steve knew, the Lynn behind the Larry Coughlin mask, was always looking for trouble. She couldn't walk away from a challenge if her life depended on it. And war was no place for overconfident kids with no idea of the real risks.

Living is a risk, my friend. Derek finally said. *Loving is, too. And we do both anyway. They'll understand. Give them a chance.*

Steve didn't respond, because there wasn't really anything to say.

Stay the course, Cowboy. Only a few weeks left, then the real work begins.

Steve snorted and threw back the rest of his beer.

I'll drink to that, Canuck. Can't happen fast enough.

Chapter 11

LYNN'S HIGH SCHOOL GRADUATION CEREMONY WAS A SATISFYING end to an epoch of her life that had almost broken her.

Was it ironic that the biggest lessons she'd learned that would stay with her for life had nothing to do with any class? Maybe school had been a life-changing education for some of her classmates, but for her it had been a series of hurdles she had to jump over to reach the freedom of adulthood with a thing in hand that employers and society at large said she had to have.

That wasn't quite fair to her teachers. Some of them had been absolute gems, and she'd truly enjoyed those classes. But most were simply trying to make a living. They shoved information at her so she could regurgitate it on a test and prove she'd been paying attention. They got their paychecks and she got her passing grades, and they could part ways with no love lost between them.

None of it made any difference to her future.

But she was still proud that she'd stuck it out, worked hard, walked the stage, and gotten the piece of paper that was her culture's rite of passage into adulthood.

Now she could get on with her life empowered by the important social lessons she'd learned in the dog-eat-dog world of public school. She could have done without most of them, but that hadn't been the choice given to her. So, she'd done the best she could with what came her way.

And then there were the friendships.

She'd cheered unashamedly when Edgar, Ronnie, Mack, and Dan's names had been called to walk the stage. They'd all passed, even Edgar, with fairly decent grades. Every one of them had been tempted a time or two to give up on school and go all in on TD Hunter. If all of them had wanted to give up at the same time, they might have tried to do it. But they'd looked out for each other and had given out the necessary kicks in the tail needed to straighten out their priorities.

Kayla, of course, killed it. She got some award for her contribution to the school's student spotlight stream, which she'd apparently helped produce. Following in her father's footsteps already.

To Lynn's disappointment, Elena and her flunkies managed to scrape by the grades necessary to graduate as well. Connor, unsurprisingly, was top of the class. Lynn supposed one couldn't have everything in life.

She was mildly surprised neither Connor nor Elena tried anything untoward at the graduation ceremony. Not a single snide comment or even a veiled look of venom. It made Lynn suspicious, as usual. Connor didn't seem like the kind of narcissistic bully to give up. But maybe how hard he'd gotten smacked down—physically by Edgar and legally by GIC—when he'd tried to bully Skadi's Wolves had taught him well: putting himself in his enemy's sights was a losing proposition. Which, of course, was why the guys were convinced Connor had been behind her many troubles that spring.

They just had no proof.

Lynn put the entire topic from her mind, happy to leave high school and its trials behind her. She'd done it. She was free.

The cap toss on the front lawn was a magical moment Lynn would always remember. The moments after, too, though for different reasons. Dan's cap almost poked his eye out when it came back down, and Mack lost his in the crowd, which made him panic because his mother wanted it as a memento and would kill him if he lost it. He ended up grabbing some random cap on the ground. Lynn was pretty sure its owner wouldn't miss it.

Matilda had tried to organize a big graduation party for them all, but the Nguyen's had a fancy dinner planned with their extended family, the Rios' were doing a joint cookout with a few of Mack's cousins who had also graduated, and

Mr. Payne had never even responded to her invite. So instead, Lynn, Matilda, and Mr. Thomas—who had *insisted* he attend her graduation— joined Edgar's family for as much pizza as they could eat at Happy Joe's. Lynn noted the conspicuous absence of Edgar's dad, and she wasn't sure if that was a good thing or a bad thing. Edgar didn't seem gloomy, so she took it to be neutral or good. Then again, Edgar seemed perpetually happy around her these days, so his mood might have had nothing to do with his family situation.

Overall, it was a good day. One she would treasure. The people she cared about were around her, she was forever done with high school, and she'd eaten *a lot* of delicious pizza.

Finally, *finally*, she could focus her whole heart, mind, and body on the biggest goal she'd ever set in her life: to win the TransDimensional Hunter Championships.

"Did you, um, like the food, Daddy?" Elena asked, walking quickly to keep up with her father's long stride. They were leaving the fancy, snooty restaurant her mother had picked out so they could look important while celebrating Elena's graduation. Her mother had already left, obviously, taking their private air taxi home so she wouldn't be subjected to sharing the same air as her husband and daughter any longer than necessary.

Elena assumed her daddy was going to take her shopping, maybe for a special graduation treat. It was what he usually did during his brief visits: lavish her with gifts, ask her how school was going, and leave again promising he would be back in town as soon as his busy schedule allowed.

It never allowed.

But instead of asking her where she wanted to go, he seemed distracted by something on his implant and acted like he was rushing off somewhere. She hoped a little conversation would remind him she was even there.

"It was fine," he said absently. "Not worth the exorbitant price, but fine." He stopped on the street corner by the tastefully decorated all-weather overhang where passengers waiting for air taxis usually sat.

"Where are we going, Daddy? I thought, maybe... maybe we could go shopping, since it's my graduation?"

He glanced at her, that familiar guilty look marring his brow.

She could have hated him so much more easily if he didn't act guilty for being such a terrible father.

"I'm sorry, sweetie pie. I've got a very important deal I'm hours away from closing. This is the big one, I can feel it. Rich oligarchs from out of country. It will turn everything around, I promise."

Elena kept her smile glued on her face, even though her heart was falling apart inside. It had already been shattered years ago. But every time he came and went, another piece crumbled off and fell down somewhere into the dark.

It was always like this. Every deal was "the big one." Every deal would change things, and he'd be home more.

All lies.

But he was the only person in her life who loved her, and she couldn't help clinging to that for all she was worth.

"That's all right, we can make it quick," she said brightly, giving him her best "adorable little girl" smile that always seemed to melt his heart.

He hesitated.

"I'm...sorry sweetie pie, but I really ought to go. I'll try to get things wrapped up by next week. Maybe we can go somewhere nice, just you and me. Or maybe since you're done with school, you can come visit me in New York! We can look at colleges there, see which one you want to go to."

That wasn't new either. He always promised she could come visit him in New York, but the "right time" had never materialized. Still, he'd mentioned college. Maybe he meant it this time.

Not that she was sure she *wanted* to go to college. Or at least, not the kinds her daddy had in mind. But if it meant escaping this horrible town and her horrible mother, she might take the chance.

But that was only if she failed. The Plan was to establish a foothold and a following so she'd be free to go and do whatever she chose—whatever the viewer wanted to see. She could envision some cute college-themed content, but it was mostly a really boring place.

She had this silly, stupid, secret dream she had never told a soul that if she could just get popular enough, get enough sponsorships, that maybe she could go live with her daddy in New York, set up a studio wherever he lived, and they could exist in each other's spheres. She didn't expect him to be around all the time. But she'd have freedom and her own source of income, and she'd get to be around a person who actually cared about her.

But she had to prove to him she could support herself first. That she would contribute, not suck off his teat like her mother did. She'd be her own boss, not a burden.

"That would be great, Daddy, I'd *love* to come to New York! But I haven't seen you in *weeks*. I miss you so much. Can't you please stay a little longer? Please?" She blinked a few times and thought sad thoughts, trying to make herself shed a few tears—it wasn't hard, with the crap her mother yelled at her. She clasped her hands together and pulled her shoulders in, making herself seem smaller, younger.

Her daddy hesitated again, looking at the sky. He no doubt had the time ticking away in a corner of his vision. Maybe even messages from his investors scrolling along the side, demanding his attention.

"*Please*," she whispered, feeling moisture gather and spill over. People thought she was shallow for being able to cry on demand. What they were too stupid to see was that she wasn't summoning tears when she needed them, she was suppressing tears all the times she *didn't* need them, pretending like everything was okay and she was confident and happy.

"Oh, sweetie pie, don't cry." Her daddy gently wiped a tear off her cheek, and Elena almost lost control. She couldn't have that. She needed to make more content later today, and she couldn't do that with puffy, red eyes. "I can probably...I can spare thirty minutes, okay?" he said, looking around. "Look, there's a park over there. It's a gorgeous day, let's go for a walk."

Elena got far more exercise than she'd ever wanted trying to keep up with her former ARS athlete teammates hunting TDMs. She only tolerated it because a toned figure was good for stream ratings, and it was nice to eat something other than salads. She nodded enthusiastically at her father's suggestion anyway, afraid to do anything but agree in case her daddy changed his mind and left.

They walked across the street together and past a sign declaring the area to be Greene Square Park. It wasn't very large, just a single city block of mostly open grass with some trees planted along the paved walkways bisecting it and a few benches here and there. It wasn't a beautifully designed park, just an average greenspace in the middle of downtown because so many of the old sprawling gas-guzzler parking lots had become obsolete and greenspaces were supposed to promote mental health.

Honestly, with those large, rectangular green transformer boxes clustered at one end, it looked like the sort of space where CRC would spend an hour killing TDMs.

Her daddy started walking down the main paved walkway and she trotted to keep up.

"So," he said, diving right in without preamble, "I think you would do very well at Cornell. Columbia and New York's MBA programs are quite prestigious, too. But I think you'd benefit from the higher quality instruction at Cornell. Cornell has a gorgeous campus, which is, of course, because it isn't in New York City. There are benefits to living in the city, certainly, but having lived in and out of the city for years, I can tell you there are definite drawbacks too."

"Wait, Daddy, what are you talking about?" Elena said, still walking faster than was comfortable in her high heels. Why was he in such a hurry even when he was supposed to be taking a leisurely walk? Maybe she could get him to sit down on one of the benches.

"Your choices for MBAs, of course."

"What is that? Masters of Business Arts?" she asked.

He screeched to a halt and gave her an incredulous look that made her skin feel hot and prickly.

"Masters of Business Administration, sweetie pie. We've been talking about this, remember? You're going to get an MBA so you'll have all the skills you need to be successful in life." *Unlike your mother* was the unspoken end of that sentence.

Elena bit her lip. Was this the right time to bring it up? If not now, then when? She dove in.

"I know how much you like business, Daddy. And I do, too. That's why I started my own stream brand. I have sponsorships and everything! Did you know I just passed twelve million followers?"

She gave him a brilliant smile, anticipating his praise for how hard she'd worked.

But he only stared at her blankly.

"Stream brand? Sweetie pie, I'm sorry, but that's not real business. I know it's all the rage with kids, but you're an adult now.

You have to act like it. Livestreaming is performative nonsense. I'm all for capitalism, but for that you need innovation, big ideas, big investments. Stream celebrities are just lazy narcissists too afraid of hard work to join the real world and produce something that actually benefits civilization. You're better than that."

Elena only heard about half of what he'd said. She stood, frozen, staring at him.

Not real business... performative nonsense... lazy narcissist... afraid of hard work.

The words ricocheted around in her chest, hitting her heart over and over again, sending crumbling pieces flying and falling down into the dark.

Afraid of hard work.

The rage started to build.

"Afraid of hard work?" she said, voice low, but growing louder. "Afraid of hard work?! Are you kidding me? Do you have *any* idea how hard I've worked for *years* to get good grades, establish social dominance in school, and build a stream brand that's actually earning me *real* money? Did you know that Mom won't pay for *any* of my clothes or shoes or makeup? She says it's a waste of money since I'll never be a real actress, so she spends all the money you give her on herself instead. I get to eat whatever she has around the house and that's it. I've been paying for everything else myself for years. And you think I'm a *lazy narcissist*? How *dare* you! You don't care about anyone but *yourself*! You're just a worthless coward too afraid of Mrs. Seville to divorce her like she deserves and take me away to give me a real life with... with..."

She couldn't get the words out, just couldn't say *a parent who loves me*, because she knew it wasn't true. She knew she'd been lying to herself this whole time. No one cared about her. She was all alone.

But she *refused* to fall apart.

"I've worked hard and earned every bit of money and influence I have. You do *nothing* but talk big and play around with other people's money. Benefit civilization? Yeah, right! All you care about is benefitting yourself!"

By this time she was screaming, fists clenched, feet planted. Her father's face had cycled through shock, then discomfort, then anger. But now his face had gone eerily blank and cold.

"Are you finished screaming?" he said, coldly.

Elena crossed her arms, glaring, too angry to be hurt anymore.

"I see your mother has been teaching you well. You sound just like her. 'I got this part' and 'I won this award.' And what good has it done her? Where's the capital? Where's the profit? What has she done for anyone other than herself? It's *my* money she lives off of, a leech on the underbelly of society. I work hard every day to provide for both of you, and this is the thanks I get? Well, that ends today. You're an adult now. If you want my money, you'll stop being a foolish, selfish little girl and let me send you to business school to build a future for yourself. If you want to chase your shallow, childish fantasies, you can do that on your own dime. I'm not going to pay for you to turn yourself into your mother. I couldn't stand by and watch that."

Elena was furious. Furious at her father for being so high on his horse, and furious at herself for still caring what he thought. How dare he pretend to care about her now, after being absent for her whole life.

"Fine! I don't need you. I've *already* made my own name. I'm going to win the TransDimensional Hunter International Championship, win five million dollars, and be so famous even your stupid investors will be talking about me. Just you wait and see!"

Her father snorted.

"Good luck with that, sweetie pie. Call me when your mother kicks you out and you're ready to see sense and go to college. I'll be waiting."

"No, you won't!" Elena found herself screaming. "You never answer my messages anyway! I can't trust you for *anything*!"

This time her father's face colored, and his jaw clenched. But instead of responding, he simply turned away and strode quickly down the path that led past the green transformers and out of the park. He'd probably already called another air taxi. He was going to run off to New York again and abandon her.

Conflicting desires warred in her chest. She could break down right now, start sobbing and beg her daddy to stay. She was sure she could convince him to give her what she wanted, if she just had the time to prove what she'd accomplished.

But that would involve pretending to admit he was right, after he'd insulted and embarrassed her. No way was she going to give him that sort of satisfaction, that selfish, arrogant—

Without sound or preamble, her father abruptly collapsed, like a puppet whose strings had been cut or a robot whose switch had been turned off.

"Daddy!" Elena screamed and took off down the sidewalk, running as fast as her heels would let her. When she reached him, she fell to her knees beside him, scraping them painfully on the concrete. She suddenly felt woozy and nauseous, like she was going to pass out or throw up or both. Her hands fluttered uselessly as she tried to breathe through her panic. Her daddy was twitching and blood slowly oozed from his scalp where he'd hit his head in the fall.

"Ma'am, are you okay?"

"I'm calling 911."

"Somebody go put pressure on his head to stop the bleeding!"

Bystanders had seen the incident and were shouting, but Elena couldn't hear or see them. All she could see was her father's limp face, surrounded by oozing blood. All she could hear was her own voice, screaming at him.

Her nausea surged and she almost blacked out. But then several people arrived and crowded around, and her dizziness abruptly faded.

She was shaking, now, and rocking back and forth, arms wrapped around her torso. People were talking, asking questions. Someone pressed a shirt to her father's head. All Elena could do was stare at him and mutter over and over, "Please, Daddy, please don't leave me. Please, Daddy. Please."

While the rest of their class in Cedar Rapids was busy partying, soaking up the sun, and generally reveling in their newfound freedom, Lynn and her team geared up and went on the hunt.

They battled from dawn to dusk. They found every "hot" spot there was and cleared vast areas, slaughtering monsters by the thousands.

And every day, it seemed like there were more TDMs than the last. Whether the game was leading up to an "event" like Mack had said over the winter or not, at least Lynn and her team never wanted for targets.

Trying to make up for lost time, they met up with Team Voodoo Girls twice to make a hunting group and wipe out some bigger, tougher mobs of TDMs than they normally tackled on their own. It was a treat to get to know the girls better, though Lynn still felt awkward around other gamer girls when ninety percent of her gaming life she'd been surrounded by male gamers and was more used to their foibles. As Lynn had assured her teammates weeks ago would be the case, the members of Team Voodoo Girls *were* solid, and they picked up the formations and movements Skadi's Wolves taught them with ease. Sure, maybe their movements weren't as polished or blows quite as accurate. But they had no trouble keeping up with Lynn and the guys.

Plus watching Ronnie blush every time he was in Quorra's vicinity was hilarious. Her presence seemed to rob him of his powers of speech, maybe even his powers of thought. Mack, Dan, and Edgar had been forced to save him multiple times when Quorra had asked him innocuous, hunting-related questions that he couldn't answer because he couldn't even string two words together. At least killing TDMs was sufficiently distracting to keep his mind in good working order whenever they were in combat mode.

Small blessings.

Lynn's birthday came and went with a necessary lack of fanfare. Not only had she strictly forbidden her mother from throwing a party, but even if her mom had, all the people she would have invited were already with Lynn all day, every day. And by the time the sun set, they were far too tired for parties.

Disappointingly, turning eighteen didn't magically make her feel more confident and grown up. But then, she'd long ago realized she had to depend on her own stubbornness and strength for that, not outside circumstances, so it wasn't much of a let down. It *was* weird realizing the house she lived in was now legally hers. But it didn't change anything about her everyday life, so she didn't dwell on it.

Despite her embargo on a party, she hadn't tried to forbid presents. So when she came down to breakfast, despite it being before dawn, she wasn't surprised to find her mom had made her a scrumptious meal of poached eggs over steak, with crisp-on-the-outside, tender-on-the-inside tater tots to top it off. Lynn grumbled that she wouldn't be able to hunt weighed down by so much food, but that didn't stop her from making it all disappear. She needed the fuel, she reasoned. Her mom gave her a huge hug and a wrapped present, which turned out to be two identical "impossible puzzles" with no picture what-so-ever on them.

"So we can finally prove once and for all who is the puzzle queen in this family," Matilda said with a cheeky grin.

Edgar showed up earlier than he needed to for them to leave and meet the others. He had a shovel in one hand and a giant grin on his face.

"Uh-oh. What are *you* up to," Lynn asked, eyeing the shovel. "Are we going to bury something? Did you bring me Connor's dead body for my birthday?"

Matilda spat out a mouthful of milk all over the kitchen floor and Edgar hooted.

"Lynn Gudrid Raven!"

"Sorry, Mom!" Lynn cackled. "Couldn't help it."

"Come out back," Edgar said, still chuckling as he jerked his head toward the back door.

Out on the back patio, Lynn found a young tree in a big ball of dirt with a pile of landscaping tools laying beside it.

"Uhhhh." She looked between the tree and Edgar.

"Happy Birthday," he said, grinning wider than ever.

"Thank you," she said slowly, "buuut what *is* it?"

"Oh, yeah. It's an apple tree. I was tryin'a think of what to get you, and I knew you don't like random junk, so it had to be useful. And you own a house and a yard now, so I figured an apple tree would be a great addition. Don't worry, you don't have to do any work. Just show me where ya want it. I've planted a lot'a trees during my summer job. Apple trees need full sun, but other'n that it can go anywhere. They look great when they bloom, they smell nice, and eventually you'll get apples." He spread his hands wide, a look of childlike wonder on his face.

Lynn laughed.

"Thank you, Edgar. That's probably the most thoughtful thing anyone has ever gotten me." Before he could drop his arms, Lynn surprised them both by hugging him tightly around the middle. She didn't mean to linger, but his solid frame was so pleasant to wrap her arms around, and the feel of his heartbeat was a soothing rhythm against her cheek. The cedarwood scent of whatever body wash or soap he used tickled her nose, and she breathed it in, feeling her body relax. Just a few seconds... he wouldn't mind...

"Uuuh, Lynn?"

"Oh! Sorry," Lynn let go and jumped back, having no idea

how long that infinite moment had actually been. His arms were still held out as if he'd been afraid to touch her. She dropped her eyes to examine the ground. Gooseflesh had broken out across her arms, despite the warmth of the sun on both of them.

"So, uh, do you wanna plant it?" Edgar asked, voice rough. She forced herself to look up and meet his eyes, covering her embarrassment with an automatic smile.

"Yeah, yeah, absolutely. Help me find a nice sunny spot for it, okay?"

"You got it, boss."

She helped him carry his tools, and they picked a spot in the middle of the open back yard nearer the fence line, past which hummed the sound of interstate traffic.

It only took Edgar a few minutes to dig out a perfect hole for the sapling, his arm muscles bunching and flexing as he efficiently cut away through the thick sod and dirt below it.

Lynn helped plant the tree, and when they were done they stood back, hands on their hips, surveying their handiwork.

"Uh, Edgar. How long does it take for an apple tree to make fruit?"

"Usually about five to eight years, for this variety."

Lynn chuckled.

"So, basically, if I come back after college I might finally get to taste the fruits of our labor?"

"Pretty much," he said, grinning.

They cleaned up and headed out, only for Lynn to get another surprise when they met up with Mack, Ronnie, and Dan. The three guys shuffled around a bit, looking everywhere but at her, until Dan kicked Ronnie in the shin and muttered something at him. Ronnie glared back at him and opened his mouth, but then Mack yanked something out from behind Ronnie's back.

"Good grief, *I'll* do it," Mack said, and handed Lynn a bundle of cloth. "Happy Birthday, Lynn. From all of us. We, uh, hope you like it."

Lynn schooled her face and held up the cloth so that it spread out. She found it was a smart-fabric high-performance workout shirt emblazoned with the stylized words:

THAT'S WHAT I DO, I EAT STEAK AND I KILL THINGS.

Lynn grinned. "Aw, that's cute, guys. I like it."

Ronnie's ears got distinctly pink, and he still wouldn't look at her. But Mack and Dan brightened up and stumbled over each other in their rush to tell her what else it did.

"The smart fabric has another pattern that's body-heat activated," Dan said, "so when you get really into your workout, the back will show the Skadi's Horde logo from your medallion augment, and the front will change to saying 'Skadi's Wolves rule, CRC drools.'"

That got a full-throated laugh from her, and she bundled up the shirt to stuff in her compact backpack.

"The custom shirt idea was all Mack's," Dan admitted. "But the heat-activated second pattern was Ronnie's idea. I helped find a place that could make it and we all pitched in to buy it."

"Thanks, all of you," Lynn said, careful not to sound too sappy. She was really, truly touched, but getting mushy might make Ronnie puke, so she kept a lid on it.

They did their usual stretch routine, and then got to work for the day.

The days passed in a tiring blur, but not the same kind of blur as their last few weeks of school. Finals had been a dreaded hurdle they simply wanted to pass and be done with. But hunting was a fierce joy, a full-body workout, and an hour-by-hour discipline in teamwork. Despite being a lot of the same thing, every hunt was different. The terrain dictated flexible formations. The ebb and flow of TDMs forced them to always be watchful, focus on every movement, every kill, instead of zoning out. Even though they'd leveled past worrying about most of the sneakier TDMs like Phasmas and Creepers, they always had to be on guard for those telltale sounds to avoid taking unnecessary damage. They never knew when they'd stumble on a brood of Strikers or take unexpected fire from a hidden Hydra. The Penagals and Managals were some of the most tactically unpredictable TDMs and a constant annoyance for everyone. And it always got fun when a Nundu showed up.

Then there was the constant checking of the leaderboards. Lynn had forbidden her team from scanning them while in combat mode, but between battles, the guys were always pulling them up, bragging about this or that rival they'd passed in some obscure ranking metric. It was amusing in an exasperating sort of way, their seemingly innate need to constantly one-up each other. But then she supposed none of them would be competing on this level if they didn't have the competitive drive for it. She did the same thing with Larry Coughlin, just in a more private, tasteful way.

During the last week before the championship, Dan finally got his wish to see a Chimera breathe fire when they were ambushed by one near a data center on the outskirts of Cedar Rapids. Most medium to large cities had a data center of some type, to support the various AI-operated systems in the public and private sectors. Data centers were always a great place to hunt because they were energy hogs, and there was plenty of node and transformer infrastructure spread out around the outskirts to attract the TDMs.

Lynn and the guys knew all about Chimeras and their capabilities from the app's TDM list and tactical simulations, but this was the first time they'd fought one face to face. It was even less fun than Lynn anticipated, despite Dan's initial enthusiasm. The thing was *fast*. And it breathed *fire*. Or, more accurately, plasma.

After fighting that Draca, Lynn was absolutely fine not facing any more fire-breathing entities.

Slowly their experience bars inched up as the days went by, getting closer to that all-important Level 40. Lynn tried not to obsessively check her kill-to-damage ratings. That battle with the Draca had really put her in a hole, one she hadn't been sure she could claw her way out of in time to beat Derek—AKA Deathshot's—rating before she hit Level 40. But to her surprise, Derek's rating dipped along a similar trajectory as her own, as if he was also up to something damage-heavy. Lynn thought about pinging him and asking about it, but instead counted her blessings and doubled down.

There was no room in her mind for anything but her team and the hunt.

And hunt they did.

Dan head-shot everything. His accuracy had gotten so good he vied with some guy from Germany for the top accuracy ranking in the entire game. The last few levels he'd won rare named augments, which only increased the deadly force of his attacks. Anything Lynn needed dead, he made it happen.

Mack had grown. All traces of that uncertain, unkempt kid were gone. He'd grown into a confident, dependable force to be reckoned with—even his beard grudgingly got with the program, no doubt cowed into submission by Mrs. Rios. Half the time Mack seemed to read Lynn's mind and was where she needed him before she said a word, scooping up loot and keeping everybody well supplied so they could focus on the fight.

Edgar was a *beast*. His enthusiasm for the game grew every day, and if any TDM so much as looked at his team sideways, that was excuse enough for him to bury it in a firestorm of raging destruction. His hard work over the months had molded his stature to fit his prowess, and sometimes Lynn had to remind herself not to stare at his wide, muscled shoulders and powerful torso.

And Ronnie, well... if Lynn had been a superstitious sort, she might have declared him a walking miracle. She couldn't even remember the last time he'd said something snide about her—though perhaps that was because her memory was so sleep deprived. Whatever the case, he seemed to have found a handbook for professionalism somewhere and then actually *took it seriously*. Who knew, maybe Steve had sent something else his way.

Lynn was amazed and gratified, and tried to find small ways to positively reinforce Ronnie's wins in the maturity department without triggering his extreme aversion to things like feelings.

Before they knew it, it was three days before the championship, and today was the day.

Today, they were going to hit Level 40, come hell or high water.

Lynn had done more poking around on the news streams and pinpointed another area of town that seemed to be struggling with grid problems. It was suspiciously close to Cedar Rapids' generating station. On a hunch, Lynn had them go to the gates of the plant itself, which was on the southern end of the city along the Cedar River.

What they found was a Hunter's wet dream. Or worst nightmare, one of the two.

Lynn's mercenary brain took precedence over her internal paranoia, so she couldn't help but bare her teeth in a feral grin once they dropped into combat mode and saw not one, not two, but *three* boss rings and enough electrovores to suck an entire city dry.

If they'd been real, of course.

Lynn's wild conspiracy theories and suspicions haunted her

thoughts in the dark of night, which she coped with by being so exhausted she passed out as soon as her head hit her pillow.

Today, though, wasn't a day to worry about anything but killing TDMs. Much to Edgar's disappointment, they didn't try to confront the bosses camped out on the edges of the plant. The trio were likely Bravo Class bosses, based on their size, but Lynn didn't have a death wish, even if it turned out they were "only" Draca.

Instead, she took her team around the south side of the plant to the long clear space between the perimeter fence and the surrounding woods where the June sun shone down hot and humid on the evenly cut grass.

And there, they danced.

Over the previous weeks, Skadi's Wolves reaching Level 40 had slowly built into a much anticipated event on their stream channel, so Mrs. Pearson and her team were on the job managing the livestream. Today Skadi's Wolves fought with mics hot, but the livestream on a thirty-second delay, just in case.

The objective today was total destruction, so the team advanced and retreated, flowing with the surge and ebb of the TDMs themselves. Skadi's Wolves were well-matched with their opponents, and the enemy's only advantage was sheer numbers. Lynn had little to do but call the timing for bait drops and ensure her team didn't get stuck in too deep. The guys barely needed any direction. It was as if they'd all developed a sixth sense for each other's positions, and staying aligned was more instinct than conscious effort. Everybody knew their area of responsibility.

Just because they were a well-oiled machine didn't mean they were silent, though.

"*Choo-hoo-HOO*, come at me bro!" Edgar sang. "I'll kill you, I'll kill your mama, and I'll kill your mama's mama!"

"That one's so ugly I think you're doing his mom a favor," Dan quipped.

"Oooh, burn, Dan my man!"

"Dan, get this Spithragani off my back," Ronnie said, "it's crimping my style."

"Your wish is my command! Nobody is allowed to crimp my boy Ronnie's style."

"Sometimes I wish a Kongamato would crimp *your* style,

Dan," Lynn said. "If you shot as much as you talked we could all sit back and sip pop while you took care of it."

"Ah! You wound me, O glorious leader."

"Only because she's right, Dan," Mack pointed out. "Not even my *mom* talks that much, and you've met my mom."

"Hey, no fair!"

"If Dan stopped talking... his brain would stop working," Ronnie grunted in between dodging and stabbing a pair of Rakshar trying to flank him. "I should know... we've been gaming together since we were in elementary school."

"So what you're saying, Ronnie, is that Dan's trigger finger is directly connected to his mouth?" Lynn asked.

"Pretty much."

"Ho-ho!" Edgar chortled. "My homies, our eardrums are doomed."

"That's right, you lot," Dan complained, "go on and grouse. Just see where it gets you when you need some proper overwatch."

Laughter echoed across the team channel while monsters raged and exploded into sparks before the wrath of Skadi's Wolves.

Lynn grinned. She didn't know exactly when it had happened, but somewhere along their crazy journey together, almost a year to the day, they'd become a team in *heart*, not just in name.

She couldn't have been more proud of them.

"Miss Lynn, you have passed ninety-nine point nine percent experience for this level."

"*Finally*. Thanks Hugo. We might be able to wrap this up and get home in time for an afternoon nap."

"Since when has it been your habit to take an afternoon rest, Miss Lynn?"

"Since today. Once I'm Level 40, woe betide anything, man or monster, that stands between me and my bed."

"I shall take note and warn all men and monsters accordingly."

"Har-de-har-har."

To an outsider, Lynn might have sounded cool and calm. But inside she was a bundle of nerves ready to jump out of her skin. She took it out on the Jotnar in front of her, sliding under its swing and stabbing up into its chest between two cracks in its armored plates. It exploded into sparks and she backed up, letting the TDMs come to her as she picked them off with ranged fire. Any of them with high enough hit points to survive Abomination she gladly introduced them to Wrath, dodging and rolling past their attacks, using every trick she knew to stay clear of even a sliver of damage.

She didn't know if it would be enough. At this point, though, she'd come to terms with the possibility that she'd sacrificed a complete Skadi set on the altar of leveling fast enough to compete in the championship. It was a sucky tradeoff, but one she hadn't hesitated to make.

Sometimes you had to keep your eyes on the prize, and let the smaller things pass by.

"Heads up, team," she said when there was a slight break in the oncoming monsters. "We've passed the last threshold. Leveling imminent!"

"Woot woot!" Dan cheered.

"*Finally*," Mack said.

"Come to papa, you big, beautiful, bastards!" Edgar shouted. "Come and taste the fiery ashes of your own demise!"

Mack laughed. "Aww, Edgar's getting all poetic."

"Less chatter, more focus, guys. I don't want anything big and nasty taking us by surprise when we level. Once we've all confirmed Level 40, we'll drop out together. There's a nap with my name on it back home."

"A nap?" Dan said. "Are you kidding me? We've almost *made it*! I'm so hyped right now I could kill a boss all by myself!"

"Okay," Ronnie said, "who filled Dan's hydration pack with sugar water?"

"Probably himself," Edgar grunted as he ducked under the widening poison spray of a Spithragani. Ronnie obligingly rolled in from the side and stabbed the monster up through its ugly head, making it explode into light.

"We'll have plenty of time to celebrate later," Lynn said. "Remember, my mom threatened to throw a party before the championship and invite all your families?"

There was a collective groan on the channel. Lynn grinned.

"You know you're not getting out of it. *Nobody* says no to my mom if she's determined."

"Duh, she's a nurse," Dan said. "She knows how to, like, kill people."

"Don't be dramatic," Lynn said. "I think Mack's mom is *way* scarier than mine."

"You and me both," Mack agreed.

"That's 'cuz you've never met *my* ma when my little sibs get rowdy," Edgar said over the roar of fire from his Snazzgun. "She'll make you wish you had a sweet, kind ma like Mrs. Rios!"

They kept up the banter, not just for the fun of it, but because their stream followers enjoyed it too. Their most watched streams by far were the ones with hot mics.

After another five minutes, Hugo gave them all a final warning. They didn't know what would happen when they hit Level 40, so they needed to be prepared. Lynn didn't expect any surprises based on their experience reaching Level 20 right before the qualifiers. Most likely the designers had instituted another graduated level cap so that no one could advance past Level 40 until after the championships happening worldwide that weekend.

Now in the final stretch, Lynn tuned out her team's banter and focused every synapse in her brain on her surroundings, her attacks, how her body moved. She bent and flowed through the storm of enemies in a seamless, graceful whirlwind of destruction. Just before her mental calculations put them over Level 40, she had Skadi's Wolves pull inward and retreat a dozen yards to disengage from melee battles and focus on picking off enemies by ranged fire.

"Congratulations, Miss Lynn, you have achieved Level 40!" came Hugo's voice after what felt like an interminable wait.

All she wanted in that moment was to stop and check her leveling notifications, or even ask Hugo to read them to her. But she forced herself to wait. She had a team to take care of.

"Great work, team. We did it!" As she said it, an adrenaline rush took Lynn by surprise, accompanied by a relief so intense she had to swallow a whoop of joy. *They had actually done it.* Suddenly she wanted nothing more than to keep fighting. Maybe take on a boss or two. No biggie.

But she quelled the triumph raging through her and reminded herself there would be plenty of that for later. Right now her team needed to *rest*. The biggest, most difficult battle lay ahead of them.

"Everyone, finish up whatever you're killing right now, we're hopping out of here."

"Aww, but Mom, I don't wanna go home," Edgar said, blasting the heads off an entire brood of Creepers at once. "Pleeease can we have five more minutes? *Pleeease?*"

Lynn rolled her eyes but didn't respond. Instead she said: "A big thanks to all our fans watching. It's been a wild ride and we can't wait to see you at the TransDimensional Hunter US National Championship this weekend!" She continued her rote closing for all their livestreams, mentioning the sponsors she was contractually obligated to mention and reminding everybody to opt in to notifications so they would "never miss a stream." Then she got everyone's attention and they all dropped out of combat mode together.

As usual, the abrupt quiet and stillness around her made Lynn dizzy for a moment after Hugo took her out of combat mode. But it dispelled quickly as she grinned around at her teammates.

"We did it!" Dan yelled, punching the air. Then he took Lynn by surprise and tackled her with a hug.

"Whoa! Dan, uh, settle down?"

"We couldn't have done it without you, Lynn!" he exclaimed.

"Ya know, he's right," Edgar agreed, sliding in from the side to sneak an arm around Lynn's shoulders. "Good job, Lynn."

"Yeah! Good job!" Mack came at the little group, arms open wide, and managed to grip half of Edgar and most of Dan in his enthusiastic contribution to their hug fest. Lynn just stood there, holding perfectly still in hopes it would encourage Dan to loosen the death grip he had around her torso.

"Yo, Ronnie, come on, team hug, bro!" Edgar called.

Ronnie crossed his arms over his chest and snorted.

"What do you think we are, a cheerleading team? Yeah, no thanks. I'll pass."

"Let's get out of here," Lynn said, not even offended. "I already called an air taxi."

The whole encounter was no doubt transmitted live by the swarm of paparazzi drones swooping around them. The guys barely seemed to notice them anymore, and Lynn had made her peace with their presence, at least for this battle. She understood peoples' desire to be a part of this moment of triumph, even though it wasn't *their* moment. The fact that Skadi's Wolves had chosen to livestream their journey to the entire world meant they'd invited the entire world into their lives. She couldn't begrudge them the emotional payoff of all the time they'd spent watching.

Which didn't mean she planned to invite them into any *other* moments of her life.

Ten minutes later they were cooling off in the vigorous air conditioning of the air taxi, hydrating from their packs and munching on energy bars. Once the taxi was in the air, it was finally safe for everyone to hop back into combat mode to check their leveling bonuses. Lynn kept her breathing calm and even as she navigated to her leveling and bonus screen...

Her heart leapt and her eyes prickled suspiciously at the sight of an obsidian black medallion with an ice-blue rune at its center. The personal augment was called Skadi's Crown, and Lynn didn't even bother to check its stats, she simply equipped it.

Lynn gasped.

"Mack! Look at your armor!"

"Whaa—*whoooa*! Look at me! Look at everybody!"

Her teammates had transformed in her augmented vision. Their eclectic mix of armor items had morphed into their own scaled suits of obsidian with glowing ice blue runes. Their armor wasn't a carbon copy of hers; rather each team member had a unique design and rune pattern. Ronnie's was sleeker, with runes running down the arms and legs, while Edgar's had giant, rune-covered plates reinforcing his chest, thighs, and shoulders. Together, they truly looked like a fearsome band of space Vikings, ready to lay waste to whatever monsters TD Hunter threw at them.

"Lynn," Edgar said softly, "look at your avatar." His eyes were on her forehead, and she fumbled in her rush to select her customizable avatar. That's when she saw what Edgar was staring at.

She wore a crown. It was obsidian black, like the rest of her armor, but its surface was covered in a Nordic design glowing ice-blue against the obsidian surface. The upper edge didn't stick up from her head in ridiculous spikes; instead it lay low across her forehead, compact and tactical just like the rest of her warlike armor.

And the ability it came with...

Lynn whistled.

"What does it do?" Dan asked eagerly, leaning forward.

"It's called Shared Fate," Lynn said, her tone awed. "I can use it once per twenty-four-hour period. When I activate it, for the next five minutes all damage and healing is evenly distributed across each member of the team."

"Whoooah," Mack said, his eyes getting big.

"Wow... that's actually pretty useful," Ronnie said, brow furrowed.

"Yeah," Dan agreed. "It basically makes us unkillable for five minutes!"

"Unless we run out of Oneg," Edgar pointed out. "Then we're *all* dead."

"Pshhh." Dan made a dismissive gesture. "Details."

"The devil's in the details," Ronnie muttered, eyeing Lynn. "It'll be pretty tough figuring out when to use something like that."

"Do or die moment," Lynn agreed, nodding gravely.

"Shared Fate," Edgar said. "All for one and one for all."

After that, Lynn almost didn't care what else the crown did, though of course she was glad to hear her teammates' muttered exclamations over the upgraded stats and special buffs their new Skadi's Armor gave them.

They truly were Skadi's Wolves, now. A single unit driven by a shared purpose—and a shared fate. They were *her* team, and the weight of that responsibility sobered her as she stared at her new symbol of office.

This wasn't about her anymore, or what she wanted.

It was about her *team*, and she fully intended to ensure they utterly destroyed this championship and took home the victory they had worked so hard to secure.

Chapter 12

"HEY, JERALD! THANKS SO MUCH FOR COMING TO OUR PARTY."

"Oh, I wouldn't miss it for the world, Lynn." Mr. Thomas gave Lynn's hand a squeeze. The skin of his hands was leathery and wrinkled but his grip was still full of warmth and strength. Then he moved past her to greet Matilda in turn.

Lynn had known there was no point telling her mom not to throw Skadi's Wolves a "Leveling" party. Matilda had been antsy, not getting to properly celebrate Lynn's graduation *or* eighteenth birthday, both huge milestones. Lynn figured this party was the release valve Matilda needed to get all that celebration out of her system.

The open layout between the living room, dining room, and kitchen area of their house was perfect for hosting a party. It was decorated to the nines, and Lynn had to admit it didn't look bad—Matilda had likely recruited Kayla to help. The petite girl had a definite eye for style, fashion, and decor. She'd chatted with Lynn a few times about convincing her dad to give her a paid internship at GIC to work as their design consultant for a gap year while she explored various design and fine art specialty schools.

The party planners had gone with black and ice blue for their color theme, and someone had produced a smart fabric banner to hang over the living room area that cycled between different messages like, "Congrats Skadi's Wolves!!!" and "Skadi's Wolves for the win!!!!!" and "We're so proud of you!!!!" Lynn assumed the presence of so many exclamation points indicated Kayla was the mastermind behind that particular bit of decoration.

It was...exclamatory.

Whatever she and the guys thought of the party decor, they could find no fault in the food. Specifically, the fact that Matilda had made bacon-wrapped steak bites. And not just *some* bacon-wrapped steak bites. A *lot* of bacon-wrapped steak bites. Enough to feed multiple families of hungry teenagers. She'd obviously remembered how much Lynn had raved about them from Kayla's Christmas party and gotten the recipe from Mrs. Swain.

"Oh my God, Lynn! I love your mom!!"

Lynn rolled her eyes, unsurprised that Dan had spotted the bacon-wrapped delicacies from across the room as soon as he set foot in the door.

"Hey, don't hog them all yourself this time," Mack protested, and took off after Dan, leaving Lynn and her mother to greet their respective families. To Lynn's relief, neither Mr. nor Mrs. Rios gave her the stink-eye, and Mr. And Mrs. Nguyen both shook Lynn's hand warmly.

"We wish you every success this weekend, Lynn," Dan's impeccably dressed mother said. The skin around her dark eyes crinkled and she leaned in closer, voice lowering. "Thank you for giving Daniel something to strive for. It's been good for him... and us." She patted Lynn's hand, then moved further into the room to greet Mr. Thomas. Mr. Nguyen nodded gravely as he passed, and Dan's older sister winked, then made her own beeline toward the refreshments, yelling at Dan to keep his greedy little fingers off the bacon.

When Edgar arrived with his family, Lynn had to keep from staring at the tall, bulky man who accompanied them. She'd never met Edgar's dad before. His skin was much darker than Edgar's, and he had the muscled-yet-thick look of someone who used to be fit but had let themselves go. From the tense postures and exaggerated smiles of Edgar's mother and siblings, it was clear they weren't very comfortable around him. But at least he'd come to support his son. That was something.

Edgar's plethora of siblings jostled their way past Lynn and Matilda, obviously having only one thing on their mind. Mrs. Johnston pulled Lynn in for an unexpected hug while her husband stood back awkwardly, hands in his pockets.

Mrs. Johnston was soft and warm, a little shorter than Lynn, and her frizzy black hair smelled of vanilla, which weirdly reminded her of Edgar. It was a nice hug, though, and Lynn found herself returning it instead of stiffening up. When Mrs. Johnston pulled back, she was smiling and there was a barely noticeable watery shine to her eyes. The kindness there was clear as day, only emphasized by the dark circles under her eyes that made her look every inch the exhausted working mom that she was.

"Thank you for making my baby boy smile," she said quietly, and moved to hug Matilda before Lynn could reply.

Edgar, who was trailing behind his parents, grinned at Lynn.

"Well, I guess I see where you get your touchy-feely side from," Lynn told him with a grin.

"That mean you won't bite me if I do *this* more?" he asked and sidled up to give her a gentle but firm side hug.

"Hm, I suppose I'll let you get away with it, if I must," she said, still smiling.

Edgar mimed a victorious fist pump, nearly making Lynn giggle. She suppressed it, though, because Mr. Johnston was still standing around awkwardly while Mrs. Johnston talked to Matilda, and the big man was staring at Lynn.

Ronnie, as usual, was late. Kayla and her parents had already arrived, and everyone was standing around with plates of finger food when he appeared at the front door. Lynn had been keeping an eye out for him, and so was the first to notice the red-haired and mustached man who stood behind him.

No way.

When Matilda had insisted she was inviting *all* of the families, she hadn't been kidding. A part of Lynn—the old her who preferred to hide in baggy clothes and pretend not to exist—wished the man with Ronnie would just disappear. But what if he was finally trying to support his son? Lynn gritted her teeth and made herself go welcome them in.

"Hi, Ronnie. Hi, Mr. Payne. Welcome to the party!" She gave the elder Payne her most winning smile and held out her hand politely. The man, as freckled and lanky as Ronnie—or at least as lanky as Ronnie *used* to be—glanced at Lynn's hand, then ignored it.

"Evenin'," he grunted, making it abundantly clear *exactly* where Ronnie had gotten his sullen jerkitude from.

Ronnie's face flushed as red as his hair, and he looked away.

"Well," Lynn cleared her throat and dropped her hand, "we've got lots of food, and, um..."

Before her attempt at hospitality went from awkward to painfully lame, Matilda swooped in and saved her.

"Mr. Payne! I'm so glad you made it. I'm Matilda, Lynn's mom. Here, let me introduce you to the other parents. I'm sure they'll be thrilled to meet you."

Matilda moved as if to take Mr. Payne's arm and guide him away, but as she reached for him, he flinched. Matilda, ever the expert at handling people from many years in the ER, simply altered her direction mid-motion and gestured toward where the other adults were standing instead.

There was a tense beat where Mr. Payne didn't move. But Matilda's welcoming smile stayed firmly in place, and finally he shuffled off after her.

Lynn let out the breath that had been stuck in her lungs.

"Hey, Ronnie," she said quietly. "Good to see you."

He gave her a combative look, as if expecting an attack, but she just smiled.

"Come on, let's go grab some bacon-wrapped steak bites before Dan eats them all."

That made Ronnie's eyes widen, then his lips quirked upward.

"Leave it to Dan to stuff his face before the competition shows up. Mack is just as bad, but at least he's sneakier about it."

"Well, then, we'd better get moving." Lynn lifted her eyebrows and tilted her head in the direction of the kitchen island where all the refreshments were laid out. Ronnie snorted and headed that way.

While Dan and Mack hadn't *quite* managed to eat their bodyweight in steak bites *yet*, they were well on their way. Lynn and Ronnie joined Dan's sister in fighting them off. In the process, though, they made the critical mistake of taking their eyes off the prize, and by the time they turned back, Edgar's siblings had descended on the bacon steak bites like starved pterodactyls, complete with screeches and hissing. Edgar took pity on his teammates' beleaguered plight and joined the fray. Eventually they chased the interlopers away and enjoyed a few moments of bacon-filled peace before the starving hordes joined forces and regrouped.

Lines had been drawn and battle was preparing to commence when Matilda's voice rose above the general chatter, getting everyone's attention.

"Thank you all so much for being here to celebrate and support our young people."

Everyone turned toward the living area where Matilda stood in front of the couch, a cup in her hand.

"They've worked incredibly hard this year," she continued, "and are now getting ready to embark on the journey of their lives."

A thrill of anticipation shivered up Lynn's spine, and she met her mom's eyes with a smile.

"I don't know about all of you, but I was definitely skeptical when Lynn told me she was going to play this new TD Hunter game."

"At least *you* knew what she was doing," called out Mrs. Rios, and Mack gulped and bent at the knees, shrinking a little as if to hide from his mother's detection behind his friends. Dan, in contrast, looked completely unrepentant, and gave his mom a jaunty wave when her critical eye landed on him.

Matilda laughed.

"Do we *really* ever know what our teenagers are up to?" she asked, spreading her hands to encompass them all. "Whether we've wanted to or not, I think we've grown as parents through this process just as much as our kids have." Matilda met Lynn's eyes across the room and smiled. Lynn grinned back, though she felt a tinge of bittersweetness within the triumph. What would it have been like to have her father there too, standing beside her mom and smiling just as proudly? The wistful thought ached in her chest like a physical thing, but she forced herself to let it go. Maybe someday soon, Steve would be standing with her mom, no longer a Tsunami employee and free to celebrate Lynn's wins alongside them.

"That's why," Matilda continued, "despite some difficulties along the way, I think we can all say how incredibly proud we are of you five, not only for what you've accomplished, but for what you've overcome." She paused, a brief cloud passing over her expression as she no doubt remembered the horrors they'd all faced. Then she took a deep breath and fixed a smile on her face. "So, here's to Skadi's Wolves, and winning the championship!" She raised her cup, prompting cheers and clapping among the gathered families. Mrs. Johnston gave Edgar a tight hug, and even Mrs. Rios cracked a smile at Mack, while Mr. Rios winked and gave his son a thumbs-up behind his wife's back.

"Please, eat lots of food and stay as late as you want, though I'm sure our contestants will want to get plenty of sleep before they head off to Austin tomorrow."

There was a general shuffle as people returned to their conversations, while Lynn and her "battle brothers" and "battle sister" prepared to meet the oncoming horde, led by Dan. He'd found a sparkly party hat somewhere and was waving a fork in the air like a sword in preparation for their charge.

Amid the low hum of conversation, though, Lynn's ears suddenly caught a phrase, and she froze.

"—just be glad when all this nonsense is over."

"Why, Mr. Payne? Isn't Ronnie enjoying the competition?"

"I don't give a hoot what that boy enjoys. The whole thing is a waste of time and I'd break him of it if I could."

The sudden silence that followed Mr. Payne's loud comment was deafening. Lynn felt Ronnie shift beside her and she glanced over to see his fists clenched and his eyes on the floor.

"What?" Mr. Payne said, glaring around at everybody's shocked stares. "Don't act all high and mighty and pretend this nonsense is what you want for your kids. They're all wasting good time and effort on pussy games that don't mean a thing. You mark my words, they'll still be living in your basements in ten years, living off Mommy and Daddy's money like manbabies."

The silence stretched on, though it had become charged like the thickening air of a thunderstorm. Lynn could see the other adults glancing at each other, some incredulous, some confused, as if wondering whether Mr. Payne was actually serious.

"I mean, look at *him*," Mr. Payne continued, gesturing at Edgar's father. "At least he set a good example for his kid, playing a *real* game like football. Why can't we get back to the days when people didn't have their face stuck in a fantasy all day long? If we did, our kids wouldn't be such pussy-whipped weaklings having themselves get led around by a *girl*—"

"Dad! *Shut up!*"

Mr. Payne spun on his son faster than a striking snake,

pointing his finger at him from across the room as if he wanted to do much more than simply point.

"Don't you tell me what to do, boy. You know I'm right, if you'd only stand up for yourself and be a man for once in your—"

"That's *enough!*"

Matilda's voice cracked through the room like a whip, and Mr. Payne flinched, though he still turned his glare on her and crossed his arms. That lasted the whole three seconds it took Lynn's mom to march across the room and stop inches from his face, her lips pulled back in a snarl. His skin blanched and he uncrossed his arms.

"How *dare* you speak like that about *anybody*, much less your own son! You are the worst excuse for a father I have ever seen, and believe me, I've seen some low-life scum come through my ER."

Mr. Payne's mouth opened and closed soundlessly, but Matilda wasn't done. Not even close.

"No thanks to your miserable, worthless hide, your son has worked himself to the bone at a *real* game with *very real* rewards. Do you realize that if they win, they get five million dollars apiece *and* a full ride college scholarship?"

"It'll probably be fake electronic money, that bitcoin stuff," he muttered, not meeting Matilda's eyes. "And it's a *gaming* scholarship. What self-respecting man studies *games* for a living? It's ridiculous!"

"*You* are ridiculous!" Matilda threw her hands in the air. "Who cares what your son studies? It's *his* life, and you should be proud of him no matter what he does, because you're his *father*, you backward-thinking, worthless cretin! Do you even know the difference between virtual and augmented reality? This game is just as real as anything else, and it's been one of the best things these kids have had going for them in their entire lives. Do you have any idea how much they've grown the past year? Have you even *looked* at how healthy Ronnie is now compared to a year ago? Have you listened to him, seen how he's matured and developed?"

Lynn glanced at Ronnie again and saw that his eyes were still glued to the floor and his face was roughly the shade of a tomato—but there was also a discernible uptick at the corner of his mouth.

A new voice spoke up, and Lynn's eyes shot over to see Mrs. Nguyen standing beside Matilda, arms crossed and perfectly plucked eyebrows arched in disdain. With her heels and immaculate pantsuit, she looked every inch the high-powered attorney she was. Her husband came up beside her as well, a quieter but just as impressive presence in his tailored suit and silver cufflinks.

"A year ago I might have agreed with you, Mr. Payne. But I would have been wrong. This is not the dream I had envisioned for Daniel, but I can't pretend it's not a serious and impressive undertaking. He has applied his passion and honed his skills to become one of the top-ranked gamers in the world, and he will end up working for the biggest company in the gaming industry, if I have anything to say about it. That is something to be proud of, and from what I have seen, Ronnie has been there the whole time as his best friend and biggest supporter. That shows loyalty and hard work, regardless of what you think of the gaming industry."

"I agree," Mrs. Rios butted in before so much as a word could come out of Mr. Payne's wide-opened mouth. She stepped up on Matilda's other side, hands on her hips. "My Maxwell has always been such a handsome boy, but he's been looking better than ever since he started competing. And with his amazing success and fame, it's all I can do to keep the girls away from him." Lynn snorted into her hand at the look of mortification on Mack's face, and she wondered what Mrs. Rios thought of her son's ill-advised foray into virtual dating. Did she even know about Mack's maybe-maybe-not-scam-bot girlfriend? Probably not. "Young Ronnie was the one who got him into gaming in the first place, which obviously shows how smart and forward-thinking he is, doesn't it, Maxwell?"

"Uh y-yeah! Absolutely," Mack agreed, elbowing Ronnie in the ribs with a grin.

"AI and automation are changing the world faster than we can keep up," Mr. Rios commented from near his wife. "Young people need to be ready for the world they're stepping into, not the world we grew up in." He spread his hands and shrugged, as if the logic of it was self-evident.

"Gaming has helped Edgar find focus and balance in life," Mrs. Johnston added, having quietly come up beside the other moms. "His team are his best friends in the whole world and they've done more for him than I ever could. You should be *very* proud of your son, Mr. Payne. We are."

Silence finally fell again, but Mr. Payne didn't say a word into it. Faced with a solid majority of the parents, several of whom looked ready to rip him a new one, he had backed up a safe distance to glare at all of them, a faint sneer lifting one corner of his mouth. Something ugly simmered beneath his expression.

"What I think about my son is none of your business," he finally snapped. "I don't have to stand here and take this abuse. Come on, Ronnie, we're leaving." He turned and strode off, arms stiff and hands clenched. It took him until he got to the door to realize Ronnie had not followed him. He spun, anger at the fore again now that he wasn't being stared down by an army of mama bears.

"Get your sorry carcass over here, boy! We're leaving."

Ronnie's eyes flicked from his father to the rest of the room, and Lynn could easily see the conflict in them. Give up in front of his friends, but avoid conflict with his father? Or stand up for himself and pay for it later?

"We've got your back, Ronnie," Lynn said, voice low so Mr. Payne wouldn't hear it. "Whatever you need, we'll be there."

"*Boy!*"

Ronnie's eyes flicked back and forth a few more times, then his expression set.

"I-I'm staying. The party isn't over yet."

His father swore viciously and the man started marching toward Ronnie.

"Get over here this instant, you worthless runt, or I swear I'll—"

The angry man pulled up abruptly to avoid running face-first into Mr. Thomas, who had stepped resolutely into his path. Lynn realized the elderly man had surreptitiously moved around the main group of adults while the argument had been going on. Without bringing notice to himself, he'd taken up a flanking position, perfectly poised to cut off Mr. Payne's route back into the house. Now Mr. Thomas stood, shoulders set and bent back straight, cane held loosely in his hands, staring Mr. Payne down like a matador.

"You will do *what*, exactly, Mr. Payne?" Mrs. Nguyen snapped, her icy voice cutting through the tense silence. Multiple other adults shifted to put themselves between Mr. Payne and the group of teenagers by the kitchen island. "Are you seriously threatening to commit domestic abuse in front of a dozen witnesses? I am a managing partner of one of Iowa's most prestigious law firms, and I recommend you think *very* carefully about your next words. What is more, my husband is a renowned surgeon. If you think he can't recognize even the most subtle marks left by physical abuse, you are more of a fool than I imagined. So again, I will ask, what *exactly* do you think you're going to do?"

If looks could kill, their entire party would have keeled over then and there. But they couldn't, as Elena's failure to off Lynn via venomous stares over the years had already proven. Fortunately, Mr. Payne had the sense—or cowardice—to not push the issue. With one last dark look at his son, he spun and stormed out the front door, slamming it violently behind him.

"Ronnie," Mrs. Nguyen said, turning to her son's friend, "you will be spending the night with us, and one of us will accompany you to your house tomorrow morning to pack your things for the championship."

Ronnie hesitated. A torrent of conflicting emotions were obvious on his face. Lynn couldn't imagine what it would feel like for the one person in the world who should have loved you unconditionally to treat you like an inconvenient piece of trash. What kind of piercing shame and sorrow must Ronnie have been hiding all this time? All the years she had known him, she'd never given him the benefit of the doubt or taken the effort to understand what his life had been like, even though she knew from veiled comments between him and Dan that his father was a pretty terrible person.

Yes, Ronnie was responsible for his own actions, and the lies he'd accepted as fact from his father. But she still felt a twist of guilt in her heart that she'd never dug deeper.

Ronnie noticed Lynn staring at him and his expression shifted toward embarrassment, quickly covered by annoyance. But the pointed look Mrs. Nguyen gave him made him glance away and shrug one shoulder.

"Yeah. Sure. Thanks, Mrs. Nguyen."

"Excellent," Matilda said, clapping her hands together and adopting a bright smile. "Now, I believe we were all enjoying each other's company and celebrating our amazing young people. Let's not let a little—" she bit back what she was about to say with a glance at Ronnie, then took a deep breath "—unpleasantness ruin our evening."

It took some time, but slowly the tension left the room and the incident was forgotten. Well, not forgotten—Lynn would never forget the look on Ronnie's face as his father had berated and insulted him. But it was put aside, for now.

"Don't you dare pity me," Ronnie said, stepping up beside her with a cup of punch. His face was set in stubborn lines, and he avoided her gaze as he spoke. "I don't need your pity, and I sure as hell don't need your help."

Anger and sadness swirled in Lynn's chest. His words hurt, but not nearly as much as she figured his father's words had hurt *him*. She wasn't about to kick him while he was down. It made her glad that, despite being tempted a few times by a guilty conscience, she'd never told him Larry Coughlin's true identity. It surely would have shattered the fragile trust building between them.

"'Course you don't need my help," she said, and shrugged. "But if you ever do, I'll be here. We all will."

He looked at her in surprise, emotions mixing in a confused tumble across his face. But she just nodded gravely and left him to his thoughts. There was still food left over, and those bacon steak bites weren't going to eat themselves.

Tsunami flew them into Austin, Texas, on a posh, private airbus—thankfully, they weren't forced to share with CRC. The free transport surprised Lynn, but it seemed Tsunami was pulling out all the stops for their Hunter Strike Teams. The championship competition was being held on Sunday, the third and last day of Tsunami Fan Con, the gaming convention Tsunami hosted every year. All the competing teams were flown in on Friday and had a bevy of events scheduled for Saturday, from signings to media appearances to a private VIP party in the evening.

Tsunami covered all expenses for each contestant and their plus one. Since they were all over eighteen, their plus one didn't have to be a parent. In fact, Dan brought his older sister who was on a brief break before her next semester of med school. Obviously, Lynn invited her mom, and Mrs. Rios came with Mack to "protect him from all those pawing fan girls." Not a single member of their team offered Mack any sympathy. In fact, they had a field day sniggering every time Mrs. Rios made a comment about how "handsome" her son was or how it was "inevitable" that he should attract so much female attention. They didn't go so far as to tattle on him about his Japanese love-bot, but it was a close thing.

Predictably, Ronnie came alone. As for Edgar, he brought the oldest of his siblings, the sister who had been doing extra babysitting duty this whole year. Lynn had offered to cover the cost of more of his siblings and his mom, but his mom didn't want the younger ones going, nor did she want to go and leave them at home. Instead, she opted to support Edgar from afar and let her two oldest go have a good time.

And good times were definitely in store, starting with the ride to Austin. The airbus had a built-in refreshment bar, full-spectrum entertainment options, and even massage settings built into the seats. It would have turned into a *real* party if Mrs. Rios hadn't confiscated all the miniature bottles of alcohol from the bar. Dan whined about it, but Lynn was secretly grateful she didn't have to be the party pooper herself. They all needed to keep their wits about them.

Mack spent the entire trip talking—very quietly and out of his mother's earshot—about how jealous Riko was that she couldn't attend Tsunami Con with him. She'd been planning to come, and he'd been stoked that he'd finally be able to introduce her to them in person. But her travel plans had been cancelled last minute over travel safety issues. Apparently, Japan's biggest and most respected airbus manufacturer had had one of their units experience catastrophic system failure and go down during an international flight, killing everyone on board. All units had been grounded pending a top-to-bottom safety review and firmware purge.

Of course, nobody had the heart to tell Mack that Riko's excuse was just an elaborate ruse taking advantage of current events to make him think she was real. After all, if she was as rich as she claimed, wouldn't she have access to private travel options? Dan bet Ronnie his favorite vintage controller that any day now the bot would find some excuse to ask Mack to transfer it money, though Dan was too chicken to confront Mack about it. Dan's excuse was that Mack was a grown man and needed to learn from his mistakes.

They arrived at their hotel in Austin around noon on Friday and were met by their management crew from GIC to do some interviews and promotional shots. The crew consisted of the eagle-eyed Mrs. Pearson, a cameraman-slash-drone-operator, their stream technician, and an assistant named simply Bill. Nobody commented on the fact that "assistant" Bill looked buffer than Rambo and seemed incredibly alert and watchful for being a simple gofer. Lynn suspected he had a hand in the scarcity of paparazzi drones at the hotel. Being a PR company, GIC probably had permits for all sorts of fancy tech that private individuals weren't allowed to use, including surreptitious devices to disable nosey drones.

Kayla was there too, much to Dan's delight. She'd convinced Mr. Swain to send her on a trial basis as their wardrobe stylist, with the dual job of helping Mrs. Pearson with fan relations, since Kayla was closer in age to the average Skadi's Wolves fan than the severe PR manager was. Lynn was less than thrilled at Kayla's presence, not because she objected to Kayla, but because she objected to the things Kayla expected her to *wear*.

Mrs. Rios, predictably, was thrilled by GIC's involvement. She talked Mrs. Pearson's ear off with suggestions for how to frame Mack's shots "just so." After a while, Matilda took pity on Mrs. Pearson and did her best to keep Mrs. Rios occupied and out of the way.

Overall, it was an emotionally exhausting day, though at least it was all indoors. It was *hot, hot, hot* in Austin, and Lynn developed a newfound respect for TD Hunter players in southern states. Hunting in that heat was probably miserable as *hell*. But Friday was all about PR, so they gratefully hid from the June heat in their hotel.

And their PR duties weren't all bad. At one point they did a live Q&A with their stream followers, and Lynn was gratified by the quality of questions and positivity of their fans. The best was when a little girl asked Dan if he would marry her so she could always have the cheat codes to the games she played. Lynn hadn't known his skin could turn that shade of red, or that he was capable of being struck speechless, but she supposed there was a first time for everything.

Then came Saturday's Tsunami Con.

If Lynn had thought Friday was exhausting, it was a drop in

the ocean compared to Saturday. Over a hundred thousand fans of TD Hunter and dozens of other globally popular Tsunami games flocked to Austin's giant convention center just south of downtown by the Colorado River. The convention had it all: tech debuts and demos, vendors selling gaming paraphernalia, influencer and pop icon events. They even had a slew of smaller tournaments running for everything from Tsunami's ultra popular Wizard Duelists card game to their BattleBot Arena virtual free-for-all.

Lynn and her group did not arrive at the convention through the front entrance. As VIP "celebrities" they had their own back entrance, and even a Tsunami security team to guide them where they needed to go and provide crowd control. Lynn felt like it was overkill, at least until they arrived, and she saw how large the crowds were. Plus, Mrs. Pearson had briefed them the night before that GIC was still receiving concerning messages meant for various Skadi's Wolves team members. From stalkerish fans to angry CRC fanatics and the usual crazy dregs of humanity, it really was enough to warrant a security detail.

When Skadi's Wolves first entered the convention center floor, people in the crowds recognized them right away. Some called, some waved, and some surged toward them, probably intent on getting selfies or autographs. There were screaming girls waving and making kissing motions in the guys' direction, which made Lynn scowl. Much worse were the men whistling and catcalling at her, which she did everything in her power to ignore. All it would take was one guy making a lewd gesture and bringing up traumatic memories of last month to ruin her entire day. Edgar stayed glued to her side, though, and Bill always seemed conveniently placed to intercept those who thought it was acceptable to abandon all social decorum and try to rush their group. As deterrents went, his muscle-bound frame and dangerous stare was more effective than Lynn would have expected. His secret was probably being a head taller and twice as wide as anyone else around other than Edgar. Between Bill and their security detail, Mrs. Pearson was able to herd everyone along, insisting that they had places to be.

As championship competitors, most of their day was planned out for them, including an equipment test and promotional appearances with Tsunami staff. Team Voodoo Girls was at the convention as well, but they weren't included in any of the publicity or photo ops. They simply had to show up for the official equipment checks and some routine admin stuff.

When Lynn tried to apologize to them for it, Quorra scoffed at her.

"You kidding me?" she said. "We get to go *enjoy* the con. You all get to *work*. Have fun!"

Quorra was not wrong.

Despite the veneer of fun and entertainment, what Lynn and the guys had to do *was* a ridiculous amount of work, with far too many cameras to smile at and hands to shake. Lynn had to remind herself that Tsunami was footing their bill, plus the various sponsors of Skadi's Wolves had paid them good money and were owed their fair time in the sun. Lynn and the guys were all decked out in their sponsored gaming paraphernalia covered in company names and logos.

There was a surreal moment when she was posing for yet another picture that Lynn remembered watching footage of Tommy Jones at this exact convention two years ago, doing exactly what she was doing. At the time she'd had a massive crush on him and had tracked down any stream vid of him she could find.

Now, there she was, a professional gamer herself, and most likely providing crush fodder for millions of guys worldwide.

The irony would have made her smile. But unlike Tommy, who had clearly lapped up the attention like a prize show dog, Lynn wanted nothing more than to hide in her hotel room. Despite having her mom and teammates there to support her, the crush of humanity and crazy, almost worshipful energy of the crowds shook her. Some screamed, some held out their hands, reaching as if they wanted to grab her and bury her in their fanatic love. Except it wasn't love, because not a single screaming fan knew her as a *person*. They were simply obsessed with the illusion of who Lynn Raven was.

Bill turned out to be incredibly helpful in keeping screaming fans from getting to them. Okay, all but *one* screaming fan, but the scantily clad girl threw herself at Mack with surprising force. Lynn didn't even see her coming, but Bill intercepted her deftly before she could get her arms around Mack's waist and start begging him to sign her forehead. Besides that crazy fan, there was a constant press of people all around them on the convention floor. It was unfortunate, since it kept them from enjoying the convention and showing their family members around the exciting games and equipment. Lynn got sick of how many girls waved booklets, T-shirts, and other paraphernalia at Edgar, yelling for "Mr. Maui" to sign their merchandise or pose with pictures of them squeezing his biceps. She didn't dwell on why it annoyed her so much—she had her work cut out for her avoiding all the guys begging her to put on lipstick and sign their pictures of her with a big fat kiss.

The only thing that kept her going were the genuine fan interactions during the paid photo ops. She signed so many batons and various pieces of TD Hunter gear, she lost count. Tsunami had special markers whose ink bonded with the baton's omnipolymer and would remain even through multiple transformations—though Dan assured Lynn that nobody who'd gotten their baton signed would be using it to hunt. They'd put it on a shelf in a glass case.

Each of the Skadi's Wolves members had their own photo op line. No one was surprised at whose line was the longest. But there were a surprising number of fans who paid extra for the group photo, and many were particularly obsessed with getting a baton pair signed by all five team members at once.

Then there were the cosplays.

Lynn almost couldn't stand them. They were simultaneously the most embarrassing and coolest thing she'd ever seen. People cosplaying *her*. The costumes ranged from cringy to so impressively detailed that Lynn assumed the wearers were professional costumers. The level of dedication put into some of them made Lynn jealous, considering she'd never actually *worn* her Skadi's Avatar armor or fought with a real Abomination or Wrath. All she had was the ultra-realistic view of them through her AR interface. Seeing people modeling the armor set and weapons in the real was fantastic fun. More than once her "handlers" had to remind her that more people were waiting in line, and she couldn't have lengthy conversations about costume-making techniques in the middle of a photo op.

Probably for the best.

The highlight of the cosplays was the guy who showed up toting a massive replica of Edgar's Snazzgun while sporting the Loincloth of Lordly Might—*only* the Loincloth, as opposed to how Edgar had worn it, which had been overtop his other armor. Lynn was too busy laughing her head off at Edgar's obvious discomfort to worry about the sight of barely covered man parts.

There were definitely cringy moments, though. Lynn found that fans overshared to an embarrassing level, as if she weren't a real person, just a stand-in for their fantasies. There was even a guy who got down on one knee and started proposing. Fortunately the Tsunami security team removed him in short order, and Edgar had no opportunity to get himself into trouble.

As difficult as parts of Saturday were, though, it was incredible to see how many people she had inspired to pick up a baton and get outside—maybe even start caring about their health and friendships along the way. Fan after fan thanked her for being a positive role model, for showing them what average, everyday people could accomplish with dedication and hard work. Plus, all the little girls dressed up in smart-fabric knockoffs of her Skadi's armor with their hair tightly braided to their head nearly made her heart burst with pride. TD Hunter required players to be at least thirteen to register an account, but that didn't stop kids from watching the streams or buying the merchandise. Lynn took extra time to kneel down to their level and ask them which TDM they were most excited to fight, once they were old enough. Those girls, more than anything else, made her certain it had all been worth it—all the sweat and tears, even the harassment and danger.

She might have only been a player, but she was proud of what Mr. Krator had accomplished with TD Hunter, and was thankful that she got to be a part of it.

While Dan, Mack, and Edgar joked around with fans and acted like the whole day was one big party, Ronnie was surprisingly subdued, considering all this fame was what he'd fought so hard to achieve in the first place. Lynn wondered if echoes of his father's words had dug their evil little claws into his brain and he was having trouble exorcising them. Regardless, she was happy to push as much attention and adulation away from her and onto him as she could get away with. He was welcome to it.

Finally, the day drew to a close, and they only had one event left to tackle: a private reception for the Hunter Strike Teams and their plus-ones.

Since Ronnie didn't have a plus one, Kayla was able to convince Mrs. Pearson to let her stay with her friends for the event. Mrs. Pearson and her staff went back to the hotel, though Bill stayed on to "watch their back" as Mack said. He'd taken quite a liking to Bill after his rescue from the unwanted fan tackle, and he and Dan had badgered the poor man all day to "show them some moves." Lynn was sure Bill would be happy to be rid of them come Monday.

The reception was on the top level of the convention center in one of their ballrooms, and since it was a semi-formal event out of the public eye, Lynn and her team had been dressed in appropriately stylish clothes picked out by Kayla. Lynn had been ready to hate whatever it was Kayla gave her, assuming her friend would use the opportunity to dress her to the nines. But to her surprise, Kayla had whipped up a tastefully simple black ensemble of slacks and blouse with ice blue accents. She'd even gotten custom-made earrings in the shape of Lynn's sword, Wrath.

Darn drat her. It was hard to say no to Kayla's style choices when she did thoughtful things like that.

Yes, Lynn's blouse did show off more of her golden skin than she'd have preferred, but it wasn't scandalous, and it made Edgar's eyes widen and his jaw hang slack for a second, so Lynn supposed she could live with it. Lynn braided her hair tightly to her head as usual, but she let Kayla put on some stunning eyeshadow that started out black on the eyelids and faded to electric blue at the edges. The guys all had similar outfits, with black slacks, an ice blue high-collared shirt, and a black blazer with different patterning on each that set them apart and harkened back to their now iconic Skadi space Viking armor in TD Hunter.

Dressed to kill, Kayla said.

Lynn would have preferred sweatpants and a hoodie.

When they entered the reception, though, Lynn had to agree that Kayla had done good work, and it was probably a good thing she wasn't allowed to make her own fashion choices. Everyone was decked out, from formal evening attire to stream glam, laid-back hipster, and edgy techgoth. Few of the teams were as coordinated as Skadi's Wolves, though, and it made Lynn proud that they were presenting a unified and professional front.

Lynn was interested to see the familiar nod Bill gave to the Tsunami security that checked their convention badges at the doors to the reception. She was reminded of the familiarity between the TD Hunter staff and the guards at the army base where they'd had their qualifiers. Did everyone just know everyone else in the former-military-now-personal-security world?

"Holy tamales," Mack said and whistled as they stood to the side of the entrance and tried to take in the huge reception area. Everything was hung with black banners trimmed by red and blue piping, emblazoned with the TD Counterforce logo—even the refreshment glasses and plates had the emblem.

Lynn's eyes darted around the dim room. There were hundreds of people present, split between players and their plus ones. From the Hunter Strike Team leaderboard, Lynn already knew there were about fifty teams competing in the US National Championship. Though the teams were grouped by region, she thought of them as being state by state. Not all states had a team that had qualified, and some states had more than one.

All in all, though, it made for a lot of people. Lynn unconsciously drew closer to Edgar's solid presence at her side as she surveyed the room full of strangers. Her mom and Mrs. Rios were chatting with Bill at the back of the group, while Dan's sister and Edgar's sister had their heads together, giggling over something on their LINC displays. For a moment, it was just her and her team.

"Remember, guys," she said quietly, "stick together. Be polite and everything, but don't forget that these are our opponents. Plus, somewhere around here is Connor, Elena, and their lackeys."

"Aye aye, cap," Dan said, then, "Oh, sweet! Is that food?" He promptly peeled off and headed for a long buffet table, making Lynn roll her eyes.

"Ronnie, Mack, go with him and keep out of trouble, okay?" She wasn't hungry, despite the delectable-looking food Tsunami had provided.

Ronnie and Mack trotted off after Dan, already debating the imagined qualities of the other teams mingling in the room. The plus ones of their group soon joined the guys, leaving Lynn and Edgar to hang back.

"Trouble?" Edgar asked, his quiet voice a rumble that she could feel through their almost touching shoulders.

She cleared her throat. "Uh, no. At least, I hope not. Though, knowing those three goofballs..." She cast a look at the buffet table and shook her head.

"Yup," Edgar agreed, a smile audible in his voice.

Silence fell between them, and Lynn suddenly realized she was standing alone with Edgar in their own quiet little bubble.

He was so close. She fought the urge to twitch her hand and find his in the dimness, to twine her fingers through his. Why would she want to do that? What a dumb idea.

"So..." Edgar cleared his throat. "Can I get you a drink or something?"

"Uh, sure, I gu—Look! Is that Connor and Elena over there in the corner?" Lynn jerked her chin in that direction, trying not to look conspicuous.

The two figures stood near the edge of the room, apart from the crowd, alone. Lynn wondered at that. No hot dates as their plus ones to make them look important and desirable? Not even a fawning parent to inflate their ego? Elena had always bragged about her daddy being some big time Wall Street investor. Surely *he* wouldn't have passed up a chance at rubbing elbows with rich and famous tech giants at this massive convention. So where was he?

"Huh...yeah, I think it is them," Edgar said.

"I wonder what they're arguing about," Lynn muttered, squinting at the two who were having an animated, if hushed conversation. Were they planning sabotage? On impulse, Lynn glanced toward Bill, saw he was still deep in conversation with the adults, then grabbed Edgar's hand and pulled him toward the far wall covered by a huge, black curtain.

"Whoa, hey there, boss. What's up?"

"Shhh, just follow me."

Lynn studiously focused on her destination and not the calloused warmth of Edgar's palm clutched in hers. Soon they reached the ceiling-high black curtain that marked the edge of the room. She poked at it experimentally, then nodded in satisfaction. Like most convention spaces, this was simply one huge ballroom divided up into smaller sections for private events. All they had to do was slip behind the curtain and they could walk behind it all the way over to where Connor and Elena were arguing.

"You up for a little recon?" she asked, grinning up at Edgar.

"Dunno if I'm cut out to be a spy. Pretty conspicuous and all that, ya know?" Edgar's mouth quirked as he made a miming motion with his hand, emphasizing his height.

Lynn rolled her eyes. "Yeah, yeah, yeah. Just stay close and be quiet, okay?"

"Hey, you're the boss lady, boss lady."

Resisting the urge to grumble about guys who weren't as funny as they thought they were, Lynn glanced around the room, then slipped between two panels to get behind the curtain. Edgar joined her soon after and they tiptoed along the curtain until they heard...

"Don't be an idiot, Elena. That will never work. There are far too many eyes at this competition. Just stick to the plan and do your part. Your job is to look hot. Leave the thinking to me."

"If I left the thinking to you, we'd never have reached Level 40. I'm the one who paid those players to level for us—"

"They weren't leveling for us, they were adding bonuses to our group."

"Whatever. The point is, without *my* money—

"You mean your father's money?"

"Don't you *dare* bring my daddy into this! I spent my own, hard-earned money. Without me, you would be just another lame player. *I'm* the one who took you back in after The Slut threw you off her team. That hussy isn't playing fair so why should we? She's got everybody licking out of her hand—I'll bet she's paid off the judges, too. Why else would everybody be pretending to love her?"

There was a pause in which Lynn could easily imagine Connor rolling his eyes and praying for patience. At least, she hoped he was, because seriously? "Pretending to love her"? She sincerely wished her fans were all fake, because then after the competition they would drop their facade and she could go back to her normal, quiet life.

Like *that* would happen.

"I seriously doubt even your father's money could buy the judges, Elena. Tsunami isn't that kind of company. Now, do *not* do anything stupid, and if you value your precious streamer reputation, keep. Your. Mouth. Shut. I told you, my plan is foolproof. We won't be competing against Skadi's Wolves come tomorrow. Trust me."

"You—you're sure?" Elena's tone wobbled and Lynn wondered what expression was on her face.

"I know what I'm doing, Elena. Now smile, all right? We're happy to be here, remember?"

"I know that! Stop treating me like I'm some newbie influencer. This is *my* world, Bancroft." Elena huffed, then Lynn heard a swish of hair as if Elena had just flicked her perfect blond ponytail behind her shoulder. "Go get me some food. I'm starving."

"Get yourself some food, Seville. I'm not one of your little lapdogs."

There was a gasp of indignation and retreating footsteps, and Lynn might have giggled in glee if she hadn't been fighting a rising lump of anxiety in her throat.

What was Connor up to? What lengths would he stoop to this time? Another scumbag to do a hit piece on them? A thug hired to assault them?

They needed to warn the rest of their team. It took a bit of skulduggery, but Lynn and Edgar got back into the reception area without attracting notice, and Lynn spotted her teammates right away.

"Should we tell someone...official?" Edgar murmured as they headed over to where Ronnie, Dan, Mack, and the girls stood chatting with some other players, while the adults stood nearby.

Lynn had been agonizing over that same question, and she still didn't have an answer. Finally, she opened up her TD Hunter app.

"Hey, Hugo," she subvocalized.

"At your service, Miss Lynn."

"I, uh, don't really know the right protocol or anything for this, but I wanted to tell someone so there'd be a record of it. Just not an official record, if you know what I mean."

"I will know what you mean once you *tell* me what you mean, Miss Lynn. For all that humans complain about the complexity of technology, humans are infinitely more confusing."

"Tell me about it," Lynn muttered, then finished quickly before she reached her teammates. "I overheard Connor and Elena talking about some kind of plan to sabotage Skadi's Wolves so that they won't have to compete against us tomorrow. I didn't hear any details, but Connor is the mastermind, and he seemed really sure we wouldn't be in the lineup tomorrow."

"I have made note of your information and will log it in my daily usage reports, where it can be found should someone go looking. Is that acceptable?"

"Yeah, thanks, Hugo."

"I am simply following my programming."

"Yeah, yeah, but thanks anyway. You're a good AI."

"I am flattered beyond measure. If I had a tail, I would wag it."

"Okay, now you're just being sarcastic. I take it all back."

After that she closed her app because they'd rejoined their group. Lynn shot off a ping to Edgar saying she'd "taken care of it," then a group message to the team warning everybody to keep their eyes peeled in case CRC tried anything. She didn't give them the details of what she'd heard. No need to get them all riled up, especially Ronnie.

The players Dan had struck up a conversation with were native Texans, one of three Lone Star teams who had passed their regional qualifiers. One of their members, a man with sandy hair, tanned skin, and sporting a bolo tie and cowboy boots, smiled at her and touched the brim of an imaginary hat—one Lynn assumed he wore outside during his day-to-day life. This *was* Texas, after all.

The handsome Texan welcomed them to the Lone Star State and started talking about the weather, which wasn't actually as boring as a non-TD Hunter player would assume. After all, their Hunter Strike Teams were out in it every single day, and the guy was curious at the climate differences that affected their daily movements and strategies.

"It's a darn good thing we have all these fancy athletic suits with built-in gadgets, these days," he commented. "Can't tell ya the number of times my team would'a plum keeled over from heatstroke without our built-in hydration monitors and temperature modulatin' technology. 'Course, it don't hurt that they show off our athletically honed figures, too."

He winked at Lynn, who felt her cheeks warm. She shifted closer to Edgar—he'd been sticking to her side like a shadow—and noticed a look of surprise cross the Texan's face. Lynn looked up and found Edgar scowling at the man.

"Apologies, ma'am. Didn't know you were taken," the Texan said, looking back down at Lynn and smiling crookedly. "The good ones always are, aren't they?"

Lynn stared blankly at him, which for some reason made him laugh.

"I'll let you two get back to enjoyin' the party. Evenin'."

He rejoined his team currently clustered around Ronnie, who was grilling them on the mesh web speed and data capabilities in Austin. Lynn stared after him, still processing the fact that he'd been hitting on her—tastefully, too—and that Edgar had been distinctly not on board.

Apologies, ma'am. Didn't know you were taken.

Lynn shook her head. She wasn't even going to touch that one, not tonight, not with everything at stake tomorrow.

With conscious effort, she redirected her attention to Ronnie's conversation, thinking it might affect how their battle progressed the next day. Lynn didn't pay attention to things like varying levels of infrastructure and mesh speeds around the country, but Ronnie knew all the big gaming hubs. He even had a wish list of top cities to live in for when he and Dan graduated and moved out together to pursue their fortune as professional gamers.

That thought stopped Lynn cold in her tracks, and for a moment the conversation flowed over her without her hearing a single word.

Now.

It wasn't "someday" anymore, it was happening *right now.*

The surreal moment was only heightened when the lights in the room suddenly dimmed and the theme music from TD Hunter began to play. Spotlights lit up a stage at the end of the room, and a screen the size of the entire wall began showing a vid. It was so expertly edited and put together that Lynn didn't realize it was clips of actual players as seen through the TD Hunter Lens app until she saw herself among them, spinning and rolling, cutting down TDMs with a precision and grace that was far more impressive on the big screen than it had ever been in Lynn's head.

"OMG Lynn!" Mack whisper-yelled. "That's you!!"

Lynn elbowed him, hard, in the ribs.

One of the Texan players whistled softly under his breath and shot her a smile. "Not bad."

She nodded woodenly.

The vid ended with a crescendo of music and the words "Humanity is counting on YOU," superimposed over the TD Counterforce emblem.

There was a spattering of applause, which suddenly increased into true fervor when an unimposing, middle-aged man stepped out onto the stage from behind the curtains and gave a wave.

"Good evening, Hunters!" said Mr. Krator, billionaire game designer and head of Tsunami.

There was another round of furious applause and whoops of delight as the room full of contestants crowded forward toward the stage. Lynn held back. She hated crowds. To her relief, Edgar stayed with her while the rest of their team pushed forward with the other players.

"I know it's late, and you've all come a long way, so I'll keep this short. Thank you, ladies and gentlemen, for being here. Thank you for your months of hard work and enthusiasm for a venture that, honestly, I had no idea would work or not. But there was a need, a...crisis, you might say, out there in the world, and I thought that my little idea could make a difference. And now look at you all!" Mr. Krator said, encompassing the room with a sweep of his arm.

The crowd went wild.

"Together, you Hunter Strike Teams have destroyed over twenty-two million TransDimensional Monsters in the last year."

A cheer went up.

"I know, I'm impressed too! But believe me, there's plenty more monsters to hunt, and tomorrow you will all be up against one of the biggest of the lot. I can't say any more, or my guys in the back will kill me." He jerked a thumb toward backstage and laughed. "You'll get the full briefing tomorrow. But try to grab a good night's sleep, because it's going to be the fight of your lives. And only the top three teams will be crowned winners of the US National Championship and move on to the international competition!"

More cheers.

"Seriously, though, I'm so proud of you. All of you. I will absolutely be cheering for every one of you tomorrow as you 'step into the real' and fight to defend humanity against these monstrous forces that have come to destroy us. They've got you to contend with now, and I wouldn't have it any other way. So stand proud, Hunter Strike Teams, and fight for glory, fight for survival—fight to keep our lights burning bright." Mr. Krator raised both fists into the air and pumped them, encouraging the crowd of players who all cheered and clapped until he finally backed off the stage and the screen came back to life, playing through various promotional reels and exclusive background content for the game.

Lynn had cheered and hooted with the rest of the crowd, even though Mr. Krator's speech seemed overly dramatic. But then, she'd never been part of a national gaming competition before, and she had to admit, it had gotten her blood pumping. It was fun that Mr. Krator had played into the storyline of the game, something Lynn had mostly ignored in favor of laser focus on performance, rankings, and stats. She'd never been one to game for the storylines like Mack and Dan did. The storyline for TD Hunter was pretty straightforward, but no less powerful for it. They *were* fighting for humanity's survival, and it wasn't at all certain that humanity would win—in game, of course. She was really curious what the storyline was building up to. It would probably have some sort of explosive conclusion at the International Championship, wrapping up the initial story arc and setting the stage for additional storylines to come after. Now that she thought of it, this entire storyline had basically been a year-long advertisement campaign to convince an entire globe of gamers to participate in this groundbreaking cultural moment.

Wow.

Lynn supposed the thousands of people she'd seen that day and the immensity of the event gave her a bigger perspective on things than she usually bothered with.

The vids on the big screen wrapped up and a DJ started talking as the TD Hunter theme song led into some pretty sweet dance music. People were eating and drinking and having fun, but Lynn wished they could skip to tomorrow's fight and be done with all this pointless hobnobbing.

Lynn stood quietly, lost in thought, and nibbled on a few appetizers beside Edgar while everybody else did their thing. She felt guilty for not chatting with the other teams like the rest of the guys—she suspected there would be a lot more working together tomorrow than most of the players imagined, and it would have been good to make some friends. But she was just too tapped out.

"Hi, Lynn. I'm glad you're still around, I was hoping to run into you."

Lynn spun at the familiar voice and gaped at Mr. Krator in his jeans, TD Counterforce T-shirt, and casual blazer. He even had on a pair of AR glasses, despite having the pick of literally any interface type on the planet. With his average brown hair and brown eyes, the man was utterly unassuming, and had obviously used that to his advantage to slip through the crowd. Lynn did notice two tall, no-nonsense-looking guys in black TD Counterforce shirts standing back and chatting with Bill. Probably a security escort. After all, Mr. Krator was worth billions of dollars.

"M-Mister Krator! Uh, nice to see you?"

Lynn felt naked with no modulator and no screen to hide behind. He was right there, *right in front of her*, staring with raised brows. Was he disappointed in what he saw? Was she not as impressive as he'd expected from the great Larry Coughlin?

"Are you ever going to call me Robert?" His lips quirked upward, and Lynn felt her face heat.

"Mr. Krator, it's an honor," Edgar said smoothly and held out a hand, like he wasn't about to touch the person they all hero-worshipped.

Well, Edgar wasn't as into gaming as the rest of them. He probably hadn't obsessively followed Robert Krator's career, nor daydreamed about what it would be like to meet the tech giant some day.

Mr. Krator shook Edgar's hand in a firm grip and gave the younger man a once-over.

"Looking sharp, there, Edgar. I'm thrilled to see what Skadi's Wolves does tomorrow. It's going to be a wild ride."

Lynn's brain was a useless jumble of thoughts. She almost blurted out then and there that Connor was a back-stabbing snake and could Mr. Krator please ban him from the game? But she restrained herself.

"Lynn," the billionaire said, turning his eyes to her, "it is truly a pleasure to meet you in person. You've come a long way since we last talked, haven't you?"

"Y-yup," Lynn fairly squeaked. She cleared her throat and nodded, face flaming.

"You've done everything I'd hoped for and more," he said with a reassuring smile. Then he leaned forward conspiratorially. "I'm not one to say I told you so, but I think maybe now you've seen what I meant when I sent you that engraved LINC?"

Lynn's thumb unconsciously brushed the mysterious "LL" cut into her black LINC ring that she'd been sent by Tsunami when she'd agreed to beta test TD Hunter. She'd always wondered what it meant and if Mr. Krator had been the one responsible for it. Now she knew.

Lynn-Larry. Larry-Lynn.

Mr. Krator's fateful words a year ago rang in her memory:

"Remember that 'Lynn Raven' is special in a very important way, not just 'Larry Coughlin.'"

"I think you are more Larry Coughlin—or should I say Larry Coughlin is more you—than you might realize, Lynn."

"Yes, sir, I think I do see," she said, gratitude warming her chest.

"Excellent. A word of advice, then, if I may?"

Lynn nodded again, hoping she didn't look like a bobblehead.

"Trust your instincts," he said, his stare oddly intense. "They've guided you well so far, and I think they'll be what get us all over the finish line, in the end."

"Uhhh, okay? Thanks, Mr. Krator."

"Robert," he corrected her with a wink, and held out a hand.

She gulped, hesitated, then dove in and shook it gingerly. "Thanks, Robert. I'll do my best tomorrow."

"I know you will." He nodded in farewell, then drifted over to his security team, stopping to say a welcoming word to their parents as he went. Of course the adults had absolutely no idea who he was, which was a tragedy. Ronnie and the guys were off mingling with the other teams, so they didn't see as Mr. Krator quietly slipped to the back of the room and out the door with his security escort.

"Hey, Lynn. Who was that?" Dan asked, walking up with a refilled plate from the buffet table.

Lynn glanced at Edgar, who shrugged.

"Just someone wishing us the best tomorrow," she said, calm purpose settling over her. "We should go back to the hotel. The less time we give Connor to get up to mischief the better, and we need the rest."

"Aww, come on, we just got here!"

"Nope. Party's over. Let everybody else stay up late, eat too much food, and drink alcohol. We put our game faces on *now*. We have one shot at this. Just one. Now go get everybody else. Skadi's Wolves has a boss to fight and a championship to win, and we're going to do it on a full night's sleep.

Chapter 13

OF COURSE, GETTING A FULL NIGHT'S SLEEP WAS EASIER SAID than done.

Despite her physical and emotional exhaustion, her brain would *not* turn off. The experiences of the day, good and bad, kept swirling in her head, mixing with her gut-twisting worry about tomorrow.

Eventually she snuck out of bed to go make herself some hot milk in their suite's little kitchenette. She was sharing a room with her mom, so she was careful not to wake her as she slipped out of the bedroom and closed the door against the light she needed to turn on in the sitting area to see what she was doing.

She'd just settled on a chair by the big window overlooking the twinkling lights of Austin when there was a soft knock on her hotel room door.

Her heart leapt into her throat, but she immediately slapped it down. A thug hired by Connor wouldn't announce his own malicious presence.

When she looked out the peephole, it somehow didn't surprise her to see Edgar's broad chest in a rumpled T-shirt.

She opened the door.

"Hey, you. Couldn't sleep, too?"

Edgar blew out a breath and scowled.

"Dan snores like a chainsaw, that idiot. How somethin' that

snack-sized manages ta make that much noise, I got no clue. I went to the front desk for earplugs. Saw your light on. You okay?"

Lynn covered her mouth, trying not to giggle at Edgar's misery. His question quickly sobered her, though.

"Uh, yeah. I guess. Just...lots to think about."

"That's why I try not to think too much. Makes my life easier."

That surprised a laugh out of Lynn.

"Hey...you want a mug of hot milk?"

"Sure," Edgar said, a little hesitant as he peered past her into the suite.

"Mom's asleep in the bedroom. You won't bother her, I promise."

"Oh. Okay, then."

Lynn got to work making a second cup of warm milk, lamenting inside that she couldn't make a proper mug of "Grandma's Favorite Recipe" because she had no spices. There was honey, though, so she sweetened it and handed it to Edgar before curling up again in the chair by the window. Edgar sat nearby and blew on his milk before sipping it. He seemed to like it, which made Lynn smile.

That feeling didn't last, though, and she looked back out the window, gritting her teeth against the wordless anxiety that was wrecking her sleep and jeopardizing her fighting readiness. Lying in bed, staring at a dark ceiling, unable to sleep was basically her worst nightmare. It gave a chance for all her fear and trauma to slither up out the black pit of her brain where she shoved them, like oily nightmares that never truly went away. You just had to look away and pretend they didn't exist.

Except that was really hard to do when she was sleepless and had just spent an entire day being screamed at by thousands of people all wanting to touch her, have a piece of her, *be* her.

"Why are they all so obsessed with me?" she said abruptly, keeping her voice low. "Why can't they just leave me alone and let me do my thing!" She'd said it at the window, not so much as a question but a cry of frustration to the universe. She knew perfectly well how publicity and sponsorships and all that worked. She knew the world was full of creeps and weirdos, hiding in the woodwork. Apparently fame brought that sort of craziness to the surface.

"It's because you're amazing, Lynn."

Lynn looked at Edgar in surprise. Apparently he'd thought she was asking him a question. Her brow furrowed.

"Uh, no I'm not. Not really. I basically just work hard, that's it."

Edgar scooted his chair closer and leaned forward, propping his elbows on his knees, cup of warm milk forgotten on a side table. The light in the room was low, but it was enough for her to see the oddly intense look on Edgar's face.

"Yeah, Lynn, you *are* amazing. You're... you're... *next level*. You fight like some mythical warrior queen, like Nafanua, a *Toa Tama'ita'i* of old. Watching you is exciting and terrifying and beautiful all at once. Have you *seen* the comments on your stream? *Uce*, people can't look away from it. Hell, I get distracted during battle watching you without realizing it. If I wasn't the point guy with you behind me most'a the time, I'd be useless. Darn near gotten me killed before."

"Shut up," Lynn said, shaking her head. "You're such a goofball."

"Yeah, I know, but I can't help it." He shrugged but didn't look away. "You're that good."

Lynn felt a flush slowly creeping up her neck. Edgar didn't look away, didn't lean back up. She shifted to face him fully and clear her throat.

"I, um, appreciate the compliment, Edgar. Really. Maybe I have some talent"—she shrugged—"but lots of other people do too. I'm just trying to game well, build something good for my future, you know?"

"But it's not just your fighting, Lynn," Edgar insisted, now gesturing with his hands, like it was important for her to understand how serious he was. "You're really nice to be around, you know? You treat people well, you don't talk down to them. You're funny and witty and interesting to talk to."

"Uhh, thanks? I'm just trying to be a decent person. I'm not even that good at it. You have no idea how many people I make cry in WarMonger," she finished lamely, thinking with a twinge of shame the secret of Larry Coughlin that stood between them.

"Lynn, stop putting yourself down. Just stop it." Edgar got up abruptly, and started pacing in front of their chairs, seeming agitated. Lynn had no idea what was going on, so she kept her mouth shut. Maybe Edgar had had a stressful day, too, and just needed to get some things off his chest?

"You don't get it, do you? You don't see how important you are, how much you mean to the people around you. Of *course* everybody's obsessed with you, how could they not be?"

Lynn's eyes widened, still having no idea where Edgar was going with this rant.

"I mean, you should look at yourself in the mirror sometime. Like, *really* look," he went on in a ramble, still pacing and gesticulating with his hands. "Your hair is long and raven black, and there's these little pieces around your face that come out of your braid that I'm always dying to tuck back in. And your eyes—good God, your *eyes*, Lynn. They're so beautiful, and they see right through you and I—I mean, people are mesmerized by that, you know? And obviously your body—I mean, you know—" he paused and turned toward her, making vague curvy gestures with both hands like outlining an hourglass "—it's—I mean, your legs are amazing, and your hips, and—and everything there and..." Edgar's face was a shade darker than normal, a sure sign of a blush, even though the light in the room wasn't good enough to see much of it.

He didn't let that stop him, though, and forged on.

"And your chest, I mean, I don't care *what* a guy likes, you'd hafta to be *dead* not to appreciate it, and—and—what I'm trying to say is that you are a work of art, Lynn. A freaking work of art. Not some fragile skinny thing you put on a shelf and forget about as soon as you look away. You radiate strength and beauty like a fire—you can feel it whether you're lookin' at it or not." He stopped pacing and turned toward her again, holding his hands out to his side like he didn't know what to do with them. "*God,* your ferocity and—and the pure freaking *joy* you take in what you do is addictive to be around. Watching you is like a shot of ecstasy right in the arm. People love you because you're freaking amazing in so many ways they don't understand, they just know it in their heart and bones and they can't help wanting to get closer, wanting to always feel your fire."

Lynn was struck absolutely dumb. She might have forgotten how to breathe. She wasn't sure if she was reading things right, or if oxygen depletion was making her loopy, because it didn't sound like Edgar was talking about what *people* thought.

It sounded like Edgar was talking about what *he* thought.

Some sliver of her realization must have shown in her expression, because Edgar's face visibly drained of color, becoming ashen in the yellow light.

"I—I—" His mouth worked, but he seemed to have spent all his words already.

"Edgar..." Lynn started, but Edgar held up both hands pleadingly, as if he thought he was upsetting her and he wanted to put her at ease.

"Don't, Lynn, I'm sorry. I'm such a goofball, like you said. I shouldn't have blurted all that out. Just—just forget about it, okay? I never wanted to make you uncomfortable or—or make you think I didn't respect you as a friend. I promise I'll keep my thoughts to myself and just be your friend, forever and always. You don't have to worry about me causing you trouble. Please don't be upset..."

He trailed off, maybe confused by the lack of anger or disgust on her face. Was that what he'd been expecting?

She wasn't angry. She was confused, and a little hurt. Did he really think all those things about her? Or was he just saying them to make her feel better? Which was it?

Oh, come on, sweetie, her mother's words echoed in her head. *He is so obviously over the moon for you. I keep waiting for him to say something.*

Was this the "something" Matilda had meant? If so, why hadn't he said it before? What guy who liked a girl didn't tell her about it? Was she not good enough for Edgar? Had she done something to make him afraid, to expect her anger and rejection? What had she ever done but be polite and kind to him? How could you care about someone, and yet keep secrets from them?

That thought instantly turned around and slapped her in the face, leaving the words *"Larry Coughlin"* emblazoned on her imaginary forehead.

We humans... we're all tangled balls of contradictions and potential.

Mr. Thomas' words came vividly to mind, bringing back other bits of advice he'd shared long ago, when she'd just been a secret beta tester trying to figure out how to stop living a lie and open up to people.

I am sure your mother and your friends will forgive your choice to keep things to yourself. You must simply approach the situation with humility and sincerity, and be as willing to forgive them their flaws as you are asking them to forgive you yours.

"Edgar..." she started again.

He flinched, eyes still fixed on her even as his body tensed like he was stuck between fight or flight.

"Thank you," she said, finally finding the right words. "Thank you for being honest."

"W-what?" he mumbled. "You're...you're not mad at me?"

"Well," a smile twitched the corner of her mouth, "maybe a little. But you're my friend. I trust you. Thank you for trusting *me*."

He seemed as struck dumb as she'd been moments before, like he'd never even considered this possible response or what he should do about it.

"I...I'm not sure how I feel about what you said. I can't process it right now." Even with what her mother had told her months ago and all the time she'd spent wondering, she'd never imagined Edgar felt *this* about her. It was a monumental thing to try and wrap her brain around, and she simply couldn't afford to handle it the night before the biggest competition of her life. "Look, we have *got* to get some sleep. But...I'm not mad. And I hope you'll still be my friend."

"Oh, *manamea*. I will *always* be your friend. Until we all go out in a blaze of glory, I'll be there. Just...just let me keep fighting by your side, that's all I could ask for."

Lynn gave a soft snort.

"Don't we both realize by now that I couldn't get rid of you if I tried?"

Edgar grinned.

"You said it, boss, not me."

"Get out of here, you goofball."

"Yessir, ma'am."

Edgar gave her a mock salute, then walked backward to the door, as if reluctant to take his eyes off her. When he finally bumped into the far wall, he gave an awkward little wave.

"Night, Lynn."

Lynn smiled.

"Night, Edgar."

After the door clicked shut behind him, Lynn stared at the abandoned cup of no-longer-warm milk Edgar had left behind.

Oh, manamea. I will always be your friend. Until we all go out in a blaze of glory, I'll be there.

That was the perfect thought to lull her to sleep, burning

bright and scaring away the nightmares. She got up, cleaned up the forgotten milk, and went to bed.

When her alarm jerked her awake the next morning, she felt briefly disoriented because everything around her seemed... fine. She'd half expected to get kidnapped in the night. She mentally cursed herself for the stress she was allowing Connor to cause her. She resolved then and there, by the light of a new day streaming into her room, that she wouldn't let Connor get inside her head. Today was all about focus. She would keep the big picture in mind, eyes on the goal.

Connor didn't deserve a single iota of her emotional reserve.

Everybody got ready in good time, and before long they'd scarfed down a hot breakfast and were being transported with their friends, family members, and GIC staff to the convention center.

They'd been given very few details about the big day, just where to meet in the morning, fully geared up and ready to go.

Once they arrived at the convention center, they found out their families would be watching them compete from TD Hunter's comfy HQ suite, far away from the milling tens of thousands of fans still enjoying Tsunami Con. The competitors, however, were to be herded off to board a group of airbuses. Lynn hugged her mom tightly in the early morning sun before they parted.

"Remember, sweetheart," Matilda said, "I love you no matter what happens. You've overcome everything life has thrown at you, fair and unfair." She gripped Lynn's shoulders and looked her right in the eye. "This, right here, is already a win. You show me every day what it looks like to live life well, honorable and unafraid. I couldn't be more proud to be your mom, and I think if your father were here, he wouldn't even have the words for how proud he was. He'd just kiss you on the forehead, like this,"—Matilda pulled Lynn toward her and planted a warm kiss on her tightly braided hair—"and he'd say 'that's my girl.'" Matilda pulled back and gave Lynn a watery smile. "Now, you go show the world what you're made of, you hear me?"

Lynn had to swallow to get past the lump in her throat.

"I will, Mom. I promise. They won't know what hit them."

"That's my girl," her mom whispered, and planted one last kiss on her forehead.

Lynn led her team onto the closest airbus, senses alert and eyes busy roving. The guys were doing the same, and their tense expressions and silent watchfulness fit right in with the other competitors. Everyone seemed on edge. She didn't see CRC anywhere on the bus, but that didn't mean much. She doubted they would try anything personally and risk incriminating themselves.

To her surprise, there were not one, or even two, but *six* TD Hunter staff on the bus. And, oddly, they all carried a pair of blue batons slid into handy pockets at their thighs. They smiled when spoken to and acted professionally, but they, too, seemed tense. They were also surprisingly athletic-looking for employees of a gaming company. But maybe Tsunami only hired people with brains *and* brawn.

The ride to wherever they were going lasted about twenty minutes. Using the TD Hunter app and subvocalization, she set the rest of her team to various tasks, like keeping tabs on their fellow players, monitoring the main TD Hunter-focused stream channels, and watching the news. She didn't tell them why, just let them assume it was all to foil CRC's plans—whatever they were.

In reality, though, she was listening to her instincts and watching for... something. Anything. She had no idea what. All she knew was that Robert Krator himself had told her to follow her gut, and her gut was feeling pretty suspicious. Was it connected to TD Hunter itself? Or was Tsunami somehow tangled up in whatever was going on globally? She couldn't help remembering the circumstances around TD Hunter's development, the strange investments from military-adjacent companies, the next-generation algorithm, the strangely rushed beta testing phase.

She just hoped it wouldn't interrupt the championship. She'd worked too hard to get interrupted by a breakout of war with China or something.

The airbus ride was smooth except for one point when all six TD Hunter employees looked at each other, seeming startled. Whatever it was, they communicated via subvocalization, so Lynn could only stew in ignorance and wish she knew what was going on.

Their landing seemed odd, too. The airbus altered course once, then circled a few times before it finally set down. Even though it was still early in the morning, the air shimmered with heat as they stepped off the air-conditioned vehicle.

"Good grief," Mack muttered, fanning his face with a hand. "Is it always like this?"

"Yup," said one of the other players in a Texan drawl. "Us Texas teams have a bet goin' for how long it's gonna be afore one o' you Northerners gets heat stroke."

While the player's friends laughed around him, Lynn mentally thanked him for the reminder.

"Everybody, I want you sipping your hydration pack constantly," Lynn subvocalized to the guys. "Plan to refill it *and* use the bathroom right before the competition starts. I don't doubt someone's going to collapse before the day is through, but it isn't going to be one of us."

"Looks like everybody's got high quality gear at least," Dan said, twisting and squinting at the growing crowd of players around him.

At shouted directions from the TD Hunter staff, the players started moving toward a low, single-story cement building that looked like it was normally used as a warehouse. In fact, the entire area around them looked like an industrial section of town, though there wasn't a vehicle or person in sight besides them. Ahead, beyond the warehouse, rose the sides of some sort of arena. The shimmering walls met in a point at the top and it looked for all the world like a giant, reflective pyramid.

Lynn nudged Edgar who walked beside her. "Any guesses?" she asked, nodding at the odd structure.

"Paparazzi," he said simply, and Lynn could have smacked herself in the forehead.

Of course.

The amount of advertising dollars that had gone into this event was no doubt mind boggling. What was the point of paying for all that air-time if viewers could just watch the event on some random streamer's channel instead? It made perfect sense that Tsunami would want the competition to happen in a closed environment. Lynn figured something like the qualifiers hadn't been high profile enough to worry about rogue drones.

Still, Lynn wondered why all the rigamarole. The Austin Convention Center surely had space enough and plenty of security to host the actual competition. So why were they on the outskirts of Austin with the high-rise skyscrapers and fancy downtown area nowhere in sight? And where were the spectators? Surely

Tsunami could have made millions by selling exclusive seating to watch the competition in person using the Hunter Lens app?

The hundreds of players slowed and waited as those in front filed inside the warehouse through a single, small door. When it was their turn, Lynn saw that there was security at the door, scanning everybody and their bags. After they passed through, they were met by a TD Hunter employee with what looked like a longer version of their electric blue batons. He had each player grip it as he explained that it was confirming their identity and matching them to a registered competitor profile.

Identity confirmed, they were ushered from that small antechamber to a long, gray hall with tables upon tables of helmets and vests. They were told to grab one each and keep moving. Lynn kept her eyes peeled and her senses alert. This was definitely not going down like she'd expected, though a small part of her wasn't surprised.

Nothing about TD Hunter had ever been like she'd expected. Why would it start now?

Coming out of the long hall, the walls opened up into a spacious warehouse with clean concrete floors, rows of chairs around the edges of the room, and a few tables with supplies like bottled water and energy bars. There was a single, large flex screen hung between two pillars at the front, but other than that the warehouse room was empty. Their TD Hunter staff escorts took seats at the back of the room while the crowd of players finished filing in, milling about in the empty center.

"*Circle up, Hunters,*" bellowed a familiar voice over the low chatter of curious players.

Lynn grinned.

In front of the flex screen stood a man of imposing stature with a salt-and-pepper buzz cut. His black TD Counterforce shirt stretched taut across his broad chest, with bits of tattoos peeking out from underneath his sleeves. Though *she* knew him to be a super cool guy, she wasn't surprised that the crowd of players which gathered around him left a healthy gap between them and the stranger.

"My name is Steve Riker, and I'm part of TD Hunter's Tactical Support group. I'll be giving you your safety and mission briefing, so move to where you can see me, then shut up and listen. I ain't saying this stuff twice."

"First, let's get you geared up. You should have each been issued a helmet and vest. If you're one of those brilliant knuckleheads who wasn't paying attention and didn't grab one, go back in the hall and get one. Come on... there's always somebody," Steve growled, and sure enough, a handful of figures in the back made their way sheepishly out to grab the required gear.

"For everyone else: congrats, you've proven yourself capable of following basic instructions. Let's keep a good thing going and everybody put your vest on. They're made of smart fabric, so it's one size fits all. If you have a backpack or hydration pack, take it off and put the vest on underneath. You can replace the hydration pack, but nothing else besides hydration and batons are allowed in the arena. No backpacks. Put them against the wall. You can get them after the battle."

There was a general shuffle as everybody followed instructions and got their vests settled. The vest fabric was thick but flexible, and it molded perfectly to Lynn's body, covering her torso completely from waist to neck. As she put it on, she glanced up and realized that Steve was wearing exactly the same vest. Its smooth, flat surface blended perfectly with his shirt, and the smart fabric of the vest had replicated the TD Counterforce logo. Now that she thought about it, she realized that *all* of the TD Hunter staff she'd seen so far that morning had been wearing these vests.

"Now, everyone with AR glasses, visors, or helmets are probably wondering, 'What the frick, Steve, how are my glasses gonna fit under this helmet you gave us?' Great question. They're not."

A storm of whispers swept through the crowd.

"In order to ensure fairness and prevent foul play, you will *all* be using the standard issue LINC and display equipment built into the TD Hunter-issue headsets you're holding in your hands."

Some of the whispers turned into disgruntled muttering, but Steve raised his hands, expression unfazed.

"If you don't like it, you know where the door is. Don't let it hit you on the way out. You're welcome to go watch the competition from the convention center with all your mommies and daddies. For everyone else, I promise, this stuff is top of the line, the very latest AR headset Tsunami has to offer. I'm tactical, not technical, support, so I can't tell you all the cool tech-y stuff about them. But suffice it to say that you'll find them perfectly adequate for the competition once you've got them on and you've loaded up your TD Hunter profile. The helmets are lined with omnipolymer to conform perfectly to your head, and they even have built-in cooling packs to keep you comfy in this heat. If that's not luxury, I don't know what is."

Lynn exchanged a look with her team. This was certainly different but not unwelcome. She liked the idea of everyone using the same equipment. She just hoped the AR headsets were as good as Steve claimed.

"The vests are linked to your headset and will display your TD Hunter handle on the chest so you can be easily identified by our medic teams in case of an accident. The vests *also* serve as a flag to identify any Hunters who reach zero health or exit combat mode for any reason once the competition begins. The entire vest will turn bright red, and if you are mobile, you're expected to exit the arena *immediately*. If that happens you will come in here, sit your butt down, and watch the rest of the show on this." Steve jerked a thumb behind him at the huge flex screen.

"If you are *not* mobile for any reason, sit tight and one of our medic teams will get you and take you to our triage room over there." Steve pointed to a door on the right-hand wall. Then he pointed to another door beside it.

"That is our Championship HQ. Keep your nosey selves out of there unless you want to get disqualified. If you need a staff member for any reason, notify your TD Hunter service AI and one of us will come running.

"Now, this should be obvious, but for lawyer-y reasons I have to state it explicitly: from the moment you fire up your TD Hunter app on your headset, everything you do and say will be recorded, and said recording is the sole property of Tsunami Entertainment. In other words, don't go do your little boy or little girl business while wearing your helmet, okay? Nobody wants to see that."

There was a titter among the players and Lynn couldn't help but grin.

"Remember, we're all professionals here, and this is serious business. No cutting up or horsing around, no hitting each other with your weapons, and no physical contact of any kind between teams. Your mission is to destroy *monsters*, not each other, and any infringement will get you red-flagged and ejected from the arena before you can say 'I'm a dipshit.'

"And I know what you're thinking. Don't freak out if you

bump into someone by accident in the heat of battle. We've got *hundreds* of cameras out there filming from every angle. I promise you we can tell the difference between accidents and deliberate fouls. We're watching your every move—so no picking your nose or scratching your ugly butt unless you want it looped and thrown up on the streams as meme fodder. My tech guys are good, but they aren't saints. They know it's a crime against humanity to deprive the watching world of that comedy gold."

Way to make a girl feel comfortable, Lynn thought. She could imagine Steve's replying grin in her mind's eye, and knew he was probably having way more fun up there than he let on with his gruff voice and no-nonsense instructions.

"Right. Now that we've got all the boring stuff out of the way, time for your mission briefing."

Steve's businesslike words made Lynn stand up straighter, and an almost tangible calm came over her. She had no idea what Connor had been, or was still, planning to do. But it was time to lock and load and do what she did best. Her team was near the edge of the crowd on one of Steve's sides, so she had a good view of him as he spoke.

Steve folded his hands behind his back and adopted a parade rest as his piercing gaze swept over the large crowd of gamers.

"As you've hopefully figured out by now, TD Hunter is a cooperative game. It may go against your bloodthirsty natures to cooperate with your competition, but that's just what you're gonna do, at least if you're smart. Your mission today is simple: destroy the Sierra Class boss out there in the arena *and* return to your rally point with any survivors.

"How you accomplish that is entirely up to you. You will be evaluated on your teamwork and tactics as well as on your individual ratings for things like overall kills and kill-to-damage ratio. Those scores will be added together for an overall team score, which will determine who advances to the international championship."

Steve held up a finger.

"There is one new factor for you to take into consideration when deciding tactics. For this championship, each team captain is allotted a single 'air strike' to use in aiding your mission. This attack is AOE, Area of Effect, and the payload is equal to about thirty standard fireball attacks. That'll wipe out most any TDMs in a twenty-foot radius. Just remember: each team has only one. So use it wisely.

"Lastly, I know there were some *questionable* tactics used during the qualifiers to defeat bosses, so I want to make it extra, super, crystal clear: *do not get within melee distance of the boss.* It's high enough class that any solid strike it lands will utterly destroy you. Melee attacks are not advisable. And if, God forbid, you're stupid enough to try and charge *inside* of it, just don't, please. You will die instantly and be given a zero score for pulling a stunt like that."

Steve did not look her way, but Lynn grinned impishly anyway. If Tsunami didn't want gamers breaking their game, they shouldn't have made a game in the first place. It was her sacred duty as a gamer to do crazy shit in games to see if it would work.

"You will have one hour, I repeat, sixty minutes, to complete your mission. You do not have to use those entire sixty minutes to accomplish it; you can exit the competition at any time by returning to the rally point. Once you return to the rally point *or* your time expires, your headset will automatically exit combat mode and your scores will be tabulated. While failing to destroy the boss or failing to return alive to the rally point will not disqualify you, accomplishing either or both of those things significantly increases your scores. So I suggest you prioritize them. Any questions?"

Inevitably, there were some clarifications, but once those were cleared up, Steve stepped to the side of the flex screen and gestured to it.

"Okay, Hunters, eyes forward. First Sergeant Bryce of the TransDimensional Counterforce will be giving you your mission brief up on the screen."

The lights dimmed and the huge flex screen lit up, showing the First Sergeant standing beside a large, square screen that mimicked the combat display from the TD Hunter app. For some odd reason, Lynn thought the First Sergeant looked tired. Maybe it was a trick of the light, but he seemed like he had dark circles under his eyes, and his expression looked even more grim and lined than usual.

Lynn shook her head. It was probably all just special effects, put there on purpose for extra realism.

"Good Morning, Hunters. I'm glad to see you geared up and

ready for action. The situation has become critical worldwide, with TDM numbers increasing at exponential rates which have begun to regularly interfere with grid networks and data systems. Through intel gathered by our global volunteer Hunter force, we've determined that the appearance of these larger entities, designated 'bosses,' causes an immediate and steep increase in TDMs spawned in an area. Put simply, these bosses are monster generators, and the more we destroy, the more we slow the spread of the entities across local infrastructure.

"We have tracked down a massive boss right here in Austin which is threatening a backbone transponder node for the downtown area. If this entity is allowed to remain, it will trigger sweeping blackouts, causing massive infrastructure and system damage to the proud capital of Texas, not to mention loss of life through accidents as well as lack of basic health and safety services. Our entire way of life is at risk, from clean water, to functional sanitation systems, to our whole communication and transportation network. It's up to you, Hunters, to protect the good people of Austin by destroying this boss."

The First Sergeant's screen came to life with an image of a huge monster in the middle of what was clearly the inside of the arena. The creature looked like a massive, mutated serpent. Its coils were as thick as an airbus and they were curled possessively around the base of a node tower right in the center of the arena. Its body wasn't uniform, though. It varied in thickness and split off in random places to form tentaclelike appendages trailing on the ground or waving threateningly in the air. Its head was large and angled, with no discernible eyes above its gaping maw full of fangs. It had strange proto limbs near the head that seemed to serve as crude appendages as well as antennae. For the moment it appeared passive, but Lynn had no illusions that it would stay that way once two hundred and fifty-odd Hunters started shooting at it.

"This entity has been designated Nagaraja, a Sierra Class-2 boss with significant reach and damage capabilities. It has been observed uncoiling and attacking nearby threats, but its movements are slow and can be avoided with proper vigilance. The hide is thick so anything less than armor-piercing or incendiary bullets are unlikely to penetrate. Based on its crushing size and pummel capabilities, direct melee engagement is unadvisable."

First Sergeant Bryce pointed at the monster's various features as he spoke. When he finished, he turned back to the camera and looked directly at them, as if he could see them standing there, listening.

"There is no backup plan, Hunters. Austin is too big to evacuate and our emergency resources are already strained dealing with similar infrastructure collapse across the country. We're depending on you to work together and eliminate this threat before people start dying. As a great commander once said: Speed is everything, surprise is everything, deception is everything, Utter Ruthlessness! Give 'em hell, Hunters, and we'll see you on the other side. First Sergeant Bryce, out."

The soldier gave a crisp salute, then his image faded to be replaced with the TD Counterforce logo.

Lynn had a weird sense of déjà vu. But this time, instead of feeling excited for the competition ahead, she felt a heavy sense of duty grip her.

No matter what she told herself, some instinct screamed that destroying this boss was about much more than racking up points and winning a gaming championship. It didn't make any sense, but neither did all her other formless suspicions and fears.

Was that why Mr. Krator had given her such cryptic advice? What was really going on? Cyber warfare with China? Shadowy hacking groups? A rogue game algorithm? If so, what did Mr. Krator know and why wasn't he fixing it himself with all his money and resources? Why not tell the public and get the military involved? Why did it seem like he was telling *her*, a nobody teenager from Cedar Rapids, to trust her instincts and, for lack of a better way to put it, save the world?

She didn't have time to contemplate the answer. The lights had come back up and Steve was barking instructions that sent the milling crowd in several directions. This was their last chance to visit the head, and this time around Lynn made sure the guys stayed in pairs. On her own way out of the bathroom, she nearly collided with a man and a woman in matching outfits of blue, green, and white.

"*You!*"

The woman's horrified gasp made Lynn tense and her eyes flew up to the pair's faces.

Elena Seville looked like she'd seen a ghost, and Connor, who stood beside her, had a momentary expression of absolute fury which was quickly hidden behind a hard mask.

"Yup, me," Lynn said cheerfully, though every sense was on high alert. Edgar and Mack, who had been watching for her nearby, came over and flanked her, arms crossed.

Elena's mouth opened and closed several times in silent denial as fury and panic built on her face.

"B-but you're not supposed to be here! Connor swore—"

"Shut *up*, you idiot," Connor gritted out.

"You promised me!" Elena hissed, spinning on her teammate. "You said—"

"Absolutely nothing," Connor declared, danger glittering in his eyes as he grabbed Elena by the arm and yanked her away like he couldn't get out of sight fast enough.

Lynn watched them carefully as they disappeared into the crowd.

"What do you figure?" she subvocalized to her teammates.

Mack glared after their departing rivals. "Sounds fishy as a fish market full of fish, as Dan would say."

"A real poet, our Dan," Edgar offered.

Lynn snorted.

"Geeear up, ladies!" Steve yelled in a drill sergeant-worthy voice. "Time's a-wastin'!"

Everyone rushed to stow their personal LINCs and AR interfaces and put on their headsets. No personal LINCs were allowed in the arena at all, Lynn assumed to prevent any cheating or pirating of the battle footage. Those with interface implants, audio or visual, could easily shut them off and switch to using the TD Hunter-issued equipment.

Lynn struggled to wrangle her helmet down over her tightly braided hair. But once she'd gotten past the braid, the headset settled easily, and she felt the interior omnipolymer padding shift, filling in the empty spaces and molding to her form so it fit perfectly. She blinked a few times as the HUD display came to life and her eyes focused.

Once everything was up and running, she was pleased with what she saw. From the outside, the headset looked like a thinner, more compact version of a visored motorcycle helmet. Lynn had initially worried she would lose her peripheral vision and situational awareness. But from inside the headset, the display screen wrapped around her head, giving her a full range of vision with crisp and vibrant images. Lynn shook her head experimentally, expecting the helmet to shift. But it stayed snug and firm. The self-cooling omnipolymer would be a sweet relief against the muggy heat, and there was plenty of airflow around her nose so things wouldn't get stuffy when she started breathing heavily.

Knowing she needed to hurry, Lynn used the voice activation controls to verify her identity and load her TD Hunter profile. Soon Hugo was giving her a cheerful "Good morning, Miss Lynn," in her ear. As the other players settled their headsets into place and logged into their profiles, gaming handles started popping up on their vests, the large white letters splashed high across the chest and back so the players could be easily identified from both sides.

"Time's up, Hunters." Steve's roar cut across the hundreds of chattering voices like a thunderclap. "Form up and follow these nice staff members to the rally point. I'll be watching you from the sky, so good luck, and remember: the brave may not live forever, but the cautious never live at all."

He stood in front of the flex screen, huge arms crossed in front of his chest as the contestants streamed past. Lynn caught his eye through her clear visor as she drew level with him, and he gave her a nod and barely suppressed grin. Then he raised an eyebrow and tapped his ear.

"Voice chat request from Steve Riker of TD Hunter Tactical Support," Hugo intoned.

"Accept," Lynn subvocalized. Now what was he up to?

"Can't chat long or I'll get my butt kicked. A little bird told me TD Hunter cyber security caught someone hacking into one of our user accounts last night and planting incriminating evidence of code manipulation."

Lynn's eyebrows shot skyward.

"I'd give you three guesses as to whose account they were targeting, but I doubt you need more than one."

"Sounds like somebody is trying to hedge their bets," Lynn said.

"Wish we could've identified the hacker and traced their funding source, but they were too slippery."

"Shame," Lynn said.

"Watch your back out there, you old snake."

"Be like that one time I was in Khartoum! There I was, surrounded by skinnies..."

A snort sounded over the voice chat.

"One of these days you gotta go public. When that happens I'm gonna sit back with a bag of popcorn and watch the gamer community lose its ever-loving mind."

"Oh, come on. Don't be dramatic. Tons of gamers use alter egos."

"Not like you, they don't," Steve chuckled. "You think I don't know about that kill list some of your fan club keeps going? There's pools out there in the hundreds of thousands on who from it you'll frag first. *No one* does what you do, kid. Now get going and good luck out there. Oh, and don't you dare pull another stunt like you did last time. Darn near gave me a heart attack, and I'm too pretty to die. If I don't skin your hide for it, your mother will."

"I'll try to be good," Lynn promised.

"You'd better. Riker out."

Whatever was going on, Lynn had one hour to deal with it. After that, she seriously needed to take a break from killing pretend things in the real and go relax killing real things in virtual. This professional gamer business was going to make her go gray like Steve if she wasn't careful.

"If this doesn't work..." General Kozelek said.

"Then what I just said, General, will occur," Colonel Bryce finished. "Which will make this *maskirovka* difficult to maintain."

"Yes, that," the general agreed. "But what I'm really thinking about is that Godzilla in New York. Because losing Austin will kill hundreds of thousands. Godzilla will kill millions."

Chapter 14

BY THE TIME STEVE SIGNED OFF, THEY'D CROSSED THE WAREHOUSE and their guides were funneling them through a pair of double doors and out into the wide-open space of the arena. Lynn's visor tinted as they stepped out into the bright morning, her helmet saving her from being slapped in the face by the muggy heat. There wasn't a breeze to be found, and the heavy air smelled faintly of hot asphalt. Looking up, she realized that the walls of the arena were made entirely of something like construction fabric stretched over a huge wire frame. Such fabric was designed to let light in, but not prying eyes, and was commonly used at construction sites and renovation projects.

Easy to put up, easy to take down.

Lynn was curious to note not a single tiny camera drone hovering around their heads. She'd assumed they'd be all over the place, catching the best angles and combat shots for the viewers back at the convention center. Nope. The air around their heads was clear. Maybe they had fixed cameras above, connected to the arena frame? The only drones in sight were a fleet of a dozen or so spread out around the outer perimeter, as far away from the node tower as they could possibly get. Lynn squinted at the closest, realizing it was the same slate gray as the new drones she'd been seeing hanging around in Cedar Rapids. Coincidence? At this point, she wasn't sure she believed in them anymore.

Once again, Lynn wondered why they'd gone to all this trouble on the outskirts of town instead of holding the competition in the Austin convention center. Maybe it was a space issue? This arena was about twice the size of an old-style football stadium, covering the area of several parking lots and a city block that looked like it had recently been cleared of structures. But the convention center was massive. The expo floor they'd walked yesterday was easily this big.

Did it have to do with the game algorithm, then? Steve had once said their engineers did not control TDM spawning locations, but that the algorithm determined all the placements. The engineers wouldn't even know where a monster would pop up until it actually spawned.

Had the algorithm gone rogue? Had it spawned a boss where it wasn't supposed to simply because of the strength of this backbone node's electromagnetic radiation?

She tried to remember exactly what Steve had said all those months ago, something about how every interaction with an AI had an element of risk. Maybe it did what it was programmed to do, or maybe it reinterpreted its programming in a way you didn't intend.

That made sense, but...she couldn't shake the instinct that something bigger, and more dangerous, was going on.

"All right, Hunters, this is your rally point," said one of the TD Hunter staff members who had led them out of the warehouse. He pointed to the large white square painted onto the concrete around them. The back edge ran along the wall of the warehouse with the double doors centered in the middle. "Once you've destroyed the boss, come back here and wait inside the white square for the game timer to expire. Please note that you should not take off any of your TD Hunter-issue equipment at any point while in the arena. We will remove and collect the equipment once you have returned to the warehouse.

"Now, you will notice that the timer on your display is in a fifteen-minute pre-countdown," the staff member continued, his voice filtering perfectly through the headset's speakers. "This is to give you all time to form up and prepare to enter combat mode. There will be a loud tone when the clock starts your one hour, and your apps will automatically take you into combat mode."

Movement drew Lynn's attention and she noticed the remaining staff heading back into the warehouse. One of them had already closed half of the double doors, and was waiting by the remaining open door.

"Good luck, Hunters, and happy hunting!"

Was it just her, or did the last staff member walk a little too fast back to the warehouse door? She was probably just imagining it, but the staff had seemed oddly relieved to be going back inside. Probably just the heat.

Pushing it from her mind, Lynn looked around.

"Could I have everybody's attention!" a voice called out over the crowd. "Yes, over here, at the front of the square. Hello! I'm Connor Bancroft and I'm a professional ARS player and team captain. I would be honored to lead our assault today and make this mission a success."

Lynn gritted her teeth and cursed herself internally for not moving faster. If Connor took charge, he would look for any way possible to sabotage Skadi's Wolves and make them lose points. Also, professional ARS player? He'd never been paid to play, it was all just high school varsity stuff. The liar.

"Hey," yelled someone from the crowd, "aren't you that douchebag who spread all those lies about RavenStriker and her team?"

"Oh yeah," someone else called out. "I watched that interview he did and then the real footage from TD Hunter. The alterations they made were super sloppy. That was low, man. Real low."

"They weren't lies, and I didn't alter anything," Connor said stiffly. Lynn shifted until she could see him standing with his back to the open arena, facing the intently watching crowd. It was hard to see through his helmet's visor at this distance, but his body language had all the tells of a frustrated individual.

"Yeah, yeah," the first guy called out. "It wasn't your fault, it was the paparazzi, blah, blah, blah. I don't really care, all I care about is scores. Your team isn't even in the top *ten* US Hunter Strike Teams. So why the hell should we follow you?"

"Oooh, burn," Dan sniggered from beside Lynn.

"I—"

"Shut your piehole, Bancroft," shouted someone else. "I'm captain of Team Florida Man, and we *are* in the top ten US teams. I say we do this nice and easy. Top team leads, simple as that. Where's Skadi's Wolves?"

People started shuffling and turning, eyeing each other's vests.

Lynn took a deep breath and shoved down the part of her

that whined and complained about not wanting to be in the spotlight, *again*.

Come on Larry-Lynn, Lynn-Larry, whatever. We've got a job to do.

"Heads up, guys," she subvocalized to her team. "Duty calls. Follow me, arrow formation."

She started toward the front of the crowd, her team following on the right and left. By the time they neared Connor, the other players had pulled back to clear their path, and Connor stood alone. Off to the side Lynn spotted Elena by her posture of crossed arms and impatiently tapping foot, while her three teammates stood around her, shifting restlessly.

"Going by score doesn't make any sense," Connor called out, ignoring Lynn completely as she led her team to the front of the square and turned to face the crowd a few yards from Connor. "What you need is leadership experience, and I led my ARS team to victory for four years."

The crowd was not impressed by Connor's supposed credentials.

"Nobody cares about your stupid high school sports."

"Y'all are jocks, not real gamers."

"I heard RavenStriker led a whole bunch of teams to kill off *two* bosses up in Iowa," someone else yelled.

"Yeah, me too, I watched her after action report on her stream. That's the kind of leadership experience we need."

Lynn wouldn't have been able to hide her self-satisfied grin if she'd tried, but she did try to smooth her expression back to neutrality as quickly as possible. She could just imagine the lemon-sucking look on Connor's face.

"Look," her rival tried again, "just because she—"

"Shut up, Connor," Lynn said. "No one wants to listen to you." Then she switched to subvocalization. "Hugo, can you make a hunting group and send invites to all players on the competition roster? I need a mass group channel so everybody can hear me."

"Done, Miss Lynn."

"We don't have much time and I hate yelling," Lynn said, pitching her voice to be heard across the whole group. "I just sent you all invites to a hunting group. Join it and let's get this show on the road." She switched to her team channel. "Guys, keep an eye on Team CRC while I organize this mess into a functional fighting force."

Figuring everybody had had plenty of time to accept their invite, she switched to the group channel labeled Operation Snake Hunt.

"Okay, everybody. I'm RavenStriker, captain of Skadi's Wolves. If you want to join my team in taking out Nagaraja, listen up. If you don't, hop out of this group now and go do your own thing, I don't care." She paused, but nobody moved, and there were no notifications about members exiting the group. "Right, then. The rest of you, we have roughly ten minutes left to organize before the clock starts, so this is going to be quick and dirty."

Lynn's mind raced at top speed, counting and organizing, reviewing what she knew and how to apply it.

"We have forty-eight teams. I'm splitting everybody into five-team squads. The top-ten-ranked teams are the ten squad leaders, starting with Skadi's Wolves as Squad 1 and going down the line by leaderboard number. I'm assigning the rest of the teams to each of the ten squads at random, so check the group chat for your assignment. Squad leaders, make squad-specific channels to keep in contact with your teams, don't go broadcasting in the main group.

"Now, Squad 1, you're front and center with me. Everybody else, form up in your squads and line up by squad around the inner edge of the square, starting with Squad 2 on the far-right rear corner." She pointed to her right. When nobody immediately hopped to it, she pitched her voice and went from subvocalization to her best Larry bark. *"Move, move, move!"*

The gathered players scattered, everybody scrambling to find their squad and their place, which Hugo helpfully highlighted for them on their overheads. Squad leaders took up posts around three sides of the square, and their squads of five teams each coalesced around them. While everyone found their place, Lynn kept talking.

"We won't know exactly what the TDMs are up to for another few minutes, but they're probably in the standard ring formation around Nagaraja. We can't just charge to the center, kill the boss, and hop out of combat mode. We have to get back here. If previous experience is anything to go by, that won't be easy, and we won't have the time or resources to destroy every TDM in this arena.

"So, we're going to spearhead formation toward the center,

spreading out and killing as we go to leave us a clear path back to the rally point. Once we're close enough to the boss to be in airstrike range, we'll *all* use our single airstrike on the boss. Hopefully that'll wipe it out, but if it doesn't, we'll set up a firing line with teams on our flanks to protect us from being surrounded.

"The most important thing is to keep moving, keep shooting, and do your best to stay together. Otherwise, we'll get overwhelmed and defeated in detail. I hope all of you have experience using your bait markers to control the flow of TDMs. Since we can't guarantee how much of a resupply of those we'll have, hang on to them for the first part. Once we're engaged with Nagaraja and retreating back to our rally point we'll use them to keep the TDM mass from swinging around and cutting us off."

"Hey, RavenStriker," said a voice over the hunting group channel. "You put the Cedar Rapids Champions in our squad, but I don't trust liars and backstabbers. Put them in someone else's squad or we're out."

Lynn glanced at the pre-countdown. One minute till they were dropped in the pot. No time for arguing, only action.

"CRC, you're in Squad 1. Amaranth, you're now in Squad 6. Make it happen!"

Players scrambled for their places. Soon the countdown clock was in the single digits, and Hugo's voice intoned in Lynn's ear.

"Attention, all contestants, you will be entering combat mode in five—"

Lynn spun toward the node tower in the center of the huge arena.

"—four—"

She whipped out her batons and gripped them tightly in each hand.

"—three—"

Glancing to each side, she made eye contact with her team. Their faces were a mix of anticipation and worry.

"—two—"

Lynn wasn't worried. They'd been fighting to arrive at this moment for an entire year. They were ready. *She* was ready. It was time to kill, both for glory *and* survival. Because this was what she did. This was what made her blood sing.

"—one—"

Lynn's world flashed into chaos, and she leapt forward, welcoming it with open arms.

"Chaaarge!"

Her team was right there beside her: Edgar in the lead to her right with his Samoan war cry, Mack behind to her left loyally yelling *"Skadi's Wolves!"* like the good team player he was. Ronnie, behind Edgar's right, was silent, letting his "Sword of Mastery" do all the talking for him, while Dan anchored the end of their V formation on the right, screaming "For the Horde!" at the top of his lungs.

They ripped through the TDMs like a hot knife through butter. The first ten feet of Delta and Charlie Class monsters simply evaporated into showers of sparks, and the next ten feet lasted only seconds longer. Within fifteen seconds their line had cleared as many yards ahead of them. And within seconds of that, the area was filling up again with higher level monsters.

The arena was packed to bursting with them. There may have been even more outside the arena that were coming in through the flimsy, temporary walls, attracted by the fighting. Lynn didn't know how the algorithm was set up to "referee" this championship. All she knew was that she had fifty-nine minutes and thirty-eight seconds to destroy Nagaraja and get back to the rally point alive.

For the first five minutes Lynn rode on a glorious high of death and destruction. Wrath flashed in her left hand and Abomination spat fire from her right. Her team kept pace around her, the runes decorating their obsidian armor glowing an unearthly ice blue in her augmented vision. Lynn wished for a moment she could be a spectator, sitting back with a bag of chips and a pop to watch Skadi's Wolves slaughter their way across the championship arena.

Her team wasn't the only one worth watching, of course. She knew from pictures and stream clips about the championships that she was surrounded by visions of warriors from history, fable, and straight-up fantasy. Her favorite were the ones in massive suits of armor with decorative pauldrons that defied the laws of gravity and physics. The finery and gravitas of their collective augmented armor was a fitting counterpoint to the ultra realistic graphics of the monstrosities they were fighting. Claws, fangs, and poisoned spikes slashed at the Hunters from limbs armored and scaled, even some covered in chitinous black carapace. Bulging eyes, roaring mouths, and gnashing teeth flashed past Lynn's vision as she slashed, dodged, and twirled through the storm of enemies hungry for their blood.

She had no time to truly appreciate it, but the sheer magnitude of what they were doing was staggering. Operation Boss Bash had only been a hundred people. This was nearly two hundred and fifty. Over the howls and screams and seething mass of enemies, Lynn would occasionally see or hear some player's special weapon ability trigger, flashing light and vaporizing TDMs in massive surges of destructive power. The Hunters around her were dressed to kill, and wielding weapons that, in her augmented reality vision, were the biggest, baddest, most lethal bringers of death she'd ever seen up close and personal.

Thanks to the power of augmented reality, she got to lead a host of warriors from myth, legend, and imagination unbound.

Larry Coughlin would be proud.

Despite the howling chaos, the teams of hunters moved forward steadily. Their lines were messy, but for having had fifteen measly minutes to organize, she thought they were doing a pretty darn good job. Wherever she saw a gap opening in the formation of blue dots on her overhead map, she called out the squad leader of that section and they rallied their teams together.

Ten minutes in, they were making steady progress, but Lynn could tell many of the teams were tiring. While most of the TDMs were no match for the Hunters one-on-one, there were just so many of them. It was like trying to mow down a field of grass by cutting each blade individually.

"There's too many of these monsters! We should use our airstrikes on them or we'll never get out of here alive."

Lynn recognized Elena's voice on the open group channel and gritted her teeth. She slashed at the Managal in front of her with more force than necessary and almost overbalanced as she tried to reverse direction and cut the Phasma that attacked her left side, opposite Abomination.

"Off the group channel, Hunter," Lynn spat out, keeping her words short and sweet to save her breath for fighting. "Do *not* use your airstrikes. We've got time. Keep grinding. We'll be in range of the boss soon."

Of course, being in range of the boss meant first getting through the ranks of Bravo and Alpha Class monsters. Said monsters had no intention of doing anything but utterly destroying the Hunters that threatened their boss. The Bravo Class ones weren't too successful, but once the lead teams hit the highest-level ranks and could no longer kill a monster with every stab or shot, things started to get *interesting*.

Lynn had never seen TDMs packed this tightly. Usually they were spread out enough that each individual monster had room to maneuver and swing without running into its fellows. But not this time. They were stacked right on top of each other. Arms, legs, and bodies mingled as the monsters rushed the Hunters in solid walls of hungry destruction.

She hated it when the algorithm decided to get creative. Could a machine have a sadistic streak?

Soon they had to start using up their bait marker stores to funnel the TDMs into firing lanes. That meant Mack would soon be in charge of managing resupply lines to the frontmost squads from the rearmost ones who were barely using anything.

The saving grace of the situation was that Mack had to do much less dashing around to pick up loot, and it looked like all the teams were still well supplied despite having mowed down thousands of TDMs already.

That was about to change, though. Lynn hadn't realized how much better her team's weapons were than even the average Hunter Strike Team until she saw how much faster Skadi's Wolves were punching through the lines of Alpha Class monsters. She actually subvocalized a few commands to the guys to slow them down and hang back so they didn't outpace the rest of her squad—especially CRC, which was clearly struggling. To Lynn's surprise, Elena fought hard alongside her teammates, face twisted in an angry grimace. But all she had was the standard team plasma cannon, which couldn't match any of Skadi's Wolves' weapons for sheer destructive force.

Let her fail. She's the enemy, her Larry brain insisted, quite vehemently.

But if CRC failed, then Skadi's Wolves might fail, too.

On a sudden inspiration, Lynn disengaged a few precious braincells to subvocalize to Hugo.

"Can I give an augment to Elena, now, mid-battle?"

"Yes, I suppose—"

"Then give her this one, now!" Lynn subvocalized, then yelled out loud, since they were mere yards apart: "Elena! Accept the augment I sent you, Holy Hand Grenade. Adds twenty-percent explosive damage to your cannon!"

"Go away!" Elena yelled back, blasting a Managal to smithereens before it could split. "I don't need your help!"

"Take the stupid augment, Elena, and *beat me with it!*"

Lynn didn't have any more energy to spare arguing. She dodged to the side in time to avoid a crushing blow from a Rakshar, which positioned her perfectly to stab it in the kidney with Wrath and send it exploding into sparks.

"Fine! But this doesn't mean we're *friends*. You're still an ugly, fat—"

"Less whining, more killing, Elena," Connor yelled at them, and Lynn gladly spun away, shooting up a cluster of Strikers trying to flank Team CRC.

What had that airhead been thinking? Why was she even still playing TD Hunter? Lynn understood the initial popularity draw of it, but why had the pop-girl stuck with it when she clearly didn't care about gaming? Lynn hoped she could find out someday what desperate thing was going on in Elena's life that had motivated her to stick it out.

Her brief moment of ruminating cost her. Lynn lunged to stab a Spithragani in its bulbous body and tripped over something uneven on the ground. She went down, hard, and rolled to keep from being skewered by several of the Spithragani's massive spiked feet. It was only seconds before she was back up, but already two more Spithragani were spitting poison spray at her, and her ankle twinged when she put weight on it.

Lynn cursed herself in fine Larry form, using every obscenity in her vast and well-researched repertoire.

"Skadi's Wolves, be careful, there might be tripping hazards around."

The panting acknowledgements of her team trickled in just as Lynn heard a cry of pain behind her. She finished off the looming Spithragani with Abomination and spun to see Elena on the ground close to where she'd fallen herself. Unlike her, though, Elena had not rolled and popped back up, but was trying to hold off a brood of Creepers on her own while struggling to her feet. Connor was nowhere to be found.

Lynn cursed and doubled back, sweeping through the Creepers with Wrath and then hauling Elena up by an arm.

"Are you hurt?"

"Don't touch me, you freak!"

"Elena, it's me, Lynn."

"I know who you are, you disgusting little hussy, and I don't need your help."

At that point Lynn was very, *very* tempted to give Elena a good shove, reasoning that it only put her back where Lynn had found her. But fortunately she was too busy shooting the horde of Rakshar charging at them to act on her impulse.

"Whatever, Elena. Just stick with your team and stop falling behind."

With that, Lynn charged forward again, fingers and wrists burning with exertion as she worked extra hard to vaporize the TDMs that had tried to push forward through the gap she had left.

Despite her best effort to keep the squads motivated and organized, one by one players started making mistakes, and it only took a few before the press of monsters piled up and the damage outpaced a Hunter's ability to chug Oneg. Lynn shouted at the squad leaders to start using their bait markers more aggressively, and that seemed to help. They weren't dropping like flies yet, but Lynn realized that for some of the teams, they needed to use their airstrike ability soon before their last member died.

They were so close to being in range. But not close enough.

That was when she realized that to accomplish the mission and destroy Nagaraja, her team would have to do something extremely unpleasant that might cost them everything they'd worked so hard for.

It was insane, and she didn't even know why she considered it.

They had *five million* dollars apiece waiting for them, a full-ride scholarship, and guaranteed jobs, if only they stuck it out, did their best, and got back to the rally point. She'd already proven her leadership and teamwork capabilities. Their scores would be good, probably good enough to finish in the top three.

But Nagaraja would survive.

Lynn wanted to beat her head against a wall and scream. She did scream, since she could, and dove between two Jotnar bearing down on her. Coming out of her roll she spun and slashed up under the beasts' armor plates in a furious flurry of moves fueled by her frustration.

Why couldn't she do the smart thing? Why couldn't she be one-hundred-percent Larry and focus only on winning the prize? She knew what she needed to do to win, so why couldn't she do it?

Because of my stupid, thrice-cursed instincts, that's why.

With one last yell of frustration, she gave up and threw herself headlong down the path her instincts were screaming at her to take.

"Skadi's Wolves, change of plans. We're going to charge ahead, cut through, and get Nagaraja's attention. We've got to draw it out so all teams can close and hit it with airstrikes. And we have to do it *now*."

"No!" Ronnie yelled. "That's suicide, and you know it! We'll never get the score we need to win if we do something that dumb."

"If you've got a better idea of how to kill this boss, be my guest, Ronnie!"

Lynn killed a few more Alpha Class TDMs while Ronnie audibly ground his teeth.

"I can't promise we won't die," she said. "I *can* promise this is the only chance to accomplish our mission. *That* is what matters."

"How can you be sure?" Ronnie complained. "They told us to get back alive!"

"I know what they said," she gritted back, spinning and ducking under a leaping Nundu. "Dan, kill that thing before it rips my head off!"

"Got it, boss!"

"Ronnie, do you trust me?"

There was a pause, then a frustrated scream that Lynn sympathized with so hard. Ronnie would never understand how much.

"Fine! But you had better not lose us the championship or I'll never forgive you!"

"Noted!" Lynn yelled. "Wolves, straight ahead. Hit that ugly snake with everything but our airstrike." She switched to her squad channel. "Fellas, been nice knowing you. We're gonna hop up ahead, get that big ugly's attention, and get it over here so everyone can airstrike it. Hold the line, make a clear path back home. See you on the other side!"

With that she pushed forward, slashing and blasting furiously as she kept in line with the massive firebombs belching from Edgar's Snazzgun and the deadly whirlwind of steel that Ronnie wielded with expert precision. Every fifteen to twenty strikes, a ring of destruction exploded out from Ronnie's sword, felling even Alpha Class TDMs.

They were a good dozen yards in before Lynn noticed the group of blue dots accompanying them.

"Connor, what the freak are you doing?" Lynn shouted on her squad channel, too focused on staying alive to even have Hugo open a private chat.

"Can't let you have all the glory, RavenStriker. I told you months ago I'm a winner. You might not think there's anyone willing to risk it all to win, but you're wrong."

What in the world—was that creep planning to trip her or do something nefarious in the heat of battle, despite the warning Steve had given? There was no way she could fight two enemies at once, one in front and one behind. So she chose the enemy in front of her and the risk it posed to everyone else over Connor's personal threat.

And that was when the Chimera jumped on her.

Or, more accurately, shot a stream of fire directly in her face.

Lynn's arm snapped up, Wrath morphing into Bastion without her saying a thing, as if her baton was an extension of her instincts. The shield caught most of the blast and Lynn dodged the rest, then ducked away from the strike of the Chimera's scorpionlike tail.

"A little backup, guys!" she yelled and dodged another strike from the Manticar upgrade. She couldn't stop moving for even a second, but with her shield she was able to fend off most of its attacks while Edgar and Dan filled it with incendiary rounds. It finally exploded into sparks—

Just in time for two more to jump them.

"How many of these things are there?" Dan yelled.

Lynn took a split second to look beyond the Chimera currently trying to eat her or burn her to a crisp, perhaps both.

"Lots," she gritted out and got back to dodging the Chimera's tail. She shot steadily, and finally that Chimera exploded too, only to be replaced by *three* more.

"I'm dropping an airstrike on these bastards," came Connor's voice.

"No!" Lynn said. She jumped, rolled, and shot a Chimera under the chin before it bit down on her. "It's not worth it. They aren't clumped tightly. We can take them. Just keep moving."

"I'm not going to get taken out by a measly Chimera because you're too stubborn to do what's necessary." Connor's cold voice was accompanied by a high whistle that sounded similar enough to the Tengu attack that Lynn glanced reflexively above her. But

Dan had already cleared the skies above them of airborne threats. The next second, Lynn's vision exploded into blinding light and there were multiple roars around her that were abruptly cut off.

When her vision cleared, she saw there was an empty area about fifteen feet across around Skadi's Wolves and CRC, but Jotnar and other TDMs were already surging forward to fill the gap and four more Chimera galloped toward them from around the far side of Nagaraja's massive coils.

"You're welcome," Connor said.

"You're an idiot," Lynn growled, but was too busy picking off TDMs with Abomination to worry any more about his short-sighted tactics. Whether the airstrike was worth it didn't matter; now she had to use the slight advantage it gave her or else waste it entirely.

"Edgar, Dan, on me. Pound the bastard until it comes after us. Ronnie, Mack, keep us alive. CRC, protect the rear."

"I'll keep you alive all right," Ronnie growled, putting his back to hers with sword raised and ready. "I'll keep you alive so I can beat the snot out of you later for dragging us through this shit."

Lynn grinned like a maniac.

"Stop yer bitchin', kid, and kill monsters."

Lynn's concentration broke for just one second as she realized not only what she'd said but how she'd said it.

She sounded exactly like Larry.

They all shut up and got to work, though Lynn noticed to her great annoyance that Connor, Elena, and their teammates were lined up a few paces away pouring fire into the boss, exactly the *opposite* of what Lynn had told them to do.

Glory hogs.

Edgar, Dan, and Lynn's firepower joined theirs, but while the bulky coils of Nagaraja shifted and twitched, as if annoyed by a mere swarm of biting flies, its neck and angular head stayed wrapped around the node tower.

"Plan B," Lynn yelled. "I'm gonna airstrike it. Get ready to book it!" She switched to subvocalization. "Target its head, Hugo, go!"

"With pleasure, Miss Lynn."

A piercing whistle filled the air, and this time Lynn closed her eyes in time to save her vision. When she opened them, it was to the sight of Nagaraja uncoiling itself, its giant head rising and turning to look directly at them. At her.

"Uh, Lynn, I think you got its attention," Dan said, shifting his fire to the thing's cluster of skinned over, spiderlike eyes. "And I think it's a little pissed off!"

The scaly neck bent as Nagaraja pulled its head back, looking suspiciously like...

"Back up! Back up! It's gonna strike!" Lynn yelled, backpedaling.

Lynn's team reacted instantly to her order, disengaging and retreating. Team CRC, predictably, did not.

"Connor!" Lynn screamed, just as the boss's head shot forward, covering the considerable distance between them as if its neck was some kind of bungee cord. "Hugo, activate Shared Fate, *now*!"

Lynn sprinted and dove, shoving Bastion up over her head as she intercepted Nagaraja's strike directly in front of Connor.

She *felt* the collision. Felt it in her bones.

Her display flashed blood red with critical damage while her body flushed with heat, like she was burning up inside. Painful tingles swept through her limbs, though they stopped short of her torso where her vest shielded her vital organs.

Bastion didn't fare so well. Her shield flared white hot and the omnipolymer burst into flames. She flung it away from her even as the force of the collision sent her tumbling backward into Connor. He half caught her and managed to keep them both from smacking their heads on the concrete.

"What the hell?"

"Get back, you idiot!" Lynn screamed in his face as she jumped to her feet. "Get out of range, RIGHT NOW!" She shoved Connor with all her might, then grabbed Elena's arm, who was closest to her, and dragged the pop-girl away, back toward her own team.

Lynn felt nauseous and dizzy, even though she hadn't hit her head on the concrete. She turned her head and took some gulps from her hydration tube, hoping it wasn't heatstroke.

"Your entire squad's health is dangerously low, Miss Lynn. If that had been you alone, you would be dead."

"Look at that, the power of teamwork," Lynn growled. "Use my Oneg, Hugo, all of it!"

"I have done so, Miss Lynn, but with Shared Fate still in effect, it will take more than that to get the entire team back to safe levels."

Lynn glanced at her display and saw what Hugo meant. Well, at least for the next four and a half minutes, no one member of her team was in danger of dying. But Lynn was still angry. She'd wasted her team's ace in the hole to save her two worst enemies. If any of her fellow WarMonger mercs could see the great Larry Coughlin now, they'd shake their heads in shame. She should have let the morons take the hit. They were the idiots who'd ignored her call to retreat.

But look what that boss had done to her *baton*. What would have happened to Connor and Elena if Lynn hadn't acted?

Well, no time to cry over spilt milk. At least she hadn't *died* saving her two worst enemies. That would have been truly humiliating.

By that time the rest of Squad 1 had managed to fight their way to her team's position at the edge of the innermost ring. A few of them must have seen her collision with Nagaraja because they were standing frozen, perhaps staring at the blackened, shriveled thing on the ground that had once been Lynn's baton.

"L-Lynn, your—" Mack began, pointing.

"STOP GAPING AND FIGHT," Lynn bellowed in full-on Larry mode. She shot a Striker in the face that was about to lunge at Mack, then another that was making for Dan. She kept bellowing until her whole team was moving again, fighting like hellions, trying to widen their attack corridor and beat back the TDMs using distracting bait markers and overwhelming firepower.

None of the monsters tried to flank them by venturing into the empty space around Nagaraja.

Lynn didn't blame them.

"Squad 1, group tight and retreat in an orderly fashion back toward the main body." Lynn's harsh, sharp commands got everybody's attention and the teams started moving. Lynn glanced at the boss and saw that it was partially uncoiled, its head oriented toward them, proto arms flared wide like bat wings as if it were using them as radar dishes, listening as it swayed back and forth. Was it trying to get a lock on their position? They needed to put distance between them and it before they used more airstrikes, or it might kill them all.

They couldn't wait too long, though, or it might retreat to the node tower and they'd be right back where they'd started.

It wasn't time they lacked, but supplies and manpower. They were going to run out of Oneg before their hour was up. No matter how many TDMs they destroyed, there were always more, pressing in from every side.

"All Squads! We're luring the boss toward you. Team captains by squad, launch your airstrike as soon as it's in range, then move back toward the rally point to make room for another squad to move up and launch. Keep the corridor clear, launch assembly-line style, and watch the boss. It has a lightning-fast turbo strike—if it coils its head, run like hell. All long-range gunners, snipers, grenade launchers, keep chipping away at the boss, every little bit helps.

"Squad 1, launch now, then scat. Squad 6, you're next, prepare to launch!"

Everything was chaos, noise, and confusing flashes of light and color. Lynn felt like a useless sack of potatoes with only one weapon, but she kept blasting away with Abomination regardless, mentally grinding her teeth the entire time.

Her team seemed hyper aware of her vulnerability, because they kept telling her to "get back" and "stay in the middle," which annoyed the heck out of her. She didn't waste time arguing, though, just kept shooting and using her spare attention to coordinate squad movements. She also had to keep transferring Oneg back to Mack, once Shared Fate expired, because he kept shoving it on her like he thought he could force feed it to her. She yelled at him to give it to everyone else and stop babying her. They were closer to the fight. They needed it more.

It would have been glorious if her plan had worked perfectly and all the teams moved in a coordinated dance of assembly line death and destruction.

Unfortunately, it was more like a royal Charlie Foxtrot of fumbling, yelling, and desperate fighting. But her squad set the example and successfully unloaded their airstrikes on Nagaraja, then pushed back, fighting like the hounds of hell were on their heels to put distance between them and the boss.

Its retaliatory coil and strike didn't quite reach Skadi's Wolves, but it was so close that Lynn drifted to the edge of the fight, ready to switch her remaining baton to Bastion and do whatever necessary to keep her people alive.

Conveniently, Connor took his team and booked it back to the rally point. Maybe he figured that with their airstrike spent, it was their "duty" to make room for other teams to get their strike in. Skadi's Wolves stayed, of course, holding back the TDMs to keep the corridor open.

At one point, Lynn made the excruciating choice to switch from Abomination to Bastion. Their Oneg supplies were down to a bare trickle, and the insane defense bonus gained from her one-of-a-kind Skadi's Bastion shield covered everyone in her hunting group—which meant every team in the arena.

The difference was tangible, and they clawed back a bit of ground.

So, instead of fighting like every fiber of her being longed to do, Lynn stood in the middle of her team, shouting orders and being a guardian angel for every Hunter in the arena.

Sometimes her life sucked.

By the time the fourth squad got off their airstrikes, Nagaraja seemed to decide it had had enough, and started uncoiling fully from the node tower.

Shit, shit, shit.

"Heads up, squads! Nagaraja is mobile, I repeat, boss is mobile! Whatever you do, keep it at the very edge of your airstrike range. It touches you, you die. Squad 8, get up here and launch!"

Four more squads got off their airstrikes, though by the last two they had to launch while retreating, because Nagaraja was actively hunting them. Instead of slithering gracefully like a snake, its lumpy, uneven body bunched up and stretched out like an inchworm, making its movements erratic and hard to predict. Weirdly, the TDMs seemed just as eager to avoid the boss as the Hunters were. The monsters didn't run from it or react to it in any way, they simply avoided it, as if they'd been programmed to stay exactly x feet away from it at all times.

Which, of course, they probably had been. It was a game, duh.

With only two squads worth of airstrikes left, Lynn was getting nervous. They had barely ten minutes remaining, everybody was low on health, and the boss's advance was starting to back them up, Hunter and TDM alike, into the space between it and the rally point. They couldn't circle around it because of the massive press of TDMs on both sides. They were almost out of bait markers, which were the only things preventing the TDMs from dogpiling everyone faster than they could be destroyed.

Already some fifty people who had bailed once their airstrike had been spent were in the white square. Lynn didn't exactly blame them, but she did wish they'd stayed to help protect the teams still waiting to get close enough to strike.

As for her, Skadi's Wolves would kill that boss or die trying. There was no other choice.

"Squads 9 and 10, get your butts up here and launch your airstrikes, or that thing is going to push you into the rally point and throw you out of the game!"

Squad 9 managed it, though two of their teams were overwhelmed and their vests flashed red right after they managed to launch. It was as if the TDMs had gotten wise to the Hunters' tactics and were focusing their attacks on whichever team came forward to threaten the boss. Skadi's Wolves, who had stayed at the tip of the spear and had been taking the brunt of every wave, was on its last legs, despite the supplies Mack had gathered from those few teams willing to share—it seemed some players were willing to benefit from Skadi's Wolves' sacrifice, but weren't willing to sacrifice for them in return.

"Skadi's Wolves," Lynn said, "we have one last squad to launch. You're doing great, I'm proud of you. Hang in there."

"Lynn, I'm running on empty," Edgar said. "Health *and* power."

"Mack, do what you can for him."

"I've got some ichor left, Edgar, transferring it now," Ronnie said.

Lynn opened her mouth to tell Ronnie he should keep his ichor, but then closed it. Instead, she gritted her teeth and shoved up between her two friends.

"Lynn! Get back! You're just going to get killed up here."

"I've got Bastion. No way in hell am I going to hold back and twiddle my thumbs while you two fall on your swords like noble idiots."

"We wouldn't have to fall on our swords if we weren't being idiotic white knights," Ronnie griped, then slashed through the neck of a Yaguar that tried to leap over them. Lynn blocked its clawed strike with her shield, and the little bit of knock back damage Bastion doled out was enough to burst the Yaguar into sparks.

"There, see?" Lynn said brightly. "I can be useful."

"We're all gonna die," Mack groaned, darting around them, picking up ichor and plates and anything else he could find.

"But we're going to look fantastic while we do it," Dan yelled, sniper rifle on his shoulder as he took potshots at Nagaraja. Suddenly, he lowered it. "Whoa, do you guys see that? It's retreating."

Lynn's head shot up. "No! That stupid, cretinous little bastard of a worm! It's almost dead, I just know it, so it's running away. Squad 10, get up here *now*. We'll push forward with you. You're the last one to launch, we can do this!"

To her team's credit, they didn't even bother complaining about running *away* from the safety of the rally zone. To Squad 10's credit, neither did they.

"Come on, Lone Stars," came a cry right behind Lynn. "Let's show this varmint some good ol' fashioned Texan hospitality!"

Lynn grinned at the player who came abreast to her. It was the captain of the team they'd chatted with during the reception last night. The one who had flirted with her. Her display labeled him as "GadsdenSnake" and he was decked out in tightly fitted leather armor with pockmarked metal plates riveted to vital areas like the chest, shoulders, and torso. The getup gave him a faintly post-apocalyptic cowboy look, complete with tasseled chaps. Naturally, he had an augmented reality ten-gallon cowboy hat on his head.

"I'd give you a spare baton if I had one," he said, focus remaining ahead as he shot with twin handheld Gatling guns. His rate of fire was mind boggling. "You're prolly the craziest, bravest lady I ever met, and I'm just sorry as hell I can't ask you out. I know where to find the best BBQ in all'a Austin."

Lynn nearly stumbled and face-planted at the comment, but managed to stay upright. Before she could reply, Edgar on her other side yelled, "Heads up, boss! It's coming back!"

She looked upward to see Nagaraja's head swinging around, like it was going to line up for another strike.

"Squad 10 launch now!" she yelled. *"Go, go, go!"* They didn't have the time or the health to push forward again if they were forced to retreat. But would all five teams be able to get in range and launch before Nagaraja struck?

"I can buy us a bit'a wiggle room," GadsdenSnake said, squinting with one eye as he aimed both Gatling guns at Nagaraja, tongue between his teeth. He triggered some sort of ability, and what looked like two flocks of tiny rockets shot out from the many barrels of his twin guns. The rockets twisted and twirled as they flew, but instead of simply covering the distance and impacting on Nagaraja, the tiny rockets blossomed and morphed in her AR vision into a ghostly stampede of raging Texas Longhorns, tossing their heads and snorting. They charged Nagaraja with explosive trumpets of fury, and as each one lowered its horned head and rammed the boss, there was a flash and roaring explosion.

To say that Nagaraja was distracted would have been an understatement. The boss writhed, its head thrashing back and forth like a battering ram as it reeled from the attack.

GadsdenSnake tilted his guns up and blew theatrically across the barrels. "Now *that's* what I call a signature move," he drawled and winked at Lynn.

All she could do was shake her head, grinning as Squad 10 moved into position to launch.

"That's what *I* call game designers having waaay too much time on their hands," she yelled at him over the noise of howling TDMs, explosions, and Hunters calling back and forth. "If I hadn't already known Tsunami was headquartered in Texas, I'd know it now!"

"Ain't nothin' worth doin' if it ain't got a bit a fun to it," GadsdenSnake said sagely, going back to mowing down the swarms of TDMs crowding in from all sides.

The lead team in Squad 10 reached the edge of their launch envelope, paused, then shouted in triumph and booked it back toward the rally point as a high-pitched whine came from overhead.

Four more, Lynn thought. But Nagaraja was already regrouping, coiling back into a strike, its mouth open and head swaying back and forth as it searched for a target.

Knowing Steve was going to kill her, Lynn grabbed Edgar and Ronnie's arms and hauled them back, then shoved them toward the rally point, hoping against hope they would make it. "Go! Shoot while you run! *Go!*"

Another Squad 10 team shouted in triumph and another high-pitched whine sounded overhead.

The airstrike explosions just seemed to galvanize Nagaraja, and it zeroed in on their group. Lynn raised Bastion and braced it in front of her. She could have run, too. It would have been the smart thing to do. But she couldn't banish the image of Mack convulsing on the ground from her mind. She had Bastion. She could stay in front and take one more hit to make sure this thing didn't touch any of the other players while they got off the last few air strikes.

After that, it would be all over, one way or another.

Lynn heard GadsdenSnake yelling at his remaining teams right behind her and a high-pitched whine reached her ears, then another.

One more. Come on, come on! she thought.

Nagaraja struck.

Its massive, fanged face came straight at Lynn, as if it were aiming for her specifically. She stumbled back, hoping to get out of range while still shielding those behind her. There were yells of alarm and she ran into someone, but kept her shield upraised.

The boss struck Bastion front and center.

The shockwave traveled through her, sending her flying backward while that hot, painful tingle swept over her body, avoiding her chest and head. Her display flashed red, then went blank as her health reached zero and she was kicked out of combat mode. Bastion flared white hot just like her first baton had, and she flung it in the direction of where Nagaraja's head had been before her display had died.

She barely noticed at first that she'd been flung back into someone. But that someone cushioned her fall, wrapping her in strong arms and taking the punishment as they both fell backward onto the pavement.

"Ooof!"

"Edgar!" Lynn yelled and twisted in his arms. "What are you doing here? I told you to run!"

"Don't be silly, *uce*. You can't get rid of me that easy. I already told you, you're stuck with me, until we all go out in a blaze of glory."

She couldn't see his grin, but she could hear it. She twisted, trying to get a good angle to smack him on the vest, which was crimson red, like hers. Nearby Ronnie was throwing his batons on the ground and cursing up a storm. His vest, too, was red. Dan was nearby, also down for the count. Both his fists were raised in the direction of the node tower with his middle fingers extended, yelling a string of obscenities at it that would have been right at home in a WarMonger match.

Mack, somehow, was still alive, though if he had more than a handful of health points left Lynn would eat her own headset.

Suddenly, a cheer went up among the players still in the game.

"We did it!"

"Take that, you big ugly worm!"

Mack looked around, eyes wide, then peered down at his chest as if he couldn't believe it wasn't red. His hands shot into the air, still gripping his omnipolymer electric blue pistols, and he did a victory dance.

"I *liiive!*" he howled.

A second later, his vest turned blood red.

Mack dropped his arms, his pistols returning to baton shape. "Well, crap."

"Back to the rally point, everybody!" shouted a voice that Lynn didn't recognize, probably one of the remaining captains.

Lynn's head swiveled, craning to see around Edgar's bulk. About half the total contestants remained outside the rally zone, but all were now pointed in that direction, some running, some still fighting unseen enemies.

"Come on, we'd better get going," Lynn said, suddenly *very* aware that she was sitting smack dab in the middle of Edgar's warm lap with his arms still around her.

"Oh! Yeah, uh, sorry." He let go of her and they both scrambled to their feet and jogged back toward the rally point, yelling at Mack and Dan to "move it," then catching Ronnie by the arms and pulling him along as they went. He was muttering and cursing to himself, and he shot Lynn a dirty look, obviously blaming her for getting them all killed.

But they'd done it. They'd accomplished the mission.

The only question was, would it be enough to win them the championship?

What Lynn had been so sure of in the heat of battle, now she second-guessed.

Had sacrificing themselves really been the smart move? Their kill-to-damage score would be absolutely abysmal, probably the worst in the entire group. And they'd never made it back to the rally point before dying. Would killing the boss make up for it?

She hoped it would, but she worried it wouldn't. Her worry was mirrored in the tense looks of her teammates through their visors as they all reached the rally zone.

"That. Was. *Incredible!*" GadsdenSnake said, spotting her and coming over to clap her on the back. His team followed, and they all shook hands and congratulated Skadi's Wolves. More teams came over, some to spectate, some to shake hands and slap backs. Soon most of the contestants were gathered together, many taking their helmets off despite the staff's earlier order. They chatted and laughed with relief on their faces and triumph shining from their eyes.

"Hey, y'all," GadsdenSnake yelled over the crowd, "three cheers for RavenStriker and Skadi's Wolves, whadaya say?"

Faces lit up and voices and fists were raised in celebration.

"Hip hip, hooray. Hip hip, hooray! *Hip hip, hooray!*"

They were still laughing and regaling each other with epic moments from their battle when the double doors opened and a group of TD Hunter staff members came out. The Tsunami employees were smiling too and they gave a round of applause, then started shaking contestants' hands.

"Congratulations, Hunters, on completing your mission! If you would please all head inside now for your debriefing and to hear the final scores."

The icy water of reality dumped itself over Lynn's head, and she exchanged a worried look with her teammates.

This was it. Had they succeeded, or failed?

They headed toward the warehouse together to find out.

Chapter 15

BACK IN THE WAREHOUSE THE AIR WAS THICK WITH TENSION and the low hum of hundreds of voices as contestants whispered among themselves. While they'd been fighting the boss, the staff had filled the empty space with rows of chairs, so everyone was able to sit down and rest after their hard workout.

Lynn was too nervous to sit. Her nerves were strung tight as a violin and her gut was all tied up in knots, making her feel nauseous and a little dizzy. Or maybe she felt that way because of the heatstroke that had given her hot flashes out in the arena?

Or had whatever force that had melted her batons affected her body as well?

What *were* the TDM bosses, and why did they cause physical effects? Why had Mack had a seizure when he'd encountered a boss, but she hadn't? Were TDMs the ones causing grid failures and making drones and airbuses fall from the sky? But if so, then how?

Questions swirled in her head faster and faster, becoming harder to ignore as more dizziness set in. Maybe she *should* sit down. Could she do it without anyone suspecting she felt sick? She was about to find out if all her blood, sweat, and tears for the last *year* had been enough. No way in hell was she letting them cart her off to a hospital to do a bunch of useless checks.

She turned her head to sip through her hydration tube, hoping some water would help soothe the dizziness.

"Thank you for your patience, Hunters," one of the TD Hunter staff members called out over the murmuring crowd. "If you could please be patient for a little bit longer, the judges are deliberating the results. In the meantime, feel free to sit down, use the restroom, hydrate, or grab some energy bars from the tables over there."

Lynn and the guys were clustered tightly together, and none made any move to disperse following the announcement. Lynn swayed slightly, unable to help herself. She was so tired. She'd trained for this sort of exertion for months, but maybe the heat had gotten to her.

"Whoa, Lynn, steady there," Edgar murmured beside her, taking hold of her elbow. "Come on, guys," he told their teammates and guided Lynn toward the nearest chair, which happened to be at the front on the side closest to the Championship HQ door. Mack, Dan, and Ronnie followed, eyeing the other teams suspiciously, as if they expected one of them to attack.

"Mack," Edgar said, "grab some energy bars for everyone. I'm starving."

Mack headed off and Edgar made Lynn sit, which she was grateful for because it gave her an excuse to rest without looking weak. It was then that she realized everybody's backpacks and gear were gone. Had the staff moved their personal effects? What was going on?

She still had her helmet on, so she pulled up the TD Hunter app—the only app available on the TD Hunter-issued LINC—and subvocalized, "Hey, Hugo, what's going on? All our stuff is missing."

"I am sure your possessions are stored somewhere safe, Miss Lynn. I am not in any way involved in the competition management, but Tsunami values its players and if you will have a little patience, I am certain all will be explained in due time."

"Hmm," Lynn hummed unhappily. "Can I send my mom a ping from here? There's no messaging app on this LINC."

"Unfortunately not, Miss Lynn. This LINC is restricted to TD Hunter app use, and will only interface with the game for the purposes of the championship. All other functions have been disabled."

Cold realization trickled down Lynn's spine.

She was completely and entirely cut off from the outside. From her mother. From the streams.

A tiny lump of panic lodged in her throat, and her body felt clammy all over.

She *never* took off her personal LINC, not even in the shower. She'd been using the technology in some form or another since she was a little girl. It felt...physically disorienting to not be able to send a ping to her mom, to tell her what was going on. It was like she'd lost a limb. Her mind kept reaching out to touch that connection with the entire world that had always been at her fingertips. But it wasn't there. Lynn looked around, seeing similar sparks of panic in the eyes of other players, mostly younger ones like her. The older players seemed more wary than panicked.

What is going on?

"Hugo..." she began, but then fell silent.

Her stupid paranoia was spinning out of control. What kind of answer would she get if she asked the AI designed by the very people who were holding them...what? Against their will? No one was trying to leave, though, so that wasn't exactly true.

And yet, here they were, cut off. No communication, in or out.

Calm down, Larry's voice growled in her head. *Wait and watch—and be ready to act.*

At that point Mack returned with energy bars, and Lynn focused on hydrating, refueling, and breathing deeply, trying to push down her nausea and pretend she wasn't still dizzy.

Finally, the door to Championship HQ opened, and Steve strode out, followed by Mr. Krator himself along with a dozen TD Hunter staff in their matching black shirts. Excited whispers swept through the gathered players, but Lynn barely noticed. She felt an odd pang of betrayal, seeing Steve up there with the owner and mastermind of TD Hunter.

Did *Steve* know what was going on? Had he helped confiscate everyone's LINC, thereby isolating them? Had he been keeping secrets from her, from her *mom*, all this time?

An even worse thought made her suddenly sick to her stomach.

Had Steve been a *plant*? Some kind of spy cozying up to her in order to...what? Control her? Watch her? Was his entire interest in her mom a sham? A lie? A psyops mission?

No, no. That was just her Larry side talking, putting up her defenses. She needed to wait and hear Steve out. There was probably nothing going on at all.

"Thank you, Hunters, for your patience," Steve said, standing at the front of the crowd beside the giant flex screen. He stood at parade rest, looking more military than she'd ever seen him.

His expression was grim. Gone was the secret humor that sparkled behind his eyes and lurked in the corners of his mouth. His eyes flicked over and met hers for the briefest of moments, then continued to sweep the crowd.

"We have an announcement we need to make before we can proceed. Due to...unforeseen circumstances, we have had to make some last-minute changes to the judging criteria of this competition."

Disgruntled murmurs began, but Steve quickly silenced them with a barking command.

"I understand everyone is confused and impatient. But we are all professionals here, so put on your big girl panties, button those lips, and for goodness' sake, take a seat. Mr. Krator is going to explain the situation. There will be plenty of time for questions after you understand what's going on."

There was a general shuffle as everyone found seats, and then quiet returned. Steve waited a few more beats, making sure every eye was fixed on him, before he turned and gave the floor to his boss.

"It has come to the judges' attention," Mr. Krator began, his voice considerably softer and more conciliatory than Steve's, "that the format of today's championship could be considered unfair with how individual scores are weighted against clear examples of teamwork. Because of the fierceness of the battle and the extreme numbers of TDMs—a factor determined by our cutting-edge algorithm and not something within our control to change in real time—it seems that those teams which contributed the most to the mission also took the hardest hits by overwhelming numbers of TDMs that they could not have defended against no matter their skill. Consequently, those teams which contributed the most ended up having the lowest individual scores.

"So, instead of opening the competition up to accusations of unfairness, the judges have decided to qualify *all* participating teams to continue on to the international championship."

There was a collective gasp in the room, and then cheering broke out. Not everyone cheered, however. Some players looked at each other in confusion, even disappointment, as if upset that those they considered inferior were being advanced to the final stage.

For Lynn, though, the announcement made her sag with relief. It was disappointing, but it also removed the sharp knife of anxiety that had been digging under her breastbone, making her chest hurt.

They hadn't exactly won, but they weren't out of the running yet, which meant her choice to follow her instincts hadn't lost them the competition.

None of her teammates were celebrating, either. They exchanged grave looks, and waited for Mr. Krator to continue.

"The caveat to this decision is that, in order to advance to the TransDimensional Hunter International Championship, every player must opt in to an NDA, a non-disclosure agreement, giving Tsunami complete access to your personal LINC and mesh web access point."

Angry mutters began to grow again, but Mr. Krator ignored them and continued talking.

"I understand this requirement may seem confusing and inconvenient, even invasive. However, in order to continue competing, contestants will be given intimate access to cutting-edge gaming technology worth *billions* of dollars, and therefore must sign the NDA to protect not only Tsunami Entertainment, but yourselves as well. The monitoring will not be active, it is simply a legal precaution giving you protection from accusations and legal suits. The access will last only for the length of the competition, and will terminate as soon as the international championship concludes.

"Agreeing to the NDA also involves your commitment to using your personal LINC as normal, keeping it on, and not attempting to circumvent the NDA by acquiring another device or concealing your actions in some way. If you have any privacy concerns, I can assure you that our servers are the most secure in all the world, and your personal information will not be kept or accessed in any way beyond ensuring you hold to the terms of the NDA. Also, in case anyone here is unaware, our minimum age requirements during the qualifiers ensured that everyone present is of majority and can legally enter into this NDA without parental input.

"So now, Hunters, you have a choice to make.

"If you object to signing the NDA and wish to leave the competition, then I thank you for your participation from the bottom of my heart. Thank you for dedicating so much time and joy to this endeavor. Each member of your team will receive a participation prize of one thousand dollars and a grab bag of Tsunami merchandise. If this is the path your team wishes to take, you can make your way now to your left, and exit the way you came in. My staff will return your belongings and escort you to our airbuses which will fly you back to the convention center where you can watch the conclusion of the competition with your families."

Mr. Krator fell silent, and for a moment, no one moved.

Then one of the contestants cursed loudly and said, "This is crazy, I'm outta here." He stood and headed toward the exit, the rest of his team trailing behind him, muttering quietly among themselves.

That seemed to give everyone else permission to move, and suddenly forty-seven teams were putting their heads together, having whispered conversations, deciding whether to leave or stay. Lynn looked at her teammates, but all of them shrugged and stayed right where they were.

Ronnie was the only one whose expression was doubtful, and Lynn wondered if it had anything to do with his father. He hadn't been back home since his dad had threatened him, and Lynn assumed Mrs. Nguyen would offer to let him stay with them as long as he needed while he looked for other living arrangements. It was a delicate, embarrassing situation. Not one he'd want Tsunami poking their nose into.

He didn't move, though, or verbally object.

In the end, about ten teams got up and left, leaving some thirty-eight behind, waiting on pins and needles to see what happened next.

"Thank you all," Mr. Krator said, addressing the remaining teams. "Our TD Hunter service AI will now walk you through the NDA on your headsets and after you have verbally agreed, your personal LINCs will be returned to you so you can grant Tsunami Entertainment the necessary permissions."

"Good morning again, Miss Lynn," Hugo said in her ear, his posh voice unnervingly chipper. As with Steve, Lynn felt a tiny sense of betrayal, even though she wasn't sure why. There was nothing strange going on, just an irregularity in the judging. No biggie. Besides, Hugo was an AI. A computer program. He had no personhood, no loyalties, no social obligations to her. He was just strings of ones and zeros.

That didn't help her tender heart. She'd *liked* Hugo.

"Let us get through this non-disclosure agreement, shall we?" the AI said, and Lynn gave a subdued noise of agreement.

It was... intense. The NDA basically said that Tsunami had the right to spy on her twenty-four-seven for the next three months until the TD Hunter International Championship. She would have no privacy at all, and she had to continue using her LINC the same way she always did—in other words, not try to hide things or circumvent the NDA. There were various clauses outlining the legal and criminal consequences that could be brought to bear if she broke the NDA and disclosed *any* of TD Hunter's proprietary secrets.

Well... this would suck. She already had mental health struggles from feeling preyed upon by paparazzi drones and gossip streamers. And this monitoring would be in her most personal space, intruding on everything she said and did.

Come on, don't get all butt hurt, she scolded herself. *Ad agencies already scrape everybody's data all the time. You can't use a single app without opting in to monitoring. Don't act like being watched by algorithms is anything new.*

She took a deep breath.

Tsunami just wanted guarantees that their secrets would be kept. She was good at keeping secrets, and there was no way she'd give up on this competition *now* just because of a weird NDA.

So, Lynn verbally agreed to everything Hugo read her. As they went through it, she noticed several more teams walk out. But everyone else, it seemed, was determined to see things through.

Once the quitters, as Lynn thought of them, had all been escorted out, the staff members helped distribute personal effects back to their respective owners, and Lynn followed Hugo's instructions to power up her LINC, and give him unrestricted access to it.

A little chill threaded down Lynn's spine as she did it, but she told herself there was nothing to worry about.

She trusted Hugo, right? The AI had consistently expressed concern for her and other players. It was programmed to keep them safe, right?

After everyone had gotten their personal LINCs sorted, the staff members collected them again, making Lynn and her teammates scowl.

That didn't bode well.

"Don't worry, Hunters," Mr. Krator said, "you'll all get your LINCs back shortly. There are just a few more things we need to discuss first." Mr. Krator clasped his hands behind his back and rocked slightly on his heels. He seemed nervous. Or excited. Lynn couldn't tell which. "Why don't you all take off your headsets. I'd love to make sure everyone can hear me for this next part. I'd rather not have to repeat anything."

Some in the crowd murmured and looked at each other, but eventually everyone started removing their TD Hunter-issued helmets, most putting them on the floor under their seats, some holding them in their lap.

When the cool air-conditioning of the warehouse hit Lynn's sticky face, she shivered. Despite the cooling system working overtime, this many sweaty people bunched together made her nose wrinkle. Not that she didn't smell, too. Her hair was probably mussed to boot, with flyaways sticking out here and there. But her braid was basically intact and secure.

Mr. Krator waited until everyone had stopped shuffling around, then began again, more slowly this time.

"This moment has been a very long time in coming, and I hope you will all continue to extend us the courtesy of your understanding and patience as we share a few more details about this competition going forward."

He paused, and the door to Championship HQ opened again. This time, though, it disgorged...

First Sergeant Bryce?

Lynn stared, brow deeply furrowed, not sure what she was seeing. But no, it *was* the same man, slightly older than Steve and not quite as tall, looking just as eagle-eyed and imposing as he'd looked in all the TD Hunter vids.

What was a game actor doing here?

But that wasn't all.

The actor was followed by several other men in military attire, their coat fronts festooned with pins and their shoulders heavy with stars. Behind them were over a dozen military members in duty uniforms, carrying standard-issue rifles.

What in the world is going on?

Lynn glanced at her team and saw looks ranging from confusion, to shock, to suspicion. While she was looking around, the various military leadership joined Mr. Krator at the front, while the armed men took up positions around the remaining teams of contestants, making the Hunters shift inward as they sent nervous glances toward the stone-faced guards.

"Good morning, Hunters," barked First Sergeant Bryce. His voice was powerful and commanding, and Lynn found herself sitting up straighter. "I'm sure you're all wondering what in the name of Jesus, Mary, and Joseph is going on. Well, today is your lucky day, because I'm here to tell you. Part of the purpose of the NDA was to grant you clearance to hear what we're about to say. You are the first civilians outside a select group of government-contracted researchers to be read in on this national security situation."

"I knew it!" Ronnie hissed, punching a fist into the opposite palm. "We're at war with China!"

Edgar elbowed him hard in the ribs, and he fell silent with a glare at his friend.

"My real name is Bryce, Colonel Manuel Bryce, United States Marine Corps, and I am the head of Force Training for Taskforce Sanctus, the US branch of a unified mobile operation unit. With me is Lieutenant General Kozelek, of the United States Army, head of the unified military command.

"Yes, I am the person who performed as First Sergeant Bryce for the TransDimensional Counterforce videos. No, I am not an actor. I have served in the United States Marines for over twenty years, and I am honored to be here today to help lead CIDER in its critical mission, which General Kozelek will now explain to you."

Lynn's heart was in her throat. What in the world was going on? Reaching blindly, her hand made contact with Edgar's warm, solid body. He shifted and took her hand in his and held it, his grip just as tight as hers.

The older man introduced as General Kozelek stepped forward.

"Hunters, I know this will be a shock to the system, so I'm just going to come out and say it plainly: The TransDimensional Monsters you've been fighting for the past year...are real."

You could have heard a pin drop in the room. The silence was absolute.

Then someone started laughing.

At first it was just one person, but then others started chuckling nervously, and more and more joined in as the laughter swelled.

It didn't even seem mocking. Just relieved—or slightly crazed—as if those laughing were comforting themselves by believing this was all one massive joke.

Not everyone was laughing, though. Nobody on her team so much as twitched. Lynn kept a close eye on the military members, noting that none of them moved a muscle or responded to the incredulous laughter in any way.

While the laughter still echoed around the large room, the flex screen in front of them lit up and Steve, Colonel Bryce, and General Kozelek all turned toward it.

The picture that came up was of the freaking *President of the United States*.

"Holy crap," Edgar muttered.

Mack and Dan were gaping, speechless, and Ronnie was watching the screen closely through narrowed eyes.

"Good afternoon, fellow citizens. I know you are reeling right now, and are not sure what to think. Because of the extreme nature of the news we have to share, we thought it only fair that you hear it from the highest authority in the land. I can confirm, on my honor as your duly elected president, that what the members of my military are telling you is correct. We have discovered the existence of entities that are destroying our power and communications grid. From where they come and for what purpose, we do not know. All attempts at contact and communication have failed. They seem to operate like a hive mind or a virus, and have been slowly sapping the global energy grid and causing infrastructure failures across the globe for at least several years, if not longer.

"In response to this threat, an alliance of countries across the world established CIDER, the Coalition for Interdimensional Dark Energy Research. It is a front for the research and military action needed to identify this threat to humanity and eliminate it once and for all.

"I apologize for the deception, but it has been necessary to prevent mass panic and social unrest. People would not react well to the knowledge that invisible monsters, energy gremlins, were causing these disruptions.

"We need every resource our unified governments, research teams, and militaries have to offer focused on this one goal if we hope to survive. The personnel assigned to CIDER from their various member nations have dedicated every waking moment to responding to this threat, for the good of all humanity.

"I will leave it to the good men and women of CIDER to explain the situation in more detail and how *you* will be involved in saving humanity as we know it. Thank you for your willingness to fight to protect your country, your family, and your species. Thank you, brave citizens. Thank you for your time, and I hope you continue on this great crusade. We have a civilization to save."

If Lynn had thought the silence was absolute before, now it was physically oppressive. Her ears rang with it, and she couldn't even look side to side to stare at her teammates, trying to grasp what was going on. No, her eyes were fixed on Steve, still standing at parade rest behind Mr. Krator, his grim face carved from craggy stone, entirely unsurprised.

He'd known. He'd known this whole time.

Oh my God... our planet is being invaded by aliens, Lynn thought, tightness gripping her chest, like some outside force was crushing her inward, making it impossible to breathe.

The TDMs were... real? Exactly as the game had been telling them all along? How was that even possible... *aliens*?

Lynn's mind reeled, flailing in panic and struggling to make sense of anything. All her instincts, all her vague paranoia, had been right. Even her *dreams* had been trying to warn her, showing her visions of burning cities and monsters running amok.

Edgar gripped her hand even tighter, as if he feared she would be ripped from him by the invisible entities around them. Five minutes ago, Lynn couldn't have cared less about them. Five minutes ago, she'd felt safe.

Not anymore.

The flex screen had gone dark, and General Kozelek stepped forward again.

"I know this is very difficult for you all to grasp, but I hope we are on the same page now."

He fell silent.

There was no laughter.

"Good. For the most part, what you have learned from the TransDimensional Hunter game is true. We *are* being invaded by an invisible, other-dimensional army of entities that seem to feed off the electromagnetic spectrum. Their activities compromise human infrastructure all across the globe, and their numbers and aggression have been increasing exponentially over the past six to eight months. You've seen this growth with your own eyes, and you've seen the destruction these entities have caused across the US. You've heard of the airbus crashes. You've experienced the grid failures. You might have heard of people across the nation mysteriously dropping dead, or collapsing with unexplained seizures—"

There was a loud gasp from someone in the audience and Lynn heard a strangled cry of, *"Daddy!"* before the person's voice was muffled, perhaps behind their own hand as they stifled their uncontrolled outburst.

Had that been *Elena's* voice?

"This is what humanity is facing," General Kozelek continued, not responding to the cry, "and, unfortunately, it will only get worse. Exponentially worse. Our scientists calculate that if the entity numbers continue increasing on their current trajectory, within six months society as we know it will begin collapsing, worldwide. For those who might have seen it, the TD Hunter WarMonger crossover game is based on our estimates of the results.

"So..." General Kozelek paused, slowly looking across the dozens of Hunter Strike Teams hanging on his every word. Lynn could see that his expression was firm, but there were dark bags under his eyes, and his posture was stiff—the stiffness of someone rigidly preventing themselves from collapsing, because that was simply not an option.

"So," he began again, "we are putting one last choice before you: formally volunteer to join the TransDimensional Counterforce—that is, CIDER—and help us fight this invasion under the guise of competing for the TD Hunter International Championship. Mr. Krator and his team are ready to update game messaging and mechanics to introduce a new storyline where the Hunter Strike Teams are now a part of the 'counterforce.' You will be working together to clear the alien scourge from our cities as part of your 'training' for the final competition. You will be given all the support the United States military can bring to bear, plus a generous salary and benefits package.

"Or, decline to volunteer, in which case we will send you,

and any family members wanting to join you, on a six-month, all-expenses-paid, vacation to an undisclosed location. For the security of CIDER's global operations, you will have no contact with the outside world for six months. Your every reasonable need will be met—I hear paperback books are quite enjoyable, if you've never tried one—but you will be under military lock and key. After six months...well. We don't know if there will even *be* a military left to keep you. Secrecy will be a moot point.

"I am sincerely sorry this difficult choice has been put before you. There was no way to provide you the opportunity to volunteer, with full knowledge of the risks, without also taking steps to isolate those who chose to decline. Our military has a long and proud history as a volunteer fighting force, and despite the direness of our circumstances, we believe that is still the best way to move forward, at this point."

Silence descended once again, and Lynn could just hear the objections working through people's brains, straining against their lips:

We have rights, You can't lock us up!

This is government-sanctioned kidnapping, I want to talk to a lawyer!

You're all crazy! This is some elaborate scam to steal our personal information, isn't it?

It was a good thing their LINCs had been confiscated. NDA or no NDA, Lynn was sure some in the crowd would have already whipped out their LINC and started livestreaming.

Once again, her instincts had been right, though she never would have dreamed in a million years that "it's an alien invasion!" conspiracy theorists would be the ones proven right.

Her brain was exploding. Everything was shifting, dropping into place.

Everything made sense now.

The full weight of what was happening finally settled on her shoulders.

Her planet. Her people. Her *mom*. They were all in danger.

And knowing that...there was only one thing to do, really.

Lynn stood up.

"I volunteer," she said, raising her hand, voice loud and clear.

Edgar stood only a split second behind her.

"I'm with her," he said simply.

Across the empty space in front of the flex screen, Lynn met Steve's eyes. They were beyond worried—they were haunted. But he gave her a small nod.

Was it an apology? A thanks? It didn't matter. She wasn't sure if she could forgive him, but she understood his actions. He had done everything he could to protect her, while also protecting his mission and the human race. She didn't think his fondness for her or Matilda had been fake. It had felt too genuine. And she'd been friendly with Fallu before Mr. Krator had ever recruited her to beta TD Hunter.

That didn't make his secrecy hurt any less.

Her mom might literally skin him alive when she found out. But Lynn didn't have time to worry about that now.

"I'll fight," another voice said, cold and hard, into the silence.

Lynn's head whipped around, and she saw Elena standing, arms crossed, a disgruntled look on her face.

Elena?

"Shut up, you idiot," Connor hissed from his seat beside her. He tried to tug her down, but she slapped his hand away.

"No, you shut up, you worthless bastard. I volunteer," she said again, louder.

"Team Lone Star's in," came a voice from behind them. Lynn turned to see GadsdenSnake wink at her. "We're from Texas. *Duh*, we're in. Li'l upset you stood up before me, miss. Just hope the grubs better'n what the Army served, back in the day." He made a face, and several people chuckled.

Lynn looked to her other side where the rest of her teammates sat. Mack looked worried, even scared. His eyes pleaded to understand what was going on as his entire world was turned upside-down. Dan, weirdly, looked thoughtful, as if this whole thing was just another gaming scenario and he was deciding if he liked the parameters enough to go all in. Ronnie looked... intense. He locked eyes with her, and didn't look away. Lynn couldn't tell what he was thinking, or what he wanted her to do. He just kept staring at her, as if waiting for her to lead the way.

Lead the way.

He didn't trust TD Hunter. His head was full of conspiracy theories and chronic suspicion from a life spent resenting the abusive authority over him.

But he would follow *her*. She had gained his trust.

Lynn gave him a rueful smile.

"You with me, Ronnie? Who wants to be a hero?"

He let out a minuscule sigh, as if he couldn't believe what he was doing.

"You're the boss, boss," he muttered, and stood. "Sign me up," he said loudly.

Edgar on her other side chuckled.

"For the Horde!" Dan said, standing and punching a fist into the air.

"Um, I think he means the United States of America," Lynn clarified to General Kozelek.

He just looked at her, then Dan.

"Son, what you meant to say was 'no pity, no remorse, no fear, for the God Emperor!' Otherwise I'm sending you to the Island."

"Uh..." Dan said.

"Warcraft is for lightweights," the General stated, then looked back to Lynn. "The US Military has many issues, Miss. But assigning a General who has never played games to this mission exceeds even the *Pentagon's* level of incompetence."

"Yes, sir," Lynn agreed, chuckling.

"For Skadi's Wolves," Mack said softly, smiling at her and standing, though there was still plenty of fear in his eyes.

"We're in," Lynn said firmly, turning back to face the General, Colonel Bryce, Mr. Krator, and Steve.

"Team Amaranth will fight," another team captain said, standing. Her whole team stood with her.

One after another, with a scraping of chairs, every single remaining Hunter Strike Team stood and pledged their support.

Lynn noticed that Connor and the rest of CRC had surreptitiously stood as well, though she hadn't heard them say anything, and Connor's face was carefully neutral—always a bad sign. While Elena wore her feelings on her sleeve, Connor hid everything behind a mask. Elena, for whatever crazy reason that Lynn couldn't fathom, seemed committed to fight. Unafraid. Perhaps foolishly so. But Connor? He would be one to watch.

"Looks like you have your fighting force, sir," Lynn said. "What next?"

The General gave her a close-mouthed smile.

"Now, Hunters, you are about to learn the meaning of 'good training.'"

While most of Skadi's Wolves looked confused, behind her she could hear GadsdenSnake groan.

"Any chance of changing our minds, sir?"

This time the General's smile was sharp as a razor.

"As much chance as the TDMs discovering diplomacy, son. Now, form up, Hunters. It's time to save the world."

Epilogue

CONNOR BANCROFT WAS FURIOUS. NO, BEYOND FURIOUS. HE WAS fuming. Seething. Outraged.

But he didn't show it. He kept his feelings hidden, smiling and going along with everything simply so he could get out of that concrete warehouse and back to civilization.

They couldn't do this.

They had destroyed his entire life's plan. They had tricked him into committing time and energy he could never get back, his whole senior year wasted, his ARS scholarships thrown by the wayside, in return for what? *Nothing.* No prize, no fame, no security for his future.

Did they seriously think they could ruin someone's life like that and get away with it? And *why* in the world take the legal risk? He didn't know, but it certainly wasn't aliens. All the other contestants might have swallowed that ridiculous lie, hook, line, and sinker, but he wasn't an absolute moron. Watching *that whore* stand up and patriotically promise to "fight for humanity" had sickened him. He would have gladly wrung her little neck.

Except he was smarter than that. He would never touch her himself, no matter how much he'd enjoy doing it. No, he had a celebrated sports career to build for himself, so he couldn't have any skeletons collecting in his closet. He let other people collect those skeletons for him.

The smear campaign had been a mistake. Even though he'd

hired someone else to break the story and alter the footage, the simple fact that he'd personally had to make the accusations against his rivals had been too much involvement. He'd learned his lesson, and had stayed far away ever since.

Which was why it was so enraging that every other plan he'd set in motion had failed to put that arrogant whore in her place where she belonged.

The faketime vid.

The stalker.

The doxxing.

The last-minute hack into her TD Hunter account. He'd waited until the very last minute to pull the trigger on that one, to ensure the cuckold officials at TD Hunter would have no time to rally to her defense. She would be disqualified and shamefully thrown out of the competition for all the world to see.

But none of his plans had stopped her. Her PR team had deftly managed the fallout of the vid, the crazy lunatic he'd put onto her scent hadn't had the decency to properly assault her, and no one else had taken advantage of her address just *sitting* there, waiting to be exploited. He'd been hoping for a few good SWATs at the very least. The negative publicity of her in handcuffs could have tanked her popularity. If he had been extremely lucky, she might have resisted arrest and "accidentally" gotten shot. But no one had made the call. And then the whore had up and disappeared. He'd put several PIs on her trail, but none of them had been able to find her new address.

Was he the only person capable of accomplishing *anything*?

So much money, time, and effort, wasted.

And now Tsunami was trying to pull the wool over his eyes and defraud him of his time and energy. He'd spent an entire year advertising their product, paying into the system under the assumption he had a fair shot at the just rewards: money, fame, and career opportunity.

But no. They'd gotten cold feet and had come up with this elaborate ruse to wiggle out of their contractual obligation to pay out the prize money. Maybe their stocks were poised to tank. Maybe there was some lawsuit pending.

Whatever it was, he would not stand for it.

So he'd gone along, agreed to the NDA, and let their sticky

fingers into his main LINC, just to get out of there and back to his hotel room, where he had *three* other LINCs that he'd been using for his various clandestine ventures.

He wasn't an idiot. Obviously this LINC would stay squeaky clean. TD Hunter would never know who had brought the righteous hammer of justice down on their unsuspecting heads.

In his hotel room he powered down and closed the TD Hunter app on his "official" LINC and tossed the thing on his bed. Then he dug out one of his other LINCs, a fashionable wrist-watch, powered it up, and connected it to his audio implants. After that he paused, considering which gossip streamer would be the best to contact. Who was the most discreet? Who was actually here, at the convention? It would be safer to meet them in person, to cut down the amount of messaging back and forth.

Finally, he chose one of his contacts, and sent him a message:

I have the biggest story of the year, maybe the entire decade, and you get to break it for me. When and where can we meet?

An answer came quickly back.

Covering top-rank competitor interviews, can it wait?

Connor scowled at the reminder of his rivals' triumph.

No. Now, or I'll take it to HotGamingCelebs and be done with it.

Ten seconds later:

Understood.

The streamer gave him a room number and said to meet him there in thirty minutes.

Good, that gave Connor just enough time to jump in the shower and wash away all the sweat and ick from that boss hunt.

Twenty-five minutes later, he was headed to another floor of the hotel, when a new message came in from his contact.

Sorry, there was a typo, wrong room number. Here's the new one.

Connor rolled his eyes. It was closer, at least.

He went ahead and initiated a voice call with the idiot. He would feel better if he had someone to berate, since he couldn't attack the person he really wanted to. She would get her comeuppance eventually, but he'd have to figure out a foolproof plan for that. Maybe something involving her mother. Or that oaf, Edgar. That would be satisfying.

"Bruce, you idiot," Connor started right in once the call connected. "A typo? Are you drunk? Or do you just have fat fingers? Should I have picked someone *else* to break this story? I'll need a substantial offer to make it worth my time. Any other streamer would *kill* for this scoop."

He spotted the proper room number on the direction screen at the three-way split in the corridor and turned right, following the hall down, steps silent on the thick rug beneath his feet.

"What, cat got your tongue? If you're too drunk to have this conversation right now, tell me. I'd be happy to take my business elsewhere."

"Apologies," his contact's muffled voice finally said. "Door's unlocked. Come right in."

Connor found the right door, turned the handle, and pushed inside. The tension in his shoulders and neck relaxed as he entered the dim interior of the hotel room and the door clicked shut behind him, signaling that he was safe from prying eyes. Now, finally, he could speak his mind.

"Where in the world are you, Bruce? You'd better not be puking in the toilet."

"Not exactly," said the voice in his ear. But he heard the voice in the room in front of him, too, just around the corner.

Connor walked forward, brow furrowed.

"*You* might be puking soon, though," the voice continued.

Connor's eyes widened as *Steve Riker* stepped around the corner, hands behind his back, expression pitying. Connor quickly recovered and retreated a step, intending to get out of there as quickly as possible. He couldn't prove it, but he suspected Riker was one of the cuckold TD Hunter employees that slut had manipulated into covering up her every indiscretion.

"Sorry, I must have come in the wrong room," Connor said.

"No, you've got the right one." Riker smiled, eyes sparking dangerously.

Connor whirled around, but two men in military uniforms had stepped out of the bathroom which he'd passed by without looking inside. They pointed sidearms at him, blocking his exit.

"Y-you can't do this," Connor stammered, whirling back to Riker. "I-I have rights!"

The big man—he was even bigger up close and personal, with biceps like bulging tree trunks and a broad mountain of a chest—was now holding something black and clothlike in one hand.

"True, you do have rights. You have the right to remain silent, for instance, and I suggest you exercise that one. Though I don't know how you could possibly screw yourself over more than you already have. Thanks for leading us right to your little stash of illegal secrets, by the way. I can't *believe* you actually *kept* LINCs used to commit crimes." Riker shook his head. "Such a waste of a decent Hunter. If only you were as smart as you think you are."

"W-what do you mean? You don't know anything! I haven't done anything illegal. I gave you complete access to my LINC. Go look yourself! There's nothing there!"

"Oh, you mean *that* LINC?" Steve pointed at Connor's wrist. "Do you not remember the part of the NDA about not using alternative LINCs or attempting to circumvent our monitoring? Did you miss the little clause in there that gives us permission to, ahem, force entry into any device used to break the NDA and disclose confidential information?"

Connor clamped his mouth shut.

"As villains go," said a new, crisp voice in his ear, "you are a sad specimen indeed."

It sounded like the default, British butler voice of the TD Hunter service AI. He'd changed that stupid voice in his own TD Hunter profile as soon as he'd been able. He preferred something feminine and sexy, but he knew a lot of people had kept the standard setting. What was it called? Hugo?

"What are you doing on this LINC, you creepy AI? I never installed the TD Hunter app here! How did you get here? You're—you're trespassing!"

"Not at all, Mr. Bancroft. I go where I'm needed, and I am currently operating fully within my programming mandate to advance CIDER's critical mission. I wish I could say it has been a pleasure working with you, Mr. Bancroft. But it most definitely has *not*. Goodbye."

Connor stood frozen, mouth agape, mind reeling as he tried to think of some objection or excuse that would save him.

The last thing he saw was Riker's wide chest, and then a black bag dropped over his head.

"Enjoy your 'vacation,'" Riker's smug voice rumbled close to his ear.

Connor felt a jolt at the base of his spine, and he blacked out.

To be concluded in
TransDimensional Hunter Book 4:
Beyond the Rift